To my family and friends,

Who believed

And to my wife,

Who is perfect

The Chronicles of Lumineia

By Ben Hale

—The Shattered Soul—

The Fragment of Water
The Fragment of Shadow
The Fragment of Light
The Fragment of Fire
The Fragment of Mind
The Fragment of Power

—The Master Thief—

Jack of Thieves
Thief in the Myst
The God Thief

—The Second Draeken War—

Elseerian
The Gathering
Seven Days
The List Unseen

—The Warsworn—

The Flesh of War
The Age of War
The Heart of War

—The Age of Oracles—

The Rogue Mage
The Lost Mage
The Battle Mage

—The White Mage Saga—

Assassin's Blade (Short story prequel)
The Last Oracle
The Sword of Elseerian
Descent Unto Dark
Impact of the Fallen
The Forge of Light

Table of Contents

The Chronicles of Lumineia 4

Map of Lumineia 8

Prologue: Setting the Trap 9

Chapter 1: Shattered 13

Chapter 2: An Eternal 19

Chapter 3: Elenyr's Hope 27

Chapter 4: Adrift...32

Chapter 5: Keys of an Eternal...38

Chapter 6: Kelindor 45

Chapter 7: A Returned King 52

Chapter 8: A Dangerous Ally 59

Chapter 9: Tardoq's Request 65

Chapter 10: The Return of Carn 71

Chapter 11: King Justin's Tale 77

Chapter 12: Kinship..84

Chapter 13: Hyren's Secret...90

Chapter 14: Vanguard...97

Chapter 15: An Ancient Friend...105

Chapter 16: The Unnamed...112

Chapter 17: The Eyes of Erasat 119

Chapter 18: Risen 127

Chapter 19: Rune's Warning 132

Chapter 20: Visitor 137

Chapter 21: Senia's Offer 144

Chapter 22: The White Dragon..151

Chapter 23: Reunion 158

Chapter 24: Retaliation 165

Chapter 25: Serak's Message...172

Chapter 26: Buried Secrets 180

Chapter 27: The First Visitor..186

Chapter 28: The Exiled Assassin..193

Chapter 29: The Assassin 201

Chapter 30: A Chance Encounter 208

Chapter 31: Lord Dallin..215

Chapter 32: Serak's Heart..223

Chapter 33: Lost 229

Chapter 34: Homeland..236

Chapter 35: The Fallen King 242

Chapter 36: Warmind 250

Chapter 37: The Alliance Council 256

Chapter 38: The Imposter 263

Chapter 39: Blackwell Keep...270

Chapter 40: Elenyr..274

Chapter 41: Wounded...280

Chapter 42: Draeken's Truth 288

Chapter 43: Draeken's Rising...297

Chapter 44: Requiem 301

Chapter 45: Conquerer..306

Chapter 46: Alliance 313

Epilogue: The Fragment of Power..319

The Chronicles of Lumineia 322

Author Bio 322

Map of Lumineia

Prologue: Setting the Trap

Serak stood on the battlements of Xshaltheria, watching the snow fall in the valley. The road and the fortress were blanketed, and the valley lay dusted in white. The clouds were dark. The air carried a bite, a chill that would not abate until spring.

He'd caged the world's monarchs for weeks, kept them captive until they could bear witness to the rising of the Stormdial. Then he'd released them without explanation. His location was now known to the kings and queens of Lumineia. It wouldn't be long until the monarchs returned in force.

The kings had taken a wagon and hastened their journey, as if afraid Serak would change his mind and again cast them into prison. King Porlin had suffered the worst in captivity. He'd lost weight, his features now gaunt, his clothing slack on his torso. He rode the wagon, urging the horses to greater speeds. King Justin flicked the reins at his side, no less tense, but his eyes were fixed on the road ahead. He'd had the wisdom of taking a sword, and the weapon lay on his lap.

Dothlore, the dwarven king, also rode in the wagon. He too, had taken a blade, and he spun the axe in his hands, the motion casual. The dwarf gazed on the high fortress as the wagon approached the trees in the valley.

Queen Erisay, the dark elf queen, rode her own steed. Serak had expected her to depart alone, but the queen remained with the group. Serak nodded his approval. They had united in captivity, at least to a degree, and that would further his plans.

At her side, the most important of the monarchs departed on foot. Queen Rynda, head of the mighty rock trolls, towered over Erisay, even with the woman on horseback. She walked with purpose, her greatsword on her back. Her liquid metal hand clenched and unclenched, but not in worry or fear. The woman was confused, and when she reached the threshold of the tree line, she paused and looked back.

The rock troll stood on the edge of the forest, her expression visible even from the distance. She'd hated him and sought to kill him, but her role was crucial in his plans. But would she obey when the time came?

"It will take them a week to return to Terros," Zenif said, joining Serak on the battlements and pulling him from his thoughts. "Are you certain they will gather an army?"

"Rynda will return," Serak said.

"Are you certain it was wise to release them?" Zenif asked. "Rynda will be a threat. You can be sure of that."

"You read her thoughts?"

Zenif scowled. "You know my mind magic is limited."

"She is a warrior queen," Serak said. "She is hardly a normal monarch."

Zenif grunted in agreement and then pointed into the fortress of Xshaltheria. "Tardoq is pacing in his quarters. The fall of the Stormdial hit him hard."

Serak released a long breath. He'd brought Wylyn and her son to Lumineia. She'd come with a group of dakorians, all dead except for Tardoq. Serak had used them, manipulated their goals, ultimately setting them up to be killed by the fragments. But if they had triumphed over Draeken, all of Lumineia would have fallen into krey hands.

The gambit had been risky, and Serak had weighed that risk for years. In the end, he knew Draeken needed to rise to his potential, and a threat like Wylyn would force him to become the guardian Lumineia required. But there was always the chance Wylyn would succeed. Serak was glad he'd bet correctly.

"What will we do with Tardoq?" Zenif asked. "I tried to use a sleeping charm on him and he didn't even notice."

Serak raised an eyebrow. Zenif's magic may have been limited, but his sleeping charm could knock out a reaver, and even make a dragon sleepy. But Tardoq had been Wylyn's Bloodwall, his body perfected by krey engineering.

10

"Will you kill him?" Zenif pressed.

Serak frowned, considered how he could. Tardoq was as old as Lumineia, and had been trained to recognize threats, to eliminate dangers. He'd undoubtedly studied Serak and Zenif. Even as allies, it was Tardoq's duty to kill them if they turned against Wylyn. Of course, Serak had never really been on Wylyn's side, a fact that would have brought swift retribution if Tardoq had known.

"The fragments will move swiftly to destroy the Order of Ancients," Serak said. "Send Tardoq to prevent that."

"I thought you didn't care about the Order anymore."

"We don't," Serak said. "All our loyal forces have been moved to our secret halls. But it's better to keep someone like Tardoq busy."

"As you order," Zenif said.

Serak realized he would have to find a way to kill Tardoq. The dakorian should have died with his master. He presented an anomaly, and Serak could not anticipate what he would do with his newfound freedom. For a time he would probably work with Serak, but eventually he would probably grow resentful and defiant.

"We are in the final hour," Serak said, "and we must tread cautiously. The dismantling of the Order of Ancients will occupy the fragments for a little while, but not long. We must begin our final preparations."

"Are you certain we must go to such extremes?" Zenif asked. "I believe my charm will work on the fragment of Mind—"

"It will not," Serak said. "Your magic is powerful, but he would crush it. Everything hinges on him, for he controls Draeken. We need him to *choose* to come."

"My son is stronger than I," Zenif said proudly.

"Which is why I gave him his current assignment," Serak said. "Zoric is talented, but not stronger than the fragment of Mind."

Zenif scowled, and Serak realized he doubted their plan. But Zenif would not disobey the order. Zenif understood what was at stake, why they needed Draeken to assume leadership. The army on the opposite side of the Dark Gate would require a powerful mind to control, one stronger than him or his lieutenants.

Serak inwardly shuddered, recalling his one and only attempt to open the Dark Gate. It had been four thousand years, and still he felt the agony of that night. The Gate had opened, smoke pouring from the opening, sentient, sinister. It had sought to control him, subvert him, turn him into one of the fiends the Dark controlled. Serak had shut the breach, but it had nearly cost him his life. That's when he'd known he needed someone stronger. A guardian with more power. He needed Draeken.

His attempt to watch Draeken had become an obsession, and Serak's plan had been born. Now he was ready, and the time had come. When the Dark Gate opened again, it would not be Serak standing in the opening, it would be Draeken.

Serak turned away from the view and looked to the volcano containing Xshaltheria, the ancient dwarven forge. A grey cloud now billowed up from the volcano, the vestiges of a thousand barrels of stonesap being poured into its mouth. The cloud would keep the Dark from entering Lumineia, allowing Draeken to control the army.

"All is set in place," Serak said, a thread of excitement spilling into his blood. All his work, all the centuries of labor, it was finally time. He turned to Zenif and nodded. "It is built. We now await the master . . ."

Chapter 1: Shattered

The fragment of Mind stood in the back of the room, leaning against a doorframe. Dust layered the abandoned inn where they had taken refuge, and not even the crackling fire in the hearth could dispel the sense of gloom, possibly because the fire had been lit by the fragment of Light. His effort had damaged the entire hearth, leaving stones and the mantle scorched and blackened.

Outside, snow drifted onto the nearby trees, fluttering through the branches to settle on the ground. The snow was the first of winter, and it would likely continue for the next few days. Mind disliked the cold, but for once he did not feel the chill. Perhaps it was because he'd absorbed the fragment of Fire when he'd been killed, and his brother's magic now filled his blood.

The other fragments gathered in the large room, the distance between them indicative of their profound grief. The silence in the room was deafening, but Mind could sense their thoughts as easily as if they were speaking.

I wonder if I could dye Elenyr's hair blue, Shadow was thinking. *I bet Fire would have liked that.*

Is there any chance Fire is alive? Water stared into the fireplace. *What if Mind managed to pull his consciousness in time?*

I'm hungry for cheese. Light thought brightly. *Fire usually kept some in his pack.* Light's features were forlorn.

Lira predictably stood with Water. Their growing attachment was palpable. Even though her mental shields were adequate, Mind caught fleeting glimpses of her thoughts, mostly worry for Water, interspersed with deep satisfaction that Wylyn had been killed. Her purpose in coming to Lumineia was complete, and she tried not to think about returning to her duties as an Eternal.

The last two members of their group, the aged Sentara and the young Rune, sat on what had once been the bar, their thoughts dark to

Mind. Touch amplified Mind's magic, but even then he could not discern their truth. Elenyr obviously knew their real identities, but Mind had been unable to discover their secret.

Light began playing with a dagger of light, a nervous action as he tried to burn off his energy. It was night, which usually meant the fragment wanted to sleep. But after his time in the Deep, he'd grown less and less observant of the hour. When he realized it was night, he would probably drop to the floor and snore, but for now, he paced nervously.

Mind turned away from his brothers and stared out the window, watching the snow settle on empty branches. There was no wind, the snow floating to a silent resting place on bough, building, and earth. The river adjacent to the inn flowed out of the trees, its icy waters dark, the current swift.

Mind stared without seeing, his thoughts on the events at the Stormdial, where Fire had been killed. Wylyn crushing Fire in a hand of stone. And Mind absorbing his essence. He could feel it now, stirring in his blood, a magic, a might.

He reached his hand up and turned away from the group, towards the window, and attempted to draw fire into his palm. The action was unfamiliar, and something he could only do as Draeken. A spark of flame ignited, the flicker of light glowing on his face. He extinguished it quickly, hating what it meant.

Of one thing he was certain, he felt stronger, much stronger. He'd just begun to master his magic of gravity, manipulating the magic to lift and move objects. With the other fragments combined into Draeken, he could even fly. He reached to the threads of gravity binding everything to the ground, and warped them, willing his boots to rise.

His feet came off the ground and he hovered a hairsbreadth above the dusty floorboards. He released the magic and settled back on the floor, never looking away from the window. He smiled to himself, pleased at the addition of Fire's magic to his own. It made him stronger, more powerful.

The shame came quickly, surging and crushing his smile. His brother had died, and he could only think about the increase in his own power. Perhaps there was more of Draeken in him than he realized.

He cocked his head to the side, wondering about Draeken, and his connection to Serak. As the Father of Guardians, Serak was dangerous, tactical, and powerful. His plot revolved around Draeken, and on numerous occasions he'd sought opportunity to reveal his desires to the various fragments. After defeating Wylyn, Mind retained the memories of when the fragments had joined as Draeken, and recalled all the times Serak had spoken to Draeken through the fragments.

Serak wanted an ally. He wanted Draeken. But for what purpose? Mind was the only one to view all the invitations at once and recognized a pattern in his words. From the moment Serak had revealed himself, he'd spoken of protecting Lumineia. His actions were not meant to destroy, but to guard.

Despite his words, Serak had invited Wylyn to Lumineia, bringing the greatest threat to Lumineia since the Dawn of Magic. He'd created the Order of Ancients, all but destroyed the Assassin's Guild, and formed the Bloodsworn, a rival guild of assassins. He'd even kidnapped a phoenix and gathered enormous amounts of explosive stonesap. His actions implied a larger agenda, a greater war that needed to be fought.

A war *against* the krey.

It was the only answer. The Krey Empire was vast, filling countless worlds like Lumineia, spreading across the stars. It was the only true threat to Lumineia, and no amount of magic would protect them against an invasion. Unless the people of Lumineia had something the krey feared.

Mind hated Serak, but could respect him for his willingness to do what he believed. His tactics were clever and bold, patient and exacting. He'd sacrificed much of what he'd built over five thousand years, all in an effort to garner a single piece.

Draeken.

How did Draeken fit into Serak's plans? What role did he play in protecting Lumineia? There could be only one answer. Light had seen the writing in Serak's office that described the Dark Gate, and others had heard talk of the same. Pulling on the memories of the fragments, Mind put the pieces together. Serak wanted to use whatever lay beyond the Dark Gate against the krey, and he needed Draeken to do it.

Mind sensed the truth to the words, and it filled him with dread. He'd seen glimpses of the future in Senia's vision, and seen Draeken standing at the head of a vast army—not to protect Lumineia, but to slaughter its inhabitants. It was a future Mind would do anything to prevent.

Elenyr and Jeric entered the room, drawing Mind's attention as they made their way to the fire. She touched each of the other fragments on the shoulder and arm, a gesture meant to comfort, but Mind kept his distance. Both her and Jeric's thoughts were guarded, as they always had been. Even with touch, Mind could not break their shields. But grief had distracted Elenyr and he caught glimpses of shock and doubt, an ocean of sorrow. As much as he would have liked a peek into the boundless secrets of Elenyr, he could not stand the grief, and so he retreated.

"My sons and friends," Elenyr said. "We have suffered a blow, but Serak remains, and we must discuss how to proceed."

"Kill the Order of Ancients," Shadow said.

"We must deal with the Order," Elenyr agreed. "And against that threat I will send Water, Lira, Shadow, and Light. The four of you can join with the forces of Talinor and Griffin to eliminate their halls and imprison those that survive."

"And Fire?" Water asked. "Any chance he is alive?"

All eyes turned to Mind, and he felt a stirring in his chest. Fire's magic was present, but his consciousness, his thoughts and emotions, were not. Mind was not Draeken, he was merely the fragment of Mind with additional magic.

"No," Mind said, his voice bitter. The hope on Light's features shattered, and Mind regretted speaking so forcefully.

"Wylyn is dead," Sentara said, stabbing a finger at Elenyr, "and it's clear Mind has sufficient magic now to fulfill your promise."

Mind frowned, and caught a glimpse from Sentara's memory of a young woman standing with Elenyr, and surprisingly, Ero? The trio stood before a strange machine, obviously krey in architecture.

"I will fulfill my oath," Elenyr said softly. "But there is something I must share with the other fragments."

"I'm not leaving," Sentara said, folding her arms.

Rune, the young girl that never left her side, glanced uncertainly between them. She fingered the hilt of her sword and jumped down from the bar. Mind wondered how one so young possessed such mental shields. It usually took decades of practice for anyone to block him so well.

Jeric sighed. "I know who Sentara is. I believe she will guard my truth."

"Are you certain?" Elenyr asked. "This is not a small truth. If it becomes known . . ."

"What are you talking about?" Water asked. "Does this have to do with Fire?"

"No," Elenyr said. "It has to do with Jeric, and his real identity."

"I thought you were the Ear," Lira said.

Jeric groaned and wiped a hand over his face. "At least sharing this truth will finally rid me of that name."

Mind looked between Elenyr and Jeric, recognizing the distance, the physical gap they had subconsciously placed between their bodies. Prior to the conflict at the Stormdial, they had been closer, as if they were reconciling what had kept them apart. Instead of affection, Elenyr looked to Jeric with borderline suspicion. What secret had he kept?

"Sentara," Jeric said, his gaze settling on her. "I know what you are, but not what you will become if Mind and Elenyr do as you desire. Will you guard my secret?"

Sentara shrugged. "You assume I do not already know it."

Light laughed. "I bet she does."

"I don't," Sentara said, and jerked her head towards the orb hidden in the pouch at her side. "But she does."

17

Jeric chuckled dryly. "I suppose that is to be expected."

Do you know what's going on?

Water spoke to Mind by thought, and he responded in kind.

We'll find out soon enough.

"You know me as Jeric," he said. "But what am I about to reveal must be kept secret from anyone not in this room."

He turned to Shadow, holding his gaze until Shadow rolled his eyes. "I won't tell anyone."

"Not even Lorica?" Jeric pressed.

"Not even the assassin," he said.

"Then it's time you understand," Jeric said, and reached up to the pendent on his neck.

His body began to alter, changing shape, the skin and tissues gradually morphing into an entirely different being. His hair turned white, his body turning grey and shrinking several inches. In the end it was not an elf standing before them. It was a krey.

Jeric was Ero, head of the Eternals.

Chapter 2: An Eternal

Stunned silence filled the abandoned inn, with everyone staring at Ero. Mind prided himself on anticipating friend and foe alike, but in this, he was not prepared. He knew Jeric as a scoundrel, a warrior, and a man prone to adventure. To discover that he was Ero, leader of the Eternals, protector of Lumineia, left him speechless.

"*Ero?*" Lira blurted, breaking the stillness. "You've been Jeric this whole time?"

"I'm sorry," Ero said. "I should have told you."

"Is this a ruse?" Shadow asked, folding his arms.

"I don't think so," Water said.

Mind watched Lira, whose shock had left her mental shields in shambles. He surreptitiously slipped into her thoughts, using the breach to scan her memories. She hadn't known Jeric's identity, and Ero had repeatedly spoken of not interfering in the affairs of Lumineia. They were supposed to protect the free races, not manipulate them. She felt betrayed.

"You told us we could not interfere," Lira all but shouted. "That the Eternals needed to stay away from the free races, and let them learn how to protect their own freedoms."

"You must understand," Jeric said. "In the Dawn of Magic I swore an oath to protect Lumineia, which I did for thousands of years. But I didn't want to just protect Lumineia, I wanted to bear witness to the lives of the people."

"You wanted to see your creation," Mind said coldly.

Ero's eyes turned on him and he nodded slowly. "I did." Jeric sighed and scanned the room, which had filled with hostility. "I am sorry for my deception, but you must understand. In the entirety of the Krey Empire there are no worlds of free humans. There are no kingdoms where men and women choose their professions, or live in families. Lumineia is unique, and I wanted to see such liberty."

Mind sensed the wealth of truth he did not say. Jeric was a krey, and had spent many lifetimes as a tyrant to the race of man. It was only when he came to Lumineia that he began to care for mankind, and desired that they be made free. Ero had seen more than just magic, and wanted to be part of it, not just protect it.

Water was upset, probably on Lira's behalf, while Sentara's expression was inscrutable. Rune seemed shocked, and for good reason. Ero was essentially a god to many on Lumineia, and to meet him in person would leave almost anyone speechless. Light was still thinking about Fire, but he too seemed surprised. But Shadow was angry.

"You've been fighting with us the whole time?" he growled. "You could have prevented Fire from being killed."

"I wish I could have prevented that," Ero said. "But I did not have access to any of my technology that would have made a difference. Here, I fought like Jeric, with only his attributes, weapons, and talents, albeit with my knowledge."

Shadow growled in disbelief and kicked a broken chair, sending wood scattering across the floor. He muttered a curse and fixed Ero with a baleful glare. Ero's expression was sad, but he did not retreat.

Water motioned to himself. "Some of the things you said to us, such as the location of the beacon in Erathan. Did you know about them before?"

"I did not," Ero said. "I learned of the beacon's location here, as Jeric."

"But you're Ero," Rune exclaimed. "You know everything."

"I am but a man," Ero said. "And while my knowledge of science and technology is extensive, my knowledge of Lumineia and its inhabitants remains comparable to your own. I could not have prevented Fire's death."

"You lie," Shadow snarled.

"Shadow," Elenyr said, her voice conciliatory, "we cannot blame Ero, even if we want to."

She folded her arms. Ero sighed and stepped to the window, sweeping a hand to the snow falling outside the glass. It had deepened in the last few minutes, with only the long grass still showing.

"I cannot explain the Empire to you. It would take thousands of years to even visit all its worlds, let alone understand the complexities of life for krey, dakorian, and human, as well as the other races. What is important right now is that you understand my purpose. Never in my lifetime have I seen snow fall upon a free people. Never have I seen a husband and wife raise their children and hug their grandchildren, free of fear. Those freedoms only exist here. Can you blame me for wanting to witness it? To feel a part of it?"

"You risked everything the Eternals have built," Lira said. "How many times have we needed you and you were absent?"

"Heth'rugal is more than capable," Ero said. "And he has handled Eternal needs during my times as Jeric."

"Times?" Elenyr asked. "You have not been here the whole time?"

"I have spent more time away from Lumineia than I have in your midst," Ero said.

"So you have a way off Lumineia." Mind scowled at that revelation. "What if Wylyn had used it?"

"That would have been impossible," Ero said. "Only the Eternals know of our Gate locations, and even if they were discovered, Wylyn would have not been able to acquire the two keys needed."

"What about the Dark Gate?" Mind asked. "Does it, too, require keys?"

"The Dark Gate?" Rune asked, her eyes flicking about the room like a squire accidently caught in a council of kings.

Ero released a sigh. "The Dark Gate is not a place on Lumineia, it is a destination."

"Serak believes there is an army through that Gate," Mind said, glancing to the others. "He believes he can use it to fight the Krey Empire."

"He is right," Ero said.

The silence was deafening, except for Mind. The scattered thoughts were like shouts in his ears. Shadow still didn't trust Ero, while Water was concerned about Lira, who was still angry. But it was Lira's thoughts that were the most disturbing, and to her Mind turned to ask the most important question.

"What lies beyond the Dark Gate?"

She glanced to Ero, who nodded in consent. "Tell them, Lira."

Lira passed a hand over her face as if to ward off the telling. "Several thousand years before the Dawn of Magic, a weapon was released on a world called Kelindor. The cloud was called the Dark, and it subverted everyone that lived, turning them into mindless fiends. Billions of krey, dakorians, and humans were killed, and the Krey Empire was forced to abandon the world. It is now forbidden, and the Empire fears the Dark spreading to other worlds."

"And Serak wants to open a Gate to such a place?" Rune shuddered. "I preferred my ignorance when I didn't know about the krey."

"I believe it is the army he seeks to use," Elenyr said. "Not the Dark."

"But if the Gate were opened," Water said, "surely the Dark will come through."

"Serak is smart," Mind said. "Smart enough to learn about the Dark Gate, and smart enough to stop the Dark while allowing the army through."

"They were once beasts, humans, dakorians, and krey," Ero said. "But now they serve only the will of their master, the Dark."

"I don't understand," Lira said. "Few know of the forbidden world, and even fewer understand how it was created. How do you know so much?"

Ero sank against the wall, his eyes sweeping the room before settling on Elenyr. He'd already revealed his identity, but in this, the truth was an even greater burden. Mind frowned, disliking his expression.

"Because my brother was the creator of the Dark," Ero said.

"*Your brother?*" Lira exclaimed.

"To my everlasting shame," Ero said softly.

"But why?" Water asked.

"It was in an age of marvels," Ero said, his voice distant. "Back when Ja'kuul, Skorn, and I were young sons of a powerful house. We wanted to forge a legacy for ourselves, and we often talked of creating a powerful weapon. Ja'kuul actually did so, and in secret, he created the Dark. Skorn and I did not see his ambition until it was too late. He released the Dark, hoping for praise. Instead it destroyed our entire house, and everything on Kelindor."

"Then you know how to stop it?" Rune asked.

"Of course he doesn't," Sentara muttered. "He's an Eternal, and all they do is destroy."

Ero grimaced but continued, "Skorn and I began our work on Lumineia because we wanted to reclaim our home. We created magic."

"And you used the race of men for the experiment." Water's voice was hard.

"You were still slaves to us then," Ero said, his voice distant. "But, for the first time, I witnessed your integrity. I saw the honor inherent to your race. We thought that allowing you freedoms would destroy you. Instead you had more greatness than the whole of the Krey Empire."

Mind grappled with the wealth of revelations, those said, and those unsaid. Lira was reeling, her mental shields in shambles. Mind slipped into her memories again, a slight intrusion before she recognized the attack. She would feel like she'd suddenly forgotten something, while Mind copied as much of her memories as he could in a few seconds.

23

For Mind, it was like stepping into a library and hurling books into a bag before sprinting out the door. Lira's consciousness pushed all her memories about the Dark, the Dawn of Magic, and Ero to the forefront of the library, so he didn't have to delve deep. He gathered what he could and slipped out. As the others fell into a heated argument, he reviewed the memories.

She'd been truthful about Kelindor, but her knowledge was limited—a handful of memories involving rumors about various krey and humans. The locations were exotic, the structures and environments shocking and exciting. Mind would have liked to explore the memories of other worlds, but he set that desire aside. Instead he listened to the conversations, and from them gleaned what he could.

For much of the Krey Empire, Kelindor was a legend. There were several such forbidden worlds, their existence steeped in mystery. The Krey Empire had made an effort to keep the populace from knowing what had occurred on the planet, probably because they feared the truth of the Dark. But rumors could not be stopped. Now the Empire considered Ero's house a disgrace, and the Empire claimed it had been destroyed by infighting, their wealth absorbed by another house, a house led by Wylyn.

Lira's memories of the Eternals were rife with information. He doubted he would get another unfettered glimpse into her mind, so he examined the memories with great care.

Skorn had told Wylyn that his new venture with Ero would repair the damage to his house. He'd never returned, and Wylyn had launched her search for Skorn and Lumineia, a search that had ended on the Stormdial with her death.

The last memory Mind had obtained from Lira proved the most fruitful, because Lira had heard another rumor, that a handful of krey had escaped the destruction of Kelindor, and they'd born witness from what they called a moon station.

"I want to see it," Mind interrupted the arguing.

"See what?" Elenyr asked.

"I want to see Kelindor," Mind said. "I want to see the depth of the danger."

24

He didn't say why, but Elenyr's eyes narrowed a fraction, as if she suspected. Mind had taken a vision from the oracle, a possible future of himself controlling the fiend army. He wanted to see what might lie in that future. He kept his expression bland and did not meet Elenyr's gaze.

"It is impossible," Ero said. "We cannot open the Dark Gate."

"The one on the moon," Mind said. "The one where you observed Kelindor's fall."

The assumption that Ero had been present could be false, but the way he spoke implied a biting regret. Mind suspected he'd seen it personally, leaving a legacy of emotional scars. Ero regarded him with doubt, and then his eyes flicked to Lira.

"A hall on the moon?" Rune was incredulous. "You say the krey live among the stars, but the moon?"

"Krey engineering is greater than you can imagine." Mind spoke without taking his eyes from Ero, again implying he'd picked Lira's thoughts.

"How would you even get there?" Water asked.

"He has a Gate to leave Lumineia," Mind swept a hand to Ero. "Surely he has a way to reach the moon of Kelindor."

"You have to be an Eternal to use the keys," Lira said.

"Then it's time we became Eternals." Elenyr nodded to Mind and then turned to Ero. "Or do you not recall your invitation?"

"You can't be serious," Shadow scoffed. "He just told us he practically destroyed another world, yet you think we should join him?"

"Ero doesn't have a choice." Mind folded his arms. "He needs us to fight Serak, and I want to see Kelindor."

"You will not learn anything," Ero said.

"So there *is* a Gate on the moon?" Lira asked.

"Do we have a deal?" Mind pressed.

"I can take you to Kelindor without you being an Eternal," Ero said.

25

"I want more than just Kelindor," Mind said. "I want to understand everything about the real threat, the Krey Empire."

Ero held his gaze, measuring the heat to his tone. Mind didn't retreat. Being an Eternal, however briefly, would help Mind understand Serak. He would never admit the truth, but he feared becoming the Draeken that brought the army to Lumineia, the one he'd seen in the oracle's vision. He feared his future.

Ero released a sigh. "Welcome to the Eternals."

Chapter 3: Elenyr's Hope

After Mind's demand and Ero's surprising acceptance, the fragments dispersed. Shadow departed with a scowl, Light reluctantly going with him. Water and Lira slipped away, while Sentara and Rune remained. Elenyr watched them go, still grappling with Ero's revelations.

Elenyr spotted Mind ascend the stairs to the second floor, his expression dark. She followed and climbed the steps of the abandoned inn, searching for Mind. It didn't take long to find him on the balcony of one of the rooms, the one looking east, where the Stormdial had been.

"May I join you?"

Mind didn't look up, and Elenyr smiled faintly before claiming a seat at his side. She did not speak, and for a while they sat in silence. Elenyr yearned to alleviate Mind of his guilt, of the weight of Fire's loss, but she carried her own burden.

It had been six days since the battle at the Stormdial. The inn where they'd taken refuge sat on the shore of Blue Lake, and had once been part of an aspiring community. But a flood had taken the other buildings. Fearing the inn would be next, it had been abandoned. The room looked out over the grey sea, the brick walls dusty, the air carrying the scent of mold. The balcony provided a wide view of the sea, the wooden railing now grey and starting to rot.

Snow drifted down in lazy swirls, settled on the evergreen boughs. Obscured by the snowfall, the grey sea rose and fell, the waves occasionally heard when they crashed against the rocks. When Elenyr entered the room, Mind sat outside, staring into the distance.

"I can't believe he's gone," Mind finally said.

"Neither can I." Elenyr rubbed her heart, the ache so painful it was hard to breathe.

"I can feel his magic inside me," Mind said, "almost like when I'm Draeken, but his thoughts are not there. I keep hoping but . . ." He lapsed into silence, unable to complete the sentence.

"Will you show me what happened?"

Her voice carried a trace of pleading, and Mind glanced her way. She'd been on the top of the Stormdial, and not witnessed the battle with Wylyn at the base. Her fragments had returned bloodied and broken, with Fire absent, their expressions haunting Elenyr's dreams. She wanted to know what had happened, needed to see Fire's final moments.

Mind regarded her for a moment and then gave her his memory. She watched the battle through his eyes, witnessed the five brothers fighting the construct around the gravity sphere, until Wylyn crushed Fire in a hand of stone. When the memory faded, Elenyr stared into the storm, tears trickling down her cheeks. The memory was tinged with Mind's shock at Fire's death, his numb agony. The memory faded, and they sat in silence for some time.

"It's not your fault," she finally said.

"It's always my fault," Mind said, abruptly rising. "I'm the one that thinks ahead, plans, finds the route to victory. But Serak is smarter than I am. He's proven that time and again."

"Because he kidnapped the monarchs?" Elenyr asked. "Or because he allowed Wylyn to raise the Stormdial?"

"Both. I cannot fathom why he would kidnap kings, or permit Wylyn to do so much damage." Mind growled and struck the railing with his fist, the wood cracking from the blow. "I failed, and I lost a brother because I failed."

He turned and leaned against the doorway, and after several moments, Elenyr motioned to the sea. "I'm the one that failed. It's my job to protect you all, and instead I was nearly killed. I was even captured—twice."

"Yet you survived," he said. "And that is its own victory."

"I don't feel victorious."

Mind sighed and swept a hand to the falling snow. "Without Fire, at least I know . . ."

His jaw tightened and he looked away. Elenyr regarded him, measured the conflict written on his face and then spoke. "You think Fire's passing prevents Senia's vision from coming to pass?"

"So you *did* see her vision," Mind's eyes narrowed.

"I did," she admitted.

"What do you know?"

"Senia shared everything with me," Elenyr said, recalling her conversation with Senia.

"Prove it," he countered.

Elenyr regarded him for several moments but decided there was no reason to withhold the truth. "It appears there is a future where Draeken controls the Dark Gate, and uses the army to slaughter many in the kingdoms."

Mind winced, and she regretted speaking so bluntly. They had both seen the vision, and both knew that it was a possibility, but reminding him of his potential, murderous fate would only cause harm. Nevertheless, Elenyr needed Mind to understand that she knew.

He released an explosive breath and looked away. "I don't understand how such a future can occur."

"Everything can be," Elenyr replied. "Even I could fall to temptation and choose brutality over honor."

"You?" Mind scoffed. "You would never fall so far."

"Everyone has the seeds of destruction," Elenyr said, her voice suddenly harsh. "There were many I thought above reproach, yet they chose to betray their oaths and even sought my life."

"But you," Mind said. "You would not do the same."

"You do not yet understand." She gripped the cold railing, the ice freezing her skin. "All may fall to their vices. All may rise above them. Ultimately the choice is yours."

"You do not seem afraid of such a dark future," Mind said.

"Should I be?" Elenyr asked.

"Of course not," Mind exclaimed. "We've been fighting to keep the people safe for thousands of years. Surely we would not open the Dark Gate."

Elenyr held his gaze again but Mind looked away. She could see the conflict on his face. Would he stand at the head of such an army? Command them to slay the very people he'd spent his life protecting? He jerked his head and winced, as if shying away from that thought, but then Elenyr noticed a touch of desire in his eyes. The destruction had been terrible, but the Draeken in the vision had such *power*. And Mind had always craved power. Perhaps that was what terrified him most, and he feared his own desires.

"When I was oracle, I could see the future as well."

"So?" he asked.

She flashed a humorless smile. "I saw the future of others, but mostly my own."

"And you saw such dark paths?" he challenged. "You saw yourself leading armies and destroying innocents?"

Unable to meet his gaze, she looked into the falling snow. "To my utmost shame."

"I do not believe you."

Elenyr's heart filled with regret so profound that it nearly swallowed the ache of Fire's loss. But that ache could not be taken, not ever. She recalled all her visions as oracle, the darker paths she could have taken, the power that would have been in her grasp.

"You cannot imagine the power of being high oracle," she said softly. "When the betrayer on the Eldress Council sought destruction, I could have united with her, ultimately claiming her life in order to make my power absolute. Kings would have feared me, the Verinai would have served me, and all peoples would have been my slaves."

She recalled those visions, the spark of desire for such might, the adoration and fear of thousands. "I knew that fate," she continued. "I felt the desire to wield such power, tasted of the infinite pleasures that would have been mine . . . and then turned away from that path."

"How?" Mind asked. "How could you abandon so much?"

Elenyr smiled faintly, dispelling the haunted guilt of what she could have been. "I saw the price required. If I had chosen that road, I would have one day fought my daughter, and her blood would have been on my hands until death finally released me from the burden."

"You would have killed Alydian?"

"She would have forced it," Elenyr said with a nod. "And the same applies for you. If Draeken were to seek such power, he and I would stand on opposite sides of the conflict."

Mind grunted and jerked his head. "What sort of depraved soul would seek to harm his own mother?"

Elenyr smiled, this time with real humor. "Exactly. Would you kill me to have such power?"

"Never," he said.

Mind was not prone to affection, but he reached out and embraced Elenyr, folding her into his shoulder like she truly was his mother. The hug was brief, but she felt the wealth of grief, regret, and doubt in the contact.

"See?" Elenyr said when they parted. "You have nothing to fear."

"I still lost my brother."

"I know," Elenyr said. "and that loss will haunt us for the rest of our lives. But we cannot let that ache lead to Draeken's downfall."

Mind's features hardened. "Fire's gone. I'm not going to lose myself as well."

He turned and strode away, exiting the overlook and leaving her alone. With a sigh, she sank onto the worn chair and stared out to sea, wishing she was a better mother. Wishing she were more. Wishing she had not failed.

Chapter 4: Adrift

Tardoq stared at the arch of black material. It had been a week since he'd retreated from the Stormdial, seven days since he and the lightning mage had passed through the Gate, leaving Wylyn behind. Tardoq's lips curled in disgust. Duty required him to seek Wylyn's body, but that would have just ensured his death. Wylyn was dead, her invasion into Lumineia terminated by those she had once called slave.

He too, had dismissed the races on Lumineia as slaves, thinking they were beneath him. That truth had been bred into his consciousness, and prior to his arrival in Lumineia he'd dismissed the inhabitants as akin to every other slave world. That was before he'd seen women pass through walls, men wield lightning like a blade, and a human fly by force of will.

Was it magic that made them different? Was it the power they wielded that commanded respect? He assumed that was the answer, for what else could it be? They led fleeting lives, the humans living for less than a single century, yet they possessed a nobility that Tardoq had never seen among the slaves of Wylyn's house—or anywhere in the Empire.

For the first time since he'd been a child, he had no master, no krey to direct his path. Bred for war, trained to kill, and granted a perfect body because of his loyalty, he now had only his own will to follow. He was a warrior without a war, a soldier without a general. With Wylyn dead, he had nowhere to go. All the dakorians he'd brought were now dead, also slain at the hands of the fragments of Draeken. Would he too perish on this unknown world?

He scowled and retreated from the Gate, avoiding such thoughts of defeat. The Gate room had been built by Serak, and once connected to the Gate crossroads belonging to the Order of Ancients. Then Wylyn had taken over, claiming the Order as her own. Those who had followed her were mostly dead, and Serak had destroyed the Gate crossroads so it could not be used for an invasion.

32

The Gate room of Xshaltheria was bare and represented typical dwarven architecture. Instead of decorations, the stone had been carved with shields and swords. They'd probably once been touched by magic, but like all energy, it had eventually faded.

He idly wondered what it would be like to wield magic, to feel pure power coursing through his body. But would that be so different to what he felt now? His perfect flesh never experienced disease or illness, did not age or wear. He healed remarkably fast and could even regrow limbs. His muscles were powerful, his bones hardened. He moved faster and thought quicker. He'd lived for thousands of years and trained to the pinnacle of perfection with every weapon. He'd guarded Wylyn against countless threats. But Lumineia had killed his dakorian companions and Wylyn herself, and all his vaunted strength and training now seemed fragile.

What to do now? Should he join Serak and his fight against Draeken and the fragments? It would satisfy a sense of revenge, but he found he had no taste for that conflict. But neither would he fight against Serak. The man had sent a beacon to Wylyn, and might be Tardoq's only means of returning home.

A faint footfall signaled someone approaching. The whisper of a cloak and the scent of oil used to darken hair, both marking him to be Zenif, a man Tardoq found distasteful. He was vain and ambitious, and thought his magic powerful. Tardoq had felt the sting of magic many times since arriving in Lumineia, but Zenif was weak compared to the fragments.

Zenif stepped to the door and Tardoq addressed him without turning. "What do you want?"

"I have an order from Serak."

"I don't take orders from him," Tardoq replied, annoyed.

"Wylyn is dead, as is her son, Relgor. Serak may not be your master, but he is an ally."

Tardoq still didn't face the mage, his thoughts inexplicably turning to Relgor. None but the fragment of Shadow knew what Tardoq had done to Relgor in the swamp outside of Mistkeep. The krey had been a fool, risking Tardoq's soldiers in a vain attempt to kill Shadow. Tardoq could have kept him alive, but out of disgust, he'd abandoned him to his fate. If Wylyn had known, she would have viewed it as a betrayal, not that she ever cared about her children.

"Will you accept your order?"

"What is your request?" Tardoq asked.

His correction was important, and Tardoq wondered what Serak would do if he used his hammer to crush Zenif. Would Serak retaliate? Or praise him for the attempt? Tardoq had always assumed he would eventually die at the hands of another Bloodwall, an honorable end. Could he defeat Serak if it came to a duel?

Tardoq disliked the doubt. Guardians on Lumineia were mercifully rare, only Draeken and Serak, as far as Tardoq knew. Both were the pinnacle of magic wielders, and in Tardoq's youth, he would have sought the contest to prove his superiority. Not now, especially because if he did kill Serak, he had no way of getting home.

"Serak believes the fragments of Draeken will move against the remaining halls of the Order of Ancients," Zenif pressed. "He desires that you go and protect them."

It was a fluff order. That much was obvious. Serak recognized that Tardoq was dangerous without a purpose, and sought to occupy him until he knew what to do with him. The man had probably expected Tardoq to be killed with Wylyn at the hands of Draeken, and might even hope that his current request would end in his death.

"I'll do it," Tardoq said. "I deserve a chance to kill the fragments for killing Wylyn."

Zenif tried to hide his relief and failed. Tardoq rotated and accepted the paper from the small man, ignoring his flinch. Then he ascended the steps toward the top level of the fortress. The servants and soldiers of Serak gave him a wide berth, but he paid them no mind. None of them mattered.

He didn't really crave a fight with the fragments, but Zenif would report his words back to Serak. It was what the man probably expected, even if it was a lie. Then Tardoq noticed that Zenif was still at his side, and frowned in irritation.

"I can find my own way."

"That is not necessary," he said. "I have a patrol outside the gates ready to accompany you to the place we believe the fragments will strike first, a village called Talon's Well."

Tardoq rounded on him. "I do not need a guide."

"You will if you want to avoid the weather," Zenif said, retreating a step. "Winter has come, and I suspect even you would not survive being frozen."

Tardoq wanted to retort that he could, but prudence bound his tongue. Although having a group of humans at his side would be an irritant, it might also provide a font of information. If they were of sufficient rank.

"I don't travel with grunts," he said flatly. "Only officers."

"Serak suspected as much," Zenif said. "The group I have assembled are only senior acolytes."

Tardoq disliked that Serak had already known what he would want. It suggested Serak could anticipate Tardoq's actions. Of course, Tardoq had been underestimating the humans since his arrival, a habit that was hard to break after ages of seeing them as inferior.

"I will be recognized," Tardoq said.

"A cloak is in the supplies," Zenif said. "It is thick and dark, and most will assume you are a rock troll. It is not entirely uncommon to see the warrior race among the kingdoms during winter. Queen Rynda likes to send her people out on sojourn, so they may understand their foes if future conflicts occur."

Tardoq snorted, a sound of praise. Of all those he'd met, Queen Rynda deserved respect. She did not have the magic of the fragments, or the Hauntress for that matter, but she was a general with cunning that matched any Bloodwall. What would she do in his situation?

He inwardly chuckled at the thought. Rynda was still a slave, her race created from the race of man. He was wondering what a slave would do without a master. His amusement faded as he realized that was exactly his position. He'd thought himself a servant, but perhaps he'd just been another type of slave, one bred to fight and die.

"Serak wants the fragments alive," Zenif was saying. "You mustn't kill them."

"I kill who I wish," Tardoq said.

Zenif opened his mouth to respond but Tardoq picked him up by his tunic and held him aloft. His eyes widened and Tardoq felt a prickling in his mind as the man sought to subdue him. A valiant but stupid effort.

"You send me, you know what I will do. If you don't want me to kill them, don't give me such a request."

"As you say." Zenif's feet dangled. "Do with them as you see fit. Just protect our halls."

He responded well, for a man held above the floor. Abruptly tiring of the man's presence, he tossed him away and the man landed in a heap. Ignoring his cry of pain, Tardoq ascended the final stairs and crossed the large courtyard to the first drawbridge, the one passing over the volcano. His boots thudded on the wood, and then he passed through the outer gate.

Five guards fidgeted next to a wagon of supplies. The captain caught sight of Tardoq and approached, hurrying to fall into step beside him. He pointed to the wagon as his other men mounted their steeds. At least they had animals to ride. Without them the humans would never have managed to keep up.

"The supplies are loaded, Master Tardoq. Are you ready to depart?"

"Leave the wagon," Tardoq said. "It will slow us down."

"We could load a pack horse," he said, almost jogging to stay with Tardoq. "But it will take time to move the load."

"Then catch up when you're done," Tardoq said.

The man tried to protest but Tardoq continued walking down the road. The captain barked orders and his men rushed to unload the supplies and load them on a pair of packhorses the stablemaster hurried to bring out.

Tardoq, the men already forgotten, descended the road towards the valley below. Snow layered the road, the white marred by tracks of soldiers and scouts. His large boots made large tracks, and he assumed he would have to figure out a way to hide his trail, especially if he had to leave Serak behind. Tardoq knew how to track a foe, but he'd rarely been the one hunted.

The road wound its way down the mountain, passing other gates and crossing other bridges. The guards scrambled to open his path, and one set of guardsmen were too slow to open the gates. He leaned in and struck the wood, crashing through the barrier with ease. Ignoring the shouts, he continued his descent. He did not have a destination. He did not have a foe. But he could only press the advance. He knew no other course. Deep down he recognized the sense of resignation casting a shadow on his heart. He was alone, and would probably be alone until they found a way to kill him. He needed a way home. But that was the very thing he lacked.

Chapter 5: Keys of an Eternal

The revelations about Ero had temporarily distracted Mind from Fire's death, but it returned quickly when they departed the inn. Elenyr spoke to Sentara and Rune outside. From the snippets Mind overheard, Elenyr promised she would meet them in Talinor, where she could fulfill her mysterious vow to Sentara. Then the two women departed in the krey ship they'd taken from the Stormdial. Mind watched them sail across the dark sea.

Elenyr trudged back to the fragments and Jeric, and they hiked through the trees to a nearby outpost, where they rented steeds. The journey was subdued, even for Light, who did not even chase a squirrel that chattered at them from a branch.

They reached the outpost, a small stable adjacent to a road, and Mind manipulated the stablemaster's consciousness in order to acquire three steeds. He mounted his horse and collected the reins, and Jeric did the same. While he procured the horses, Elenyr embraced the other fragments.

"Are you certain?" Water asked when Mind exited the stables.

Elenyr nodded. "We'll join you later. Start with the Order of Ancient halls in Talinor and move into Griffin. If you move quickly, you can dismantle much of the organization before Serak resumes control."

"As you will," he said.

Water conjured his traveling wheel, while Shadow and Light mounted a pair of wolfsteeds conjured by Light. Then he turned to Lira and embraced the woman, speaking in low tones. Elenyr noticed the exchange and turned to Jeric.

"What's happening there?" she asked.

Jeric motioned to Lira. "I have been on Lumineia longer than I anticipated, and the Eternals must be informed of what is happening. I'm sending Lira in my stead."

"You're sending her away?" Mind asked.

"I must," Jeric said. "Serak is not the only dire threat Lumineia faces, and it's imperative the Eternals continue to operate."

Lira glanced to Jeric, and Mind noticed the anger in her look. She didn't want to leave, and hated the order to return to the Eternals. Water caught Lira's attention and the two kissed. Mind looked away, uncomfortable with the expression of affection.

"She'll return soon," Jeric said.

Mind noticed Jeric's reserve, and realized there was much he did not say. His orders to Lira were obviously important, but they had not been made public. Too weighed down with his thoughts, Mind barely spared Lira a look before the group parted ways. Water watched Lira stride into the trees, his features clouded. Then he looked to Mind.

Can we trust Ero? He thought.

It's not like we have a choice, Mind replied.

Water scowled before climbing into his water wheel. He, Shadow, and Light turned south, disappearing from the clearing. When they were gone, Mind released the charm on the stablemaster, who blinked in confusion and looked about.

He spotted Elenyr mounting her horse and scratched his head. "When did you three arrive?"

"We're just leaving." Mind tossed him a small pouch of coins.

The man opened the pouch in puzzlement. He'd been quite irritating before Mind had seized control of his consciousness, wanting to know who they were and their business. As Mind, Jeric, and Elenyr departed the grounds of the stables, Elenyr frowned.

"You didn't have to curse him so hard."

"I didn't like him," Mind said flatly.

Normally Mind prided himself on using the exact amount of magic to accomplish his needs, but ever since gaining Fire's magic, a

39

side of him wanted to punish and cause harm. His anger at losing Fire elicited a desire for brutality that proved difficult to suppress.

Traveling east, the group joined the main highway going north and south. The road was carpeted in snow, but many travelers were still present, their wagons or horses leaving ruts and hoof prints in the newly fallen snow. This time of year normally saw many rushing to reach their destination, but rumors slowed the progress of the people.

The caravans and individual travelers talked to each other, whispering rumors of a great tower that had mysteriously appeared in the sea, and then quickly disappeared. Others still argued about the absence of the kings or worried who could be behind the events. Some whispered in fear, and believed Skorn had risen and the calamities heralded his return.

Mind listened to their words and their thoughts, annoyed by the current of doubt and fear. The people didn't know that Wylyn had been killed or that the Stormdial had been destroyed. They didn't even know that it was called the Stormdial, and the Shard of Midnight was on everyone's lips. They were sheep, frightened by the notion of danger, even when Draeken and Elenyr had destroyed the threat.

Mind suddenly realized his irritation bordered on anger and reined the emotion with a tight clench of willpower. Too much had occurred in recent weeks, and he was still grappling with his newfound control of gravity magic, let alone the battle with Wylyn, the death of Fire, and the revelation by Ero.

He glanced to Jeric, who also seemed lost in thought. Mind couldn't blame him for what he'd done. He had wanted to see what he protected for thousands of years, and once he'd met Elenyr, he'd fallen hard. It had not been planned, but once it had occurred, he'd embraced the persona as his own, and the lie had grown too large to admit. Then Mind frowned at a sudden realization.

"Did you know the location of the Stormdial?" he asked.

"I did."

Elenyr's features darkened. "Yet you did not speak?"

Jeric stared straight ahead, his tone heavy. "I hoped we could stop Wylyn before she raised the Stormdial."

"We could have destroyed the tower before Wylyn arrived." Mind ground the words out, struggling against a surge of anger. A nearby wagon lifted off the ground an inch. "She used the construct to kill *my brother*—because of *you*."

"Mind," Elenyr murmured, her voice urgent as she pointed to the wagon.

He followed her gaze and clenched a fist on the pommel, relinquishing his hold on his magic. The wagon settled into the snow with a bump, the motion unnoticed by the man at the reins. Mind's glare turned on Jeric.

"I was reluctant to let such knowledge loose on Lumineia," he said, unflinching before the heat in Mind's gaze. "You should know more than anyone, thoughts are not private when memory mages are present."

Mind went to shout—and then held the anger in check, suddenly realizing it did not come from him. He was not prone to anger. That had been Fire's attribute. He looked away, unwilling to let the others see the tears in his eyes.

"I'm sorry," Jeric said softly. "I never imagined—"

"I think that's enough truth for one day," Elenyr said.

Jeric inclined his head, and the group fell silent. Winding toward the north, they worked their way across the snowy roads to a small city called Orinfall. Named after a soldier who had fallen in battle protecting the village from marauding pirates, the settlement marked the only port for several days north and south. Situated against the main highway and the lake, the city provided quick transportation from northern Griffin to the sea.

They passed between brick structures and thatch roofs. A handful of larger buildings dotted the city, most collected around a large fort based on the waterfront. Much of the Griffin military passed through the fort at some point, and a large gate in the seaside wall permitted full vessels into the enclosed harbor.

Mind dismounted at a stable near the fort, and relinquished the steeds to the stable master. Much more amenable than the previous stablemaster, the large man laughed and smiled often, his thoughts on his new wife.

They left the stables behind and Mind followed Jeric down the crowded street. As a rule he skimmed the thoughts of those nearby, a habit that Elenyr disliked, but Mind considered only prudent. Those with lethal intent could hide beneath a cowl or a smile, but could not keep their thoughts from Mind. He did not linger with his magic, and considered many of the minds of men and women to be unsavory.

They were like a sea of whispers, angry and happy, annoyed and mischievous, lustful and fearful. A young child raced about, his thoughts on escaping his younger brother, whom he'd just pushed into a pile of snow. Mind heard his laughter in his ears and head, and his mother's worry about their farm's food reserves for the winter.

Others were not so easily discerned. Those with firm minds, such as those trained for combat or magic, held a strong focus. These thoughts were muffled, like voices in an adjacent room. With enough effort Mind could hear them, or by touching their bare skin.

He passed a soldier, their arms brushing, and Mind caught the tinge of lust in his thoughts. The man was hurried, just off his watch, and focused on the house of ill repute at the southern end of the city. Disgusted, Mind subverted his thoughts, adding a worry for his family, and a layer of guilt that would lead to confession. The man stumbled in the street and spun about, but Mind had already passed on.

Jeric led them north and west, toward the fort. The main gate was flanked by two towers and manned by guards. Avoiding the point of entry, Jeric led them around the structure, to a small stone well. Situated close to the sea, the well stones were worn, the bucket absent, the rope rotted.

Jeric stepped behind the well to a small alcove made by the roof of a nearby building, the placement set against the fort's wall. Withdrawing a small knife from his side, his pressed the knife into the crack in the wall of the fort.

The stone shimmered into a Gate, and he stepped through the wall. Elenyr and Mind followed. The opposite side reeked of moisture and salt, and Mind looked upward, sensing the wealth of other minds above ground. In the dim light, it was obvious they stood beneath the fort, granting the hidden chamber the protections of the fortifications above.

Domed and open, the space contained an assortment of odd machinery against one wall, and a collection of shelves on the opposite. More strange machines sat on the shelves, but Jeric passed them by.

"Normally a new member of the Eternals would be celebrated," Jeric cast over his shoulder. "You would meet some of the others and receive more instruction on what we do. If you remain an Eternal after this conflict, that ceremony will likely occur."

The *if* was noticeable, and suggested Jeric was not certain Draeken would remain an Eternal. The doubt indicated he would not be giving Mind full access to everything the organization possessed. It was a temporary appointment, but all Mind needed.

Jeric stepped to wall opposite the entrance, to a large arch that resembled the Gate on the Stormdial. Withdrawing a second dagger, he pushed one into a slot on the right of the arch, and the second on the left. The Gate glowed to life, a silver liquid flowing into view.

"These keys are now yours," Jeric said, motioning to the Gate. "Welcome to the Eternals."

Mind remained in place, shocked and disturbed. Mind had seen this moment before. This very room had been in the oracle's vision of the future. In the same vision where Mind had seen Draeken leading an army into Lumineia.

"Mind?" Elenyr asked.

He forced himself to advance towards the Gate, ignoring Elenyr. They had defeated Wylyn and destroyed the Stormdial, but this moment proved they had not stopped Senia's vision. Draeken could still open the Dark Gate, could still become the threat the oracle had foreseen. The chilling prospect brought Mind to a halt and he lifted his gaze to the Gate.

By stepping through the portal he would be able to get answers that might lead him to stop Draeken's rise to power. Or he could refuse and abandon Serak, Elenyr, even the other fragments. Draeken could not be whole without the fragment of Mind.

43

But even as he thought it, Mind knew he would never forsake his brothers or Elenyr. Serak would never stop hunting, and the war would just continue. Mind might be headed towards Senia's vision, but he still believed he could defeat Serak and Draeken's dark future.

A touch of a smile came from inside, and he sensed Draeken was pleased. He wanted to come forth, to reign supreme, and Mind's choice to advance through the Gate would bring him one step closer.

"Are you certain you wish to do this?" Elenyr asked.

Mind glanced her way and saw the worry on her features. "Of course," he said evenly.

He turned back to the Gate, and without another hesitation, advanced through the material. He felt a tug near his chest and it seemed his body moved thousands of miles, yet it was just another step. A step to another world.

Chapter 6: Kelindor

The chamber was smaller than expected, not much larger than the Griffin fort. Another domed roof curved above Mind, the surface opaque. Around the exterior of the room were an assortment of panels and runes, with a small Gate on the opposite side. The Gate was a local one, but the arch was broken, the sides ripped apart, the damage obviously intentional.

Elenyr stood at his side, also surveying the room with interest. Jeric strode to one of the panels and began touching runes, the symbols lighting up as he activated the chamber. Lights glowed to life, illuminating the space.

Have you ever been away from Lumineia? Mind thought to Elenyr.

Never, Elenyr replied in kind.

Mind spared her a glance, uncertain if she was being truthful. Since Fire had perished, she'd seemed broken, her words forced, her eyes fallen. She had not smiled even once, and Mind knew the only thing keeping her upright was the need to deal with Serak, and her desire to protect the other fragments.

Jeric motioned upward. "I'll have the view open in a moment."

"The view?" Mind asked.

Jeric passed a hand over a symbol and the domed ceiling changed from opaque to transparent, the coloring gradually fading to reveal that the ceiling was actually a window. Mind sucked in his breath as their position was revealed.

They were on a grey landscape, the rocky expanse empty except for scattered boulders and ravines. The inhospitable ground lacked any markings of any kind, no roads, buildings, or even footprints. It was as if the outpost had simply dropped from the sky. Mind noticed it, but his gaze was drawn upward.

An infinite sky stretched in all directions, stars dotting the dark expanse. The sun glowed on the horizon, brighter and larger than seemed possible, only it wasn't the yellow of Lumineia, but a vibrant red. There was no haze of wind, no clouds, only pure, dark sky.

Mind turned a slow circle, his eyes wide. He'd spent lifetimes on Lumineia, seen forgotten cities, ruins of ancient structures, read more books than almost anyone alive, and come to view himself as one with supreme knowledge. In one glance he realized he understood so very, very little.

Jeric noticed their expressions and offered a faint smile. "I'm sure you have a host of questions, but you wouldn't understand the answers. It would be like you trying to explain magic to someone who had never seen it, never heard of it, and couldn't even comprehend the most basic of answers. For now, you'll have to accept that we are on a small observation structure on one of Kelindor's moons."

"One of?" Elenyr asked.

"Yes," he said, and turned back to the panel of symbols. "We are out of view from Kelindor, so I'm going to move us lower into orbit."

"You're going to move . . . the moon?" Mind asked.

Jeric pointed to his feet. "Beneath the surface is a small world engine. It will allow me to move us to a lower orbit."

"Orbit?" Elenyr asked.

"Like I said," Jeric replied. "Too much to explain. Give me a moment."

A slight tremble came from Mind's feet, and then the entire sky moved. He reached out to stabilize himself, but the motion was unnecessary, and the stars seemed to drift aside. Shocked, Mind could only watch in awe as a small orb in the distance grew closer, until it seemed to fill the entire sky, an enormous arc.

"Is that Kelindor?" Mind asked, approaching the view.

"It is."

To see a world—from beyond the world—made him feel small for the first time in his life. The disconcerting sense was powerful, but a surge of another emotion caused him to clench a fist. Draeken too, found it disturbing.

Mind wrestled with Draeken's consciousness, and Draeken retreated, the conflict going unnoticed by his companions. Mind assumed it was because he had merged with the fragment of Fire, for he'd noticed an increase in Draeken's emotions since Fire's death.

"Kelindor," Jeric said, rising to his feet and approaching Mind and Elenyr. "It used to be my home, the central world of my house. Now it is a place forbidden, and the location has been erased from the archives of the Empire."

His voice was bitter and laced with regret. Mind spared him a glance, and saw the conflict written on Jeric's features. He had not wanted to return here, probably avoided it since the incident claimed Kelindor.

"I don't see anything," Elenyr said.

"We are as low as we can be without the moon falling to the surface," Jeric said. "But what you see is the Dark, a cloud that covers the whole of the world."

"Tell me everything," Mind said.

"I will show you," Jeric said.

He leaned to a panel of runes and pressed a symbol, and the domed ceiling changed again, gradually brightening to reddish sunlight and towering buildings. White, purple, blue, and green, the buildings seemed to reach to the heavens. A handful of floating vehicles sped across the sky, passing through clouds and shrinking as they disappeared into the stars. Mind blinked and looked upward, and spotted the crescent moon above—the location where he stood.

"We are still on the moon," Jeric said, pointing to the panels and the floor at their feet. "But you now see what it looked like on Kelindor, shortly before the Dark's release."

"You do not need to show us this," Elenyr said.

Mind looked to Jeric and found him leaning on the panel, his features dark, his jaw clenched. To reveal what had happened here pierced him with a dagger of shame, and sweat beaded his forehead.

Elenyr reached out to him in a gesture of comfort, but Mind jerked his head.

"No," he said. "If we wish to stop Serak, we must see what he desires."

Jeric inclined his head and turned back to the panel. Mind kept his gaze on the people walking the streets of the city in Kelindor. Dakorians and krey walked beside each other. Beasts were also present. Large, doglike animals played in the walkways with young krey. Larger creatures resembled scorpions without the tail, and carried riders up and down sides of buildings. The aura of tranquility was marred by the sight of the men and women.

They walked with their heads bowed, their backs filled with items to carry. They tended to the doglike creatures and the larger beasts, and labored over a section of wall that needed to be replaced, a krey woman standing over them.

"Why are the humans obedient?" Mind asked.

"Humans belong to a certain house," Jeric said, "and they have an earring that marks their owner. The earring also acts as a primary means of enforcement."

Mind didn't need to ask how it worked. A woman working on the wall had gotten distracted, and begun talking to the man at her side. The krey watching them frowned, and abruptly the human woman fell to her knees, shaking and crying out in pain.

"Did you hurt slaves?" Mind asked.

"My crimes are too many to enumerate," Jeric said softly.

"We do not need to discuss who you were before Lumineia," Elenyr said, her tone becoming reproachful.

Mind rounded on her, his voice gaining an edge. "His crimes are the reason we are here. Becoming an Eternal didn't erase what his family did, it only buried it, and now Serak wants to see it risen."

Jeric glanced to Elenyr and then nodded. "As you desire, but brace yourself. What you are about to witness is haunting."

"It would be worse to witness the Dark on Lumineia," Mind said, turning back to the city.

Jeric stepped to a panel and pressed a rune, and in the distance an explosion drew every eye. Krey, dakorian, and human all squinted to see the fireball rising skyward, but it was the plume of smoke that commanded attention.

Rising and bending like a beast breaking free of restraint, the dense smoke formed the features of a face, its mouth open in a silent roar. Taller than the buildings, the face turned about and devoured the fireball, consuming it before turning on the city. In a rush of wind it descended into the streets.

The people fled. By beast and machine they rushed to escape, but the cloud overtook them, and those it caught began to change. The krey and humans saw their skin darken, their bodies becoming malformed and nearly indistinguishable from each other. Dakorians tried to fight, sending blasts of power from their hammers into the cloud, but the power only made it stronger, and the cloud caught the warriors.

One dakorian bellowed in anger and fell to his knees, his bone armor turning stark white, his eyes darkening, and then glowing red, his horns growing, his skin turning black. Rising to his feet again, he turned on his companions, striking with abandon.

"The Dark," Jeric spoke in a trembling voice. "It feeds on the lives of its captives, subverting them, twisting them to his will. Beast, krey, human, or dakorian, it changed them all, until everyone left became a vast army. No weapon caused it harm, not from the surface or from ships. The Dark absorbed it all."

The cloud overtook their viewpoint, until the scene was plunged into darkness more opaque than the blackest night. Heavy footfalls and screams filled the area, and Mind gripped his fist, calling magic to his palm. Even knowing it was an illusion, he wrestled with the desire to fight, to flee, to act. His heart pounded in his chest as he listened in the Dark to the dying and the twisted.

Jeric shifted their perspective, and it seemed their little platform soared off the ground and into the sky, where they watched the Dark gradually expand across the bright surface. Cities were overtaken, forests and sloping lands were absorbed. At such a height, Mind could see the teeth of the Dark, and watched it swallow the entire globe.

Ships fled, rising into the sky with refugees. For those too low, the Dark reached upward, its clawed hands grasping the ships and consuming the energy within. Then it seeped inside, subverting those trapped.

"In a matter of weeks my home was destroyed." Jeric's voice was hollow. "Some escaped through the Gates, others to ships. The Empire ordered all access Gates to Kelindor be destroyed to prevent the Dark from reaching another world."

"The army of the Dark," Elenyr said, her expression one of horror. "They were the people of Kelindor?"

Jeric swept a hand to the surface of the world. "Pets became what we called sipers, transport beasts became skorpians, dakorians became krakas, and krey and humans became quare. They number in the billions, and remain to this day, fed by the Dark, which now absorbs sunlight to survive."

"And Serak would open a Gate to such a place?" Elenyr asked. "Release the Dark on Lumineia—"

"No," Mind wrestled with what he'd witnessed. "Serak would know the Dark cannot be controlled. He would prepare a way to block the Dark from entering, while allowing the army through."

"You think he would use these poor souls?" Elenyr pointed to the Dark.

"Serak would not hesitate," Mind replied.

"But can he control it?" Jeric asked, and pressed another rune.

The scene returned to the outpost on the moon, moving forward in time, when a flotilla of ships arrived to reclaim Kelindor. The group of ships attempted to destroy the Dark, raining blasts of power down on the cloud. The weapons only served to strengthen the enemy, and the Dark reached great claws upward, grasping a ship that flew too close to the surface, dragging it into the cloud.

Mind watched until Jeric ended the memory, and returned the dome to present day. Mind gazed into the stars, shocked to realize that he'd fought battles and wars, but never understood what was truly at stake. Deep down he wondered if Serak was right, and one question seemed most important. Even with magic, could Lumineia stand against the Empire?

Chapter 7: A Returned King

Jeric led them back through the Gate to Lumineia, to the underground chamber beneath the fort at Orinfall. After what he'd witnessed, Mind struggled to bring his thoughts back to the surface of Lumineia, and to Serak. Jeric removed the daggers from the two sides of the Gate and offered them to Mind.

"Guard them carefully," he said.

Mind accepted the two small blades. They were light, but Mind felt a great burden settling on his shoulders. He was an Eternal now, and the whole of Lumineia needed his protection—from enemies within, and without.

"I will guard them with my life."

Jeric held his gaze and then nodded. Somber and silent, the trio exited the secret room. Jeric guided them to the northern part of the city, to a lighthouse situated on a prominent outcropping of stone at the waterfront. The enterprising owner had altered the towering structure's initial design, adding a single room at every level, turning the lighthouse into an inn.

Glass walls connected floor to ceiling, providing an unparalleled view of Orinfall, the forest of northern Griffin, and the sea. Enchanted to prevent others from seeing inward, the walls permitted the central fireplace to shine outward, turning the lighthouse of Orinfall into a tower of light, a beacon that guided many sailors to the safety of its shores.

Jeric spoke to the owner in the adjacent structure, and without argument was led to the highest floor of the lighthouse. They ascended the exterior staircase on the landward side and entered the circular room. A pair of beds were set against the inland wall, while a towering fire roared in the central hearth. Comfortable couches and finely crafted desks and tables were set around the room, positioned so seats pointed outward, towards the view.

"I own the lighthouse," Jeric said, removing his pack and placing it on the floor. "We can stay for the night while we figure out our next move."

Mind claimed a seat by the western window, his eyes on the sea. After a while Elenyr and Jeric fell into a subdued conversation about the Krey Empire. Normally Mind would have listened in, but he did not hear them, his thoughts on Kelindor, the Dark, their foe, and himself.

He'd always imagined their various conflicts as a sort of game, with pieces being played or sacrificed. A king might send in a unit of cavalry to flank an army, knowing many of his soldiers would die, the act providing time for the archers to get into position for a lethal volley. Mind saw it all, imagining which pieces had to be sacrificed in order to obtain victory.

Water had once accused Mind of being callous, of letting others die to serve his own goals. Mind had retaliated by giving Water a single memory, a moment when Mind had been connected to a soldier as he'd died. It was one of the few times Water had cried, and Mind had looked on with pity. Mind had been connected to thousands when they'd perished, friends and foes alike. He'd experienced their panic, their pain, their anger and regret, and felt their spark of life fade into oblivion. He'd felt it when Fire died, and never had Mind experienced such agony.

What Mind had witnessed on Kelindor had left him shaken, not because of the Dark or the army beneath, but the threat of the Krey Empire. The Dark controlled a single world. The Krey held thousands, perhaps tens of thousands. If they came for Lumineia—and they would—no amount of magic would stop Lumineia's destruction.

Elenyr sank into a seat at his side. "Jeric went to gather supplies."

"You sent him away," Mind guessed.

"I did," Elenyr replied. "You do not trust him, and I wanted to speak to you alone."

Mind did not respond.

"Are you well?" Elenyr pressed.

53

"Did you know all of that?" Mind asked. "Did you know of other worlds and the Empire?"

"I knew *of* them," Elenyr said quietly, "but I had never seen them for myself."

Mind released an explosive breath and stood, all the tension boiling into action. "The Empire is enormous, greater than anything we on Lumineia understand. It is difficult to comprehend, let alone fight."

"You speak of the Empire," Elenyr said. "Not the Dark."

"The Dark is a weapon," Mind said. "The Empire is the enemy."

"Would you use the Dark's army, if you could?"

The question hung in the air, the ramifications of the answer settling on Mind's shoulders. He saw the merit to using the Dark's army, or at least Draeken did. Draeken craved the use of such might, but Mind was not so certain. He wanted to lie to Elenyr, to deny the appeal of using such a weapon against the krey, but Elenyr would know it was a lie. She always knew.

"It is tempting," Mind said, unwilling to meet her gaze.

She rose and stepped to the large window, gazing out to sea. "Power is tempting to us all," she said softly. "We believe it will solve our problems, hurt our enemies, but most importantly, we think it will keep us from being afraid."

"I'm not afraid."

"Aren't you?" Elenyr asked.

Mind met her gaze, and realized what she meant. He was loathe to agree, but he *was* afraid, not of the Dark or its army, not of Serak, but of the Empire. He feared the Empire's might, their unfathomable machines, their vastness. And the Dark was a means to fight that fear.

Elenyr nodded as if she understood. "Serak, too, is afraid of the Empire. He does not believe that they can be defeated by the people here on Lumineia."

"We would not survive a conflict," Mind scoffed. "We would be as an insect to them."

"All it takes is one voice," Elenyr said. "One leader that becomes hundreds, then thousands, and then millions."

"We cannot fight the Empire," Mind said. "We would be destroyed, the survivors left to become experiments."

"On our own, yes."

Mind frowned. "What do you mean?"

"The Empire may be vast, but it will have its share of enemies. Humans that wish to be free, houses that are sympathetic to the plight of slaves. There will be groups that desire the end of the Empire, even if it means changing the very fabric of their existence. There are always dissenters."

"Is that what the Eternals do?" Mind asked. "Look for dissenters?"

"Among other things," Elenyr said.

"How do you know so much about the Eternals?"

"The high oracle always learns about the Eternals," Elenyr said. "But as the Hauntress, Ero has sought me to join their ranks. He even thought you a candidate."

"You refused?"

"Of course," she replied. "I had other duties here, and you were far from ready to be on your own."

"And now?"

"Draeken is stable," Elenyr said. "You proved that at the Stormdial." Her features tightened and she looked away, obviously thinking of Fire. "Your training is complete," she added, quieter than before. "And your path is now your own."

Mind considered the offering, wondering what path he would choose. She was right, of course, they could be Draeken, permanently, or they could remain as fragments, living separate lives, battling separate foes.

Mind disliked both options. As the fragment of Mind, he felt a deep yearning to merge with the other fragments. Usually he suppressed the emotion with the knowledge that they could not be merged, but that doubt was now gone. Mind also didn't want to let Draeken have control. Although he never said it, Draeken had a darker heart when they were merged. Water's integrity usually tempered Draeken's darker inclinations, but Mind didn't care for the prospect of being Draeken forever.

"I don't know," Mind finally said. "Especially now that Fire is gone."

Draeken stirred in his chest, a burst of heat, of anger at the words. Draeken wanted revenge for the killing. Even though Wylyn was already dead, Draeken wanted to punish the krey. Mind did not disagree.

"You feel Draeken more since Fire's death," Elenyr said. "Don't you?"

Mind hesitated, and then nodded. "Since absorbing Fire's magic, I can almost hear his thoughts, but I am still a fragment. I'm not sure what it means."

"Draeken gains strength based on how many fragments are present," Elenyr said. "His magic makes you stronger."

"I am uncertain I care for the feeling," Mind admitted. "We are apart but also together." He didn't say that he enjoyed the extra power that came with it.

"Draeken wants to come to power," Elenyr said. "We both know he has seen Senia's vision."

Mind grimaced and looked away. It was the second time Elenyr had confessed to knowing Senia's vision of the future, where Draeken led the Dark army. Mind hated that she possessed such a vision of him. Mind ground his hand against the glass, abruptly angry.

"I cannot imagine committing such an atrocity," he growled. "Yet I saw a piece of the vision be fulfilled this very day. I feel as if I'm on course to see it occur, and nothing I can do will stop Serak's plan. I feel powerless."

He struck the window, sending cracks spiderwebbing outward. The helplessness, the anger, the loss of Fire, the weight of everything burgeoned up inside him, and it was all he could do not to scream and shatter the window. His chest heaved and he clenched his eyes shut, wrestling with the anger.

Elenyr's hand settled on his arm. "Do you want such power?"

The question was earnest and not condemning, said with love as only a mother could. All the emotion gradually drained from Mind and he turned to face her. Elenyr looked up at him, waiting, her expression full of trust.

"A part of me does," he said. "And I don't know if it's Draeken or me."

"You have felt others die," Elenyr said. "Would you want such power, knowing the slaughter it would cause?"

He recoiled at the thought of purposely ending the lives of so many, and in that reaction he saw Elenyr's truth. He would not become the butcher of the vision, would never lead the Dark army, would never betray what Elenyr had taught. He did see the merit to Serak's plan, but he was unwilling to pay the price.

"I can't let Draeken fall to Serak," he said.

Elenyr smiled. "And I won't let you fall to Draeken."

Mind smiled, grateful for Elenyr. Before he could say as much, Jeric burst through the door. Shouts came from outside, filling the city, not fearful, but excited. Mind tried to listen to their thoughts but they were too distant. Then Jeric caught Elenyr's hand and dragged her towards the open door.

"What's going on?" Elenyr asked.

"You have to see for yourself," he said.

They reached the balcony outside the lighthouse and Mind surveyed the city. Thousands were in the streets, shouting and calling, their words rising up in a giant swell. At first so many voices made it impossible to hear, and then Mind caught the refrain.

"The king has returned!"

"King Justin has arrived in Terros!"

Mind raised an eyebrow and looked to Jeric, who smiled and nodded. "The news is sweeping the city. And it wasn't just King Justin. All the monarchs have appeared."

"They escaped from Serak?" Elenyr asked.

Jeric jerked his head. "They were released."

Mind scowled, disliking the news. Captives were always freed for a purpose, either because of pressure from outside, or because it served the captor's needs. Knowing Serak, he'd released the monarchs for his own purpose, and Mind guessed it was not for the benefit of the people.

"Serak has begun final preparations," Mind murmured. "And the final conflict is set to begin." His words elicited a burst of dread, but from Draeken came a different emotion.

Anticipation.

Chapter 8: A Dangerous Ally

Tardoq traveled with the group of Serak's soldiers south and west. He set a blistering pace that left the humans struggling to keep up. Taking smaller trails, they journeyed across southern Griffin to and passed through the elven forest of Orláknia to reach Talinor.

Tardoq had donned a large cloak and cowl, obscuring his dakorian identity so he resembled a rock troll. The Order soldiers were disguised as a merchant caravan and joined a wagon on their way to Talon's Well.

Tardoq kept to himself, refusing to engage in conversation with any of the humans at his side. After a while they stopped trying, with the captain casting him uncertain looks from the head of the group. Tardoq sighed and looked to the sky, wondering how he was going to get home.

He had no allusions about Serak. The man was an ally of circumstance, and intended to occupy him until Tardoq proved no longer useful. The more Tardoq considered his options, the more he realized he had one viable chance to return home, through the fragments of Draeken and one they called the Hauntress. Only they could connect him to Ero and the Eternals.

It was a vain hope. They were his foes and would never return him to his home. Tardoq knew how to bring the Empire to Lumineia, and the Hauntress would fear the repercussions of his return to the Empire. He was an enemy with too much knowledge.

Tardoq grunted in irritation and watched the other travelers on the road. It had snowed in the west, but here the winter had yet to hit. The roads were cold and nearly frozen, ice forming in the hollows of tree roots. The frigid temperatures rattled the Order members, who shuffled in their saddles and pulled thick furs tighter about their shoulders. The icy wind cut through the clothing, making them curse.

Tardoq felt the chill, but it did not pierce his armor or flesh. His perfected body could withstand extreme temperatures, and to him the wind was a soft breeze. But this time it seemed sharper, and he found himself chilled by a deeper emotion. Doubt.

They passed a family traveling together. The father guided the horse while the two daughters played inside a cart, sitting atop barrels of ale. They giggled and laughed, hiding beneath layers of cloth every time their father looked. The father hid a smile when the children hid anew, and feigned confusion until they appeared. A game of love between father and children, one Tardoq had rarely seen among the humans in the Krey Empire.

Like most of his kind, Tardoq had been taught that man was a lesser race, their bodies and minds inferior, halfway between beast and krey, capable of labor and little else. Tardoq had helped harvest worlds where the humans had propagated across the globe, their need to build only matched by their desire for blood. Wars were common, and many slaves had perished. But here they were not slaves. Here they were free. As disturbing as it was to witness, Tardoq saw parallels to his own family, to his own father and brothers.

The two girls caught sight of him and their eyes widened. They whispered to each other and then waved shyly. Tardoq regarded them with cold eyes that did not seem to intimidate, and eventually the little girl reached out of sight and withdrew a small, wooden sword. She held it up, and offered it to Tardoq.

"I do not need a toy," Tardoq said.

The father glanced back and a touch of fear tightened his features, his eyes traveling up and down Tardoq's towering frame, noting the horns in the hood, which he probably assumed came from a helmet. Then he seemed to shake himself, and impossibly, assumed he was a friend.

"You'd better take it," the man said. "It will hurt her feelings if you don't."

Annoyed, yet unable to deny the girl's wide eyes, Tardoq reached his large hand out and the girl placed the wooden sword in his palm. It was smaller than his smallest finger, the weapon hardly a sliver in his hand, yet the girl smiled like she'd bequeathed a weapon of legend.

"Be careful," she advised in a tiny voice, "'tis real sherp."

"You mean sharp," her older sister hissed.

"That's what I said," the girl retorted. "Sherp."

A faint smile crossed Tardoq's lips and he straightened. "I'll be careful, little one."

The two girls fell to giggling and ducked under the layers of blankets, their laughter muffled but clear enough to realize they were excited a rock troll had liked her gift. The father smiled and slowed his horse to walk beside Tardoq, who noted he'd fallen behind his companions, several of which were looking back.

"Where are you traveling, stranger?" the father asked.

"Talon's Well," Tardoq said.

The man lit up. "My wife is there. Perhaps you can stop by. My girls would love to hear tales from a—"

"I'm sorry," Tardoq said. "But I must hasten."

He lengthened his stride, leaving the confused man behind. He caught up quickly to the Order soldiers and made to throw the wooden sword into the ditch. But at the last moment he hesitated, and opened his palm to examine the tiny toy.

On another world, the girls would have trembled in fear before a dakorian, especially one with the rank of Bloodwall. Their father would have been terrified that Tardoq would take the girls to be sold, a completely normal action. This time, such an action seemed repugnant. He growled to himself and again sought to discard the wooden weapon. Again he hesitated, and with a sigh he tucked it into a fold of his cloak.

"Speaking to the locals?" Captain Borne asked, a trace of suspicion in his tone.

"Keeping up appearances," Tardoq said.

"Stay with the group," he said.

Tardoq closed the distance so quickly the man nearly fell off his horse, and the mount whinnied in fear. Borne gazed into the blazing eyes of the dakorian, and his courage abandoned him. Tardoq's voice quivered with anger.

"I do not take orders from one such as you."

"My apologies." The man trembled in his saddle, and flicked the reins, taking him away.

Tardoq followed behind, annoyed that he'd almost snapped the man's neck. In the Empire, he would have killed any slave that had spoken with such idiocy. He scowled, and realized the freedoms of men were a two edged sword. They made a young girl happy, but made grown men think they could issue orders to a dakorian.

After the encounter, the other Order guards kept their distance and muttered to themselves as they cast Tardoq suspicious looks. Tardoq didn't care. Their mutterings were like squawking birds. Still, it would not be wise to antagonize the men who served Serak, not when he was Tardoq's only ally.

The group reached the edge of Talon's Well, entering from the eastern road and passing between the remains of hundreds of walls that resembled the fins of fish. They'd obviously been intended to encompass the city but were abandoned as the city grew too quickly.

Built into the saddle between two hills, a large well marked the gathering place of the village, and they passed around it, many of the villagers pausing to stare at Tardoq's cloaked figure. On the opposite side, the group ascended a curving road to a large estate situated on the eastern hill, the home of Lord Hyren, a former Order member who'd been killed by the fragments.

The group entered the main gates of the estate to find the courtyard in turmoil, men and women rushing to load carts for departure. A large wall had been opened like a door, revealing a secret tunnel descending to a subbasement. It too was occupied by wagons rushing to depart.

Captain Borne dismounted. "What's going on?"

"The fragments of Draeken attacked the Order halls to the east," someone said. "We believe they are coming here next."

Captain Borne barked orders and the groups began to depart, the wagons ambling down the road in an attempt to escape before the powerful fragments struck. Tardoq stood in the middle of the courtyard, wondering if he should care. These men and women had betrayed their world, their people, to follow Serak and Wylyn, whom they'd thought to be gods.

Tardoq knew he should consider them allies, even help them survive, but he couldn't muster any concern. They were slaves that had betrayed other slaves, and deserved their fate. He cocked his head to the side, wondering why he disliked calling them slaves.

Captain Borne spotted Tardoq in the courtyard and called to him. "Can you help them load those crates?"

"Do I look like a beast of burden?" Tardoq retorted.

He did step out of the way, allowing others to help with the loading and unloading. He wondered what he should do. Help? Or simply depart? Both were unappealing, and he snorted in disgust, wondering how he'd gotten himself so trapped.

Temporarily ignored in the shuffle of wagons and men, he drifted to the side of the courtyard. Crates were lifted onto wagons and departed, but there seemed to be dozens more from below. In the last few months he'd overheard some talking of Talon's Well, and knew it to be a central location to the Order of Ancients in Talinor, a hub where weapons and soldiers could flow to their destination.

Then he heard a distant whisper, the sound of steel on wood, a blade coming free. He cocked his head to the side. Then he heard a voice, one he'd heard before, a voice of someone excited for a coming conflict. He drifted deeper into the tunnel and waited. But it didn't matter. He knew the name.

The fragment of Shadow.

The fragments were here, and getting ready to attack. He focused his hearing, not magical like the humans, just enhanced, and marked their location. Shadow was in the building, third floor, while Water and Light were outside the gates. They had a host of soldiers, probably Talinorian guards, taking up position around the estate.

Tardoq scowled, disliking his choices. He could fight with the Order, but most would probably be killed. Or he could try to talk to the fragments, who had just lost the fragment of Fire. They would probably blame Tardoq. Then he heard the sound of a large blade clearing a sheath, and realized his one course to play. Turning away from the courtyard, he descended into the bowels of the estate. The attack came moments later.

A bellow of pain came from above, and the all the Order members came to an abrupt halt as a man tumbled out of a third floor window and crashed into a wagon. Shadow appeared in the opening and smirked as he twirled a dagger.

"I love it when they fight," he called.

Then the fragments launched a barrage of strikes on the wagons in the courtyard. Wood was broken and cloth torn, the contents spilling on the ground. In seconds the estate dissolved into battle, with shouts and the clang of blades echoing to Tardoq's position.

Ignoring the cries of battle, Tardoq descended deeper into the fortress, searching for the sound he'd heard. He ducked into a storage chamber when a group of Order soldiers rushed by. A shout came from below, and then a *thunk*, a large fist collided with a face. A battle erupted, and Tardoq turned toward it, descending the stairs to a small group of soldiers that sought to escape. They'd met a towering figure. She had entered from below, and probably intended on fighting her way up the estate, eliminating stragglers that sought to flee. She came to a halt when Tardoq stepped into view.

"Queen Rynda," Tardoq said, removing his cowl. "I did not expect to see you here."

The rock troll queen regarded him with surprise, and he hoped his plan had merit. He couldn't talk to the fragments and Serak would never be an ally. He needed an intermediary, one that could speak on his behalf.

Rynda flicked her bloody sword and tossed the body of a man aside. "I've been looking forward to another fight, and here it comes."

Chapter 9: Tardoq's Request

"I just want to talk," Tardoq said.

"That's what I have a blade for," Rynda said.

She charged the gap, her large sword swinging for his throat. Tardoq twisted, ducking into a storage room lined with crates. The handful of Order members scrambled for an exit. Their departure went ignored by both combatants, who were locked in a duel.

On their first encounter, Tardoq hadn't drawn his weapon until forced. He'd assumed her skill to be beneath him. Instead she'd manipulated the duel to scout her position, employed clever feints to elicit anger, and fought with skill befitting a dakorian. He wouldn't underestimate her again.

He pulled his hammer from his back and spun the weapon, deflecting her swing. She picked up a crate by the strap and launched it at his head. Instead of avoiding the blow, he leaned in, using his horns to shatter the crate. Broken wood, straw, and glass orbs fell across his shoulders and he swung his hammer, the weapon passing through air.

The dust cleared and he heard a whine of steel, the distinct sound of metal slicing through air. Rynda had used the crate as a distraction to shift to his right, her weapon coming for his leg. He let his bone armor absorb the impact, wincing as the blade chipped his armor— deeper than expected. She was stronger then he'd thought. But the slight wound allowed him to swing his hammer at her shoulder. With both hands on her sword, she was forced to duck, the hammer swinging over her back. She kept her momentum and rose into a retreat, a wise tactic, as the momentum had shifted.

He kept up the assault, his hammer swinging down, across, and into a brutal swipe that could have taken her head. She used the hilt of her sword, knocking the hammer upward. She retreated to a stack of crates, and then swung her blade down and behind, slicing the support.

A dozen crates fell into Tardoq, a curtain of wood, allowing Rynda to slip out of his grasp and return to the center of the room.

"I owed you a duel," Rynda said. "But you're holding back."

"So are you," he said.

"I'd rather not kill you too quickly," she said.

"What are you even doing here?" he asked. "I thought you'd return to your homeland."

"The kings and I encountered the fragments of Draeken," she said, "and I saw the opportunity to strike back at Serak. Light sent a message to my people, and I got the chance to come after Serak's organization."

She lunged, swinging her blade at his waist, a feint. At the last moment she spun, whirling so quickly her blade came at the opposite side. He jammed his hammer shaft into the ground, her blade bouncing off. But he didn't see her free hand coming for his gut, the metal knuckles extending into spikes.

He admired her tactics even as he sought to sidestep. Her fist grazed his side, the spikes cutting into his flesh—and then turning into hooks. They caught on his bone armor, bringing him to a halt. His hand was close to the end of his hammer, so he aimed a blow to her head, forcing her to duck. Then he caught her metal hand and twisted it away, removing the hooks. She flipped her sword behind her back and swung across his midsection, forcing him back and away.

"Your talent is impressive for one so young," he said.

"I hate compliments."

He grinned and retreated from her flashing blade. Until now he'd kept himself in check, but this time he unleashed his full might, deflecting her sword with his hammer, and then swinging the shaft at her leg, forcing her knee to buckle. She growled and went down, into a forward roll that took her out of reach.

He swung his hammer forward, too quickly to block, too quickly to sidestep. Rynda should have retreated, but she actually stepped forward, her metal hand balling into a fist. She leaned in and *punched* his hammer. His hammer bounced off her metallic hand, and both recoiled, the sound of the impact echoing in the room.

He hoped the space would allow him to speak, but she flipped her sword into a reverse grip and charged. Ducking inside his guard, she swung by fist and hilt, striking on both sides, the blows strong enough to damage his armor. He grimaced, and then landed his own attack, bringing his skull into hers. His horns dug into the skin of her forehead and she rocked back, giving him space to swing his hammer.

She recovered quickly, and for several furious seconds they dueled, their weapons clashing, bouncing through stacks of crates, spilling goods and straw onto the floor. Rynda took most of the damage, but despite Tardoq's superior body, skill, and history, her sword and fist left him bloodied. When she raised her sword to block an overhand blow, he saw his chance, and kicked her in the chest, knocking her backward. She grunted as the wind was knocked from her body, and managed to roll to her feet. He remained in place.

Each impact of his hammer had added energy, the runes glowing to life. He aimed the hammer at her chest and pressed the symbol, releasing half of the contained energy. The power would be enough to kill a human, and against a rock troll, would probably leave her with severe burns. But she swung her sword up and turned it sideways, holding it by the hilt and her hand on the flat of the blade. The blast of power hit the sword, and she'd braced well, her feet sliding backward. The power of the weapon was scattered, and she stood, smoke curling off the unscathed weapon. She wiped the blood from her cheek.

"Is that all you have?"

He chuckled. "You have the heart of a Bloodwall."

"I told you—"

"I know," he said. "You don't like compliments. Doesn't mean it isn't true."

"What are you doing here?" she demanded. "We aren't friends. We aren't allies. So why try to talk to me?"

"I need your help."

"And you think I would help you?" she scoffed.

Captain Borne rushed into the room, a trio of Order guards at his back. Blood from a wound to his head dripped down onto his tunic. He spotted Rynda and skidded to a halt. He pointed his weapon at her and barked at Tardoq.

"The hall is fallen. Get me out of here before—"

Tardoq aimed his hammer at the man and pressed the rune on the shaft, sending a blast of power into Captain Borne. He and his companions disappeared in the explosion, their bodies tumbling into the hall. Rynda scowled at the killing.

"Is that what you do to friends?" she asked.

"It's what I do to foes," he replied.

She regarded him with a curious expression, seemingly unaware of the blood on her shoulder, waist, and knee. He probably looked the same, and he spared a smile. Every time he encountered the woman, he was forced to acknowledge her caliber.

"Why?"

It was the obvious question, and the only reason she did not resume the fight. He'd fought for this moment, so she would listen, yet found the words difficult to express. He released an explosive breath.

"I'm not used to being at the mercy of someone like you."

"A slave?" she sneered. "I know what you and the Krey Empire think of us."

"You are no slave," he said quietly.

"I'm a queen," she said.

"How many souls are in your entire race?"

Surprised by the question, she jerked her head. "What does that have to do—"

"How many?" he pressed.

"Thirty thousand," she said.

It was an underestimate, probably by half. She wouldn't want to reveal her full strength. She was too smart for that, but it didn't matter. Tardoq motioned to her. "Well my race numbers a million times your own, all hardened and trained for war. You are undeniably formidable, but how long would you last against an army of dakorians?"

"Long enough to prove we aren't slaves."

The sounds of battle had diminished above, and it was only a matter of time before they began to search the rest of Lord Hyren's estate. He was running out of time, and Rynda still wanted to fight. He could tell by the way she held her sword, the way her fingers twitched.

"I need you to convey a message to the fragments," he said.

"Why not tell them yourself?"

"They would try to kill me," he said.

"And I wouldn't?"

"You wouldn't be able to." She raised her sword, and he raised a hand to placate her. "You know it's true. We've fought twice now, and you are talented enough to recognize a superior."

"I prefer to see for myself."

More calls from above. They were beginning their search. He subtly shifted his hold on his hammer, positioning his thumb over a different symbol. Rynda noticed the motion, but wouldn't know what the symbol meant.

"I don't belong on Lumineia," Tardoq said. "And with Wylyn dead, I have no way home."

"And Serak?"

"Will eventually betray me," Tardoq said. "I am too unpredictable, and he will eliminate the threat."

Her eyes flicked to the dead captain. She understood. Serak had no choice and would kill Tardoq because he was not part of his plan. It explained why Tardoq was coming to Rynda, and why Tardoq wouldn't risk asking help directly from the fragments.

"They told me everything about your Empire," Rynda said, beginning to stalk around him, between him and the exit. "If they help you, they will be giving the Empire the location of Lumineia."

"Nevertheless," Tardoq said. "I ask their aid."

"You are their foe."

"I *was* their foe," Tardoq corrected, gradually putting pressure on his hammer. "I could be their ally."

"Against Serak?"

Tardoq nodded, and heard the approach of several outside the door. "Give them my message, would you?"

She shrugged. "I'd rather they hear it from your lips."

"Make sure they understand," Tardoq said. "I help them finish Serak. They help me go home."

"Rynda?" a voice called from the hall outside.

"In here," she called. "And just wait until you see what I have caught."

"Until next time," Tardoq said.

He slammed his hammer into the floor, the impact powering the weapon anew. Then he pressed the rune and clenched his eyes shut against the burst of blinding light. Rynda cursed and shielded her face, the light so bright the reaction was instinctual. His eyes closed, Tardoq glided around her and out the door, descending the steps to the lowest subbasement. By the time she recovered Tardoq was out the lower exit and into the city, a cowl over his head.

The action was a gamble, and it had burned the only ally he had. Serak would never be an ally again. If the fragments refused, Tardoq would be alone. It would only be a matter of time before he was killed.

He paused on the edge of the city and looked back, watching the group of soldiers search for him. With a sigh, he turned into the woods and departed. For the first time in his long life, he was well and truly alone.

Chapter 10: The Return of Carn

As Elenyr, Mind, and Jeric traveled south, the news of the kings' return spread like wildfire, with every village buzzing. The threat of Serak was quickly growing, and an order had been issued. Griffin was headed to war against the Order of Ancients. What came as a surprise was the whispers of an alliance with other kingdoms.

Including Erathan.

Elenyr heard the news from a town crier a day's ride north of Terros, and her blood boiled. The people hailed King Numen as a hero who'd fought the Hauntress and Serak. He'd returned to Griffin alongside King Justin.

"Even now!" the crier shouted. "The mighty King Numen sends word to his armies, which will shortly join our own great nation. The king has spoken, to arms! Let us eradicate this vile Order of Ancients from our lands, before the bloodthirsty Serak can destroy the people. But be wary of the Hauntress, who has been deemed an enemy of the people!"

"I wish I'd slit Numen's throat," Elenyr muttered.

The trio passed outside the crowd and returned to the street, working their way past the knot of men reporting to their captain. A campaign in the winter took time and carried inherent risks. It would take months to gather the forces, and the king would likely march after the snowmelt in the spring. If the armies of the other nations gathered as well, it would be the mightiest assemblage of forces Lumineia had ever seen. But Serak was not the only one being hunted, and bounty posters were everywhere, showing the faces of Elenyr, Jeric, and the "five brothers of Draeken."

"We used to protect them." Mind's voice was dark. "Now they call for our execution."

Elenyr spared him a look. Mind's expression remained clouded, and she knew he felt the ache of Fire's death. What they'd witnessed with Jeric only served to heighten the danger, but it was the first time the people wanted their blood. He felt betrayed.

"The people are fickle," Jeric murmured. "In a few generations you will be admired again."

"We shouldn't have to fight for their affection," Mind snapped. "We've saved them a thousand times over, and now they've turned against us. We even have to wear these blasted cloaks."

All three wore cloaks, the cowls pulled low over their eyes. The bitter cold and frequent snowfalls made it seem only prudent, yet the group had never walked in fear. The irritation was expected, but Elenyr sensed a deeper current from Mind, a darker anger that seeped into his words.

They passed out of the city and made their way south, towards Terros. Upon hearing the news in Orinfall, Elenyr had insisted they speak to King Justin. The words of the criers and rumors were one thing, but she needed to hear the truth from his lips. Jeric offered to stay with Mind, but Elenyr argued that they should stick together. Elenyr didn't say it, but she no longer trusted Jeric. He may have been Ero, head of the Eternals, but Elenyr wasn't certain she could believe his motivations.

The trio managed to acquire hardy steeds and made their way along the wintery road. The recent storm had cleared, leaving the road muddy and icy. The few men that braved the road were bundled in furs.

Elenyr spoke little, still brooding on everything that had occurred in recent weeks. Fire's death and the revelation that Jeric had been Ero were both added to what she'd seen of the Dark and its army. Her mind jumped from topic to topic, and she wrestled with the murky tides of recent events.

When they reached Terros, they found it heavily guarded. Five thousand troops were busy constructing a wall around Outer Terros and emptying the farms to make room for arriving troops. Roads were guarded, and the settlements inside the wall were heavily patrolled. Troops from Talinor had already begun arriving.

"I'll go in alone," Elenyr said.

"King Numen is in there." Jeric dismounted and led his horse to an inn called the *Wailing Wind*, located outside the wall "I don't like the idea of you going in alone."

"I appreciate your worry," Elenyr said. "But I have no intention of striking at him. It's King Justin I wish to speak with."

"We'll wait here," Mind said. "Just be careful. Justin may not know that Numen is his enemy."

"I'll be careful," Elenyr said.

Night was falling, so she left Mind and Jeric at the inn and made her way into the dark trees. The bright moon reflected in the snow, which sparkled like tiny diamonds. She circled the wall, looking for a point of ingress.

She could drop into the earth, of course, but that wouldn't let her see what lay inside the expanding camp. Built of rough-hewn logs lashed together, a barrier already reached for a mile. Military camps lined the interior, and the constant thudding of axes continued into the night.

Elenyr drifted to the wall and phased to ethereal. She entered the wood and peeked onto the opposite side. As she'd expected, the bulk of the attention was on top of the wall, where a thin walkway allowed soldiers to patrol. She watched the guards and then passed through, drifting into the darkness on the other side of their torches.

They could not harm her in her ethereal form, but being spotted would alert King Justin—and King Numen—of her presence. Numen would be ready for her, and seek to stop her conversation with Justin. Elenyr turned corporeal and advanced into Outer Terros, pulling her cloak about her shoulders as if to ward off the chill.

Until now, Outer Terros had been a sprawling village. Collections of inns and taverns were interspersed by farms and silos. Instead of an expensive wall, past kings had ordered great towers erected, each armed with dwarven ballistae set on various balconies. The towers had no entrance at their base. Instead, they connected to an underground network of tunnels that reached back to the city, allowing them to receive support from the city in times of war. Mind had helped King Justin's great grandfather design the system, but it had never been put to the test. Not yet.

73

Elenyr ducked behind a stable to avoid a patrol and passed through the wall when they searched her position. King Justin was taking no chances, and whatever he'd said had inspired the men to increased vigilance. She reluctantly dropped into the earth and glided west.

To her sight, the earth and stone was nearly transparent. Boulders were darker, while earth was lighter. The tunnels between the towers were visible, each branch stretching to connect to each other. All connected to two squat guardhouses where soldiers in Outer Terros could enter the underground system. Large stones were placed above the tunnels at intervals, rigged to collapse in case of need.

Avoiding the tunnels, Elenyr glided through the earth until she reached the city, and from there to the castle. The city itself contained several districts, each with their own walls. The poor lived in Outer Terros, while the merchants, moneychangers, craftsmen, and officers lived in the more opulent homes in the city.

Elenyr glided under the outer wall of the castle and ascended into the gardens. Steeped in darkness, the gardens were illuminated by the sun and large light orbs, the light washing across the snow, passing through the empty branches of the trees. She swept her gaze across the gardens, marking the location of patrols and guards before descending back into the ground, and passing into the fortress.

She slowed at the intersecting corridors, eyeing the hallways. King Numen would probably be in the guest quarters, and although she'd promised Mind and Jeric she wouldn't, she turned in that direction, her hand closing about her hilt. She'd never been an assassin, but Numen deserved killing.

Shoving the doubt aside, she passed through the thick walls of the fortress, just feet from patrols of guards. They surveyed the empty corridors while she glided through the stone, just inches from their swinging arms. She reached the guest corridors and found them to be heavily guarded, the soldiers bearing the mark of Erathan. She rose into the ceiling, and crawled across its surface until she lay on the ceiling above the large bed.

Numen was awake, and sat at a desk at the side of the room. He seemed lost in thought, and tapped a dry quill against a paper. She drew her sword, and even in the stone above, there was a whisper of steel on the scabbard.

Numen looked up, eyeing the ceiling, before turning back to the paper. Elenyr came to a halt, confused by what she saw. The man looked like Numen, right down to the scars on his cheek, which had obviously been repaired by a healer. But there was something off, something different.

Elenyr glided through the ceiling and spun to descend the nearby wall. There she paused on the threshold of stone, watching the man secretly known as Carn, the lightning mage. Again he seemed off, and again she stayed her blade.

There was a knock at the door and Numen stood. All at once his manner changed, his features turning more imposing. Elenyr's lip curled with hatred as he called for the guard to enter. The door swung open and a guard entered, conveying a letter on a platter. He passed it to Numen, who motioned him to depart.

"That will be all."

"Yes, my lord."

Numen waited for the door to shut and then sat at his desk, undoing the letter. Elenyr shook her head in confusion. While the servant had been present, the man had resembled Numen. But now he seemed to lack the imposing air, the royal bearing. After all the times Elenyr had seen a persona, she could not shake the obvious feeling.

The man was not King Numen.

She didn't want to believe it, but everywhere she looked she saw evidence that he was an imposter. There were no lightning charms in the room. Surely the real King Numen would have sought to protect himself from an attack by Elenyr. She knew his identity, and could reach him through the very walls. But nary a spark of power marred the bed or the stone walls. She did notice a sword leaning against the bed, a matching dagger on the man's hip. Both exuded power, revealing the lightning magic within. He had the weapons and the face, but the man was not Carn.

Scowling, Elenyr reluctantly sheathed her sword and glided upwards. The castle of Terros resembled a sitting griffin, with the great hall between its front paws. The left wing contained guest quarters, servant quarters, and storage chambers. The right wing contained the offices of the military, as well as a small barracks and the armory. At the top of the fortress sat the king's private chambers, a spacious series of rooms with large windows that overlooked the sea on the west, and Outer Terros on the east. Elenyr glided into the council chamber and stepped onto the thick carpet.

The furniture of the large council room were fashioned of rich linens and fine wood. Moonlight filtered through the many windows, which were shaped like a large octagon. Toward the griffin's head and above the great hall sat the king's private office, while the opposite direction led to the king's private quarters.

Elenyr noticed a glow coming from beneath the door to the office and glided past the large oak table. She listened for any sound of guards, and when she heard nothing, passed through the thick wood. On the opposite side, an expansive office contained an assortment of couches, cabinets, and bookshelves. Large windows lined three walls, granting an expansive view of the city and the surrounding region. A small fire crackled in the fireplace at Elenyr's side, while across from her a tall man sat at his desk. He looked up at her entry, his eyes going wide.

"King Justin," Elenyr said. "I hope I'm not interrupting."

Chapter 11: King Justin's Tale

King Justin came to his feet, his hand going for his sword. It came free in a hiss of steel and he pointed the blade at her. He was a gifted swordsman, but nowhere near her equal. Obviously he knew it, for he darted to the bell set against the wall, the one that would summon the guard. Elenyr got there first. She slashed once, her weapon striking his sword just above the hilt. It tumbled from his grip and he withdrew.

"Are you here to kill me like you tried to kill Numen?" he spat.

"Don't be a fool," Elenyr growled. "I've served your ancestors for thousands of years. I'm not going to kill you."

"Yet you left us to rot as Serak's captives."

"I could not save you," she said.

"And Numen?" He retreated another step, rubbing his hand. "Half my guard saw what you did to him. You tried to kill him in the grounds of this very castle!"

"They did not see what he did to *me*," Elenyr snapped.

He recoiled at the heat in her voice, and she wrestled her emotions to a halt. Numen had nearly killed her, but Justin could still be an ally. She needed him to believe she was a friend, and shouting would not lend credence to her words.

"What are you talking about?" he demanded.

"King Numen goes by another name," Elenyr said. "With his magic, he goes by the persona of Carn, and serves the very man that held you captive."

"Serak?" He snorted in disbelief. "And you claim Numen has magic? I've known the man his whole life. He's never shown any sort of power."

"He's a lightning mage," she said.

77

King Justin actually laughed, the sound low and incredulous. Elenyr clenched a fist, struggling to keep her anger in check. Justin was mostly a good man, cautious and clever. But he was also arrogant, and she was asking him to believe he'd missed multiple hidden qualities by one he'd called friend.

"You really have lost your wits," he said.

She took a step forward and he hastily retreated a step. "Serak sent Numen to kill me in my home." She rolled up her sleeve to show the ugly scar. "He would have succeeded if not for Jeric, who managed to get me to the elven healers at Ilumidora."

He frowned, revealing that he knew of her time in Ilumidora. He probably hadn't known the cause, but rumors had been rampant about her near death. Justin would have heard them all, and known the Hauntress had lain injured at the elven capital.

"You think I'll believe anything you say?" he asked. "Numen is a friend, and his mother was my aunt. He would not follow one like Serak."

"I don't know his motivations," Elenyr said. "I merely know his actions. He has been an acolyte of Serak for some time."

"He was in prison with me," Justin protested.

"An excellent means of establishing credibility," she said. "Tell me. Was he there when you escaped?"

Justin shook his head. "Serak had taken him a week prior."

For the first time there was doubt in his voice, and Elenyr advanced. Justin withdrew a step, but she did not make for him. Instead she walked through the couch and to the eastern wall, where she swept her hand to the sea.

"You've heard the tales of the great tower?"

"The Shard of Midnight." He nodded. "Word is it rose, and then shortly after fell into the sea. The azure people claim it's a sign from Ero. Others say it heralds the return of Skorn."

Elenyr grunted at the reference to Jeric, and turned to face him. "Nine days ago I stood on the tower. I fought the krey woman, and King Numen. Wylyn was killed and the tower destroyed."

78

Justin regarded her with a scowl, clearly not wanting to believe her words, yet unable to refute them. He knew of the tower and Numen's absence at the same interval. Numen had probably been the only king taken by Serak for a mysterious purpose, and Justin was enough of a tactician to see a reason to doubt.

"Even if what you say is true, it does not explain why Serak would have taken us in the first place."

"That's what I do not understand," she said. "While I have been battling Wylyn, you have been in Serak's grasp. I wish to understand his purpose."

Justin folded his arms and stared out the western window. For several moments he did not respond, and she guessed he was deciding whether or not to trust her. Spotting his fallen sword, she reached down and picked it up. Then she set it on the desk, the hilt pointed to him.

"King Numen was here on Serak's order," she said. "He infiltrated Wylyn's ranks and sought to assassinate me a second time, here in this castle. That is what your guards witnessed. They saw me fighting back, defending *against* the Order of Ancients. I have never given you cause to distrust me, so now I ask for your faith. Believe that I am your ally, just as I was to your father, and his father before him."

She retreated a step, leaving the sword on the desk. Justin's eyes flicked to her, and then to the sword, and he picked up the weapon. He released a long breath and then slowly sheathed the blade.

"Your words are convincing," he said. "But I am uncertain. Nevertheless, I will tell you what you wish to know."

"Where did he hold you captive?"

"Xshaltheria." King Justin pointed east. "Ancient forge of the dwarven race."

"How did you escape?"

"That is what is most disturbing," he said. "We didn't. Queen Rynda broke our cell and helped us escape. When we reached the gates, Serak ordered his men to leave it open. He *allowed* us to leave."

Elenyr frowned. "Why?"

"Serak did not give a reason." Justin's voice was dark. "He just let us depart, even gave us horses and a wagon of supplies."

"Just like that?"

He shuddered. "After what I witnessed, I fear for what he could do."

"Tell me everything about your captivity," she said.

He regarded her with a frown, and then consented. He spoke of waking in a cell, and a small prison with the orc king and the dark elf queen. One by one the other kings arrived, with Rynda and Dothlore arriving last. King Numen came and was removed, twice.

As King Justin told the tale of his imprisonment, Elenyr began to wonder if the kings were ever in any danger. It was almost as if Serak simply wanted them to become allies against him, to perceive him as the greater threat. He'd forced them to gather against him, and now the races knew his location, and were raising armies to come to his door. Then Justin's tale took a darker turn when he spoke of the Cleansing, and the Dark Gate.

"He called it a cleansing?" Elenyr asked.

Justin shrugged in confusion. "Serak claimed it would prevent something from exiting the Dark Gate while allowing an army through. I would think him mad, if he wasn't so calm."

The news was disturbing, for it revealed Serak knew exactly what lay behind the Dark Gate. Where did he gain such knowledge? How did he know such secrets? He'd even devised a way to stop the Dark while permitting the army of fiends to pass through the Gate.

"He's not mad," Elenyr said absently. "Two of my sons found his stonesap mine. He'd been gathering the resource for over a decade."

"So he truly can do as he claims?" Justin passed a hand over his face. "Ero save us."

After what she'd witnessed on Kelindor, Elenyr finally understood Serak's plan. Serak had used the Cleansing to stop the Dark from entering Lumineia while allowing the twisted creatures on Kelindor through the portal. The army would vastly outnumber even the combined forces of the kings. There was only one thing left to his plan.

Draeken.

Serak needed Draeken. The reason may not have been clear, but it explained all his machinations, all his attempts to speak to the fragments. He'd talked to Water in Keese and spoken to Light in the north. He'd spoken to Shadow in Mistkeep, and indirectly revealed his desires to Fire and Mind, through the Incinerake at Beldik and then Gendor's strike against the Assassin's Guild. He didn't want the fragments. He wanted Draeken.

"Why does he wait?" Justin was asking. "If he has the Gate, why not just start the invasion?"

"There is more to his plan," Elenyr said, unwilling to reveal Draeken's role.

She realized the truth of Wylyn. The krey invasion, the dakorian soldiers, it had all been a feint. Even his Order of Ancients. It was all a ruse to draw Draeken to the fore, to force the fragments to use all of their power. Serak had planned for thousands of years, built everything on a single goal, to bring Draeken into the fold.

She clenched her jaw. She would not let him have her sons. Not now. Not ever. No amount of intrigue would stop her from protecting her family against his vile plan. But she needed a plan of her own, one that would keep them from falling to Draeken's baser ambitions.

"How much time to do we have?" Justin asked.

"I suspect that when your army arrives, he will be ready," she said.

He passed a hand over his face, looking old for the first time since she'd known him. "Rynda said as much, but I didn't believe her."

"Will she fight with you?" Elenyr asked.

"She said she would," Justin said. "Then she met three of your sons and went south. She said Serak would expect her to return to her people, so she journeyed with the fragments to destroy the Order halls in Talinor." He sniffed in irritation. "She should have come to Griffin first."

Elenyr didn't argue the point. With all the forces gathering to Griffin, they would have an abundance of swords at their disposal, while Talinor would be dispatching their armies out of the kingdom. Rynda's tactics were flawless. Elenyr also liked the idea of her fighting alongside Water, Shadow, and Light. If Elenyr could not stand by them herself, Rynda would be her chosen replacement.

Mistaking her silence for concern, Justin came to his feet and pointed to the map table set against the window. "Should we not gather our army?"

"That's your decision," Elenyr said. "I go to thwart Serak's plans. If I succeed, the Dark Gate will never open."

"And if you fail?" he asked.

"Then pray that your army is strong enough to stop his," she replied.

She turned to leave, but he called out to her. "Wait, that's all you'll say? You come for answers and give none of your own?"

"Be grateful you do not shoulder my task," Elenyr said, and then thought better of her reserve. Sharing a secret would help Justin trust her, and she certainly needed the king on her side. "I will tell you this, the man in your castle is not King Numen. He is an imposter, probably here on Serak's order."

Justin blinked in surprise. "I've known the man my whole life. I would know if he were not who he says he is . . ." He frowned, and Elenyr guessed he was recalling subtle inconsistencies that spoke to a larger lie.

"Find him out," Elenyr said. "But be cautious. If he is on Serak's errand, his purpose will be dangerous."

"If what you say is true, where is the real King Numen?"

Elenyr had not thought to question his fate, but now that she did, she realized only one answer made sense. Numen had failed to kill her in Cloudy Vale, failed at the king's castle, and failed again at the Stormdial. Each time Numen had suffered a great deal, and on the latest attempt, he'd nearly perished himself. He'd shown his weakness to Serak, a man who despised weakness. Serak would not risk another failure.

"I wager he is dead," Elenyr said. Justin leaned against the desk as if his strength had failed him, and Elenyr looked on in pity. "You have my sympathies, good king. I hope when we meet again, it is not to draw blades."

She raised a hand in farewell, and then passed through the door. She paused before entering the council room, ensuring it was empty before retreating from the castle. She did believe King Numen was dead, but she was not fool enough to believe Serak's goal had changed. He still wanted her dead, and the fact that he'd failed gave her an idea, the start of a plan. For the first time since Fire's death, she smiled.

Chapter 12: Kinship

Mind watched Elenyr depart towards the Terros castle and then followed Jeric into the *Wailing Wind*, a large structure with vaulted ceilings and an enormous fireplace. Several soldiers sat around the hearth, speaking in low tones. A group of workers sat on the opposite corner, obviously miners, their dirty gear marking them as returning rather than departing. A handful of women and children were also present, most families of soldiers that had been summoned to Terros.

The room itself was made of rough-hewn logs, the wood crafted by hand rather than magic. A woman worked at the counter, her husband in the kitchens behind. She was kind and swift, serving the needs of the many patrons while balancing the needs of her young daughter, who played behind the counter.

Out of habit, Mind sifted through the thoughts of those in the room, noticing the gnome in the corner. He was an exile from his own lands, and trying to avoid attention from the soldiers. The others in the common room hadn't noticed the gnome in his cowl. But he wasn't a threat. He just wanted to be left alone. One of the soldiers looked at Jeric and frowned, remembering his face from a wanted poster. Mind redirected his attention and altered his memory. He hadn't gotten a good look, so Mind didn't need to touch him to create a permanent memory.

Mind frowned as he sensed the depth of the spell, the permanent change in the soldier's consciousness. Even from a distance. He'd never been able to do that before. Perhaps the addition of Fire's magic had enhanced his own magic.

"I'll get us a room," Jeric said.

I'll get us a meal.

Mind spoke through a mental link. Jeric had sufficient mental shields to prevent his mind being read, but Mind's silent words would still be heard. Mind preferred to communicate using his magic, especially in public. It kept him from being overheard, and remembered.

Mind separated from Jeric and strode to the kitchens. The wife noticed him and Mind shifted her attention. She turned away and he entered the kitchens, where the husband worked over a stove. Mind slipped into the man's consciousness, and picked up his name. William. He was a good man and a good father, evident by the son working at his side. There were memories of laughter and smiles.

"Can I help you?" William asked, busy with frying a pan of potatoes.

"I like the sounds of a kitchen." Mind gave a disarming smile. "Do you mind if I just sit and listen?"

"Have a seat." William pointed to a worn chair by the door. "Hungry?"

"A bowl of stew for my companion. And bread and steak with mushrooms, if you have them."

"I might have a handful," he replied with a smile and wink. "Where you from?"

"Nowhere," Mind said. "Everywhere."

William dished up the plate and passed it to his son, who rushed it out of the kitchens. "Sounds lonely."

Mind leaned back into the chair and watched the steam rise from the pot over the fire. "What would you say to your son, if he felt lost?"

"I'd tell him to come home." William began cutting mushrooms.

Mind chuckled at the easy response. How easy it must be for the commoners to live their lives, only worried about their families, their inns and houses, their farms and children. Then Mind frowned, catching a string of thoughts from William.

William had another son, his eldest, who'd fallen in with a group of bandits. William hadn't seen him in three years. He and his wife spent much of their coin searching, hoping to see his return. Behind the man's affable smile and care for his children lurked an aching worry for one that was lost. William feared that he'd been killed.

85

Mind released a sigh. He should have known better. He'd listened to the thoughts of thousands of commoners over the years and knew the weight of their lives. But in all the recent events and the conflict with Serak, Mind had forgotten just how much the people carried. They had lost loved ones, a pain he hadn't understood until Fire's death.

He may have lived for thousands of years, but was his life so different? He had a family, brothers and Elenyr. The other fragments even had friends, including Shadow, who'd never had a friend until now. They'd had a home, at least until Serak had destroyed Cloudy Vale.

Mind looked about the warm kitchen and watched William's son stir the stewpot before filling a bowl. This was their home, what kept them safe, protected them against the weather. And Serak would see it destroyed. William didn't even know it, but his family was in grave danger.

Mind stood and accepted the plate and bowl, absently erasing his presence from William and his son's memories. William stared at him, his eyes unfocused, his features slack. On impulse, Mind leaned in and brushed his fingers across William's hand.

The contact heightened his magic, and Mind dove into his thoughts. Picking a memory of his lost son, he crafted a new memory of his son's return, when the boy had been alive and happy, excited to labor with a craftsman in Erathan. He wouldn't be back for some time. He embraced his father before departing.

Mind broke the contact and stepped away, leaving him to his stove. William blinked in confusion and then hurried to peel potatoes. His smile remained, but his shoulders were not as hunched, and his features were happier. Mind picked up his meal and slipped outside, adding the same memory to the wife as he passed.

Jeric caught his gaze and pointed upward, and Mind followed him up to their room. They settled into their room and began to eat, and Mind pondered his conversation with William. Since the conflict at the Stormdial he'd felt adrift, but not now. He glanced to Jeric.

"Tell me of the Krey Empire."

Jeric regarded him with a doubtful expression. "You do not wish to know of Serak?"

"If you knew more about Serak, you would have spoken," Mind said. "I wager you know as much about Serak as we do."

"True." Jeric took a bite of his bread. "What do you wish to know?"

"Everything."

"I'm not sure that's wise," Jeric said. "It will distract you from the current conflict."

"Am I not a member of the Eternals?"

"You are," Jeric said, leaning back into his seat. "But be patient with such knowledge. When Serak is dealt with, I'll tell you what you wish to know."

Mind disliked the lack of trust in Jeric's words, and a burst of anger welled in his chest. Seething in silence, he stabbed a piece of meat. He'd never been quick to anger, but the emotion was hot and hard, like it wanted to burst out of his flesh. Mind had lost a great deal, including his own brother, in order to extinguish a threat the Eternals should have prevented.

A distant part of him recognized that the anger was unfounded, that Jeric had not killed Fire. Mind wrestled for control, ultimately rising and retreating from the room. Jeric watched him go, and Mind realized Ero had always been watching the fragments. He'd visited on occasion, speaking to Elenyr, and occasionally the fragments. Ero had wanted their power to help fight the Krey Empire, same as Serak, and everyone wanted him for their own purposes.

Mind stalked down the hall, a spark of flame curling up his fingers and under his sleeve, burning the cloth. He shouldered the door open into his own room and all but slammed it shut. Breathing like a raging bull, he stood in the room, wondering what Elenyr would do if he killed Jeric.

The shocking thought drove him to the balcony. He stumbled outside, breathing deep of the crisp wintery air. Had he really thought of killing Ero? The krey had been the protector of Lumineia for ages, so why such a burst of animosity?

He noticed light coming from his hand and discovered the fire curling up his fingers, sinking into his flesh. The heat blackened the wood under his grip. He'd seen Fire do the same thing, get angry and accidently burn whatever lay nearby.

The anger abandoned him and he leaned against the railing, the grief sudden and sharp. His brother was dead, yet every time Mind felt Fire's magic, he saw his brother in himself. Breathing deep of the cold air, he stared into the dark forest and listened to laughter from a nearby inn, the music spilling from the open door as a trapper departed.

Was that the source of the anger? Fire's magic? Or was there a chance there was more? It was almost as if the thoughts of another had seized him, and for a moment Mind had almost lost control of his own body. But that could only come from Draeken.

Mind cupped a handful of snow in his hand and watched it melt between his fingers. Was it possible? Had Draeken attempted to seize control on his own? Such a thing had never occurred, suggesting the addition of Fire's magic into his body had somehow affected Draeken. Made him stronger, closer to the surface.

Mind dragged a chair out of the room and sat on the balcony, lost in thought. The icy wind could not pierce his skin, for Fire's magic burned in his flesh. The power simmered beneath the surface, always present, even though Mind had been reluctant to use the power. It felt as if he were betraying Fire's memory by doing so.

Snow began to fall, drifting through the canopy of empty branches to settle on the ground, gradually filling the balcony and chair on which he sat. He did not see it and instead examined the events of the previous weeks in a new light. This was not the first outburst, and Mind recalled other moments where a second consciousness attempted to assert itself. Draeken wanted to be in control, and adding Fire had brought him closer to being whole.

But could that mean Fire was alive?

Mind dared to consider the thought. If Draeken's mind was stronger, it could be true, for Draeken's consciousness only appeared when the fragments merged. Mind delved deep into his own consciousness, searching every corner of his being for any shred of truth.

At first he found nothing, no trace of his brother, or Draeken, but as he sifted through memories of the last few days, he recalled a fleeting thought that was not his own, a touch of emotion not of his heart. Like a wraith passing in his peripheral vision, he could not locate the source. Still, it's very presence—only after the battle at the Stormdial—revealed a single truth. Draeken *did* have more power, and it was his thoughts lurking within Mind.

The revelation was startling enough, but the explanation brought Mind to his feet. Draeken was only aware when a second fragment merged with Mind, suggesting Mind had absorbed more than Fire's magic that day in the tower. Mind sucked in his breath as he realized the truth.

The fragment of Fire might be alive.

Chapter 13: Hyren's Secret

Water slammed his palm onto the table. "We cannot trust Tardoq!"

Rynda folded her arms and raised an eyebrow. "I thought Fire was the angry one."

Water looked away, ashamed for his outburst. He refused to admit that Fire was gone, but a seething anger had settled into his gut. He knew he should accept that his brother had been killed, but he wasn't ready to give up hope.

"Whatever Tardoq's intentions, we need to deal with him." Water drew in a breath to steady his tone. "He has proven to be our foe."

"I'm not so certain about that." Shadow was using a longsword to pick the dirt from beneath his nails. "He let Relgor die outside of Mistkeep. I think he was beginning to doubt Wylyn's cause."

They were still in Talon's Well. The attack had gone smoothly, with only a few of their allies having fallen. The Order members had been killed or imprisoned, and wagons loaded with Order soldiers were winding their way towards Herosian.

The three fragments and Rynda were in the secret room Shadow had discovered. Sitting adjacent to the Lord Hyren's private quarters, the small chamber contained a treasure trove of Order records, including maps of halls, lists of names, and even amounts paid to bribe officials in Herosian, Ilumidora, Keese, and Erathan. As the Talinorian guard finished dismantling and carting off the resources of the estate, the four pored over the newfound information, preparing a list of potential targets. That's when Rynda had revealed Tardoq's presence.

"I don't see what the problem is," Light said, shrugging as if it didn't matter. "Tardoq isn't so bad." He held his hand over a paper, his fingers glowing across the table.

"He's a Bloodwall," Water said. "The moment he returns to the Empire, he'll send an army to our skies, just like Wylyn planned."

"I'm not so sure," Rynda wondered aloud. "He was different, almost lost. He doesn't have Wylyn, and he certainly doesn't trust Serak."

"Yet he trusts us?" Shadow snorted and tossed the sword away. It clattered against the walls and fell on a bookshelf. Water picked it up and hung it back on the wall.

"He had no choice," Water argued.

Light darted away, disappearing from the room without a word. Water watched him depart, saddened by Light's refusal to speak. He was used to Light being impulsive, but this was different. Light had taken to disappearing and returning without explanation, only the tears on his cheeks revealing his lingering struggle to accept Fire's absence.

"I don't care what you do with Tardoq's request," Rynda said.

"It's been three days since the battle," Water said. "You should have told us then."

Rynda cast him an annoyed look. "I don't report to you."

Water rubbed the back of his neck, wishing it would ease the crick that had appeared. "We can deal with Tardoq later. Right now we need to stay focused on the Order. How many elves arrived last night?"

Shadow leaned back in the chair and put his boots on the table. "Queen Alosia added fifty of her elite guard to our cause."

Rynda shoved Shadow's boots off the table in disgust. "That brings us to a hundred."

"The Order of Ancients in Talinor is nearly gone," Water said. "I think we should let the king's soldiers finish here and move to elven lands." He pointed to one of the papers they'd deciphered. "It seems some of their largest halls are there."

Rynda produced a map and placed it on the table. Then she pointed to a spot on the parchment. "We can make a central camp here, and strike the halls in Ilumidora, Gerthorn, Whitebark, Swallow Falls, Lentwood, and Riverdon."

"In the woods?" Shadow protested, and put his boots on the table again. "You want me to sleep in the snow?"

"It's just snow." Rynda shoved his boots off the table again. "Next time you put your legs on the table, I'm going to cut off your feet."

"That's a little extreme for getting mud on parchment," Shadow said, and put his boots on the table again.

Rynda drew her sword and swung, but Shadow turned his legs to shadow form, and the sword crashed through the wood, slicing through several papers. As they fluttered to the floor, Shadow stared at Rynda.

"Look at the mess you made!"

She took a step towards him but he disappeared out the door, his laughter echoing back. Rynda cursed him and sheathed her large sword. Then she rotated and stabbed a finger out the door.

"I'm going to kill him."

"I won't blame you," Water said.

He looked at the map, examining the locations she'd marked. Rynda had vocally wondered if the entire map was a feint, luring the fragments into an extended conflict with the Order. If it was, Water doubted it had been intentional. Despite all his planning, Serak could not have known how many would follow Wylyn, or how many halls would remain unscathed until now. No, the Order still needed to be eradicated.

"I've lost soldiers too, you know."

He didn't look up. "Fire was not a soldier."

"I've lost family," Rynda said, her tone distant.

Water finally met her gaze. "I didn't take you to be the consoling type." His voice was colder than intended, but he didn't apologize. He didn't want to talk about Fire, especially to the hardened rock troll. She regarded him with heavy eyes.

"The burden you carry is one I shoulder," she said.

"He was *part* of me," Water abruptly shouted. "Not a soldier or a brother or a friend, but *part of my soul!*"

He glared at Rynda, daring her to challenge his words. He even hoped she would draw her sword and strike, forcing him into the heat of battle. Anything so he didn't have to feel the rising ache. But Rynda regarded him with unflinching eyes.

"You aren't the only one to lose a piece of your soul."

Her unexpected words punctured his anger, which gradually drained away. Her expression, pained and filled with regret, implied she'd lost much more than he'd assumed. But how could she understand?

"Who?" he finally asked.

She looked away, and the silence stretched between them. He wondered if she would share at all. Her personality bordered on belligerent, and he'd never known her to speak her feelings, or her past. Then abruptly she shrugged.

"I had a sister," she said. "In our youth we were occasionally rivals, but we were always blood. She was the only one to match my skill. Except for Bartoth." Her features hardened. "She fell in love with Bartoth, admired his strength, his magic. She thought he deserved to be king. I had my doubts, but I trusted my sister."

"And Bartoth showed his brutality," Water said.

She swept her hand to the table. "He had more cruelty than the whole of the Order of Ancients, and it seeped out of his heart the longer he sought the throne. In the end I led a rebellion and my sister sided with me. She lost her life. I lost my hand." She held her steel hand aloft.

"Bartoth killed her?"

"I can still see her face," Rynda said, her eyes like fire-hardened steel. "She always believed Bartoth could change, that he would listen to reason. She believed right up until his hammer broke her ribs."

Water wanted to reach out to Rynda, but attempting to embrace a rock troll would probably be misconstrued. Still, it was the closest he'd ever seen a rock troll come to tears. Then Rynda shook herself and met his gaze.

"I know you're a fragment, but the pain you feel is the same as anyone else who has lost a loved one."

"Fire wasn't just a loved one," Water said quietly. "He was a part of me."

"My sister was my twin."

Water's eyes widened. Twins were uncommon for rock trolls, and highly regarded. It explained her people's reverence, and why they'd paid such a heavy cost for her hand. They loved her as their queen, as their leader, as their general.

But the tale gained new significance, and for the first time since Fire's death, he realized he was not alone in feeling the bitterness of loss. Men and women had lost fathers, brothers, children, and sisters. He'd assumed he was different because he was a fragment, but that assumption diminished the weight his friends carried.

"I'm sorry," he said.

"Don't apologize for losing a member of your family," Rynda said. "Apologize for failing to honor their memory."

"Still sorry," he said.

She held his gaze and then gave a nod of approval. "Maybe you aren't a total loss."

They were the words she'd said before the battle with Bartoth in the north, and they brought a smile to his lips. "Does this mean you don't hate men anymore?"

"I still hate men," she said. "But I'm making an exception in order to kill Serak."

"I just hope to be tolerated."

"That's a good goal," she said. "Achievable even."

He laughed, grateful for Rynda's words. She had an armored exterior, but her heart had been shredded. Perhaps that was how he would end up, forceful and borderline belligerent because of Fire's passing.

He wasn't going to stop hurting because of Fire's death. He couldn't. But at least he could set aside the simmering anger that kept burgeoning up. Fire deserved that much, and apparently so did Rynda.

Shadow entered the room, munching on a slice of cheese he'd cut with an axe. It had obviously been mangled, and bits of cheese still hung from the blade, which he carried in his free hand.

"That's not used for food!" Rynda snapped.

"Worked well enough," he said with a shrug.

Rynda glared daggers at Shadow, who continued to eat, seemingly oblivious to the fact that Rynda's hand twitched toward the hilt of her sword. Water spotted the glint of amusement in Shadow's eyes, but it carried a darker tinge. He too was trying not to think about Fire.

Light skipped inside with a wedge of meat. He spotted Shadow's axe and his eyes widened. "Oh, can I use that?"

"Get your own cheese slicer."

Light scowled and muttered, "Selfish."

Light conjured an even larger axe out of light and placed the meat on the table. Rynda bellowed in protest but Light slammed the weapon down on the table, the axe thudding into the wood, the meat parting, pieces spinning about the room. The largest struck Rynda in the face and fell on the map. Light casually picked it up and offered it to her.

"I thought you'd be hungry."

"Thank you Light." She ground the words out, and took the meat from his hand. "Did you happen to think of plates? I'm not a savage."

"Right." Light conjured a plate the size of Shadow's axe and offered it to her. Water stifled a smile. Rynda had a soft spot for Light, but her patience would not last forever. Pushing the meat aside, he bent over a paper, but just as he did a man burst into the room.

"Water," he said, breathless. "You need to see what we just found."

"Please tell me it's edible," Shadow said without moving.

"What did you find?" Light asked, happily chewing on a piece of meat.

"Lachonus," Water prompted the man. "What did you find?"

The man was a gifted warrior, one assigned to them by the Talinorian army. He boasted a shock of borderline dwarven red hair,

95

and his strength was legendary. Unusually, he was also fast and lacked the slowness to his dwarven heritage.

"We found another secret room," he said, his eyes lit with delight.

"Is there food inside?" Shadow asked.

Rynda glared at Water. "I told you what I'd do to him."

Water raised a hand to placate Rynda. "Spit it out, man, what did you find?"

"A Gate," Lachonus said. "And the script says it goes straight to Serak's fortress."

Chapter 14: Vanguard

The group followed Lachonus to the base of the estate. Behind a wall of crates, Lachonus and his men had discovered a loose section of wood paneling. Upon removal, a secret doorway led to a small chamber.

Anti-magic weapons and foodstuffs were present, as well as sacks of coin, all covered in dust. The Gate sat at the rear of the room, its smaller size indicating it connected only to Lumineia. Water entered and picked up a sack of coin, coughing as the dust rose into the air.

"This room looks forgotten."

Rynda brushed the dirt from a small barrel. "Looks like a stash by someone of rank."

"Lord Hyren?" Water guessed. "Mind and Fire killed him when they were searching for Serak. He must have been embezzling goods in case of attack."

"He's got enough here to last a while," Light remarked, and his eyes lit up with excitement. "And look at the ale. It's Dwarven fire ale by Master Kismet."

He hefted the keg and fastened it to the wall with a band of light. Then he cast a dagger and stabbed the cask. As the liquid fell, he drank directly from the crack, seemingly oblivious to the staring by those in the room.

"Do you need a mug?" Lachonus asked dryly.

"We're good," Shadow said. He nudged his brother out of the way and drank his fill.

"Do you have to be so irritating?" Rynda rubbed her forehead as if their actions caused her pain.

"Always," Shadow replied.

Water pointed to the cask and used his magic to stop the liquid from flowing. Shadow and Light protested, but Water stood his ground. "Don't get distracted."

"Distractions make life worth living." Shadow sat onto a crate and began opening another.

Water shook his head and turned back to the Gate. If it had been Hyren, he'd placed the Gate here as an escape route. Did it really go to Serak? The script on the side, which matched Lord Hyren's looping scrawl, claimed as such.

"It might go to Xshaltheria." Rynda examined the runes on the sides of the Gate. "It could be our way in."

"Could he come through?" Lachonus asked. "Could he use it to launch an attack?"

"Probably," Water said. "But I don't think he will. For now, he probably doesn't know it's in our possession."

"We have to go through," Rynda said.

Water regarded the Gate, disliking the choice. Send someone through? Or leave it be? It seemed like a golden opportunity, one that could get them to Serak in an instant. At the same time, he found himself hesitant. After what happened to Fire, he questioned the wisdom in sending someone through a Gate to an uncertain fate.

"I'll go," Rynda said.

Water jerked his head. "If anything happened to the Gate, you'd be stuck. Shadow is the best at infiltration, and Light is the fastest at travel. They should go."

He should have just sent Shadow, who could infiltrate any castle, any keep, but Water didn't want to risk Shadow alone. Light could be unpredictable, but he was strong enough to face down nearly anyone. And he was the fastest of any of the fragments, so he could help them escape if needed.

"Shadow?"

Shadow looked up, a handful of seasoned steak in one hand, a handful of cheese in the other. "Water?"

Water frowned. He could be so insufferable, sometimes, but Water didn't have the heart to reprimand his brother. Not right now. Not after what they'd lost. Light was sneaking away to cry, while Shadow kept trying to pick a fight. Water motioned to the Gate, his expression expectant.

"What do you think?" Water asked.

"I think it's a Gate."

Rynda clenched a fist while Light smothered a laugh. Water groaned. "I think you and Light should go through and then report back."

"Why us?" Shadow asked, taking another bite of his prize.

"If you're not able to get back to the Gate, the two of you can escape and fly back."

"You think it's a trap?"

"It's always a trap," Rynda said.

"Not always," Light protested.

"Assume it is," Rynda folded her arms. "Or be disappointed, and by disappointed, I mean dead."

"Are you always such a pessimist?" Shadow asked.

"Or only after you lost your hand?" Light added.

Rynda looked to Water, her expression exasperated. "They're worse when they're together."

"True," Shadow said, and hopped down from the crate. "But it's as good a plan as any. We'll scout ahead and be back soon."

"I want the ale," Light pointed to the cask of ale, still hanging from the wall.

"You can drink your fill when you return," Water said. "Just see what's on the other side and then come back. Don't get caught."

"I never get caught," Shadow said.

Rynda issued a bark of laughter. "Even I know that's a lie."

Shadow grunted in annoyance and tucked his food into a pouch at his side. Then he sauntered to the Gate. Light joined him, obviously reluctant to depart. Water hesitated, uncertain if the plan was sound, but Rynda spoke first.

"We don't have much time," she said. "After you scout the terminus, we still have to plan and prepare an assault—before he figures out that we have the Gate."

"Scout. Return. Get swords. Kill foes." Shadow shrugged. "How hard could it be?"

"Will you take this seriously?" Water asked. "For once?"

The heat in his voice brought a sigh from Shadow. "You've gotten a lot angrier since . . ."

He looked away, his features contracting. The pain was palpable, and Water regretted his condescension. Light's head bowed and he looked so forlorn that Shadow tossed an arm about his shoulders and gave a forced smile.

"I'll watch out for you."

"Really?" he asked.

"Always," Shadow said.

"Be careful," Water said.

"Never," Shadow smirked.

Water abruptly embraced his brother. It was a simple scouting mission, easily completed. Shadow and Light had done similar assignments a thousand times, and Water forced himself to remember the power of his brothers. But he couldn't shake the sense of vulnerability.

"You've got the heart of a grape," Shadow said. "It squishes so easily."

His teasing smile brought one to Water's lips, and he nodded. "Thirty minutes. No more."

"Perhaps less," Light said, eying the cask of ale.

Shadow grinned and pressed the rune to activate the Gate. The glass shimmered like a ripple on water, and then went still. Shadow caught Light's shoulder and pushed him through. Then he stepped through as well.

Water, unable to shake the sense of foreboding, stared at the Gate. He wished he'd gone with them. At least then he wouldn't feel helpless. Thirty minutes felt like a lifetime, and he wished he'd gone through in their stead.

Water motioned to the Gate and looked to Rynda. "How long do you think until—"

Shadow burst through the Gate, his strangled shout causing Lachonus to curse, Rynda to draw her sword, and Water to conjure his staffblade. His heart collided with his ribs as he flinched into a combat stance. Then Shadow began to laugh.

"You are so easily startled," he said. "It's adorable."

Rynda's eyes narrowed and she pointed the massive sword at Shadow's head. "There's no threat?"

"Nope," Shadow grinned. "Just an empty room. See you in thirty!"

He ducked back into the Gate, disappearing from sight. Rynda reared back and punched a crate, spilling anti-magic daggers onto the floor. Her chest heaved, her hands trembling with rage.

"If Serak doesn't kill him, I will."

She stomped from the room, but Water remained, all his previous foreboding gone. Shadow had seen Water's fears and exploited them for a laugh, and Water half hoped Serak found him on the other side.

"Brothers can be infuriating," Lachonus said.

"You have one?" Water asked.

"A cousin," he said. "But we grew up together. And he's insufferable."

"Aren't they all," Water said.

As Water waited, he dismissed his previous fears as unfounded, brought on because of Fire's death. This was like any scouting assignment, which Shadow could do in his sleep.

Boots thumped in the hall, and a moment later Thorilian himself appeared. The towering elf barked orders and groups of soldiers filled the hall, drawing weapons and shields. When they were in position he glowered at Rynda.

"I should have been informed of the Gate and your choice to send a scouting party."

"We had to act quickly," Rynda exclaimed. "It's only a matter of time until Serak learns that we have the Gate. Then it will be useless to us."

"And if he attacks us?" Thorilian demanded.

"He won't," Rynda said. "He's had plenty of opportunities to strike against us and hasn't. The most he'll do is shut the Gate."

The group fell silent, all eyes on the Gate. Water resisted the urge to pace, but after twenty minutes could not stop himself. They should have returned by now. Shadow could scout a dark fortress in minutes, but Water had told him to be cautious.

Twenty five minutes came and went, and still nothing. The others began to fidget, and only Rynda remained still. She regarded the Gate with unflinching eyes, the point of her sword resting on the stone at her feet. Water envied her patience.

"Two minutes left," Lachonus said.

"What do we do if they do not return?" Thorilian asked.

"I go through," Water said.

"*I* go through," Rynda said.

"You can come with me," Water said, and stood before the Gate.

She snorted and joined him, and Lachonus took up position on Water's other flank. Water glanced his way but he shook his head, his jaw set. Water saw in his eyes that an order to stay behind would be refused.

The final minute trickled past, and Water grasped his staff blade. At least he would not be stuck waiting. But even as he gathered his focus, he worried about Shadow and Light. Were his worries grounded in truth? Or based on fear?

"Ten seconds," Lachonus said. "Perhaps we should—"

Fire burst through the Gate, and all three flinched backward. The explosion picked up the anti-magic daggers from the broken crate and flung them about the room, one grazing Water's leg. He grimaced at the searing pain, and then noticed another dagger hovering an inch from his heart, the hilt firmly in the hand of Lachonus, who'd caught the dagger before it could pierce Water's chest.

"If you were any slower, I'd be dead," Water said.

"My cousin is faster," Lachonus said.

The weapon clattered on the stone and Water hurried to the Gate. He reached to the glass but the silver liquid had hardened, the surface reflecting his worried features. He pressed the rune but it did not budge, and the Gate remained locked.

"They could be trapped on the other side," Water said, smashing his fist on the rune, and then again, his panic rising like bile in his throat.

"Or they could have destroyed the Gate to prevent it falling into Serak's hands," Rynda said.

Water continued in his attempts, and the others each took turns. But none of the runes functioned. The glass remained hard, the material shadowed, as if it had been permanently broken.

After several minutes the truth settled in, and Water growled. He stepped back and regarded the Gate, a once promising opportunity, now broken. Whatever had happened, he would have to wait until Light and Shadow found their way back.

If they came back.

He shoved the sinister whisper aside. Fire had been killed, but his brothers were still powerful. They'd survived for thousands of years, and a simple scouting assignment would not get them killed.

"We planned for this," Rynda said. "That's why we sent Shadow and Light."

"Did I just get them killed?"

She placed a hand on Water's shoulder. "Rest easy. They are capable warriors, and they'll find a way home."

103

She strode away, and after a moment, Lachonus and Thorilian went with her. Water continued to stare at the Gate, wishing he'd gone in their stead. His previous doubts had returned, and Water could not shake the renewed sense of foreboding.

Chapter 15: An Ancient Friend

Mind sat on the balcony of the inn until Elenyr returned that night. He sensed her approach and rose to his feet, watching the dark forest for the Hauntress. In her ethereal form, Elenyr passed through snow and trees, greenish smoke hovering about her cloak. She spotted Mind standing on the high balcony and turned into the stables, which she used to leap to his position.

"What news?" he asked.

"King Justin is indeed gathering for war, but I believe he is inclined to trust me."

They entered the room and he shut the door. Elenyr shivered, so he pointed to the fireplace, igniting the wood with a streak of fire. The sparks sputtered against the wood, and gradually built to flames. Elenyr raised her eyebrow and Mind hesitated, uncertain if he should reveal his thoughts on the fragment of Fire.

"Fire would have done better," he said.

She looked away, but not before Mind saw the moisture in her eyes. "Every time I look at you, I wonder if he could still be alive."

Mind almost told her, but doubt pressed against his throat. If he was wrong, the truth would merely crush her anew, and Mind could not bear that thought. Until he knew for certain, he needed to keep his guess to himself.

"I miss him," Mind said.

She chuckled without humor. "Do you remember the gauntlets of fire he made for me? Said they would keep me warm forever."

"Didn't they ignite and burn our camp to the ground?"

She laughed again, but wiped the tears from her eyes. "Shadow kept yelling that he could have burned the entire forest down."

"Fire felt so bad," Mind recalled. "He kept apologizing until Light tried to fix the forest and made it worse."

"I should have been there," Elenyr said, her tone abruptly bitter. "I should have been with you to fight Wylyn."

"What's done is done," Mind said. "Right now we can only press forward."

She nodded, but held her arms across her stomach as if it would keep her emotions in check. Facing the window, she remained silent for several moments, and when she spoke again she'd regained her reserve.

"King Numen was present," she said. "But he was an imposter."

"Are you certain?" The revelation implied a great deal, and Mind questioned the wisdom in such an act. King Numen had been grievously wounded at the Stormdial. Was he still recovering?

"I am," she said.

"Who is the imposter?"

She shook her head. "I cannot say, but I suspect he had memory magic. I wager it is how he's fooling King Justin and his guard."

"So what happened to the real King Numen?"

"I'm not sure."

Mind considered the options, discarding them quickly. Numen could have died from his injuries, which Elenyr had described as quite severe. But he'd made it through the Gate, probably to Xshaltheria, so Serak could have kept him alive. Serak would have needed Numen to still be king, but his injuries would have prevented that, which explained the imposter. But what would Serak have done with the real king?

"I suspect Serak killed the real King Numen," Mind said. "He has failed three times in his single mission, killing you. We are now prepared against him, and his chances of success shrink with every attempt. Serak cannot risk another failure, not while many regard Numen as a hero. Better to kill him now and use and an imposter than allow Numen to destroy what he had built."

106

"My thoughts as well." Elenyr was nodding. "King Justin suspects the imposter now, but I do not know what he will do."

"You don't think we should unmask him?"

Elenyr shook her head. "Serak will just send another, perhaps one we will not see coming. And with all the armies gathering to Terros, it would be foolish to risk King Justin any further."

"Indeed," Mind said.

He didn't mention that Serak may have *wanted* the imposter to be discovered, and that other spies were already present. They could spend years hunting all of Serak's minions, but right now they had more pressing concerns.

Elenyr spotted the leftover bread from Mind's meal and picked it up. Tearing off a chunk, she took a bite and chewed methodically, her eyes distant. She collected the mug Mind had ordered for her and drank, thanking him by raising the mug. He absently waved in dismissal. He'd known she would be hungry when she returned.

"We have three months until the snow melts," he said. "Assuming this alliance does not crumble, the gathered races will dispatch their armies to Xshaltheria."

"Serak released the kings," Elenyr said. "They didn't escape."

Mind sank into the other chair by the fire, confused at the turn of events. "He would have known the kings would return to Xshaltheria. He pricked their pride and all but invited them to his door?" He scowled. "He *wants* them to come to Xshaltheria."

"Perhaps I know why," Elenyr said. "Justin spoke of a Cleansing, where Serak used the stonesap from the mine of Beldik to alter the air around the volcano. He believes it will prevent the Dark from entering Lumineia while permitting the fiends through."

"If he is ready, then why would he wait?"

A burst of excitement filled his chest, rising and crashing over him. Draeken recognized that Serak was waiting for him. Mind clenched his jaw, shackling the emotion. Draeken reluctantly withdrew.

Mind stared into the flames of the fire, wondering why Draeken behaved differently now. When all the fragments were together, Draeken had fought Wylyn, battled against Serak. What had changed?

Elenyr shook her head, not noticing his conflict, and even still she knew the answer. "It all comes back to Draeken. He wants you, and in the next three months, we will see the culmination of his designs."

"We cannot stop what we cannot see," Mind said.

"And Senia is still absent," Elenyr said. "The elves aren't the only ones to seek her, but she won't be caught unless she wants to be found."

"Oracles are certainly crafty."

Elenyr smiled faintly at the reference to her former life. "I do not think we can rely on Senia at this time. We must have our own plan."

"What do you suggest?"

"We go to the Bladed."

"Why?" he asked, surprised by the suggestion.

"One destination," she said. "Three answers."

"Three?"

She ticked them off with her fingers. "We know the Bladed are connected to Jeric, so we can learn more about his past."

Mind nodded in agreement. "We know he is Ero, but he still possesses more secrets than an oracle."

"Indeed," she said, and ticked off a second finger. "The second benefit is that I can finally fulfill my vow to Sentara."

He shrugged, dismissing the benefit. It wouldn't help the war, but it would help Elenyr, and that was enough. Besides, neither reason would really further their fight against Serak, indicating the last reason to be the most important.

"And the third?"

"You," she said. "Second in the Bladed is a memory mage, a powerful one named Dek. Not on your level, of course, but strong enough to help you understand why Serak would want Draeken."

He leaned back in his seat, contemplating the suggestion, and Elenyr's purpose. Speaking to Dek would not likely bear fruit, so why go to the Bladed? Then another thought caused him to frown. Serak wanted Draeken, and the quickest way to prevent that would be to remove Mind from the situation. After what Mind had felt the last few weeks, he could not deny the appeal in stepping away from the conflict.

From deep inside, Draeken stirred, displeased with the prospect, and Mind smiled, suddenly grateful for Elenyr's foresight. She might not understand why, but she recognized the need to remove Mind from Serak's sight.

"Who is Sentara?" he asked.

"One that used to be a friend," Elenyr said.

"You don't get to do that," he said, anger rising in his voice. "Not anymore. Your secrets have been damaging enough."

His anger was sudden and strong. Elenyr regarded him with doubt in her eyes, and he realized he'd spoken with Draeken's anger, not his own. At least not entirely. Elenyr still had a secret about Draeken, one she'd spoken of in the memory orbs he'd found at Cloudy Vale.

Elenyr finally agreed with a nod. "Before I tell you of Sentara, let me tell you of another woman, one I knew in the Age of Oracles, a woman half mad."

"What does a woman five thousand years ago have to do with Sentara?"

Elenyr's eyes flicked to him, a touch of disapproval in her gaze. Annoyed, he settled into his seat, and Elenyr leaned forward in her chair. She absently picked up the last piece of bread, tearing it apart as she spoke.

"This woman struggled to control herself from an early age, and her magic hurt many, especially her brother, who eventually gave her to the Verinai in an attempt to keep her safe. This proved to be a mistake, and ultimately the brother sought to free his sister from the clutches of the Verinai."

"What made her so dangerous?"

"Her magic was not a part of her," she said, her voice in the past. "Her magic had its own consciousness, a second identity, a second mind."

"I've never heard of such a thing." He was intrigued.

"I, too, did not understand at first," she continued. "The woman was fearless, but her magic was volatile. I began to realize that the second consciousness was not aging as quickly. She acted erratically, each action more impulsive than the last. I would have thought her a threat, but she saved my life, more than once."

"What did you do?"

"I sought Ero's aid," she said. "I sought to merge the two minds into one, creating a single woman. I convinced her that it would be for the best, and becoming united would prevent any future accidents. She refused. But shortly afterward, she nearly killed her brother's young child, and out of fear, she accepted my offer.

"I brought her to what had once been the capital city of the krey nation, the City of Dawn. There we used a special machine built by the krey to attempt merging the minds. To my horror and everlasting regret, we failed."

"What was her name?"

"Marrow."

Mind recalled the name. Her brother had been a shadowmage, and a friend of Elenyr in the early years. He'd mentioned his volatile sister a few times, but Mind had been occupied with trying to control his magic and keep Draeken from destroying Cloudy Vale.

"What does Marrow have to do with Sentara?" he asked.

"Sentara seeks a remedy to her mind, much as Marrow once did," Elenyr said. "We tried with krey engineering before, and because of my failure, I feared a second attempt. I refused, but promised I would try in the future."

"You think I can help her," he said, recalling Elenyr's words speaking to that idea.

"You are the strongest mind mage that has ever lived," she said. "I hope you can heal the harm that has been done to her."

"You never said what happened to her."

Elenyr held his gaze. "Yes I did."

Mind frowned—and then realized her meaning. Both stories were the same. The damage to Sentara had been done to her by Elenyr and Ero in the City of Dawn. Her story was not similar to Marrow's, she *was* Marrow.

"She lived broken," Elenyr said slowly, "for five thousand years."

She passed a hand over her face, the regret palpable on her features. Mind finally understood Sentara's hatred for Elenyr and the Eternals, and why Elenyr now felt such a need to help the woman.

"I promised her healing and instead I tore her apart." She rose to her feet and Mind stood as well. She pointed to him. "You are divided, just as she is. If you can reconcile my mistake, perhaps you will find a way to resolve the fragments with Draeken."

Her reasoning was sound, and he found himself intrigued. Sentara and Rune had departed after the battle at the Stormdial, but Mind had heard snippets of their conversation in the abandoned inn. Elenyr had renewed her promise and sent them to Talinor, where the Bladed made their home at a fort called Stormwall. Elenyr had sent them there, indicating she'd thought ahead.

"It appears we journey to the Bladed," he said.

She placed the last crust of bread on the plate before departing, leaving him to his thoughts. He'd thought helping Sentara would be a distraction, an unnecessary task that had nothing to do with Serak. But Elenyr spoke as if it were essential. He remained in his seat after the door shut and stared into the flames, pondering why he had agreed. Ultimately it wasn't because helping Sentara would help him. It was because Draeken disliked the option. Mind smiled, but could not shake the feeling that the war was not with Serak.

He was fighting himself.

Chapter 16: The Unnamed

The next morning the trio departed Terros. Elenyr had informed Jeric of their plan and they retrieved their horses before heading onto the southern road. Mind rode behind the others, brooding on Draeken, who remained quiet. He disliked the animosity Draeken felt for Elenyr, but could not deny that he felt the same anger at Elenyr's continued reluctance to speak the truth. What did she know about Draeken?

They rode to a village south of Terros, outside the reach of the army, and then sailed west. Winter had fallen hard and the freezing air pierced cloak and skin, causing all to shiver. Mind alone remained warm, Fire's magic embedded in his flesh. He would have chosen the cold if it meant he had his brother back.

He avoided the others, even Elenyr, and spent much of his time using his magic to dive into his own memories. Most thought a person's mind an easy thing to understand, but he knew the truth. Looking into the consciousness of another was like opening the door into a labyrinth, only this labyrinth was constantly shifting, old pathways merging with new. The older a person was, the larger the labyrinth, and Mind had lived for thousands of years.

He sought for Draeken and Fire in his consciousness. Mind was stronger than Draeken, at least as a fragment, but Draeken carried considerable power. Mind had always thought of himself as part of Draeken, not as two separate beings. Now he was uncertain. Or he could be going mad.

His efforts proved to be in vain, and six days after boarding the ship, they landed in Stormwall, home to the Bladed. He had yet to locate Draeken or Fire in his consciousness. His failure left him irritable, and both Elenyr and Jeric took to avoiding him.

Covered in a blanket of snow, the small fortress overlooked the arena used for the summer games. Adjacent to the arena, a small wharf connected to the fortress. As Mind descended the gangplank of the ship, he realized it had just been a few months since they'd stood at the arena, and seen a dakorian for the first time. So much had happened in so short a time.

While sailors unloaded the shipment of goods bound for the mercenary guild, Jeric led them to the entrance gate. The guild of Bladed contained exactly one hundred members, but the fortress employed guards, the youths and adults hoping to be selected into the guild. Former soldiers from across the kingdoms, the guards watched Jeric ascend the path to the gate.

The fort of Stormwall sat atop a hill. A single approach led to the fort, its winding path ascending a road to the portcullis, the gate permitting entry into the courtyard. Too small to use for larger training purposes, the Bladed used the nearby arena to train. The tower itself was reserved for private quarters, guest quarters, and the armory.

Jeric offered a curt bow to the two apprentices, one a human, the other a dwarf. "Is Mox present?"

"Former Steward of Talinor," the dwarf said, his eyes suspicious. "What business do you have with the Bladed?"

"Ask any of the guild," Jeric replied, folding his arms in irritation. "They will permit us entry."

The dwarf jerked his head to the human and the man slipped through the gate, returning a moment later with a woman bearing the number 64 on her shoulder. She bowed to Jeric and barked an order, allowing the group inside the gate.

"Master Jeric," she said, motioning them inside. "My apologies, but some of our guards are new." She glared at the two sentries. "We received your previous message. Even now, Mox is gathering the others. Soon we will march for Terros."

"You're joining the war?" Mind asked.

"We have our orders," she said. "I'll summon Mox to your quarters."

"No," Jeric said. "What we need is below. Also, is Dek here?"

The woman shook her head. "She has not yet returned from a contract in Keese."

Elenyr frowned and glanced to Mind before motioning to the gates. "Has a woman arrived? One with a young charge?"

"They did, but were not permitted entry," she said. "They are staying in the village."

"Have them brought inside," Jeric said. "And lead them to the Eyes of Erasat."

"As you will," she said.

She bowed and departed, and Elenyr brought them to a halt at the end of the corridor. "Jeric," she said, "perhaps it's time you told us why the Bladed answer to you."

Jeric looked between Elenyr and Mind, who folded his arms. Then Jeric motioned to the statue set in the adjacent alcove, which depicted a large man carrying a sword and shield, his features hardened from battle, his eyes sad. Mind recognized him as Whitecloak, founder of the Bladed.

"Do you see the resemblance?" Jeric asked.

Mind muttered a curse. "You're saying that Whitecloak was you?"

"It's possible the Bladed belong to me," Jeric said, a faint smile on his face.

"No," Elenyr shook her head in disbelief.

"Whitecloak was one of my personas." Jeric lowered his voice when a guard passed, and then pointed to the guard after they turned the corner. "The Bladed do not know it, of course, but Whitecloak transferred ownership to another of my personas, and another, continuing until Jeric inherited the guild."

"You founded the Bladed." Elenyr shook her head, half in admiration, half in disgust. "Why am I not surprised."

"It's rather clever," Mind said. "Having a guild of trained warriors would allow you to subtly subdue conflicts on Lumineia."

"And give you access to all the kingdoms," Elenyr said. "Every royal family on Lumineia has employed the Bladed at one time or other."

114

"And they say the Eternals only fight threats outside of Lumineia," Mind said. "Just how many conflicts have you helped resolve?"

"Not as many as you," Jeric said. "I prefer to let the Bladed run autonomously."

Jeric turned down the corridor. Mind and Elenyr exchanged a look before following. Mind wasn't really surprised. Now that he knew Jeric's true identity, it was clear that Ero had sought to preserve the peace on Lumineia as much as he'd sought to protect its secret. It did beg an obvious question.

"With all the krey technology," he said, "why did you never attempt to elevate the people on Lumineia?"

"You want to know why I did not give our technology to the people?" Jeric chuckled as if the answer was obvious. "A people cannot rise unless by their own choice. As much as I would have liked to provide eons of knowledge and technology, it would not be received unless the people wanted to learn. Growth cannot be forced, it must be chosen, and the people of Lumineia chose to explore the bounds of magic rather than technology."

"Do you think they will ever be ready?"

"In time," he said. "And when they are, I will use organizations like the Bladed to disseminate new innovations."

Mind imagined such a future, when the world had evolved to the level of the krey. What would happen then? It was obvious that the world would eventually become known to the Empire. Perhaps Serak was right in wanting to stop the threat before it came.

Passing uniformed Bladed and a handful of apprentices, Jeric led them downward, into the underbelly of the fortress. It quickly became clear that the entire hill had been hollowed out to create a network of chambers, training halls, and storage rooms. Jeric turned down a smaller corridor to a steel door set in the stone. He produced a key to unlock the door, and then guided them inside. He pointed upward, into the darkened ceiling.

"The Bladed call them the Eyes of Erasat, named for their creator."

Mind advanced across the smooth stone, peering into the gloom. Then Jeric stepped to the side and activated the light orbs in the chamber. The chamber was much larger than Mind had thought, and contained a pair of giant glass spheres. The two orbs glowed faintly with purple light, the magic swirling within. His magic. He reached up to one of the orbs, a smile spreading on his face as he felt the wealth of power.

"What is this place?" Elenyr asked.

"An idea I got from you, actually," Jeric said. "This allows two warriors to fight in the realm of memory, a trainer and a student."

"You built a requiem," Elenyr said, her voice tinged with praise.

"I didn't have a group of oracles," he said, "so this is a poor substitute."

"And you think this will help us?"

Mind turned to find Sentara in the doorway with Rune at her side. The young woman stared in wonder at the two orbs, while Sentara had her arms folded, her expression hard. Elenyr motioned them inside but the two women remained in place.

"This is the best chance we have of healing you," Elenyr said.

"How?" Sentara challenged.

Jeric pointed to the two orbs. "These are tools that allow you to step into the mind of another. In essence, the Eyes of Erasat takes the consciousness of one and place it inside the mind of another. It should allow Sentara to connect with her detached second mind."

"But this is temporary," Sentara said flatly. "Not permanent."

"If it was just Sentara using the Eyes, that would be true," Jeric said, and gestured to Mind. "Elenyr believes Mind will be able to complete the transition, allowing you to remain bonded, permanently."

"Could it do more damage?" Sentara asked.

Mind answered before Jeric could. "When you deal with the mind of another, there are always risks. This attempt could kill you, or destroy your minds forever." He looked to Jeric, who after a moment's hesitation, nodded.

116

"He is correct," Jeric said. "But this is the only chance for you to be whole."

Sentara regarded the two orbs like they were enemy combatants, the silence stretching until Mind glanced to Elenyr, raising a questioning eyebrow. She shrugged, and made a motion to Sentara. It was her risk to take.

Mind frowned, disliking this option. Attempting to merge two minds could destroy them both, and there was no telling the damage it would cause, especially considering one of the minds was a sentient shard of magic.

Sentara reached into the pouch at her side, removing a spiked ball of pure white light. Mind shielded his gaze as the ball pulsed with power, and he sensed the power of the consciousness inside. Sentara held it aloft and gazed into the object. Tuned to the mental magics in the room, Mind heard the whisper coming from the orb.

It is time.

Sentara inclined her head and stepped forward, but Rune caught her arm. Glancing suspiciously at Elenyr, Rune lowered her voice. Although Mind could not hear her words, he heard the hiss. The girl was afraid.

"It is time," Sentara said.

"I don't want you to risk this," Rune said, clenching Sentara's arm tightly. "You have lived lifetimes without her."

"I know," Sentara said. "But I have prepared for this moment for many years, because she does not belong in a cage."

"Please," Rune said, tears forming in her eyes. "Please don't do this."

Sentara smiled at the girl, the expression of a mother to a daughter. Mind realized the two were family, much like Elenyr and the fragments of Draeken. The girl did not want to see Sentara perish.

"Do you trust me?" Sentara asked.

Rune swallowed and nodded. "Always."

"Then trust me now," Sentara said.

117

She opened the girl's hand and placed the pulsing, spiked ball into it. The girl stared in confusion. Elenyr sucked in her breath. Jeric's eyes widened in shock. Mind realized her plan and shook his head, grappling with her intent.

"I wasn't seeking to heal myself," Sentara said softly, her eyes on Rune. "I was looking for my heir. It must be you who shoulders this mantle."

"Me?" Rune's voice was barely audible.

Sentara smiled again. "She chose you, and it's time for you discover who you were meant to become."

Chapter 17: The Eyes of Erasat

Rune shook her head, but her eyes remained fixed on the spiked ball in her hand. Shocked by Sentara's action, Mind looked to Elenyr, who bore a scowl on her face. Elenyr approached Sentara and Rune.

"I do not think this is wise."

"I didn't ask you," Sentara snapped.

"Sentara," Jeric said, his voice conciliatory. "You have no idea what will happen if you attempt this."

"*She* knows." Sentara whirled to face them both. "You failed me once before, and I will not permit you to persuade me into your course again. If this fails, then so be it. Your conscience will be clear, and I will bear the guilt until my death."

"This is dangerous," Elenyr protested.

"And I am old," Sentara said. "She prolonged my life so I could find a replacement."

"But she's part of you," Elenyr said.

"No," Mind said. "She wasn't."

All eyes turned to him. While the others had been talking, Mind had reached out to the consciousness contained in the orb, attempting to understand. What he found left him reeling, because the mind in the sphere was not young. It was old—older than all of them except Jeric.

"She was born in the Dawn of Magic," Mind said.

"That's not possible," Elenyr said.

"You always think you know everything," Sentara said. "You don't."

"Then who is she?" Jeric asked.

"One of the Unnamed," Mind said.

"There's *more* of her?" Elenyr's eyes widened.

"When you activated the Forge of Light and the races gained magic," Mind said, "two of the Unnamed were created. Both had so much power, their physical bodies were absorbed, leaving only their magic. She does not know who she is, or what she was. She only knows that she was alone, and spent a lifetime looking for a companion."

"She found it in me," Sentara said, her voice soft. "When I was a child, she joined my thoughts. At first she was like an older sister, and only later did she try to merge us together. She didn't know that merging with one so young would alter her consciousness to match mine. She became a child like me, and even aged slower than me."

"Toron didn't know," Elenyr said.

Sentara nodded. "I never told anyone, especially my brother. He would have wanted us to be separated."

"Then why did you let us try and separate you?" Elenyr asked.

"She'd begun to remember who she was," Sentara said. "And she wanted to find the other Unnamed. We thought it better to do apart, and she didn't know how to separate us."

"And you think Rune can carry her?" Elenyr asked.

"She believes in Rune," Sentara said, turning to the girl. "She has chosen you as she did me. This time, she knew to wait until you were old enough to endure the merging."

This is madness, Elenyr thought to Mind.

He glanced her way and responded in kind. *You once said that the secrets of magic run deep. Is she not so different than me?*

You are different.

I am a being of magic, just as she is.

Anger crept into his voice. Elenyr did not understand—she could not understand. The Unnamed had once been like him, perhaps even more powerful. And she *wanted* to be whole. How could Mind deny her?

"I will do what has been asked," Mind said, "if Rune is willing."

The girl finally looked up from the spiked orb. "I . . . I think I am."

"Good girl." Sentara nodded her approval and turned to Elenyr and Jeric. She folded her arms and waited.

Elenyr looked to Jeric, who shrugged helplessly. Obviously torn, Elenyr shook her head, and then again. Mind knew her fears but did not share them. The Unnamed had spent thousands of years wrestling with her own identity, and the fact that she finally knew what she wanted gave Mind hope.

"Bring her forward," he said.

Elenyr reached out as if to protest, but did not, and Rune advanced to offer the orb to Mind. He accepted the orb, sensed its power, and for a split second, desired to possess it as his own. Mind swallowed Draeken's ambition and motioned Rune to stand below one of the two spheres.

"Will it hurt?" Rune's voice was small.

"Only if it kills us," Mind said.

"Was that necessary?" Sentara glared at Mind.

"She needs to know what can happen," Mind said.

He stepped beneath the second sphere and looked to the girl. She was trembling, but her jaw was set, and her eyes were bright. She straightened and gave Mind a curt nod, her hands balling into fists. She looked young, hardly fifteen, but her gaze conveyed a resolve that belied her age.

"I'm ready."

Jeric strode to a rune set on the wall and reached up to it. "Once you begin, you will not be able to stop until it is finished."

Mind accepted the warning with a dismissive wave. "I'll keep her safe."

"Mind?" Elenyr called. "Be careful."

"Always," Mind said.

Jeric, his expression reluctant, reached out and pressed the rune on the wall. The two purple orbs brightened, and threads of magic reached down to Mind and Rune. Attaching to their bodies, they lifted them off the ground, and pulled them inside.

Mind looked up as he entered the sphere. It had appeared solid on the exterior, but the sphere was almost liquid. Entering was like entering a pool of warm water, without getting wet. He knew the pull of memory magic and did not resist as the enchantment reached for his thoughts.

He felt a tug and his mind was yanked in another direction. He blinked in surprise, and when he opened his eyes he found himself standing in a field of grass, the sways of green stretching to the horizon, the scene blurred and hazy.

"Where are we?" Rune asked.

Mind turned to find Rune standing a short distance away. "This is the construction of a memory," he said.

"You've been inside one before?"

"I've put others in one," he said.

"So how is this supposed to work?" Rune asked, clearly nervous.

"I can answer that."

Both turned to find a beautiful woman striding towards them. She was a human, her long golden hair flowing to her waist, waving in the wind. She wore a simple white dress, giving an aura of elegance and regality.

"The Unnamed?" Mind asked.

"I may have power, but I am little more than a memory. But in here?" She smiled and swept her hand to the expanse. "Here I am home."

Mind noticed a scar on her left hand, as if a blade had been plunged through her palm, the damage sufficient to scar even in memory. She regarded him in turn, examining him with new eyes.

"You are not like the others," she said. "You are like me."

"I am."

"But you are but a fragment," her eyes narrowed, "and there is one greater."

Mind glanced to Rune, who stared at them in confusion. He swept his hand to her and her expression turned unfocused, her eyes growing distant. She'd proven she had mental shields before, but in this place, she'd already opened her thoughts. He used his magic to shut Rune's mind, for the moment. The Unnamed frowned at his action.

"You harm my friend."

"She is not hurt," Mind said. "I merely wished to speak to you privately."

"Is this why you agreed to help?"

"A part of the reason," Mind said.

What's taking so long, Elenyr's thoughts intruded on his own, and he brushed them aside.

"What do you want?" she asked.

"I am a fragment of Draeken," he said. "But I want to know if another fragment is inside of me. I want to know if my brother is alive."

"And you think this is something I can do?"

"I wonder if Draeken holds him trapped," Mind said. "He has more power when we are merged, but I cannot find either of them on my own. I ask for your aid, as you ask for mine."

"There is evil lurking within you." She approached and passed a finger down his shoulder. "I fear that to do as you request will bring blood and ruin, for Draeken is not what you presume."

"Help me, or I do not help you."

It was an ultimatum, and brought a scowl to her features. Her eyes flicked to Rune, who stared into the distance, her features relaxed, her body still. The Unnamed folded her arms and her lips curled with irritation.

"So be it."

He smiled, but she raised a hand of warning. "I do not trust you, so we will do both actions together."

"You want me to merge you with Rune, *while* you search my thoughts for Fire?"

"One magic for another," she said. "For I have yet to determine if you are friend or foe."

He considered the offer. Forcing both of their magics to work on each other—at the same time—would be the pinnacle of risk, yet she folded her arms, daring him to refuse. Did he have a choice? He needed Fire. He needed his brother. And the Unnamed could be the only way to free him from Draeken's ambition, the only way to restore balance to the fragments.

"It appears we have an accord," he finally said.

She inclined her head and snapped her fingers. Rune blinked and shook her head to clear it. By the time she had, Mind and the Unnamed had approached. Before she could ask what had happened, Mind imagined a staff.

Gnarled wood appeared in his fingers, extending in both directions, a construct of his own imagination. The wood darkened and turned purple, the wood only an overlay for an extension of his magic. He raised it high and plunged it into the earth.

"Hands on the staff," he commanded.

He put his hand in the center, Rune below, the Unnamed above. Then he steeled himself for what was required. He'd altered memories before, changed personalities, even fates, but never had he merged two minds into one.

"I will draw the Unnamed into myself," Mind said, "and then I will extend her into Rune's consciousness." He raised an eyebrow to the Unnamed.

"I know what to do," she said.

Mind closed his eyes and reached to his magic, the power building and wrapping around his torso, swirling outward to encompass the Unnamed. The woman grimaced as if in pain, her eyes closing. She relinquished her mental shields, allowing him to latch onto her being. For an instant he caught glimpses of her past:

A brother and a sister, both staring up at a sky on fire, flaming objects falling to the earth. A mother screamed at them but the two children could not respond. Both were weak, their bodies broken from birth . . .

124

. . . she lay in a dark room as a wave of power washed over her. A spark ignited inside, rising into a fire, which became an inferno that engulfed her, burning her body from the inside. She screamed and didn't stop screaming, the power devouring her flesh. A woman shrieked and leapt to her, her arms wrapping around her body, holding her tight. But the effort was in vain, for her body disintegrated into the rising swell of power, until her clothes fell empty in the woman's arms . . .

. . . ages of sadness, of loneliness. Her power was unbound, and without a body, she was helpless. Then she found a babe whose mind matched her own. A mother called her name, and for the first time the Unnamed found a home . . .

It's not nice to poke into the memories of another.

Sorry, Mind said.

The Unnamed spoke as if from inside his ear, her voice echoing inside his skull. Then she flitted away, searching into his consciousness. Mind struggled as she rifled through his thoughts, wrestled to keep her power from shattering his will. If that happened, they would both be destroyed. He gritted his teeth, sweat beading his forehead. Outside, the Eyes of Erasat began to brighten, and distantly he heard Jeric and Elenyr begin to shout.

Not much time, Mind called.

Then stop distracting me.

He felt a pull, a breaking as if an iron bar had been snapped in half. He sucked in his teeth, the pain wrenching and sudden. He called for the Unnamed but she did not answer, the power within growing, swelling, like a tidal wave that would tear them both apart.

His hope turned to desperation, and he bellowed for the Unnamed, shouting for a response. Had she found Fire? Was it a desperate hope? His fear raged, his doubt rising, but he fought to hold to his hope. Outside, the sphere continued to brighten, the light forcing Elenyr and Jeric into the hall. Still the light grew, beginning to burn the stone walls of the chamber.

Mind fought to keep the Unnamed inside, but the power proved too great, and he reached his hand out, both physically and mentally, knowing they had only seconds. If she did not come out of his consciousness they would die, and it would all be for naught . . .

He bellowed for her—and abruptly the hand of the Unnamed closed on his. On instinct he shoved her into Rune's thoughts, using the staff as a conduit. The woman leapt into Rune and the girl recoiled as if she'd been struck. Mind sealed the merging, closing off Rune's thoughts and forcing her mental shields to rise. But the Eyes of Erasat had endured too much, and they began to spark and spit fire. Mind raised his hands and shouted a warning—and the spheres exploded.

Mind was thrown to the ground in a sea of purple and red fires. He caught a glimpse of Rune standing tall, her features filled with wonder as fire burned across her flesh. She was beautiful and powerful, the merging a success, even though the room was destroyed. Mind experienced a crushing regret when their eyes met—and then a third person rose from the flames.

The Fragment of Fire.

Chapter 18: Risen

Fire stood in the remains of the Eyes of Erasat, the flames arcing up and down his body. He held his arms down and out, his features shocked. Mind heard his thoughts, felt the surprise. He recalled being crushed by Wylyn, and dying at the hands of the Construct.

He stared about the room, confused by the change. Was he still on the tower? Had Wylyn been killed? The confusion washed across him, expanding through the mental link and into Mind, who lay where he'd fallen.

Mind struggled to speak, to call his brother's name, but the word lodged in his throat. All the grief he'd suppressed, all the hope he'd fought to constrain, bound him like steel shackles. His hand was on the cool stone, the surface rough, the fires burning close enough to burn his thumb.

He felt the rush of heated air, the surge of lingering mind magic tickling at the back of his skull, like a memory forgotten. His breath was ragged, strained from the magic he'd performed, and the sight of his fallen brother, returned to life.

Fire noticed him and turned, his eyes wide. "Did we win?"

Fire's bewilderment brought Mind to his feet. Heedless of the fires, Mind surged across the gap, engulfing his brother in a crushing embrace. Tears blossomed in his eyes and trickled down his cheeks, but he did not retreat. His brother hugged back, clearly confused, his thoughts chaotic. Fire had no idea what had happened, but Mind could not explain. Never had Mind hugged him so fiercely, and Fire began to laugh.

"What happened?" Fire asked.

Shock, relief, and joy bound Mind's tongue. Fire still wore the clothes he had at the Stormdial, the cloak burned and rent from the conflict with Wylyn. His wounds had healed, but his skin carried a faint scar over the chest, where Wylyn's blade had pierced.

"What's with the hug?" Fire asked. "Did someone die?"

Mind choked on a laugh. "You."

"Me?" Fire seemed startled, and Mind stepped back.

"You."

"That's not possible," Fire protested.

Fire then noticed the room, the lingering fires, the shattered mind magic scattered about the room, some of the shards sticking out of his flesh. He pulled one out, grimacing before tossing it away.

Mind heard his thoughts, the doubt and worry for Soreena, even though she had not been at the Stormdial. He sought for the other fragments, wondering if they had died as well, but Mind shook his head.

"You were the only one that died."

"Do I still have my magic?" Panic burst in Fire's mind and he raised his hand, the fire burning hot and bright.

"That's what you're worried about?" Mind asked. "Your magic?"

He flashed a lopsided grin. "It's my most attractive asset."

Elenyr and Jeric appeared in the doorway. In her ethereal form, Elenyr rushed inside, dodging the purple fires, her eyes searching, her features twisted with fear. She called Mind's name—and then spotted Fire.

She came to a stuttering halt, her hands going to her mouth. She stared in shock, tears leaking from her eyes, her fingers trembling on her lips. Then she crumpled, her knees hitting the floor.

"It cannot be."

Mind parted from his brother and reached to Elenyr. "It's true."

"Was I really dead?" Fire asked.

Elenyr began to weep, and then surged to her feet and closed the gap. Mind retreated, allowing Elenyr to wrap her arms around her son. Fire grunted as the wind was forced from his lungs, and managed a protest.

"Do you have to break my spine?"

128

Mind began to laugh, the emotion bubbling out of him. He wanted to shout, to yell, to exult at the victory over Wylyn, but it all came out as laughter and tears. He wiped them away before they were seen by Jeric, who still stood in the doorway, dumbfounded.

"Are we still in the Stormdial?" Fire asked.

"We destroyed the Stormdial weeks ago."

"And I missed it?" Fire looked disappointed.

Elenyr laughed and wiped at her tears. "You died, and you're disappointed you missed a fight?"

"What did you expect?" Fire asked.

Elenyr hugged him again, her laughter relieved, the tears coming anew. Mind stood back with a stupid grin on his face, wondering why his legs trembled. He felt light headed, and when he put his hand on his forehead his fingers were bloodied, probably from a piece of the broken spheres. Then a groan came from the side of the room, and Sentara gingerly sat up.

"I swear, the fragments destroy everything," she muttered.

"Sentara," Rune said, darting to her side.

She reached out and touched the wound on her arm, and the skin began to knit, healing in seconds. Astonished, Rune held her hand up and looked at her fingers. Sentara grinned at the burst of magic.

"Hello, old friend."

Rune smiled. "She says hello."

"Is the merging complete?" Sentara asked, taking Rune's hand and regaining her feet.

"It is," Rune said. "Or at least, I think it is—no, she says it is." She laughed.

"What about him?" Sentara said, catching sight of Fire. "Where did he come from?"

Mind had no desire to share how Draeken had held Fire bound, not when he didn't understand it himself. Fleetingly he was aware that Draeken was back to his normal place. Not gone, but Mind no longer possessed two fragments inside, so Draeken could not rise up again.

"The Unnamed helped me heal Fire," Mind finally said, motioning to Rune.

"So he was inside you?" Elenyr asked. "The whole time?"

"He was," Mind said, struggling with a reasonable explanation. "When I absorbed his magic, he was nearly destroyed, and it took time for him to recover. I began to suspect he was alive, and asked the Unnamed for help."

"She helped you?" Rune asked.

Mind nodded. "A gift, in return for my aid."

That's not quite the truth, the Unnamed whispered into his thoughts.

Close enough, Mind replied, and then aloud. "She has my gratitude."

Elenyr faced Rune, her features turning sober. "I cannot express my own."

"She was happy to return the balance of Draeken," Rune said.

"Can someone please explain to me what is going on?" Fire asked.

Elenyr laughed and patted him on the arm. "I will. For now, perhaps you could extinguish these fires?"

"Right," Fire said.

He swept his hand to the lingering flames, stopping them from spreading. Jeric coughed in the smoke and waved his hand, lifting his gaze to where the two orbs had once hovered. Pieces of mind magic littered the floor like broken glass.

"Sorry," Mind said.

"A cost worth paying," Jeric said.

The thudding of boots sounded as a group of Bladed burst into the room. The rock troll in the lead, the first Blade, came to a halt and stared at the remains of the Eyes of Erasat. Then he swept his war axe at Jeric.

"What in Skorn's name happened?" Mox demanded. "The entire tower shook like it was going to collapse."

"All is well," Jeric said. "But I suspect our companions could use a meal." He raised an eyebrow to the group.

Fire looked down at his stomach. "It feels like I haven't eaten in weeks."

"You haven't," Mind said with a laugh.

The amusement spread to the others, and Mind gloried in the return of his brother. Serak may have his war, his intrigue and deception, but in broken shards of the Eyes of Erasat, Mind didn't care. He had his brother back, and with all fragments together, nothing could stop them. Not even Draeken.

Chapter 19: Rune's Warning

Mind and the rest of the group followed Jeric up into the tower, where Jeric requested a meal be set. They were led into a spacious dining hall near the top of the tower, which boasted views of the countryside and the sea to the north.

The stone was old but well cared for, scrubbed clean. Weapons of every age adorned the walls, one even dating back to the Dawn of Magic. The banner of the Bladed also hung on the wall, a white strip of cloth with a shield embroidered at the center, and a host of weapons poking out from behind the shield.

A dining table with a dozen chairs occupied the center of the room. Servants and apprentices were quick to set dishes and fill mugs of ale. Jeric departed for a time and spoke to Mox in the hall, explaining what had occurred and that the Bladed needed to continue to Terros.

Mind and Elenyr stood with Fire, who bombarded them with questions. Mind tried to explain the events after the Stormdial had fallen, while Sentara and Rune were locked in conversation nearby. From what Mind overheard, Sentara wanted Rune to use magic, but the girl was reluctant to try.

Chefs appeared with roasted meats and magically grown fruit. Warm bread was added, and they claimed chairs. After all the haste and travel, Mind hadn't sat for a meal in weeks. He relished the sumptuous fare next to his brother.

Elenyr caught Fire up on what had occurred since the Stormdial. He didn't seem to understand, but he accepted the tale at her word. For once, Mind did not look to the future, and merely basked in the moment. Fire's death had shaken him to the core, and he'd never thought he could feel whole again.

Mind realized the other fragments did not yet know, and with Fire's help, crafted a message to send. As they dug into dessert, three tigers bounded out of the fortress and disappeared into the trees. Mind smiled, imagining Water's face when he realized Fire had survived. How could Serak stop them now?

Throughout the meal, Mind watched Rune. The girl had been trained by Sentara, and Mind knew her to be an accomplished warrior. Now she was linked to a powerful mage from the Dawn of Magic. He wondered what she would do with her newfound power.

She sat in her chair, more sober than the rest, and after a time she slipped away to a balcony. Mind followed, joining her outside. The girl leaned against the railing, breathing deep of the cold night air.

"She says you do not need to worry about us," Rune said.

"It is not worry I feel," Mind said. "It is curiosity."

"Is that what I am now?" Rune asked, "a curiosity?"

Mind leaned against the cold railing and admired the stonework. "I am much like you," he said. "And I am curious because your merging has made me wonder about my fate."

"She says that we can live for a long time," Rune said. "Maybe forever—if we aren't killed."

"Living forever means watching others die."

Rune glanced back into the room, where Sentara sat at the end of the table, searching through a bowl of strawberries for the best one. She smiled when she found it, and promptly dipped it into the center of a nearby pie.

"Sentara won't live long without her," Rune said quietly.

"She lived to see you and the Unnamed become one," Mind said. "She will die happy."

Rune sighed. "I guess even magic has limits."

"What will you do now?" Mind asked.

"I'm not sure." She conjured a soldier of flame in her hand, and then morphed it into water. "I have power, but I do not know what to do with it."

"You find a cause," Mind said.

"Is that what you did?" she asked, her eyes lifting to his.

Mind swept his hand to the dining hall. "My cause is to protect my brothers and Elenyr, and the families that are threatened by people like Serak."

"Is that what I should do?"

"What does she say?" Mind asked.

Rune chuckled sourly. "She wants to find the other Unnamed, if he's still alive. But for now, the choice is mine."

A thought occurred to Mind and he reached into his pocket, his fingers closing on the two Keys of the Eternals. Then he hesitated, and realized that whatever he did, Draeken would see. And remember.

Mind had never before sought to deceive Draeken, never had a reason to. But the last few weeks had taught him that Draeken was not as he believed, and in this, he did not want Draeken to bear witness. Frowning to himself, he reached into his own thoughts, turning his magic on himself, obscuring his own memory . . .

"You have my gratitude," Rune said.

Mind blinked in surprise. "For what?"

Rune smiled and patted her pocket. "Thank you for what you did for us."

Confused, Mind struggled to recall the last few moments, but they were just a blur. He'd been about to do something he believed was right, and then nothing. Rune was already returning to the dining hall, so he shrugged. Perhaps it was just an effect of separating with Fire.

Elenyr spotted him standing on the balcony and joined him. She stepped into a warm embrace, and he hugged her back. He'd never been effusive, but Fire's return had left him with a warm glow in his chest, like a hearth holding a merry fire.

"I don't know exactly what happened," Elenyr said. "But I don't care. You have my eternal gratitude for returning my son to me."

"We both lost him."

Mind watched Fire cast a gremlin of fire that began throwing food at Rune. The girl conjured her own gremlin that raced about, dodging

134

the edible missiles. Seated at the head of the table, Jeric protested when a pile of potatoes smeared his chest.

"Do you believe the Unnamed to be dangerous?" Elenyr asked.

Mind recognized the question for what it was. Had they made a mistake in merging her with Rune? He'd been in her mind, sensed her power, felt the light and darkness of her soul. Mind shook his head in dismissal.

"She is not exactly an ally, but neither is she an enemy."

"What will they do with their lives?" she wondered aloud.

Again the thought that Mind had forgotten something. "I'm not sure," he replied. "But I suspect it will be for the benefit of Lumineia."

"We can hope." She suddenly began to laugh. He raised an eyebrow to her.

"Is something amusing?"

"No," she said. "I am just surprised at the depths of magic. Even after all these years, there are still wonders to behold."

He grinned. "You and me both."

She threaded her arm through his elbow and dragged him back to the meal. He sat by his brother, relishing his company, even when a piece of meat struck him on the face and slid down his cheek. In the ensuing laughter, Sentara and Rune slipped away. When their absence was noticed, Jeric leaned forward.

"It looks like your friends have departed."

"They have no reason to stay," Mind said, eyeing their empty plates.

"I liked them," Fire said. "Rune strikes me as a young woman of caliber."

"Despite being raised by a madwoman," Jeric murmured.

"She wasn't that bad," Elenyr said.

"How many times did she almost kill you?" Jeric countered.

"She saved my life too, you know."

135

Mind didn't join the conversation, his thoughts still on Rune and the Unnamed. He wondered what he'd forgotten, and why it seemed important. Then Fire leaned over and nudged him on the elbow.

"How are Elenyr and Jeric?" he asked.

"I don't think she loves him," Mind replied. "But I suppose they're friends."

"I still don't like him," Fire said.

"You never did."

Fire shrugged but did not refute the statement. Mind would have liked to reveal Jeric's true identity, but servants kept entering to add food to the table, and Mind didn't want to risk Fire reacting badly. He was terrible at keeping secrets, so Mind resolved to wait on sharing the truth of Jeric and Ero.

After the meal, Mind retired to the quarters Jeric provided, and collapsed into the bed. A smile on his face, Mind wondered at his good fortune, and allowed the fatigue of the day to pull him into slumber. But just as his eyes closed, he spotted a sliver of purple glass on the table by the bed. He picked it up, and the voice of the Unnamed came into his thoughts.

Be wary, Fragment, she said. *Draeken did not want to release Fire. His power comes from the combined fragments, and trust me when I say, do not let him be whole. I have never met a more malevolent being.*

The magic faded, and the sliver disintegrated. Mind stared at where it had been, sensing that Rune had delivered it on her way out the door. She hadn't known the purpose, and merely done as the Unnamed had requested. Mind settled back against the headboard of the bed and stared at the sword hanging on the wall across from him. Fire was back, but Mind had learned more of Draeken's identity. And he didn't care for the revelations.

Chapter 20: Visitor

Tardoq stalked his prey. He slipped through the trees, keeping to the drier patches where the snow would not crunch. He'd stolen a longbow from a nearby camp of soldiers, and although the weapon felt like a toy in his hands, it served its purpose. He spotted the deer again and drew the bow to his cheek.

The longbow was well made, as tall as an elf, but he was careful not to break it. The released arrow sped through the trees and plunged into the deer's flank. It fled, and Tardoq pursued, quickly gaining on the wounded animal. He caught up and smashed his bony fist into the creature's back. It folded in half and bounced down a slope. Satisfied, Tardoq strode to the kill and slung it over his shoulder.

As he retreated back to his camp, he watched the dark trees. The sun had set hours ago, only his enhanced night vision allowing him to see. The forest of Orláknia contained pine, oak, cedar, and poplar, a motley collection of trees that lent a sense of wild beauty to the rolling hills. Tardoq steered clear of roads and trails, and retreated to the gulley where he'd built his camp.

He dropped the carcass next to the fire and began to clean the beast, stripping it of hide and removing the unwanted portions. He could eat anything, but preferred the tastier meat. It was one thing he liked about this world. Meat in most of the Empire was not from an animal, it was manufactured and didn't have the same flavor. Real meat was rare and expensive.

He prepared the carcass to be smoked over the fire, all the while retaining his awareness of the area. The slightest crunch of snow beneath a boot, the snapping of a twig, the rustle of brush, none of it went unnoticed by the dakorian.

He set the meat over the fire, a slight smile on his face, a memory of another time. As a child he'd often hunted. Although the prey was far more fearsome, it had been a thrill to camp in the woods of his homeland, to train with his brothers and father. He recalled the laughter and smiles, the first wounds and scars. His family had meant a great deal to him in his first life. None had been chosen by the krey, and all had died by age or battle.

Leaning against the rock, Tardoq watched the snow just beginning to fall. His bone armor protected him against extremes in temperature, but he still felt a touch of chill. The small gulley was hardly a crack in the ground, just deep enough that he could stand upright. A pine tree had fallen above the deeper end, the boughs partially obscuring the gulley and providing shelter. His fire lay beneath the boughs, allowing the smoke to filter through the branches of the recently fallen tree.

Tardoq kept his eyes away from the fire, preserving his night vision as he listened to the wintery forest, the sounds muffled by the snow. He hadn't felt solitude in ages, and he appreciated the peace, for however long it would last. Rynda would certainly have told the fragments about his request, and it was only a matter of time until he was found. He'd hidden his camp well, and obscured his tracks, but they possessed magic, and he was still coming to terms with their abilities of mages—

"You are not what I expected."

He whirled and reached for his hammer, discarding the shock. The voice had come from *inside* his camp, from the back end of the gulley and beneath the tree. How had they entered? How had he not heard or seen them? The voice was female, and relatively young. Human or elf, at first guess. Not one of the fragments. The thoughts were fleeting as his fingers closed about the shaft of his weapon.

In less than a second he was on his feet, spinning the hammer to strike the source of the voice. But his hammer passed through empty air. He scowled, spinning about, searching for the intruder. The gulley extended further, but ended on rock. The branches of the fallen tree prevented entry, but he was certain that was where the voice had come from.

"What did you expect?" he asked, hoping they would answer.

"More anger," came the reply.

The voice still came from the back of the gulley, and he approached the spot. It was magic, but a type he had yet to experience. Then he spotted a faint glow of orange light on the stone, cleverly

138

placed so it was not visible from the campfire. He picked it up and examined the small disc of orange light, the color indicating sound magic.

"Why do you not show yourself?" he asked.

The disc glimmered as the response came. "You are Tardoq, a Bloodwall, and I would be a fool to surprise one like you."

"Smart woman," he replied, scanning the trees and forest. She must be above. "What do you seek?"

"You."

"Have you come to talk or to kill?"

"Undecided."

He scowled, disliking the doubt in the woman's voice. She was clearly confident, and if she'd managed to infiltrate his camp without detection, she was obviously formidable. In the past he would have dismissed the threat, for it came from a member of the lesser race. His lips tightened and he rejected the thought. They were no longer lesser. Inferior in combat, perhaps, but not lesser. It was a hard lesson to be learned, but the people of Lumineia—with or without magic—were not the humans of the Empire.

"I think you'll find me hard to kill," he said. "But I am willing to talk."

"Prove it."

He chuckled at her caution. She wanted to see if it was a ruse, a tactic he had no qualms of using. He held his hammer up, and then tossed it to the other side of the fire, towards the entrance to the gulley. It landed in the snow, the handle coming to rest on the side of the gulley, as if by accident. But it would be easier to grab if it wasn't on the ground. He could reach the weapon in half a second.

He waited, tense and ready to leap to the weapon. The woman could have just convinced him to relinquish his weapon, thinking it would make him vulnerable. But his body was the weapon, and if that was her gambit, she'd made a lethal mistake.

A cloaked woman detached herself from the trees and advanced into the gulley. She was uncomfortably close, just thirty feet from his position. How had she gotten so close? He hadn't seen tracks, bent twigs, or any other sign of a watcher. Definitely a mage.

The woman wore a dark cloak with a fur collar. Her blond hair hung down, and under the cowl he made out her bright blue eyes, and a hint of the pointed elven ears. The elf picked her way through the snow, descending into the ravine until she reached the hammer, which she nudged off the stone, knocking it into the snow. She met his gaze and smiled.

He chuckled at her anticipation. "Your caution is admirable."

"Only being prudent. Do you mind if I sit?"

He motioned in invitation, grateful for her first mistake. Sitting made one vulnerable, slower to rise, slower to react. He gauged the distance, preparing himself in case it came to an attack. The woman swept her hand to the earth and it rose up, reshaping into a comfortable chair. She sank into it with a sigh and warmed her hands by the fire.

"I've waited quite a while for you to return."

"You are welcome to my fire," he said. "And my meal."

"You have my gratitude," she replied.

She never took her eyes off him, and he had the unsettling thought that she knew his thoughts. He'd encountered a mind mage in Zenif, but the man had been unable to breach his mental strength. Perhaps this woman was stronger? No, he'd felt no such intrusion, and he had from the Fragment of Mind.

The two regarded each other in silence, and Tardoq considered her purpose. He heard no hint of companions, suggesting she was alone, but why had she sought him out? What did she want? She did not seem in a hurry to explain herself, and he noticed her tense posture. She too, was ready for a fight.

"Why did you come?" he asked.

"I require your aid."

He frowned. "You obviously know who I am. Why would you think I'd help you?"

"Because I can convince the fragments that you are not a threat."

"Who are you?"

She sidestepped the question. "Why have you kept your horns?"

He scowled, disliking her knowledge. He'd considered cutting his horns from his head. It would allow him to move freely among the populace, and the people would more easily assume him to be a rock troll. Cutting his horns would be temporary, as they would grow back. But the grooves on his horns could not be applied without a master of a krey house, who could sear the bones so they would not heal, marking his rank. Cutting his horns meant relinquishing his title as Bloodwall.

He stepped to the deer and used a knife to slice a section of meat. It took him closer to the mysterious woman, but she did not tense further. He tossed the meat to her and chose a slice for himself. She ate carefully in order to prevent the juices from dripping on her cloak. One trained to be fastidious. Royalty?

"My horns are my rank," he replied.

"Your race is fascinating to me," she replied. "And your tactics are flawless. You've kept yourself from being spotted by Rynda's scouting parties, and that is no small feat."

His scowl deepened. For the last several days he'd been watching Rynda and the fragment of Water. They and a group of soldiers had created a semi-permanent camp at the edge of Orláknia, using it to strike at the Order halls in the region. Tardoq had kept his distance, and not been spotted by the sentries of the camp.

"I have not seen you," he said.

"I do not watch with my eyes," she replied.

Disliking her answers, he leaned against the wall of the gulley as he ate the meat in his hand. She'd obviously been watching him for several days, and chosen this moment to reveal herself. She didn't look like much, but she spoke with such confidence that he wondered what power she possessed.

"Are you going to tell me your name?" he asked. "Or are you going to make me guess?"

She chuckled at his bluntness. "You already know my name. I'm the one both Wylyn and Serak feared."

"You're the oracle," he stated.

She finished the piece of meat and used a flurry of snow to wash her hands. Her lips twitched with amusement, as if she were playing some game. But it confirmed her identity, and why she'd been able to follow and infiltrate his camp. She was the only person on Lumineia—in the entire Krey Empire—that could see the future.

"Senia Elsheeria," she said, inclining her head in greeting.

He cocked his head to the side, curious. "You are the size of a youth, yet your reputation is formidable."

She smiled, an expression that was obviously quick and easy. "Some of it is earned, some of it is merely rumor."

"Do you know your value to the Empire?"

She carefully sliced another section of the deer for herself. "Tell me."

"Your ability to see the future would make you worth more than an entire krey house," he said. "The emperor would probably give half his ridiculous wealth to own a slave like you."

"Is that what you see in me?" she asked, a touch of steel creeping into her voice. "A slave?"

He regarded her, so small and yet shouldering such a powerful mantle. The krey would have seen her as an untold wealth, and several months ago he would have seen the same. Now? He shook his head.

"A queen does not require a throne to be royalty."

"What does that mean?"

"There are no slaves on Lumineia."

"Well spoken," she said.

"You said you wanted my help," he said. "Why me?"

"Because the world battles the foe they see. I seek to fight the foe yet to appear."

"And who is that?"

142

Her smile returned. "Will you help?"

He considered the request. She clearly wouldn't reveal the whole truth, least of all to him, but that matched what he'd learned of oracles. But should he help the woman? Would she attempt to kill him if he didn't? Did she already know what he would do? He voiced the last question, to which she laughed lightly.

"They always think I know everything," she said. "But I only know what you have already decided. Beyond that . . ." she shrugged.

"Will you at least tell me the task?"

Her eyes glowed with delight. "I need to capture a dragon."

Chapter 21: Senia's Offer

"A dragon?"

She nodded, her eyes bright with amusement. "A dragon."

"Why not ask the fragments?" he asked. "Or the Hauntress?"

"They are occupied, and I need someone just as strong."

"Is it going to get me killed?"

For the first time she hesitated, and he read the uncertainty in her expression. She didn't know. After arriving on Lumineia, he'd studied the oracles, and knew their farsight to be flawed. Each oracle's strength in the ability varied, and it appeared hers was not as strong as she portrayed. She grimaced as if she understood his doubt.

"Your assumption is correct," she said. "I do not know."

He folded his arms. "How gifted are you in farsight?"

"A day is clear, a week is clouded, a month is faint, a year is mud."

There was a touch of rancor in her voice, bitterness and disappointment. She was preparing for a conflict she could not see, which meant much of what she said were guesses based on knowledge, which could be even more dangerous. More importantly to him, she'd offered to help him convince the fragments.

"Was your offer sincere?"

"It was."

"Do you know what I will do if you lie?"

Her expression was sober. "I do."

"Then I will be your ally."

She inclined her head in gratitude, but for an instant he noticed a touch of relief. She hadn't known he would accept, and hadn't wanted to fight. Was it because she didn't want to kill him? Or because she didn't want to die at his hands?

"Meet me outside of a village called Gent," she said. "It's four miles north. Tomorrow, just before the evening meal, at the dead oak tree."

"Which one?"

"You'll know it when you see it."

"I'll be there," he said.

She rose and retreated, pausing to lift the handle of his hammer so it leaned back against the wall, a tacit acceptance that he was not a threat. For now. Then she was gone, the snow swirling in her wake to fill her footprints.

Tardoq ate the rest of his meal, considering the conversation until deep into the night. When the moon was high, he extinguished the coals of his fire, packaged the meat, and abandoned his camp. Then he turned north. Trudging through the snow, he wondered if she was following him, but guessed that she would not. She'd already said she didn't watch with her natural eyes.

He reached Gent well before dawn, and found it to be a dilapidated village of humans, just outside of Orláknia. Homes were poorly maintained, and men guffawed loudly from the one tavern, well into their drink. One person lay sprawled on the porch of the tavern, oblivious to the biting wind gradually adding snow to his boots. Home for a handful of rough trappers, the village reeked of smoke and dirty men.

He wrinkled his nose in disgust. Why would a dragon come here? The place was a hovel filled with dirt and grime. Hardly the place a dragon would strike, especially considering the treaty between the oracle and the king of dragons. He wondered if she'd been wrong, but clearly Senia knew what she was doing—

"You're right on time."

He growled and spun, and found Senia a short distance away. "Will you stop doing that?"

"No."

145

"I could kill you by accident."

"Not me," she replied, coming to a halt at his side. Apparently she knew he wouldn't hit her, and he considered a blow just to teach her a lesson.

"Why tell me tomorrow when you knew I'd come tonight?"

"Because telling you to come right away would have made you suspicious. And what I said was true. He doesn't get here until later today."

"Do you always deceive?"

She regarded him with a look of disapproval. "One with more knowledge always deceives, not by intent, but by necessity. I would think you'd know that lesson."

He grunted in annoyance and looked away. "How do you plan on catching this dragon?"

"I'm leaving that to you," she said. "But this dragon is young, and won't be overly large."

"What type?"

"White," she replied. "So its breath will be frost, capable of freezing a man's flesh in seconds."

"My flesh is not human," he retorted.

"Does the bone hurt when it grows out of your skin?"

"Our bones do not grow on the outside until our sixteenth year," he said. "They cut the skin and push outward, gradually growing to cover our whole bodies."

"Yet they do not prevent your ability to move and bend," she said. "Almost as if you were created."

"What's that supposed to mean?"

"One more thing." She ignored his question. "This dragon is a druid joreia. Do you know what—"

"Of course," he said. "Two minds, linked as one. The man can turn into the dragon."

"You are well read."

"Did you really expect me to travel about Lumineia without knowing what I might face?"

"I suppose not," she said. "But your other dakorians did not survive."

"They were not Bloodwalls."

"What will be your purpose now that Wylyn is dead?"

"Your questions are tiresome," he growled.

"My apologies," she said. "I'm just curious. Figure out how to capture him and I'll see you tonight."

She stood to depart and he rose as well, again considering striking her in the face. At least it would teach her a lesson. She shifted her feet, subtly retreating out of reach, the motion causing him to sigh.

"You want my help?" he asked. "Tell me everything."

"His human name is Rake. He'll be running out of the tavern at sunset, headed west. When he reaches the trees he will shift into dragon form and flee. Don't let him escape."

"I won't."

She turned away, and then rotated back. "And don't kill him."

He discarded his first idea.

"And don't break his wings."

He discarded his second.

"Any other rules?" he asked.

"Just try not to hurt him," she said.

"Is he your next victim?" Tardoq asked.

"Don't be jealous."

She smiled and slipped into the trees, and he decided he didn't like oracles. The future was better left to itself. Releasing a snort of irritation, he turned away from the village and made his way to the location she'd indicated, where the man would turn into a dragon and depart.

He descended through the trees and crossed the road, not bothering to hide his presence. Anyone in the village would be too into their drink to notice. Advancing through the dark forest, he approached the clearing, a short hill with a single, towering tree at its summit. The enormous oak had lived for ages, and like a jealous king, its roots had prevented any other trees from growing. The slope faced the village. Tardoq imagined the man racing up the hill, his body turning into a dragon before he leapt from the summit into the sky. This is where he would flee, and where he'd be most vulnerable.

Senia obviously wanted to talk to the man, and Tardoq merely needed him to be still long enough for Senia to speak her will. He frowned, realizing he was now effectively working for one he used to call slave. But it was hard to deny her caliber. In two conversations with Senia he'd seen more integrity than a lifetime with Wylyn—a fact that defied everything the Empire stood for.

"The humans are beneath us," Wylyn used to say. "They were born to be slaves because they lack the ability to lead."

He thought of all the humans he'd killed, those who'd resisted or tried to protect others. He'd been taught such behavior as the instincts of a beast, but what if they were the markings of more? He recalled women battling like a dakorian for their child, even at the risk of death. He'd thought them akin to animals. But stripped of the trapping of the Empire, he'd begun to see the race of man in a new light. What if—like Senia, Rynda, and the Hauntress—they were women of greater caliber?

And he'd killed them.

Like a needle in his chest, the pang of regret brought a scowl to his lips. He'd never felt guilt for what he'd done, but the people of Lumineia inspired him more than any krey ever had. Releasing an explosive breath, he turned away from the site of the trap and entered the trees, headed south.

On his way to Rynda's camp, he wrestled with his thoughts. He hated the prickling of guilt, as if he'd done something wrong by killing slaves, and separating them from their families. Around midday he slowed and leaned against a tree, feeling the bite of winter sink deep into his flesh. They'd called him a monster. And maybe they'd been right.

Shoving the thoughts aside, he reminded himself that he just needed to return to the Empire, resume his position as Bloodwall for the newest head of Wylyn's house. Then he could return and level Lumineia to the ground. A part of him recoiled at that prospect but he'd reached Rynda's camp, so he put the disturbing doubts aside and snuck through their lines.

A small force of rock trolls had joined Rynda, a vanguard for a larger army. They'd brought with them weapons and gear large enough for Tardoq. They were gone, as he'd known they would be. He'd heard them talking about raiding another Order outpost, and none of the trolls would have wanted to miss the fight. Like all good warriors, they'd brought extra shields in case one was broken, and he retrieved one from the armory tent. He also collected other supplies, among them a thick chain.

Retreating from the camp, he passed through the handful of remaining guards and made his way north, picking up the pace in order to arrive before nightfall. Avoiding his previous camp, he chewed on smoked meat, trying not to think about what he would do if he ever made it back to the Empire.

He reached Gent an hour before nightfall and quickly set up his trap. Then he crept behind the buildings to the tavern. With his newly acquired shield on one arm and his hammer in the other, he positioned himself just below the back window, allowing him a view into the interior.

Senia sat in a corner, her cowl pulled low. The rest of the patrons were all from the previous night, and Tardoq waited, guessing the man would enter any moment. Just as the sun kissed the horizon, a newcomer opened the door.

Short and slender, Rake didn't look like much. His brown hair was long and tied back, haggard, as if he hadn't seen a settlement in weeks. His clothes were old and torn, and lined with fur to stay warm. Ignoring the curious looks in his direction, he strode to the bar and settled in, calling for ale and a meal. Tardoq thought Senia would take her time to watch him, she certainly had shown herself to be patient, but she stood and claimed the seat at his side.

"How is life as a white dragon?"

149

The man stared at her, and then panicked. Crashing through chairs, he bolted out the door. Cursing the oracle, Tardoq whirled and sprinted parallel to his path, his long stride and increased stamina allowing him to reach the hill first. He slid to a halt behind a tree just as the man burst into view. Racing up the slope, Rake's body began to change, and white wings sprouted from his back. Just as his hands turned to claws, Tardoq leapt from behind the tree and collided with the man. Tardoq wrapped his thick arms around the human, careful to not break his spine, and dragged him to the ground. They landed hard and Tardoq held him in his grip.

"I'm not here to harm you," he hissed. "We just want to talk—"

The man's body swelled in size, forcing Tardoq's arms outward. He strained to hold him, but the beast continued to change shape, his arm gaining scales, the cloak ripping and tearing. The half formed dragon rolled to the side, throwing Tardoq up the slope and into the tree trunk. He fell to his knees as a dragon's claw appeared over the hill, followed by a very angry looking dragon.

Chapter 22: The White Dragon

The white dragon opened its jaws and roared. Tardoq reached behind the tree trunk and grabbed the shield, ducking behind the trunk as the dragon unleashed its freezing breath. The breath blasted off the trunk, covering it in ice, bursting around it to cool Tardoq's flesh. He shivered, shocked to feel the chill pierce his armor.

Tardoq dropped to the ground, hooked a root, and launched himself skidding down the slope, towards the dragon's legs. The dragon spotted him and twisted, snapping its jaws at Tardoq's frame. Tardoq was moving too fast, and he dug into the snow, collecting the object hidden there.

The chain was already positioned into a loop, and Tardoq picked it up as he tumbled by. Streaking past the dragon's leg, he tossed it around and caught the free end. Then he pulled a hay hook from where he'd looped it through a link, and pushed it through the end of the chain. With a savage burst of strength he bent the hook, locking the chain together.

The dragon bellowed and sought to fly, rising several feet, the blast of wind scattering snow. The chain pulled from the snow, all the way to the tree at the base of the hill where Tardoq had fastened the opposite end. It yanked the dragon to a halt and it came crashing down. Tardoq rolled to the side, avoiding being crushed as he caught the second chain hidden beneath the snow.

He grabbed the chain and reached for the dragon's claw, but the beast leapt in the opposite direction and turned its breath on the chain, blasting the iron with white breath. The iron links turned icy, quickly growing brittle. Looping the second chain around his forearm and fist, Tardoq closed the gap and punched the dragon in the face.

It recoiled, and Tardoq saw an opportunity. It wasn't part of his previous plan, but he uncoiled the chain and tossed it over the dragon's neck. The beast swung back and snapped at him, but he ducked under the neck and caught the end of the chain. He dropped to the ground,

151

using his weight as an anchor to drag the dragon onto its side. Its snarl was cut off as the chain brought his neck down, and Tardoq reached into the snow. His memory was perfect but the rumble had shifted the location of what he sought, and he reached about until his hand closed on the human sword he'd collected. Then he plunged it through a link, embedding it into the frozen ground.

With one leg chained and another chain across its neck, the dragon flopped about, its wings swinging in desperation, its claws digging into the soil. But the frozen chain was groaning, and Tardoq realized he didn't have much time. He picked up the shield he'd lost in the shuffle and used it to deflect the burst of frost breath, and then leapt onto the dragon's head.

Catching the spines, he dragged the head to the ground like a farmer's son felling a calf. He forced the jaws shut, closing off the plumes of frozen breath. His fingers going numb, Tardoq held the dragon's head to the ground as the beast writhed, tearing furrows in the snow, its wings flapping about. Straining, Tardoq noticed Senia at the base of the hill, her pose languid as she leaned against a tree.

"Care to help?" he growled.

"Looks like you have it under control."

"Are all oracles this irritating?" Tardoq demanded.

"Pretty much," she said.

She advanced up the slope, picking her way up the hill like it was a spring morning and she was looking for a place to read a favorite book. Tardoq growled at her calm, and almost released the dragon.

"Don't," she said, her tone filled with warning. "We need him."

What do you want with me?

The mental voice was tinged with desperation and fear, betraying the man's youth. Tardoq had seen the dragons in the south, and guessed the white to be little more than the age of a man. Senia approached and came to a halt close to the dragon's head. The oracle regarded the dragon with interest.

"If my companion releases you, will you change back to human form?"

152

You would just kill me.

The voice was bitter, meaning others had tried to kill him. He struggled anew, and Tardoq tightened his grip. The spikes on the dragon's head were small but sharp, cutting into his flesh. Tardoq ignored the scratches. Then Senia chuckled.

"If my desire was your life," she said, "my companion could have killed you with ease."

"It's true," Tardoq said.

The dragon's eye narrowed at him, and he wondered if the beast would attempt to escape again. The effort was futile, and it seemed the dragon realized that. Its eyes shut and the white scales began to change, sinking into the dragon's body. Tardoq retreated, collecting his hammer from where he'd stashed it in the snow.

"How many weapons do you have stashed in the snow?" Senia asked.

"Enough to ensure victory," he said, hefting the hammer and laying it across his shoulders.

"You have my gratitude," she said.

"It wasn't a favor," he replied. "Make sure you deliver your end of the bargain."

"I will speak to the fragments on your behalf," Senia said.

The dragon wings sank into the man's back, his claws shrinking into fingers. Tardoq disliked watching his flesh change. The krey possessed such abilities to alter flesh, but it was rare and expensive, highly controlled. The Empire didn't like its members walking around with the faces of others. One krey had actually attempted impersonating the emperor. Even Wylyn had not possessed a morphing amulet. To see the power used by a mage, allowing him to turn into a beast of tremendous power, left Tardoq unsettled. Every time he thought he understood the limits of magic, he witnessed more.

The man fell to his knees, his chest heaving from the transformation. He collected the remains of his clothing and held them about his waist. Barefoot, he straightened and regarded Tardoq and Senia with suspicion.

"What do you want?"

"How about we get you some clothes," Senia said. "Then we can talk."

A group of trappers from the village rushed into view, brandishing weapons. Obviously they'd heard the dragon's shouts and came to investigate. They came to a halt when they spotted a half-naked man, a towering armored dakorian, and an elf woman in a regal cloak.

"Perhaps not here," Senia said.

"Where's the dragon?" one man called.

"Gone," Senia said.

A bearded man pointed a sword at them. "By the sound of it, the beast was young, but the bounty doesn't discriminate on age."

"Aye," another said. "Its heart alone will fill our pockets with coin."

"Be gone," Senia said.

"We'll not let you keep the bounty to yourself," a woman growled.

Tardoq noticed Rake had retreated a few steps, panic in his eyes. Snorting in irritation, Tardoq slammed his hammer into the ground, powering the weapon. Then he aimed at the tree nearest to the group of trappers, and released a full blast. The energy struck the trunk, shattering through the thick wood, sending splinters into the group of huddling men. The tree fell to the earth, the branches cracking on the ground.

"I think you should look elsewhere," Tardoq warned, idly spinning the hammer.

The trappers fled, slipping in the snow in their haste. Senia chuckled as they scattered and looked up at Tardoq, her smile one of admiration. Tardoq shrugged liked it didn't matter. A bunch of cowards were not the greatest of foes.

"Who *are* you?" Rake asked.

Rake stared at them like they were mad, and Tardoq found a smile on his face. From his perspective, they were an outlander and an elven woman with a mysterious agenda. His fear was obvious.

"I'm the oracle," Senia said, and inclined her head. "Senia Elsheeria."

"And him?" He jerked a thumb to Tardoq.

"He's harder to explain." She reached into her pack and withdrew a set of clothes, which she offered to him. "For now you can call us friends."

His eyes flicked between the clothes, the oracle, and Tardoq, but eventually he shivered and accepted the offering. Pulling on the tunic and pants, he cast furtive looks to the sky. He still wanted to escape.

"Are you going to tell me what this is all about?" he demanded.

"War is coming," Senia said.

"Serak?"

"You know of him?" Tardoq asked.

"Word is, he kidnapped the monarchs." Rake shivered as he donned the cloak. "But they've returned now."

"There is much the people do not understand," Senia said.

"There is much *you* don't understand," Tardoq said.

Senia frowned at him, obviously not liking being challenged in front of Rake. Tardoq couldn't resist the smile. She may be an oracle, but she did not know everything. To his surprise, he found that he liked her. She reminded him of his younger sister before she'd died. She too, had thought she'd known everything.

"And what do you want from me?" Rake asked.

"I want you to fight with us," she replied.

"Me?" he snorted in disbelief. "I've been hunted since the moment I bonded with Isray. How am I supposed to fight with you?"

"The request was for both of you."

Senia turned and regarded Tardoq. He frowned, realizing the oracle's invitation extended to him. Senia had promised aid if he

155

would capture the white dragon, but that was not her sole intent. Manipulative.

"If I refuse?" he asked evenly.

"I will still speak to the fragments," she replied. "But if you refuse you will be alone. I cannot foresee your fate."

"What's going on?" Rake asked.

Tardoq ignored him. "I do not care to be manipulated."

"That's why this is a request," she said. "No promises. No games. No threats. Just the truth. If you help me, you can help Lumineia—and the fragments. If you do not, we might very well see defeat."

He considered the choice, torn between the prospect of attempting to ally with the fragments—who he'd once regarded as an enemy—and facing Serak, who he'd once considered an ally. Perhaps the world of Lumineia was not entirely unlike the Krey Empire.

"One condition," he replied.

"What's that?" Senia asked.

"You tell me everything you know of the Eternals."

She obviously hadn't expected his request, because her features hardened. "Why would you seek such knowledge?"

He understood her real question. Tardoq sought to return to the Krey Empire. If he did, and he knew the identity of the Eternals, nothing would stop the Empire from descending on Lumineia.

"Wylyn called the Eternals her enemy," he replied. "And I believed as much. If they are my only hope of returning home, then I must know what they seek. If I can provide it, perhaps they will provide what I need."

She held his gaze, and ultimately nodded. "Your condition will be met." Then she turned to Rake. "Your turn. Will you join us? It will lead to your freedom."

"Will?" Tardoq questioned.

Senia rolled her eyes and then amended, "Probably."

156

Tardoq grinned. Rake looked between them, obviously confused. But Tardoq knew what he would do. He had no choice. He'd been hunted long enough that he lived in fear. And Senia was offering the only chance he had of living free.

"I guess," he finally said.

Senia smiled. "Excellent. Now it's time we hunt our first target."

Chapter 23: Reunion

Elenyr, Jeric, Mind and Fire departed Stormwall, headed east. Instead of horses, Fire conjured four tigers, and Elenyr rode on the back of a large feline. She couldn't keep the smile from her features, not after what she'd gained.

She kept looking to Fire, half expecting him to be gone, that it was all a dream. That he was still dead. But Fire rode his tiger, bombarding Mind with questions on what had happened while he'd been gone. When Mind explained Jeric's real identity, Fire whirled to face Jeric.

"*Ero?*"

"Indeed," he said.

"No," Fire jerked his head. "I don't believe it. This must be a ruse to catch me unawares."

Mind chuckled. "I'm not Shadow."

"Doesn't mean you're not above *some* intrigue," Fire said.

"It's true," Elenyr said with a smile.

Fire's expression remained dubious, until Mind transferred the memory of seeing Jeric change into Ero. His eyes widened and he began to laugh. He leveled an accusing finger at Elenyr.

"You kissed a krey."

"*That's* what matters to you?" Elenyr asked.

"Yes," Fire laughed. "What did Shadow say?"

"I don't think he was focused on that part," Mind said. "We were rather broken up about your loss."

"I get to tell him," Fire crowed.

Elenyr groaned and looked to Jeric, who shrugged. "It's true, in a way."

"Who's side are you on?" she protested.

The group laughed, and Elenyr basked in the teasing, even if it was at her expense. She recalled all the similar moments of her and the fragments embarking on dangerous tasks, the smiles, the laughter. She'd thought that broken forever. She imagined future moments with the fragments, her beloved sons.

As they road east, the narrowing roadway prevented them riding together. Mind and Fire took the lead, while Elenyr rode beside Jeric. The four tigers rushed across the road, melting snow in their passage and muddying the dirt. Merchants and travelers forewent the roads in the winter, but soldiers had taken their place, the entire Talinorian army gathering for war.

The foursome sped by, the soldiers startled, but not shocked by their presence. With King Porlin's return, Jeric was no longer the Steward, and he'd altered his clothing so he would not be recognized. Elenyr knew he did not want to be the Steward and had only claimed the mantle out of need.

Soldiers assumed they were mages headed to join the conflict, and Mind enhanced those assumptions, smoothing their passage. He also picked up on the news of a camp in Orláknia where the rock troll queen, a handful of her soldiers, the fragments, and a group of Talinorian guards were hunting the Order of Ancients. Thousands had been taken to the Talinorian prisons.

"Looks like the fragments are dismantling the Order of the Ancients," Jeric said.

"If Serak wished to keep his Order, he would have kept it better protected," Elenyr replied.

Jeric motioned to Mind and Fire riding ahead. "He thinks to possess Draeken, but I believe he has no idea what he is attempting."

"That is my hope," Elenyr said.

"Do you regret our relationship?"

She swiveled in her seat to face him. He held the reins and did not meet her gaze. Snow from the trees drifted onto his hair and shoulders, the sunlight making him seem to shine. But his features were doubtful.

"Why would you ask that?"

159

"Now that you know the truth," he said, "It must have changed your opinion of me."

"How could it not?"

"Well?" he pressed. "Do you regret our relationship?"

The question was earnest, given by a man who'd kept secrets his entire life. But he really had loved Elenyr, and she had returned that affection. The knowledge of Jeric's real identity spoiled those memories, making the moments seem filled with lies. Still, she recalled times of happiness.

"I loved Jeric," she said softly. "But that season has come to an end."

He swept a hand to the wintery forest. "And all has grown cold in winter?"

"It has," she replied.

"Will spring come?"

The question cut to the heart of what he wanted. Could she love him again? She looked away, the answer coming quickly, but difficult to voice. She hesitated, considering a future with Ero, and she knew the truth.

"Jeric was once my love," she said. "Ero is a friend."

He sighed and inclined his head. "Perhaps it was inevitable. But can you fault me for falling in love with you?"

"Of course not," she laughed in an effort to ease the moment. "I know I'm a catch."

"You are," he said, smiling faintly. "And whatever the future may hold, I want you to know, I'm sorry I didn't tell you earlier."

We're almost there.

Mind's mental voice intruded on her thoughts. Ever vigilant, Mind had picked up the thoughts of the camp ahead, and they turned in that direction. Jeric made no mention of their conversation, and she sensed a shift in their relationship, a settling of the uncertainty. She'd said her peace, and their friendship had returned. She hoped.

Torn between regret and relief, Elenyr flicked the reins of liquid fire, accelerating her mount to catch the fragments. Jeric did the same, and she noticed a tinge of sadness to his features. Then Mind swiveled in his seat to look back at them.

"Two hundred," he said. "Mostly humans, but elves and rock trolls are also present, as is Water."

"How many rock trolls?"

"Three," he said. "Queen Rynda is among them."

"She didn't return home?" Jeric asked.

Elenyr shook her head. "Her people are in the north. The fight is here."

Elenyr had known Queen Rynda for many years, even met her sister when the girls were children. She was like a wolf, always seeking the conflict. Elenyr was not surprised the queen had stayed in the south.

"And rock trolls love a good fight," Fire said.

Elenyr imagined what would happen if the Dark Gate was opened, recalling the hordes of fiends waiting in the Dark. Even the rock trolls would be swept aside, their mighty nation going extinct in a matter of weeks.

With Fire's return, Elenyr considered the prospect of what Serak would do if Draeken refused him. Would he open the Dark Gate on his own? Or would he continue to subvert Draeken's will? Elenyr guessed the latter. He'd been patient for ages, and would not act in haste now.

The road ascended a hill and dropped into a large clearing, where a camp of varied races were gathered. A man in the Talinorian army stood to bar the foursome entry into the camp, and after speaking with Jeric, they were permitted through. Fire dismounted, and promptly dismissed the four tigers. Elenyr landed on her feet but in the snow.

"You could have let us dismount," she said.

"Why?" Fire asked.

He reached out and mussed her hair, like he was her big brother. He then laughed and spotted Water, who stood a short distance away.

He had a map and a quill in his hands, both of which fell from his fingers.

"Fire?"

"Why does everyone think I was dead?" Fire released an annoyed breath. "Have you no faith? Or did you not get my message?"

Water looked to Mind, who nodded, a smile on his features. Closing the gap in a rush, Water engulfed Fire in an embrace. Tears came to Elenyr's eyes as she watched her sons come together. Water began to cry, which Fire promptly teased. When they parted, Water's smile was bright.

"How is this possible?" Water demanded. "I got your message, but I thought it was Shadow's attempt at humor."

Mind explained how Fire had been inside his thoughts, the damage having left Fire effectively unconscious. Mind had begun to suspect he was alive, and with Jeric's help, returned him to life. Elenyr noticed he did not mention Sentara, Rune, or the Unnamed. Nor did he explain details of Fire's presence on Draeken.

Water listened with rapt attention, and Elenyr examined the camp. Formed of elves and Talinorian soldiers, the group also had the rock trolls. Elenyr spotted Queen Rynda, who spoke to several of her people at the edge of the camp. She'd clearly noticed Elenyr's arrival, but remained distant.

Elenyr liked the queen. She was a force of reckoning that had exiled Bartoth, the former king, and led her people with courage and integrity. She cared nothing for political intrigue and preferred walking right up to her foes and demanding surrender. She'd done it before, twice. One had been foolish enough to fight and lost his head. The second had wisely heeded the previous warning and sworn an oath to stay out of rock troll lands.

"Where's Light?" she asked, suddenly noticing he was absent.

"And Shadow?" Mind frowned. "I don't sense their minds here."

"We found a working Gate at Hyren's Estate a few weeks ago," Water said. "We sent them through to investigate, but the Gate was damaged. We assume they are traveling the long way back."

"Should we be concerned?" Elenyr asked.

Worry spiked, gripping her heart and lungs, extinguishing her breath. She knew it was because Fire had been killed, but it didn't relieve the emotion. With Serak, nothing was certain. Water seemed to understand her concern and shook his head.

"We had a plan in case the Gate went dark, which it did. They would have to travel back over land, and even with wings, it would take some time."

Elenyr's concern eased a little, but she would have felt better if they had returned. Even with Fire alive, she couldn't shake the feeling that Serak was still in control, always watching, always plotting. She fleetingly wished Senia were here, but according to what they'd learned she was still missing. Whatever the oracle was doing, she would be helping the cause.

Rynda caught her eye and tilted her chin, an invitation to speak privately. Excusing herself from the fragments, who were locked in conversation, she drifted over to the queen, who separated herself from her companions.

"Hauntress," Rynda said, offering a curt nod. "I heard of your battle at the Stormdial."

She frowned at Rynda's use of the real name for the krey structure. Rumors were rife of the Shard of Midnight, but none knew its krey name. Rynda's knowledge suggested she'd gained it from her time as Serak's prisoner.

"I heard Serak released you," Elenyr said.

Her jaw tightened. "We'll speak more on that later. For now, you should know I was visited by a certain dakorian."

"Tardoq sought you out?" Elenyr asked.

"He did," she said. "Seems he thinks you and a group called the Eternals can help him get home. He asked me to pass on the request."

Elenyr was surprised by the Bloodwall's bold actions. Tardoq had been a blood foe, servant to Wylyn and head of her forces. Elenyr had thought little of the dakorian since the Stormdial, but now realized he was on his own, bereft of friend or ally. Serak probably considered

163

him a liability, and he'd realized his sole chance of reaching the Empire would be through the Hauntress and Ero.

"I'm not going to help him," Elenyr said.

Rynda shrugged like she didn't care. "I was just asked to give you the request. Light and his brothers thought as you did, but I wouldn't put it past Tardoq to attempt speaking to you directly. I'd suggest you watch your back."

"You have my gratitude for the warning," Elenyr said.

A rock troll appeared through the trees and sprinted into the camp. Like all rock trolls, she was girded with strips of leather to her waist and carried a soulblade on her back. The woman had crafted a weapon with an axe on one side and a hammer on the other, a vicious weapon that reflected the host of tattoos marking her kills.

"Valdur," Rynda said, noticing her haste. "What news?"

"My queen," she said. "A large force of Order members is on approach. Looks like they want to retaliate."

"Excellent," Rynda said. "Inform Horn of the elven guard and Lachonus of the Talinorians." Then she turned to Elenyr. "Your timing is excellent Hauntress. Looks like the battle has come to us."

Chapter 24: Retaliation

Elenyr rushed to the fragments, gripped by an unnatural fear. She knew it was foolish to be worried and yet the feeling settled on her throat like strangling fingers. The Order had come to the camp moments after she and the fragments had arrived. Was it a coincidence? Or intent?

Rynda barked orders, and all the gathered races rushed to obey. The attack was coming from the west, and the group hurried to fortify the hilltop. Humans lifted short barricades out of the snow, bracing them with wooden poles. Elven archers claimed position behind the barricades, their mages in their midst, summoning the snow to protect the walls.

"What's going on?" Water asked.

"Looks like the Order got tired of your attacks," Elenyr said.

"How many?" Fire asked, looking to Mind.

Mind's brow was furrowed. "Five hundred," he said.

"That many?" Water seemed surprised.

"You've been hunting their halls for some time," Elenyr said. "I wager they grew tired of defending."

"Fire, Water," Mind said. "Right flank. Elenyr and I will handle the left."

"I return from the dead and I get a battle?" Fire grinned. "It's like a holiday gift."

"Just don't die again," Water laughed.

"I only allow one death per lifetime," Fire reasoned. "And since I've already used my allotment, I will now live forever."

Elenyr struggled to keep her fear from showing on her face. Fire had been dead just a few days ago and now they made light of his passing? But they were fragments of the same soul, and perhaps the agony of loss had been repaired with Fire's return. Then Mind noticed her expression, and silently spoke to her thoughts.

Put your worries to rest. He has returned.

Mind's words were kind, not dismissive, and that is perhaps what brought the tears to her eyes. He did not understand. She'd lost a son, and it had taken all her willpower to bury the agony for the sake of the war. But Fire's return had eroded that wall, and the mountain of emotion had nowhere to go.

Unwilling to let them see her tears, she turned away and cast over her shoulder, "Be cautious. We do not know why they have come."

Mind glanced to the other fragments, who seemed perplexed, and then followed Elenyr. She managed to wipe at her eyes before he caught up, and then pointed to the quickly forming line of soldiers.

"This could be Serak's doing—"

He folded her into an embrace, his arms wrapping around her shoulders. Mind had never been demonstrative, and the contact cracked the remaining wall. Tears leaked from her eyes, wetting his tunic. Mind didn't speak aloud.

I know you fear for Fire, he said. *But he is as strong as ever. Rest easy.*

He is my son! I can't lose him again! Unable to vocalize her fears, she shouted her mental anguish.

You won't. I swear it.

He released her and held her gaze, to which she nodded. The surge of fear could not stand against Mind's conviction, and she began to laugh, a sour note of gratitude for her sons. They were maddening, confusing, and difficult, but she loved them fiercely.

"Are you ready for this?" he asked.

"To fight the ones that killed Fire?" her voice carried a challenge, a craving for retribution.

He grinned. "Sorry, foolish question."

She wiped the last of her tears and then advanced to join the line. Mind claimed a place at her side, and they watched the downward slope as dark shapes appeared in the trees below, the shadows converging into the shape of soldiers. She glanced to the side and found a giant elf at her elbow, eldest son of the House of Runya.

"Horn," she said in greeting.

"Hauntress," he replied. "I'm glad you arrived. We would have been hard pressed to defeat them without you."

"Your arrival is opportune," the human at his side said.

"This is Lachonus," Horn said. "He's a decent fighter, if a bit short."

"As I recall, I killed twice the number you did."

Elenyr realized the man had bright red hair, the color more dwarven than human. He was shorter than Horn, but only by two fingers, and showed a powerful frame. His weapon of choice was not one but two katsanas, elven long swords. He noticed her curiosity.

"My father was a dwarf," he replied. "Don't ask about family gatherings. It's awkward."

"*All* family gatherings are awkward," Horn said.

"Says the exiled one," Mind said.

Horn grinned. "I told you that you'd like them."

The line of foes filled the bottom hill and began to advance. At the center of the defenders, Rynda raised her huge sword and bellowed her defiance, the call answered by the rest of the group. Elenyr glanced to the opposite side of the soldiers and spotted Fire and Water, both grinning like it was their first battle. She snorted and shook her head. Brothers.

"They have anti-magic weaponry," Mind murmured. "I'm letting Fire and Water know to be careful."

"Will you watch them during the battle?" she asked.

"Always."

"Do you think less of me for my worry?"

"One who worries is one who loves. And you're not the only one who's worried."

She smiled at that and turned her eyes forward. It had been some time since she'd stood with an army. The five companies at the foot of the hill began their ascent, their officers barking orders, their voices oddly distorted, wooden and empty.

She frowned and looked to Mind, who shrugged in confusion. Then the group drew their weapons and charged, some slipping in the snow. Rynda shouted to the archers and a volley of elven arrows pummeled the attackers, thudding into shields and burying into flesh. None cried out, not even a shout of pain. The injured grimaced and struggled on, their expressions set in a determined line.

"What's going on?" Horn asked. "Why do they not cry out?"

"Magic cannot control their will," Mind said.

"But it can take their voices," Lachonus said.

Another volley of arrows and several men perished. One woman took an arrow in the chest and soundlessly tumbled backward, her sword falling from her grip. Still they advanced, a disturbingly soundless army, now close enough that Elenyr could see what made them different.

Their eyes were closed.

"What is this?" Lachonus asked.

"I don't know," Elenyr said, and then spotted a dark elf at the center of the line, her eyes also closed. "But we should ask Princess Melora."

"Who?" Horn asked.

"A high ranked member of the Order of Ancients," Mind said. "And second daughter to the dark elf crown."

"She looks asleep," Lachonus said.

The gap closed to a hundred feet and a final volley of arrows filled the ranks of their foes. More fell, again in silence, and then Rynda barked an order to draw swords. Blades cleared sheaths and the entire group braced. But in the cold afternoon air, the voices of the enemy rose together.

". . . *Fragments*," they intoned, "*the final battle is upon us . . .*"

168

"That's not disturbing at all," Lachonus said.

"*. . . if you seek to save your people, the fragment of Mind must come to where dawn used to break, but will never again see daylight. . .*"

The collection of voices came from the charging army, spoken, not shouted, a disturbing, collective timbre. The Order force did not know they were attacking. Officers raised their swords, their eyes shut, their features tight with terror, as if they were fighting a nightmare.

"Serak is forcing them to fight," Mind said.

"*. . . I speak especially to the fragment of Mind . . .*"

"Who *is* that?" Lachonus asked.

Elenyr's hand tightened on her sword as she recognized the voice. "It's Serak," she said. "He's using the attack to speak to us."

The charge closed the gap in a rush, and the clatter of blades filled the air. Blood stained the snow, and defenders cried out in pain. The Order members crashed into the line of shields and barricades. Elenyr wanted to give the attackers mercy but they fought with unbridled terror, and finally one snapped their eyes open.

He stared about in shock, stumbling back in fear as he cried out. Others joined him, beginning to awaken, responding in kind. Elenyr turned ethereal and leapt through the line. They swung their swords, the blades flashing through her form.

A dwarf blasted her with fire but she passed through it and turned corporeal, slicing backwards once, a blow meant to incapacitate, not kill. The dwarf's eyes snapped open in shock. He cried out and went down, but she was ethereal once more, streaking for Melora.

The dark elf had woken, a cut on her arm bringing her to consciousness. She caught sight of Elenyr and spun, raising her sword. Her eyes were wild with anger and confusion. Elenyr frowned when she saw the crackle on the blade. Lightning magic. Elenyr came to a halt, and the dark elf sneered.

"I don't know where you came from," she said, "but I'm not going to pass up the opportunity to kill you."

"You don't know where you are?"

"Last thing I knew I was asleep in my bed," she snarled. "Then I wake up here on the battlefield."

Elenyr spared a look at the battle, and found dozens crying out in surprise, and fending off the defenders weapons. Those still asleep continued to speak, their words a swelling intonation punctuated by sounds of combat.

"*. . . come alone, and you will learn my purpose . . .*"

Melora darted in, her sword flashing. Elenyr drifted to the side, allowing the trunk of a tree to absorb the impact. Lightning crackled, the bark exploding off the tree. Elenyr leapt around it and turned corporeal, swinging her own sword. The dark elf retreated and claimed the higher ground on the slope.

"You and your fragments have destroyed everything I built." Melora waved her lightning blade. "I stole one of Carn's swords so I could take vengeance."

"And reclaim Serak's favor?" Elenyr asked.

"*. . . If you fail to come, you will never see your fragment brothers again . . .*"

Shadow and Light.

Fear gripped Elenyr and she whirled, spotting Mind in the midst of the conflict. His features were clouded, his blade cutting through the throng. Many of the attackers were now awake, and officers struggled to seize control, shouting orders, reforming ranks. Many were already dead or wounded, and Rynda waded into the conflict, her Soulblade slashing through the Order soldiers. Elenyr noticed she too, struck to disable, not to kill. She wasn't a murderer.

On the other end of the line, Fire forced the sleeping attackers into Water's traps, and the snow snapped shut like great jaws, sealing groups inside. Mind too, fought to disable, and the wounded piled around him. His newfound gravity magic made him especially dangerous, and men were sent tumbling down the slope with a wave of his hand.

Melora used the distraction and sliced across Elenyr's arm. Elenyr grimaced as the blade split her flesh, and blood came down her sleeve.

She spun, deflecting the strike meant to take her head, and then unleashed her full skill.

Elenyr knocked the dark elf's sword aside and up, parrying and slicing, forcing an opening. She swung her sword low, cutting across the dark elf's leg. Melora sought to block but Elenyr's sword was already up and going for her shoulder. Again and again Elenyr cut the woman, nicking her on the arm and side, even her face, each blow a scathing reminder that Elenyr could kill her at any moment. Melora's features reddened with embarrassment as Elenyr put her skill to shame, until finally Elenyr stood with her sword on the hollow of her throat.

"Your ambition means nothing to me." Elenyr spit the words at her.

Her chest heaving, Melora tried one last time, swinging her sword at Elenyr's head, risking her life for a killing blow. Elenyr ducked and flipped her sword, striking the lightning blade from her grasp. The blade twirled end over end until it plunged into a tree, blasting it apart. As the explosion faded, the last of the sleeping Order members spoke one final time.

"... *a word to the Hauntress. You have fought well, but Carn was not the only weapon that can kill you, and your days are numbered . . .*"

Chapter 25: Serak's Message

Mind listened to the last of the message, absently parrying a few desperate strikes. The attackers had been coerced using a powerful sleeping charm. In essence, they'd been walking into battle as if it were a nightmare. Upon waking they'd fought with fury born of desperation and confusion, but most were quick to surrender.

Queen Rynda and her group of rock trolls were the only ones disappointed. Mind had seen her mercy, and was grateful to see she had not outright slaughtered the sleeping attackers, even if they were foes. Rynda ordered the captives to be bound and a messenger sent to Herosian for more soldiers. There were too many for their group to guide back to the prisons.

While Rynda finished the battle and healers worked on the injured, Mind joined Elenyr. She'd forced Melora at sword point to Water's tent. Mind, Fire, and Water joined her, and a moment later, Rynda and Jeric entered as well.

"This is between us," Mind said to Rynda.

"Not when I fight a sleeping army," Rynda barked. "I want answers, and the dark elf will give them to me."

The dark elf glared at her captives, blood trickling from a host of shallow wounds. Her features were haughty, but a touch of fear ignited in her eyes. She'd been defeated, and Mind caught a handful of memories from her thoughts. She had been trained to shield her mind, but lacked the discipline to shut it entirely. The failed battle was the remnant of the Order of Ancients.

"This is the last of the Order in Talinor and the elven kingdom." Mind spoke the dark elf's thoughts. "Melora had gathered them to flee to the halls in Griffin, and the last thing she remembers is falling asleep. Then she woke up on the battlefield."

"Stay out of my head," Melora snapped at Mind.

"One more thing." Mind managed to pick a final, desperate fear before the princess shut her mind. "It appears Serak abandoned them entirely after they followed Wylyn."

"He never reclaimed authority?" Fire asked.

"Tell us everything," Rynda commanded Melora.

Rynda placed her sword on the bottom of the tent, the bloody weapon a chilling warning if the dark elf refused to speak. Melora swallowed in fear. Like the rest of her people, she was trim of build, her skin a shade of ash. Against a rock troll she would be helpless, and Rynda's weapon was larger than she was. She eyed the blade and then grimaced.

"After the defeat at the Stormdial we expected Serak to return and reclaim what he'd built, but not even a messenger arrived. Then you began destroying our halls, and we were forced to retreat."

"Are these really the last forces of the Order in the south?" Jeric asked.

"The last of those who followed Wylyn," Melora said. "Most of the Order still followed Serak at the split. He has other halls. Can I get a healer?"

"No," Mind said flatly.

Melora scowled. "When Wylyn forced Serak out, many chose to follow her. She was a member of the ancient race, after all, and we believed her claims of superiority. But she was haughty and dismissive, always calling us slaves, and by the time the Stormdial crumbled, we were glad she'd been killed."

"You won't curry favor with us," Mind said, catching the faint hope from her thoughts. "You're lucky we don't let Rynda send you back to your kingdom in pieces."

She flinched, and for a moment Mind felt sorry for her. She'd joined the Order seeking power, betrayed her people and her family, even helped Serak kidnap her mother. Melora had then abandoned Serak and followed Wylyn, again seeking power. It had led to ruin, with Wylyn dead and Serak unwilling to lay claim to the treacherous woman.

"What can you tell us about the sleeping charm used on you?" Elenyr asked.

"Zenif," she said with a scowl. "He's a mage with mind magic. His skills are limited, but his sleeping charms would surprise even you." She looked to Mind. "I hear his son is even more powerful."

"Son?" Mind asked.

He'd known of Zenif, but not of a son. Did Serak have a secret lieutenant? If so, where was he? What task had been assigned to him? Melora's ambition and conniving were dangerous to those she worked for, but a gold mine for him. She probably didn't even know the value of her information.

"Never seen him," she said. "But Zenif would boast about his son's talents, claimed he was even better than the fragment of Mind. That he'd avoided detection for decades. I don't even know his name."

"So Zenif put you to sleep and then walked you out to battle?" Fire asked.

"Apparently," Melora said.

"Just to deliver a message?" Rynda hefted her sword. "If you have nothing else . . ."

Melora retreated a step. "One more thing I can tell you, one that I wager even you do not know."

"What is that?" Mind asked.

"Serak sought four generals," she said.

Mind exchanged a look with Elenyr. It was news neither had known. "What for?" Elenyr demanded.

"He's obsessed with the Dark Gate," she said. "And he believes he needs Draeken and four generals to control what comes through."

"Do you know the identity of these generals?" Fire asked.

"I don't," she said. "But each general has a purpose. An assassin, a destroyer, a devourer, and a warmind."

Mind sensed a touch of petulance from the woman, suggesting she'd spied to learn such information. Serak didn't know she knew, making it the most valuable piece of information Mind had been able to acquire.

"Why four generals?" Rynda asked.

"Something to do with the fiend army," she said. "The will of the fiends has to be leashed, and the life of the four generals ensures they will obey their master."

Elenyr's eyes flicked to Jeric, who stood silently in the back. *Is she lying?* Jeric asked.

Mind replied in kind. *I don't think so. She's too smug to be deceitful.*

"What is the other weapon that can kill Elenyr?" Jeric asked.

"I don't know," she said.

"I think you're lying," Water said.

"I'm telling the truth," Melora replied. "Serak has always been secretive and only revealed what he claimed we needed to know."

Mind heard a wealth of bitterness to her tone. Melora had attached her ambitions to Serak, but the man had used her, refused to give even half of his plans. Wise on his part. She would have betrayed him the first moment she saw an advantage for herself.

"What do we do with you now?" Fire asked.

"Send her to her mother," Elenyr said. "She will provide justice."

Melora's sneer faltered. "You won't send me to the Herosian prisons?"

"I'd rather just kill her," Rynda said.

"No," Elenyr said. "Her mother deserves justice for Melora's betrayal."

Rynda grunted in agreement and motioned the woman out. Calling to one of her soldiers, she organized a group to take Melora to the dark elf outpost. Melora sought to convince Rynda to take her to the prisons in Herosian, her fear evident. Her words faded as she departed, leaving Jeric and Elenyr with three fragments.

"Does Serak really have Shadow and Light?" Water asked.

Elenyr passed a hand over her face, and Mind knew the worry she felt. Serak had attempted kidnapping them at Mistkeep, but Mind had gained the impression the failure was part of his plan. This felt different. From the beginning, Serak had sought to manipulate the fragments of Draeken, and he was in the final stages of his plan. He needed all of them.

"I believe he does," Mind said. "And in the coming weeks, I suspect he will come for all of us."

"We can't let that happen," Elenyr said flatly. Her hand went to her throat, where her pendent hung beneath her tunic. Mind knew it contained memories, but she'd never spoken of it, and the enchantment was too strong, even for him, to break.

"We should go after Light and Shadow," Fire said. "I'm not letting Serak have my brothers."

"We also need to protect Elenyr," Water said. "You heard him. Carn wasn't the only weapon he has against her."

"And I need to go to Dawnskeep," Mind said.

Elenyr rounded on him. "Why?"

"You know it's the location he spoke of," Mind said.

"You can't really be considering going there," Jeric protested, stepping away from the side of the tent. "It's exactly what he wants."

"Jeric is right," Fire said. "You can't go."

"It could be a trap," Water added.

"I must," Mind said. "We cannot defeat a foe we do not understand. And Serak is a foe we do not understand. He craves power but not as we first thought. Every tactic he has employed was to get to us, and we do not even understand why. Until we do, we should play his game."

"I'll go with you," Fire said.

"Not this time," Mind said. "You three need to join the gathered armies at Terros. Now that the Order has been dealt with, we need to focus on the army."

"They're months from being ready to fight," Fire protested.

"Doesn't matter," Water said, nodding as he caught Mind's intent. "What Serak wants most is us, and if we're surrounded by a large army, it will be harder for him to get to us."

"Sit and wait?" Fire grunted in irritation. "I didn't come back to life just to be bored."

"Better bored than dead," Elenyr said.

Fire grunted in disagreement. "Marginally."

Water grinned. "It's a sound plan, except for the part where Mind goes to see the enemy all by himself."

"I'll follow Serak's trail," Mind said, and raised a hand to forestall Elenyr's protest. "You three can watch each other's backs, and Serak will not harm me alone. Perhaps he'll even be there, and I can put an end to this once and for all."

"This is foolish," Elenyr said.

"It's the only plan worth discussing," Mind said. "Unless you have a better one?"

Elenyr scowled and looked away, but not before he noticed the doubt in her eyes. He did his best not to allow his true desires to show on his face. He needed to understand Serak's purpose, and the man had invited him to discover the truth. By meeting his foe, he could gain answers about Serak himself. Of course, it could also get him captured, but Mind considered it worth the risk.

"What about the four generals she mentioned?" Water asked. "Surely we should attempt to identify them."

"You can figure that out while you are in Terros," Mind said. "They will have to be specific individuals, so preventing him from getting his hands on them will obviously disrupt his plans."

"The Warmind has to be Bartoth," Water said. "He's the only one that fits that description."

"Or Rynda." Fire pointed to the door of the tent.

"Rynda would die before joining Serak," Elenyr said. "Bartoth has already followed him."

"I agree with Water," Mind said. "Where was he taken after the battle in the north?"

"To the rock troll citadel," Elenyr said. "I'll talk to Rynda and see what I can learn."

"We'll get there first," Water said with a nod.

"No." Mind grimaced as he considered the tactics. "If he's looking for Water and Fire, it could be a trap. And Astaroth is weeks journey north. Go to Terros as planned, and attempt to discover the remaining three generals."

"Are you certain this is wise?" Elenyr asked.

"I am," Mind said. "I'll do what he expects. You do what he least expects. I'll send a message soon."

Water and Fire did not appear to be convinced, and Elenyr looked even more doubtful. But one by one they all consented with a nod. They trusted him, as they always had. But they could not understand Mind's true motivations. While Fire had been inside his body, Mind had heard Draeken's voice, and it was not as he was with all the fragments combined. Mind wanted the truth about Draeken, and for the first time, he didn't trust Elenyr to provide the answer. Serak had manipulated, killed, destroyed, and threatened the very fate of Lumineia, but he had not lied to Draeken.

Elenyr's voice softened. "Be safe, my son."

Mind offered a faint smile. "I'm always cautious. It's you that needs to be careful. Mark my words. Serak will come for you. And he will be ready."

They exchanged a look, and Water's jaw tightened. "We'll be careful."

They exchanged farewells and then Mind gathered a pack of supplies. The camp was filled with captives, many of which were bound with fragment magic. Mind spoke to Rynda briefly before waving to his brothers and Elenyr. Then he turned and headed into the trees.

As he left the camp behind, a touch of excitement lightened his step. For the first time since the conflict began he was alone, and the

178

answers were waiting. He suppressed the twinge of guilt at abandoning Elenyr and set his face forward. She'd had her chance to speak the truth. Now it was Serak's turn. Mind had no intention of following Serak.

But he intended to listen.

Chapter 26: Buried Secrets

Mind took his journey south, heading deeper into the elven forests. The roads were filled with soldiers, the armies being sent to join the allied races in Terros. Even though the queen of the elves had not been one of those kidnapped, she'd pledged ten thousand troops to the effort. The remainder were being dispatched to the smaller forts and citadels scattered throughout the forest of Orláknia.

Mind slowed as he approached Ilumidora and came to a halt on a hill overlooking the city. The lake surrounded the island that contained the great mother tree. The bright lights had been subdued, and soldiers marched in the streets. The huge trees that ringed the city were filled with even more guards, fortifying the capital against any threat. Then a horn bellowed, and all activity in the city ceased.

Merchants, nobles, and commoners all thronged to the upper roadways built into the branches above the lake. They lined the railing, craning their heads to watch. Mind felt a chill as he watched the lake itself begin to move.

Rising in a wave, the lake swelled up and outward, answering the summons of thousands of water mages. The water rose up the banks and passed around homes and shops, washing past stables and leaving the straw dry to the touch. The water reached the city fortification, a wall of aquaglass that connected the greater outer trees, and the lake rose up the wall.

The water joined the city walls, rising and hardening as charms were added. The lake ran low, leaving fish flopping in the mud, and grimy plants laying on their sides. For the first time since its creation, the outer wall of the city had been raised, leaving the fortifications four feet thick, the water capable of enduring massive amounts of damage without breaking.

Mind admired Queen Alosia for her foresight. The effort required to convert the lake into the outer wall required weeks of preparation and could not be done while an army stood at the gates. Although the allied races would be at Terros, she was leaving nothing to chance.

Turning away from the city, he made his way around the outer wall, careful to keep himself out of sight from the elven archers. He had no desire to get into a pointless fight. They were fidgety enough to mistake him for an enemy.

He circled the city and entered at the southern entrance. The guards recognized him and allowed him past. The crowd was packed with people, many that had come seeking protection from Serak. The man's name was on everyone's lips, and some even called him the Father of Guardians. Mind frowned, disliking the awe and fear to their voices.

Mind threaded his way through the press to reach a squat, dilapidated structure in a poorer section of the city. The age of the building was evident in the graying wood and stone supports. The rest of the houses had been built more with magic, their walls fashioned of pristine aquaglass or living trees, their roofs intact. Mind's destination had a roof that was crumbling, and the nearby travelers avoided it like it carried a disease. Many had tried to purchase the building, if only to remove the blight from the city. But the seller had always refused to sell. None except the queen knew the owner of the house to be Elenyr.

Mind circled the building and entered the back door. Dust covered the interior of the home, blanketing couches, tables, and the floor. Footprints marred the dust, and the skittering of rodents indicated critters had taken up residence. It didn't matter. What Mind sought was not inside the home. It was hidden beneath.

He picked his way down the rickety stairs to the basement. He coughed at the dust and surveyed the handful of barrels. Twisting his way past them, he examined the wall behind the barrels. Beams of light came from a small window at the rear of the room, illuminating a faint rune on the stone footing. He touched the rune, running his hand around the exterior before pressing the center.

A faint clanking echoed, and then the entire floor shifted. The walls remained in place, but the floor, the barrels, even the stairs began sliding into the earth. As the secret platform descended, he drew his sword, the steel coming free in a whisper of sound. This could be a trap, but he didn't sense the presence of any other minds. Of course, after his experience in Beldik, Mind had learned Serak's ability with golems.

The room glided downward, deeper and deeper, until the air gained the scent of must and water. Then the ascender came to a halt, and Mind stepped into an enormous cavern. Squat and stretching for miles, the cavern reeked of age. Buried since the Mage Wars lay the ruins of a bright city.

Dawnskeep.

The city had endured the brunt of the conflict between the oracles, leaving buildings shattered and the fortress itself in ashes. The races had ordered the city covered by the earth, but the queen of the elves had decided the secrets could not be buried, and ordered the cavern built, the earth to be placed above. Separated by five hundred feet of earth, the ancient city of Dawnskeep slumbered beneath the bright lights of Ilumidora.

Mind picked his way down the slope and entered the ruins, watching for any sign of movement. The luminescent plants of the Deep now covered the walls of the cavern, their glow providing dim light.

Mind had no destination, but he made his way to the fortress at the heart of the city. The enormous tower had been felled like a giant log, and now lay on its side. Mind entered through the main gates, the wood long since rotted away, the metal brackets bent and cankered in rust.

He came to a halt in the courtyard, his eyes lifting to the stump of the fortress. Gaping holes marred the smooth material, the supports covered in moss. Water trickled down from above, and the faint dripping echoed in the background.

Mind turned a slow circle, wondering why Serak had chosen this place to meet. It wasn't the first time Mind had visited the ruins. Elenyr had many memories of the location. She'd grown up here, lived in a tower for her bloodline, raised her daughter, and guided kings and queens. She'd become head of the Eldress Council, effectively the most powerful person on Lumineia. It had not stopped her from being betrayed.

182

Elenyr had brought all the fragments to the ruins, each on individual trips. Mind only knew about Fire's visit because Fire never guarded his thoughts. The other three had returned shaken, and Mind guessed that Elenyr had told them much of the tale, pieces the history books had long since forgotten.

Mind's own visit had been revelatory. Elenyr had spoken of her time as an oracle, of her life as a leader of nations, the weight of responsibility she'd carried. She'd spoken of her becoming the Hauntress, and the pain of donning a new life.

Elenyr had shown him the remains of her time as an oracle, a thousand years devoted to serving the people, an effort that nearly failed when a member of the Eldress Council had betrayed them all. Yet Elenyr had still defied the attempts to take her life, fought those with more power.

She'd shown Mind the stables where she'd grown up, or what was left of them. She'd shown him the gardens where her mother had taught her plant magic, and the secret chamber she'd crafted out of stone, her first effort to hide when she'd fallen to mischief.

The visit to Dawnskeep had been the first moment Mind had seen Elenyr as more than a protector, and if he was honest, a captor. Elenyr had trained them, but she'd also controlled their movements and assignments. In the early years he'd thought of himself a prisoner. It wasn't until his visit to the subterranean ruins of Dawnskeep that Mind had learned the truth. Elenyr was not just any guide. She was *the* guide. Ero may have protected the world of Lumineia from the Krey Empire, but Elenyr protected the people from themselves.

The other fragments viewed Elenyr akin to a mother, but Mind saw her as something more. She was the very heart of Lumineia. While other kings, nobles, guildmasters, and master craftsmen fell to greed, ambition, and other vices, Elenyr stood tall, a beacon of morality in a craven world.

Mind frowned, and wondered if he'd made a mistake in accepting Serak's invitation. Guilt pricked his heart, and he questioned his motivation in coming. It was not a direct betrayal, but by listening to Serak, he was making a choice, to not wait on Elenyr's timing.

He scowled, and abruptly turned away from the fortress. Eager to depart, he turned to the gates, stepping over scattered stones and growths of mushrooms. Just as he reached the portal, he heard a faint footstep.

He whirled, his sword extending into the gloom. The ruins were only accessible from a few points, and all were hidden. The sound had been distinct, the scuff of a boot on dusty stone. Serak? Or one of his servants? But there was no sound from the chamber until a figure advanced into the light.

It was a golem, that much was obvious, but this golem was in the shape of a man. Clothes adorned its body, including pants, a tunic, and boots. The disturbingly realistic statue even had a cloak and a cowl, which he pulled back to reveal Serak's features.

"You have my gratitude for coming," Serak's voice came from the statue.

"I cannot say the same," Mind said cautiously, glancing about.

"No one else is present," the statue said.

"What sort of magic is this?" Mind asked, using his sword to point at the statue.

"An echoin," Serak said. "It is magic rarely used, for it connects a living mind to that of a golem. I am quite vulnerable in my present position, for I cannot even see the room I occupy. But this charm will allow me to speak to you without fear of your blade."

"You think I would attack you?" Mind asked.

"Of course," Serak said. "I have given you little reason to trust me. And I suspect you would take the opportunity to kill me."

Mind could have argued, but it would have been a lie. Although he'd come to listen, he would have undoubtedly seized an opportunity to kill Serak if it presented itself. The Father of Guardians was simply too dangerous to let live, whatever his purpose.

"You have spoken to all the fragments," Mind said. "And we both know you wish to enlist Draeken to your cause."

"I do."

Mind advanced and placed his sword on the golem's throat. It did not move, and merely waited for the lethal blow. Killing the echoin would not harm Serak, but would certainly send a message. Mind was no pawn.

"Give me one reason why I should listen to you."

"Hidden in these ruins you will find the truth of why I seek the Dark Gate," he said. "When you understand that, you'll understand why I need your help to open it."

"I am no man's servant," Mind spat.

"I do not seek a servant," Serak said, his eyes boring into Mind. "I seek a master."

Chapter 27: The First Visitor

Mind regarded the echoin, surprised by the response. Serak might be lying, but the way he spoke, as if the weight of the words had been held for ages, bespoke a yearning for this moment, to speak the truth to Draeken. Serak actually believed Draeken to be his superior.

Serak had proven himself to be cunning and powerful, capable of tremendous feats. Most may have led to destruction, but feats of legend, nonetheless. Yet he claimed he wasn't seeking a victory for himself, but preparing for one he considered greater. Draeken.

A touch of ambition ignited in Mind's heart. He tried to suppress it, but it came anyway. This was what Serak had desired from the very beginning, not to enlist Draeken as a servant or ally, but as a master.

The prospect left a disturbing thrill, as if he could taste the power. Everything from the conversations with the fragments, to the invitation to Wylyn, to all the battles had been crafted to bring Mind to the ruins of Dawnskeep, to speak the truth. The plan was flawless in its execution, perfectly ordered for all contingencies. All except one.

Bringing Mind to Dawnskeep was obviously meant as a reminder of what had come before, of the battles waged and great threats extinguished. Much had been sacrificed during the Mage Wars to destroy the Mage Empire before it could take root. Serak saw the Krey Empire as the same and wanted Mind to recognize the need. Bringing Mind to these ruins did indeed bring such thoughts to his remembrance—but they also reminded him of Elenyr, and all she'd done for him. She'd given him a home, trained him, raised him, and no matter his doubts, he would never betray Elenyr.

"I refuse," he said.

He raised his sword, but Serak lifted a hand to placate him. "Before you make that choice, allow me to show you the truth."

It was a gambit to continue the conversation, but one Mind could not refuse. He thrived on information, especially when such knowledge could win the war. Regardless of the fate of Serak, Mind wanted the truth.

"You want to share secrets?" he asked. "Who am I to refuse?"

The echoin inclined its head, and then beckoned him to follow. Turning away, he departed into the ruins of Dawnskeep. Mind frowned and looked back towards the exit. Then he reluctantly followed the golem into the fortress.

"I'm sure you know all about the conflict at Dawnskeep," Serak said. "So I won't bore you with the details."

"Wise choice by one whose life hangs by a thread."

Mind wasn't really threatening Serak. He had no way of knowing Serak's true location, but it was a reminder that if Mind grew tired of Serak's words, he would kill the echoin and depart. Serak's echoin lived on Mind's mercy.

"What do you know of the guildmaster of the Verinai?" Serak asked.

"Elsin?" He shrugged. "She fell to ambition."

"Indeed," he said. "She was my first love, and I would have given my life to her. She invented the charm that created all guardians. It is because of her that you and I possess our power."

"The granting of power is not a gift," he quoted Elenyr. "The training in how to *use* one's power is the true blessing."

Serak exited the fortress and made his way into the streets. Gaping holes and rents pockmarked the city, with many buildings in shambles. The battle at the city had been devastating, and few buildings remained intact.

"Guildmaster Elsin and the Verinai actually created several new spells," Serak said. "And the guardian charm was only one of them."

"I know all about Elsin's perverse experiments," Mind said.

"Some may have been perverse," Serak said. "But you cannot deny the boundaries she pushed in the name of magic."

"Like Marrow?"

The echoin came to a halt and turned, his features surprised. "Elenyr told you of Marrow? That is a truth I am surprised she would admit. But then, Elenyr does not like to speak of her failures. I doubt even I could have helped such a mad woman."

"At least Elenyr tried," Mind said.

"She and Ero killed Marrow," Serak said. "That is hardly offering aid."

So Serak did not know about the Unnamed, or Sentara and Rune. Mind had started to think Serak had discovered all of Elenyr's secrets, but apparently he thought Elenyr had killed Marrow when they separated her from the Unnamed.

The knowledge that Serak did not know of the now powerful Rune gave Mind an advantage, one that might prove the difference between victory and defeat. It would not be the first time a single soldier had turned the tide of war.

Mind recalled one of his early journeys alone with Elenyr. They'd gone to settle a dispute between a king and a duke, who aspired to the throne. They'd arrived before the council to ensure the conflict went as planned. The tension in the chamber had been palpable and quickly rose to heated words. Just as it erupted, one of the king's men drew a sword and sought to slay the king. An assassin's attack, orchestrated to perfection.

A servant girl had happened to be passing by, and instead of cowering she'd stepped in, raising the empty tray in her hands like a shield, deflecting the blow. In the ensuing conflict, she'd drawn a dagger, and with skill and courage protected the king. The duke had been executed, and the king had eventually married the girl. A single act of defiance, altering the course of a kingdom.

Mind considered his own role, how he could defy one like Serak. Destroying the echoin would provide little, but Serak wanted Mind to come to him, expected it, and that would be the moment he was most vulnerable.

"What did Elsin know about the Dark Gate?" Mind asked.

"Everything," Serak said, striding through the ruins. "She'd gathered every book, every tome, every record detailing the events before the Dawn of Magic."

"You mean the details of Ero and Skorn."

"The people worship them as god and devil," Serak said. "But the people do not understand the truth. They were both devils."

"I know about Kelindor," Mind said.

The echoin cast an approving look over his shoulder. "You are well informed. How did you gain such knowledge?"

"Knowledge is to be gained by those who seek," he replied.

Serak chuckled in agreement. "As you say, but knowledge of the Krey Empire is scarce on Lumineia. I wager your understanding came from the Eternals."

"Perhaps," he said. "And you? How did you learn of the Dark Gate?"

He gave a knowing smile but dodged the question. "The Krey Empire has a dark history," he said. "One more dangerous than you can imagine."

"I thought you were going to give truth." Mind frowned at the evasive answer.

"In due time."

Serak came to a halt before a large structure. The roof was gone, as were the upper floors, but the bottom floor had survived. The aquaglass enchantments on the wall had perished but the carvings remained, suggesting the building had been regal in nature.

"The hall of the Verinai," he said.

Mind had seen the building before. The Verinai had been a powerful guild of mages with multiple talents. Their capital had been a city called Verisith, located adjacent to Cloudy Vale. He'd explored the ruins in his youth, avoiding the guardians still present. They, unlike him and Serak, had gone mad, and were little more than ravenous beasts craving a kill.

"Have you been to Verisith recently?" Mind asked.

189

Serak shook his head. "It was my home, once, but now it is a reminder of my beloved."

"I was created in the secret chamber behind Guildmaster Elsin's office," Mind said.

It was an easy truth to share, one that Serak probably already knew, but in the sharing Serak would see a kinship. If Mind wanted to gain Serak's trust enough to get close, he needed to reveal a piece of himself.

"I know the chamber," he said, and smiled softly. "It was the very place I first kissed Elsin and knew that she was my beloved."

Serak entered the building through a hole in the wall, avoiding the door, which was blocked by rubble. The echoin picked his way through dark corridors, and withdrew a light orb from a pouch at his side. Igniting it, he held it aloft as he guided Mind into the darkened interior.

Debris and broken stones littered the room, mushrooms growing in one corner, and moss glowed on the ceiling and walls. The echoin picked his way around piles of collapsed ceiling and entered the back stairwell, where he descended to a subterranean level. Serak stepped over a pile where the wall had caved in and made his way to the back of the room. There he pulled on the bracket of a light orb, allowing a secret tunnel to open.

"A secret hall inside the secret ruins," Serak said, a smile appearing on his stone lips.

"Where does it lead?" Mind asked, hesitant to enter.

"I do not seek to capture you," Serak said. "I may have two of the fragments in my possession, but you must come of your own volition, for you possess the greatest portion of Draeken's consciousness."

"You didn't answer my question."

"Answers lie inside."

Serak motioned down the tunnel, and then led the way, as if that made it safer. But Mind sensed no deceit from the Father of Guardians. Instead it seemed Serak truly wanted to reveal everything. Against his better judgment, he followed the echoin.

The tunnel proved to wind downward, obviously to a secret chamber beneath the hall of the Verinai. While the city above had suffered much, the corridor was devoid of damage. The air smelled stale, tinged with dust. The end of the corridor opened into a single chamber, which contained a prison cell.

The bars were old and rusted. Water pooled in the corner, the moisture adding to the decay. The echoin stepped to a bracket and placed the light orb in the socket, flooding the room with illumination. Other than the cell and chains on the walls, the room was empty.

"You brought me to see an empty cell?" Mind asked, annoyed. "I thought you were here to reveal the truth."

"I did," Serak said, "and so I shall."

"Who did the cell belong to?"

"Five thousand years ago it contained a single occupant," he said, and turned to face Mind.

Mind folded his arms. "I'm growing tired of half-truths."

"Two revelations remain," Serak said. "Do you recall the beacon I used to summon Wylyn?"

"The one where Water and Light first met you?"

Mind had picked the memory from Light. The two, along with Jeric and Lira, had gone to the beacon and fought Wylyn. Serak had met Wylyn there, and it was the moment the fragments had learned of Serak.

Serak leaned in. "I wasn't the first one to use the beacon."

Mind frowned, disliking his tone. The way he said it, as if the news was the most significant, especially linked to what he'd said about Elsin, all suggested the beacon was connected to Elsin. But that only left one possibility.

"Elsin opened the Gate before you did," Mind guessed.

"She did," he replied. "She didn't know as much as I did, so she made crucial mistakes. She opened the Gate to Brimbor, a world infested with ravenous beasts and raging volcanoes. It belonged to House Ger'Vent, one of the smallest houses, but one renowned for its cruelty. They sent a group of dakorians and slaves through the Gate. In

191

the ensuing battle, the Gate was destroyed, and all the outlanders were killed. All except a single slave."

"One of them survived?" Mind asked.

"It is from him that Elsin learned about the Empire and the Dark Gate," Serak said.

"You met him?" Mind asked.

"I *was* him."

A chill crept up Mind's spine. "That cannot be true."

"I wasn't born on Lumineia." Serak said, the features of the echoin intense. "I was born in the Empire."

Chapter 28: The Exiled Assassin

Tardoq released an annoyed breath. "If I wanted to be bored, I would have stayed in the woods."

"For one that's lived for so long, you can be rather impatient."

"It's been five days," he pointed out. "And we're just sitting here."

After adding Rake to their little band, they'd journeyed south and west. Giving Herosian a wide birth, they worked their way through the snowy expanse to the farms adjacent to Terros. There they'd made camp in a thicket overlooking a farm, where a farmer labored.

"Why are we watching this man?" Rake asked.

The druid had kept his distance from them both, obviously still uncertain if joining them was the right course. He ate alone and frequently eyed Tardoq. Senia had explained Tardoq's identity, but Rake didn't seem to understand. He was a simple man, a druid that had lived in a quiet village until he'd summoned his animal companion, and the dragon had appeared.

"Serak wants the farmer," Senia repeated for the hundredth time.

"Why?" Rake asked.

"I don't know," she replied with a shrug, and then glanced to Tardoq. "Are you certain this man was Gendor?"

"I never forget," Tardoq replied. "He may look like a farmer, but he used to be an assassin."

"How well did you know him?" Rake asked.

"Enough," Tardoq motioned to the farmhouse. "He served the Order of Ancients, but Serak sent him on various assignments. The tales speak of him as formidable."

"If he truly was the Blade Ghost, he was feared by many," Rake said. "I didn't expect him to be taking care of cattle."

193

"The fragment of Mind changed his memory," Senia said. "The charm stripped his years of becoming an assassin from his consciousness, returning him to the man he was before becoming an assassin, a farmer. He doesn't know anything about his time as a member of the Assassin's Guild."

"Then why are we waiting?" Tardoq asked, annoyed.

"For Serak to come."

A thought crossed Tardoq's mind and he frowned. "You don't know when he is coming. Do you?"

Senia's lips thinned. "An oracle does not see everything."

"Do you tell *anyone* the full truth?" he demanded.

She regarded him with anger in her gaze. "Does anyone do that?"

"What *have* you seen?"

Rake looked between, retreating a step and wrapping his cloak around his shoulders. Senia regarded him for several long moments but Tardoq did not retreat. She'd grown accustomed to others showing her deference, even reverence, but Tardoq was not one to bow.

"Serak shows up at his door," she finally said. "He comes with a woman at his side, a mind mage, as far as I can tell. I believe she used to be a member of the Assassin's Guild before she was cast out for her actions. She used to work with Gendor."

"Name?"

"The Demoness."

Rake's eyes widened. "She's real?"

"Most of the tales are based in truth." Senia spared him a look. "The Demoness serves Serak, but from what I have seen, the pairing is fairly recent. She's a mercenary now."

"What do you know of the woman?" Tardoq asked Rake.

Rake shuddered and swept a hand toward Herosian. "There are plenty of rumors, of nobles and commoners, knights and bandits, all dying by their own hand, their features twisted in terror. The Demoness warps their minds, until they see nightmares and terrors

194

brought to life. Eventually they fall on their own sword, or leap from buildings, shrieking their desire to end what they have seen."

"My mind is not so weak," he said, and then turned to Senia. "Why bring a former assassin to a lost assassin?"

"I do not know," she said. "And that is why we wait."

"Because you don't know when they arrive."

Her features became annoyed. "No."

"What do you intend when he does show up at Gendor's door?"

"We stop him from getting what he wants," she said.

"And kill him," Tardoq added.

"If we can," Senia said evenly.

Tardoq nodded his approval and returned to surveying the farm. Rake sat silent, obviously wondering if joining them was the wisest course of action. Tardoq didn't care. The prospect of killing Serak—which would undoubtedly grant him favor among the fragments and the Hauntress—made him hopeful for the first time in weeks.

Located on the outskirts of the nearest settlement, the farm sloped down a hill into a lowland. A river ran adjacent, trees growing tall on its banks. The ground lay covered in a thin layer of snow, the white blanket also covering the house and the barn.

The house itself was small, barely more than a receiving room, a bedroom, and the kitchens. The barn was much larger, and contained an assortment of animals, all housed comfortably in neat stalls. The harvest of grain occupied a second, smaller barn. Tardoq and Senia had snuck in for a closer look when Gendor had gone to town for supplies.

For two days they continued to watch the quiet house as Gendor cooked meals and cared for the animals. When Tardoq had known him, he'd been vicious and cold, a killer. Here he smiled often, and patted the animals with an affectionate hand. Whatever Mind had done to him had left him broken. At sunset of the sixth day of watching, Senia abruptly rose to her feet.

"What?" Rake asked. "What is it?"

"They are here."

Rake swallowed and shook his head. "Will we have to fight them?"

Tardoq snorted. "For a man bonded to a dragon, you're rather timid."

Rake's features hardened, and his skin began to whiten, a pattern of scales appearing on his neck and face. Horns sprouted on his head before he clenched his jaw and reined in the emotion. He glared at Tardoq.

"I have been hunted for years," he said. "Do not mistake my caution for fear."

"Too late," Tardoq said.

"Enough," Senia said. "We need to get closer."

Tardoq followed Senia back into the trees. Passing their tiny camp, they threaded through the trunks of pine trees. Tardoq sniffed the air, sensing a prickling on the nape of his neck. A smile touched his lips. After lifetimes of combat, he could practically smell the impending blood. The excitement came as a surprise, until he realized its source. For the first time in his long life, the fight he faced was one of his own choosing.

"How are they arriving?" he asked.

"I don't know," she replied.

"Any others with him?"

"Not that I know of," she hissed. "Now be quiet."

They picked their way to the edge of the trees just fifty paces from the smaller barn. Tardoq scanned the farm and sniffed the air, which carried the scent of pine and snow. Rake sniffed as well, and to his surprise scowled.

"Two people are approaching from the opposite side of the house."

"You can *smell* them?" Tardoq asked.

"A dragon's nose," he said, a faint smile on his face. "Perhaps better than your own."

196

Tardoq chuckled at the man's response. Perhaps he was not a total loss. He'd been timid for the last several days, flinching at the slightest hint of danger. But now that they stood before a conflict, his face was set, his eyes grim.

"Shouldn't we just surprise and kill them?" Tardoq asked.

"Not yet," Senia said. "First I want to see what they intend."

"Why?" Rake asked. "If he is our foe, we should just kill him and be done with it."

"It's not enough to defeat a man," Tardoq murmured. "You must defeat his cause."

"Well said," Senia said. "Even if we did kill him, those who follow may continue his work. Information first, then we strike."

"Let's get to the farmhouse," Tardoq said.

Senia led them from the trees, her eyes half closed in what Tardoq took to mean she was watching the present and the immediate future. She would keep them from being spotted, but Tardoq watched the house anyway. No reason to become complacent, even next to one who could see the future.

They stuck close to the barn wall, passing the structure before darting across open ground to the house. One of the horses in the barn caught Tardoq's scent and whinnied in fear. A footfall sounded, and Tardoq sprinted the remaining distance, sliding into the side of the house as the rear door opened.

The opening spilled light onto the snow, and Gendor took two steps out, calling out to comfort the steed. He scanned the yard before returning to the warmth of his home. When the door shut, Rake hurried across the frozen ground to join them. His passage caused the animals to buck in their stalls. Apparently they could smell the dragon on him. Footsteps came from within as Gendor approached the back door, but a faint knock came from the front door of the house. Gendor reversed direction and swung it open. Through the window his voice was muffled.

"Can I help you folks?"

"May we come in?" Serak's voice was even.

"Of course," Gendor said. "I don't have much, but you're welcome to some bread and soup."

"We didn't come for food," the Demoness said, her voice scornful.

"What can I help you with?" Gendor sounded confused.

"You used to be a great assassin," the Demoness said. "And look at what they've done to you."

Gendor laughed lightly. "You must have me mistaken with someone else. I've been a farmer my whole life."

The front door shut and Serak said, "Demoness? You know what to do."

There was a shuffle of feet, as if Gendor had retreated. "I don't know your purpose, friends, but perhaps its best you get going."

Tardoq risked lifting his head and peeking in the window. Gendor reached for a tool on the wall. Catching the handle, he pulled it into view, and Tardoq got a full look at his weapon of choice. Instead of a sword, hammer, or axe, it was long handled, the curving blade on the end. A scythe.

Ignoring it, she advanced upon him. "This is going to hurt," she said.

"Now?" Tardoq whispered.

"Not yet," Senia said.

Gendor raised the scythe, but purple light burst from the Demoness's fingers, reaching out to strike Gendor in the head. He cried out, a bellow of pain before falling to his knees. She advanced a step, more light spilling from her fingers, wrapping around his head, digging into his flesh.

Rake grimaced as Gendor screamed. "Now?"

"Not yet," Senia said.

"She's killing him," Rake protested.

"She is returning his memory," Tardoq guessed.

198

Gendor clawed at the floor, the scythe forgotten at his side. His screams were agony, but the Demoness did not stop, and pushed harder, the purple light filling the room, spilling out the windows.

"Why aren't we stopping this?" Rake hissed.

"Trust me," Senia said.

"But what is she doing?"

"The fragment of Mind has powerful magic," she hissed through clenched teeth. "Gendor's memories are buried deep."

Tardoq spared Rake a glance. The druid's fists were clenched, and scales appeared and disappeared on his skin. The protective instincts in the man were obvious, and Tardoq again elevated his opinion of Rake.

"Don't let him die," Serak warned the Demoness. "Or you'll suffer the same fate."

"Almost there," the Demoness snapped.

Gendor shrieked again, and then abruptly the purple light winked out. Gendor was on his knees, gasping. He lifted his head to Serak and the Demoness, and then leapt to his feet, the scythe in his hands.

"What happened?" he growled. He stumbled back, grimacing. "Why do I remember a life of blood . . ." His features widened in horror.

"You are Gendor, the Blade Ghost, a member of the Assassin's Guild," Serak said. "And I've come to lay claim on your fate."

Gendor regarded him, the confusion on his face gradually turning to anger, and then, surprisingly, guilt. His grip tightened on the scythe and he shook his head, his eyes flicking between them, and spoke in halting words.

"I . . . remember what I have done," he said. "But I also remember my time here." He straightened as he spoke, his jaw setting in a firm line. "I'm not going back to killing."

"You surprise me," Serak said. "But it wasn't a request. Demoness, the cloak."

There was a whisper of cloth, and Tardoq sensed a ruffle of power. He frowned, attempting to identify the faint disturbance, but it was elusive, like a rumble of thunder, except there was no sound, merely a disturbing impression that made his skin prickle.

"What was that?" Rake asked.

"The answer we came for," Senia said. "Tardoq, it's time for you to earn your coin."

"You're not paying me," he said.

She grinned. "Just stop him, and whatever happens, don't let Gendor put on the cloak."

Chapter 29: The Assassin

Tardoq caught the handle of the window and jumped, crashing through the glass. His sudden appearance startled all three, who whirled to face him. Tardoq used their surprise to dart across the space and swing his hammer at Serak's head.

The man flinched and raised his hands. A wall of earth burst through the floor, but Tardoq was too close. His hammer swung through the wall of earth, grazing Serak's cheek. He recoiled and retreated, the wall of earth forcing Tardoq back.

"Tardoq?" Serak asked, grasping the blood trickling down his cheek. "What are you doing here?"

"He's with me," Senia said, climbing through the broken window.

Rake followed, his features grim. Serak's eyes narrowed as he looked between the sudden foes. Gendor had pulled back from Tardoq, keeping his distance. His eyes scanned the room and Tardoq guessed he was wishing for a real weapon.

"Oracle," Serak glared at Senia. "Your timing is not ideal."

"You kept me distracted long enough," Senia said. "And I don't like being manipulated."

"Get used to it," Serak said. "When this is all over, there won't be a need for you and your bloodline anymore."

"There will always be a need for an oracle," Rake said, straightening.

"Look at the one in love with the oracle," the Demoness mocked. "He's adorable."

Rake flushed, and Tardoq looked to her. The woman had recovered from their sudden entrance, but did not seem perturbed that she now faced a dakorian, the oracle, and Rake. She actually seemed excited at the prospect of a conflict. Purple light flowed up her fingers, circling the short dagger she'd drawn. Dressed in a dark cloak and

201

purple tunic, she looked the part of an assassin, right down to the dark elf skin and pointed ears. Her free hand held another dark cloak, only this one rippled like ink.

"I'm not letting you have him," Senia said. "And I brought enough to stop you."

"If it was just you against us, perhaps you'd be right." Serak was angry, his features twitching at Tardoq's betrayal. "Fortunately we are not alone."

He put his lips to his mouth and whistled, the sound like a master calling his dog. Tardoq spun his hammer, glancing to the door. Then he heard a flapping of wings and a thundering roar. Rake turned white, and not because of his dragon companion.

"No," he breathed.

A large claw ripped into the top of the nearest wall—and the roof was ripped off the house in a *crunch* of wood. All except Serak and Tardoq flinched as the top of the house was tossed aside, sending a shuddering through the floor as it landed. The large head of a red dragon appeared in the rent.

As smoke curled from its maw and sparks came from its throat, Serak smiled. "Meet Underigal, my mount."

"At least I brought my own," Senia said. "Rake?"

Rake drew in a breath, his flesh and body changing, wings sprouting from his back, his body hardening to white scales. The white dragon's appearance unleashed the mounting tension, and Tardoq lunged for Serak while Senia leapt to engage the Demoness. Tardoq half expected Gendor to flee, but he charged Serak.

Tardoq swung his hammer, but Serak ducked and jumped out the door, landing in the yard. There he summoned the earth, the ground rising about him, forming two large golems. Tardoq leapt to the first, swinging his hammer. The golem reached a large hand out—and caught the head of Tardoq's hammer.

The golem continued to swell in size, surpassing Tardoq's height and still growing. From within the house the white dragon leapt to the red dragon, attacking its neck, both tumbling through the wall and into the field. Half the size of the red dragon, Isray fought with surprise and fury, evading the claws and snapping teeth. Fire and frost breath erupted, igniting trees at the edge of the field and freezing the earth to ice.

"You should not have betrayed me," Serak growled.

"You would have killed me."

Tardoq activated the power inside his hammer, blasting the golem's hand to pieces. Then he ducked the swing by the other arm. The golem was now fifteen feet tall and boasted four arms. All reached for Tardoq, forcing him to retreat and evade. He swung his hammer, bashing the golem's hands, keeping them at bay and powering the weapon, the runes beginning to glow.

Tardoq spared a glance at Senia. Locked in mortal combat with the Demoness, she hurled bursts of light at the assassin, but her normally forceful features were twisted in a grimace as she endured the mental assault by the woman. Tardoq recognized the fear in the oracle's eyes and scowled, the desire to protect the woman sudden and forceful.

Tardoq ducked a large earth fist and swung, striking the elbow. The elbow shattered, dropping the hand into Tardoq's outstretched hand. He hurled it at the Demoness, the hand catching her on the shoulder and knocking her sprawling. She rose to her feet and glared at Tardoq.

"You'll die for that."

"Not by you," Tardoq retorted.

A fluttering attack struck his consciousness, and for an instant the world vanished, the scene replaced with dark creatures breathing flames onto dying men and women. Huge monsters crushed a nearby home, the image blurry, the Demoness struggling to make the image real. Great jaws opened at Tardoq's side, and a great horned creature burst across him, its jaws clamping shut on his head. All was an attempt to elicit fear, but Tardoq burst into a laugh.

"You assume I have not witnessed real monsters."

He swung his hammer up, where the golems arm had been coming towards him. He felt the reverberation in his arm, and heard the impact, the grinding of stone as another arm shattered on the head of his weapon.

"I don't need my eyes to fight," he said. "And your false memories will not frighten me."

The image faded, revealing the Demoness scowling, her black hair billowing as she ducked a streak of fire from Senia. She was forced to retreat, until a third golem joined the conflict, lunging for Senia. She ducked the swing and raised a pillar of ice from the snow, impaling the golem. But another charged from behind.

Tardoq saw his chance and unleashed a blast of power into the chest of the large golem, shattering a hole through and leaving an arm falling to his feet. With a groan of earth it fell to the side, leaving the field empty.

A fireball blasted into the pine trees, the sudden illumination revealing the two raging dragons. The white dragon was on the red's back. It rolled, snapping trees like they were twigs in an effort to dislodge the smaller creature. Frost breath covered the red scales in ice, and the dragon roared in pain, tumbling into the creek.

"Care to explain what is happening?" Gendor demanded, evading his golem. He used the scythe to slice the fingers from the hand.

Tardoq surveying the dark trees, searching for Serak. "Wylyn is dead. The Order is all but finished. The world gathers to destroy Serak at Xshaltheria."

"Then why did he come here?" Gendor asked.

He leapt to one of the golem's arms and jumped high, swinging the scythe to take the golem's head. He landed on the golem's chest, riding it to crash on the frozen earth. He swung the scythe in disgust and looked to Tardoq.

Tardoq grunted his approval. "Apparently he thinks you'd choose to be an assassin again."

Gendor scowled, and then jerked his head. "I didn't choose to be an assassin in the first place. I wouldn't choose it again—especially now."

"You'd rather be a farmer?" Tardoq asked, wondering what he'd do if he wasn't a soldier.

"I'd rather choose my own battles," Gendor said.

The golem beneath his feet began to reshape, rising around Gendor's legs. He sought to break free, but the stone and earth climbed, wrapping around knees and waist, sealing him to his neck. Tardoq leapt to engage but Serak appeared behind Gendor.

"I told you," Serak snapped. "It wasn't a request."

He placed the hood of the ink cloak over his head, and then retreated as the cowl closed over Gendor's neck, the cloak advancing on his shoulders like a snake coiling about its prey. Tardoq reached him and swung his hammer, but the ground rose up and smacked him aside. He hit a patch of ice from the dragon duel and skidded, the ice scrapping his cheek and drawing blood. He slammed his hammer down and stood.

Gendor screamed, the sound so harsh that Tardoq winced. The stone bindings shattered, knocking Tardoq back a step, bits of stone pelting his armor. Gendor's skin lost its color, his flesh draining of light. Still the assassin screamed, his clothes darkening to ash, the magic of the cloak threading into his clothing and body, extending down his hand and into his fingers, and sinking into the handle of the scythe.

Red veins appeared in the wood, growing and pulsing with power. The light extended up the wood and into the steel blade, darkening it further. Then Gendor released an unholy shriek, the sound even greater than the dueling dragons. His eyes darkened to black—and brightened into glowing red embers.

He fell to his knees, gasping for breath. Serak hovered in the background and Tardoq leveled his hammer at the guardian. But Gendor rose to his feet and looked to his hands, which had turned skeletal, the flesh gone, only bone remaining.

"What have you done to me?" His voice was filled with horror.

"You were an assassin of renown." Serak's voice was filled with triumph. "Now you are an assassin of legend."

Gendor whirled and charged, moving with inhuman speed. He burst across the ground, the scythe swinging for Serak's throat. The blade whistled through the air—and then came to a halt against Serak's skin. Gendor strained to complete the killing blow, but Serak regarded him with a small smile.

"The cloak has taken your life," he said. "And your very will. You cannot disobey me, and the cloak will require absolute obedience."

"I swear I will end you for this," Gendor snarled.

"You will kill who I wish you to kill," Serak said. "And from this day forth you will be one of my horsemen, the very essence of Death."

Gendor's red eyes pulsed with anger. "I will—"

"Not speak for a day," Serak said, and Gendor fell silent. "Go, and kill the hero known as Yorth."

Gendor whirled and leapt away, crossing the ground with such speed that he disappeared into the trees. In the ensuing silence Tardoq regarded Serak with surprise, but the look in return was pure hatred.

"Why not send him to kill me?" Tardoq asked.

"Because I'd rather kill you myself," Serak said.

He whistled and a pillar of stone carried him aloft. Tardoq darted forward, swinging his hammer at the column of stone. But the red dragon burst from the trees next to the farm. Snow and frost streaming off its damaged wings, it banked to Serak, who leapt onto his back.

"You cannot stop me," Serak called. "No one can."

The dragon turned and flew into the night, leaving the burning house and field behind. Tardoq spotted Senia laying near the building and hurried to her side. Just as he knelt, the white dragon crashed next to him, his body reshaping back into the body of a man. He clung to a burn on his shoulder, and blood dripped from a wound on his face.

"Is she dead?" he asked, his eyes on Senia.

Tardoq could hear the beating of her heart. "No," he said. "But she needs a healer. Grab a horse and take her to the village."

"What about you?" he asked.

"I'm going to deal with the Demoness," he said.

206

Rake took one look at the dark elf Serak had left behind and then sprinted to the barn. Tardoq regarded the dark elf, who stood thirty paces away, a sneer on her features. Her tunic was bloodied, as was her hand, but she regarded him with curious eyes. Then Tardoq's vision began to alter, his memories beginning to change.

"Let's see how formidable a Bloodwall really is—"

In a flash of movement Tardoq raised his hammer and pointed it where he knew the assassin to be. Thumbing the rune on the handle that activated the full power of the weapon, he unleashed a blast of pure-white energy. The beam struck the Demoness in the chest, blasting her into the field. She landed on ice and slid all the way down the slope, dead before she came to a halt.

Tardoq's vision returned to normal and he lifted his eyes to the sky, where Serak's dragon disappeared into the night. Gendor had spoken of choosing one's own fight, and he realized he wished for the same choice. It was an easy one to make.

"You wanted a foe?" he said to the departed Serak. "You've got one."

Chapter 30: A Chance Encounter

Mind watched Serak's echoin disappear into the ruins of Dawnskeep, wrestling with the knowledge he'd gained. After Serak had revealed the truth of his identity, he'd spoken of his time in the Empire, where he'd lived for twenty six years. He described arriving through the Gate, when a dakorian had haughtily told Elsin to kneel. The battle had left them dead, the Gate damaged, and Serak a captive of Elsin.

Mind had heard countless tales of the Verinai in his early years. Once regarded as near royalty, the Verinai had gained a reputation for villainy after the Mage Wars. They'd sought for power, pushed the bounds of magic into forbidden realms, and ultimately resorted to murder and war to attain their desires. Many of Elsin's ambitions had come from the truths Serak had shared with Elsin.

Mind turned toward the ascender that would take him back to Elenyr's house in Ilumidora. It was evident from Serak's tale that Elsin had not understood the Gate she sought to operate, and her actions could very well have doomed everyone on Lumineia. Fortune had been in Elsin's favor, because instead of destroying all life, she'd gained the greatest gift she could have hoped for, an ally who understood the Krey Empire. Serak's knowledge had sparked greed and ambition, and set her on a course to war. She'd jealously guarded the truth of Serak's origin, keeping him hidden, and killing those that knew of his identity.

Mind used the ascender to return to the decrepit house at the edge of Ilumidora. As the gears clanked and the floor climbed through the earth, he wondered if Elenyr knew Serak's true origin. He guessed not. She would've had no reason to hide such knowledge. Mind knew the woman still held a secret regarding Draeken, but she had not known of Serak.

208

"I know the threat we face," Serak's echoin had said. "I have seen it with my own eyes. I cannot defeat them alone, and I require a master with even more power than I, a guardian, a leader, a king."

"And what if I don't want it?" Mind had asked.

"Then our world will come to an end," Serak had said. "Maybe not today or tomorrow, but eventually the krey will come. And we will be defenseless."

"We have magic," Mind said.

"Magic will not be enough," Serak had said. "And you of all should know, it has its limits. We need hope. We need an army. We must open the Dark Gate. Come to Blackwell Keep, alone, and I will reveal everything, in person."

"Am I supposed to know where that is?"

"Search for the location in the King's Library," Serak had said. "You'll find the answer there."

"Why not just tell me?"

The echoin had smiled. "I want you to see the army gathering at Terros before you arrive."

The clanking came to a halt, the movement pulling Mind from his thoughts. He absently strode to the stairs and ascended the steps to the receiving hall on the first floor. Then he came to a stop and looked out the window at the group of elven soldiers in the street.

They were geared for war, their armor burnished, their blades sheathed, their bows on their backs. The whole of the elven might had been assembled, the presentation eliciting shouts of delight from children, the women waving colored strips of cloth and tossing small creatures of light into the air, the charms bursting into an array of colors. They thought themselves invulnerable, a small assignment to destroy Serak and his forces. They had no inkling of the Krey Empire, and the threat they posed. Mind hated the truth in Serak's words, hated his assumption that magic could not prevail against a krey invasion. Yet it was true, and Mind realized he faced a choice. Trust Elenyr's silence, or believe Serak's words.

He heard a faint creak of the boards above his head. Frowning at his lapse in attention, he focused on his surroundings, and noticed a new set of footprints entering through the back door. They marked the dust on the staircase leading to the second floor. He followed, avoiding the boards he knew had the tendency to creak. He reached the top floor and sensed the mind of a woman in one of the bedrooms. She was alone, and he stepped to the door.

The woman was dressed in a regal dress of red accented with white, the colors matching the streaks of color added to her blonde hair. The red highlights were unusual among the elven people, who disapproved of the coloring of hair. She faced away from Mind, and sat at the desk, a quill scribbling as she bent over the paper.

Mind could sense her mind but not her thoughts, revealing her high training. She was a noble, and the ring on her finger marked her as a member of House Erlan, second house to the crown. A princess of the city, and from the tales Mind had heard, probably Serania, who had a reputation for rebellion. For one who was third in line to the crown, she had little regard for her rank.

"Princess Serania," Mind said in greeting.

Serania leapt to her feet. Whirling and toppling the chair, she drew a dagger from a hidden sheath and pointed it at him. He'd obviously startled her, but the blade did not tremble. Good woman.

"Who are you?" she demanded.

"The owner of this house."

It was a lie, but close to the truth. Elenyr actually owned the house, but she'd always said that what belonged to her, belonged to her sons. She frowned, not liking his answer, and her eyes swept up and down, noting the fine blade on his back.

"I do not believe you," she said. "This house is always empty."

"Not today," he said. "What are you doing?"

Fear flitted across her features, the emotion cracking the guard on her thoughts. He caught a single worry, not for her own sake, but that of another. Horn, high captain in the queen's personal guard, outcast member of the House of Runya, and her beloved.

He raised his opinion of the woman. Horn had the caliber of a king, even if Shadow had gotten him exiled from Talinor, where his family resided. Without a house to support him, he'd joined the Queen's guard, and quickly risen through the ranks.

"Leaving notes for a certain captain?" Mind asked.

Her eyes narrowed and she reached behind her back to push the paper out of sight. "I know not of what you speak."

"Horn is an elf with integrity and honor." Mind motioned to the desk. "Make sure you lock the door when you're done."

He turned to leave, but she called out to him. "Please don't tell anyone. Horn has respect at the castle, but the House of Runya is not well regarded among the elven people, and Horn was exiled from Talinor. If it becomes known that we are together, it will be bad for him."

"His deeds stand for themselves," Mind said. "And you have nothing to fear from me. I have weightier matters to consider."

He turned and descended the stairs, again returning to the receiving room where he could survey the soldiers in the street. He didn't really care that Serania was using the house as a place to send notes to Horn. She wasn't a threat, and unless the war turned against Ilumidora, she was unlikely to ever be queen.

A creak came from the stairs and the elven princess approached him. She kept her distance, her hand close to her dagger, which had resumed its place in the sheath in her dress. He noted another knife hidden at the small of her back.

"You are one of the fragments," she said.

He didn't answer.

"The one called Mind?"

He still didn't speak.

"There is a touch of purple in your eyes," she said.

"What do you want, princess?"

"What weightier matters are you concerned about?"

He sighed. "You wouldn't understand."

She raised her chin. "I don't care. I'd like to know."

Torn between applauding her boldness, and condemning her petulance, he swept a hand to the soldiers. "What would you do if you knew of an impending threat, one that would destroy your entire kingdom? Would you join an enemy to prevent it? Or trust your family, and destroy the one person capable of preventing the destruction?"

She fell silent, and then shrugged. "I'd rather lose my life than my soul."

Surprised by her response, he faced her. "You would let your people die?"

"Death comes to us all," she said. "And every age has an end. Surviving is not enough, especially if it comes at the cost of our humanity."

He chuckled. The woman had Elenyr's fearlessness, and her wisdom. She would make a great queen, not that she'd ever get the chance. The rival house that had claim to the throne had two daughters, both elder.

"You speak with wisdom beyond your years," he said.

"My mother calls that irritating."

"Then she is a fool."

She laughed lightly. "She is indeed. Good day, fragment. May your journey be guided by Ero."

He managed to prevent the snort of derision as he thought of Jeric. The Princess inclined her head and then slipped out the back door, a moment later appearing on the streets. Guards spotted her and admonished her for walking the city without her personal guard. He expected her to feign fear, or pretend to be lost. Instead she shrugged, and said she had no need of guards. Glancing back to Mind, she nevertheless followed the soldiers into the upper boughs of the city.

Mind chuckled to himself, pleased with the encounter. With the weight of knowledge he'd obtained, he'd come from the ruins of Dawnskeep wondering if he should betray his home, his family. But

212

for all Serak's planning, all his cunning and conniving and plotting, there was one element he could not control.

Chance.

Mind recognized the encounter with Serania for what it was, a random event, an arrow striking a general on a battlefield, a king's horse tripping on a half-submerged rock. Elenyr and Serak stood on either side of the conflict. Serania had appeared in the center, the conversation doing what neither friend nor foe could do.

A slight smile formed on his face, but instead of departing he decided on a new course, one none would expect. He gathered his magic and reached his consciousness outward, calling into the void, not for anyone nearby, but one in particular.

Rune?

He wasn't certain he would get an answer. Rune and Sentara had disappeared from Stormwall, and he'd guessed Sentara would seek to train Rune. Without the strength of the Unnamed, Sentara would not live long, perhaps no more than days or weeks.

Mind waited, wondering if the Unnamed would answer, if she even could. Mind's magic was significant, but he could not reach another person's thoughts beyond the size of a large city. The only way to reach the Unnamed was if she wanted to be found. But he could think of no other ally. The fragments were being hunted, and Serak was smart enough to create opportunities to take them. Mind could fight, and ultimately fail, or permit Serak a taste of victory, and then land a lethal blow.

I have no wish to speak right now.

The voice of the Unnamed entered Mind's thoughts, distant, and tinged with sadness. Mind didn't have to ask what had happened. Sentara was either dying or already dead, and Rune and the Unnamed mourned her passing.

My apologies, Mind sent. *But I have need of your aid.*

Why would you think I would help?

Because you don't want to see Serak victorious, and I want to learn more about him. I want you to show me where he once lived.

213

Silence. The absence stretched for several minutes, until Mind began to wonder if she would simply refuse to respond. He couldn't blame her. After all she'd been through, she obviously wanted peace.

Meet me at the bandit camp of Horndall. Five days' time.

Any sooner?

Make it six.

The touch of warning to the change implied that would be her final offer. Mind agreed, and sensed the Unnamed withdraw. He considered his course one final time, pleased with the plan that was just taking shape. After their conversation in the ruins of Dawnskeep, Serak probably thought Mind would join him, that his plan was assured, but Mind had made his decision.

And he'd chosen his family.

Chapter 31: Lord Dallin

It took three days for Mind to find the bandit hideout, more time than he'd anticipated. The hideout turned out to be located on a large hill, two days outside of the highway between elven lands and Terros.

Many bandit groups dotted the landscape of the kingdoms, some big enough to pose a threat to larger caravans. Horndall kept his group small, with only fifty members. He had a litany of robbery and murder to his name, but staying small ensured the bulk of the guard's attention did not fall upon him.

Mind tracked the man to his lair, picking details from those who'd been robbed, to where they'd escaped, and finally locating one of the bandit scouts. Ostensibly a tavern owner, the man sent a lightcast bird every time a group of wealthy passed by. Mind picked the location from the traitorous elf and pushed through the woods to find the hide.

He expected to find the bandits hiding in a cave or crevasse, or perhaps an abandoned mine. To his surprise, they had chosen as their lair the former estate of a noble, the large house resting on a hilltop.

Mind surveyed the place from the tree line below the estate. The grand home contained four levels, two above, and two beneath. The home was old, the worn stone obviously dating back for ages, the wood and windows having been replaced recently.

Large arches graced the windows and the doors, the keystones engraved with the house of Dallin, a minor lord of the area. Mind had thought it to be false, but the name proved to be legitimate.

The estate had been owned by the Dallin line for ages, with each generation adding to the home. The outer wall, the guard towers, the winding road that passed through the main gates, all had been added by a single generation, the efforts of each Lord to expand the estate. But the newest addition, the spacious stables, were far more grand than the rest of the estate, suggesting Lord Dallin had recently acquired a surplus of coin.

In addition to the exterior, Mind viewed the interior through the eyes of its members. Corridors were lined with rich, elven cedar, while floors boasted carpets made in Erathan. Large chandeliers hung from ceilings, the light orbs of expensive elven make. All suggested Lord Dallin was a man of rich tastes, and explained why he'd become the murderous Horndall. As a minor lord, he received coin based on the production of his region, but the man's region had little but rocky foothills and a few small mines. Farms struggled to compete with the richer soils of Talinor, or the valleys of eastern Griffin. Even the neighboring estates boasted deep mines and coin to spare. Lord Dallin wanted more.

The entire personal guard had obviously joined his nefarious activities. The soldiers wore gold brackets for their cloaks, their daggers encrusted with jewels, their boots made of fine Talinorian leather. The servants cowered in silence, and Mind gleaned fear and despair from their thoughts.

As he waited, tension tightened his chest, an apprehension of things to come. He assumed it was merely worry for his plan. He was counting on his fragment brothers being captured, and then arriving as Serak expected. If anything went wrong, his brothers could very well be killed. Mind was risking their lives for a victory. He'd done it before, but this time the tension clenched his gut and kept him awake at night.

On the dawn of the sixth day, Rune appeared in the trees. She looked older, taller even. Gone was the youth to her features, replaced with determination and conviction. She was a young woman of strength, destined to live for ages and eras. But the sadness was evident in her eyes.

"When did Sentara die?" he asked.

She opened her thoughts and he saw a memory, of Rune and Sentara sitting by a fire in a small room, warm with smiles and laughter. Sentara knew her time had come, and she reached up to Rune, the daughter she'd always wanted.

"Take care of each other," Sentara said. "This world is not kind to young women."

"They had better learn," Rune said. "Or they will invite our retribution."

Tears were shed, and then the fire faded. The next morning Rune had buried Sentara's body, leaving a tombstone with a final eulogy, describing a woman who'd lived several lives, and died forgotten by all but a few. The final words had clearly been chosen by Sentara herself.

Marrow, friend to those who deserved friendship,

foe to those who deserved a noose.

"You have my gratitude for sharing the memory," Mind murmured.

"You helped all three of us," Rune said.

"I forced her to help me."

Rune chuckled, the sound echoing a maturity that had been absent before. Even a few weeks with the Unnamed had changed the young woman. He fleetingly wondered what Rune would become.

"I wasn't certain you would help."

"She said I should," Rune said. "She says there is still hope for you."

"Elenyr would say the same thing."

Rune smiled and swept a hand to Lord Dallin's estate. "What have you learned?"

"Horndall and Lord Dallin are one and the same," he replied. "He is a cruel master, his guards even more so. He's a cunning man to have evaded detection for so long."

"That's it?"

The voice was loud and right behind, startling Mind. He whirled, whipping his sword from his scabbard, nearly cutting the newcomer's head from her shoulders. Laughing, the old woman ducked the blade and approached.

"Sentara?" he demanded. "I thought you were dead." It had been some time since he'd been caught unawares, and the woman's smug smile heightened his anger.

217

"Not dead yet." Sentara waved her hand in dismissal. "And I wanted to have some fun before it was over."

"I saw the tombstone." He glared at Rune, who shrugged apologetically.

"I had it made," Sentara said. "Do you like it?"

Mind rubbed his forehead. "You are the strangest woman I've ever met."

"Thank you," she said, obviously pleased.

"Just tell me why we're here."

Sentara seemed annoyed. "I like Shadow better." Then she pointed to the house. "What do you see about the house?"

Mind frowned, his eyes flicking towards the home. "The foundations are old, the house is new. The interior has as much wealth as the king's castle."

"You wanted to know about Serak's youth. There it is."

"He told me he came through a Gate," Mind said. "He claimed he was born and raised on a different world."

"Really?" Rune's eyes widened. "Even the Unnamed didn't know that."

"I doubt anyone but him and Elsin knew his true origin," Mind said.

"Wherever he came from," Sentara pointed to the house. "He lived there for a time before becoming a guardian. I don't know what you expect to find."

"He's a tactician," Mind said, wondering why he still felt such tension, as if he were tearing in two. Could it be Draeken? "All tacticians have an emotional epicenter, and Serak's is Guildmaster Elsin. I need to know about their relationship, what happened, and what drove him to make this plan."

"Why wouldn't he destroy any secrets left behind?" Rune shook her head in confusion. "Surely he knows they would be a threat."

"He knows," Mind said, thinking of Elenyr and his brothers. "But you cannot erase what you love."

218

Sentara drew her sword and flicked it to the side. "Then what are we waiting for? Let's find a secret room."

She turned and sprinted down the slope. Rune sighed and swept her hand at the very old woman running like an excited toddler. "She's been like this since I was joined to the Unnamed—who says she was always like that."

Mind started after her, striding down the slope with Rune at his side. "Marrow was one who loved life," he said. "And now that she knows you're strong enough to stand alone, she gets to enjoy a little more. Just make sure it doesn't kill her."

"She's going to make that hard," Rune said, accelerating as Sentara charged the gates.

The guards looked at each other in bewilderment when a wrinkled old woman charged them, cackling like she'd gone mad. Then Sentara reached them and sliced one across the leg before plunging her sword in the second. Both tumbled, the shock of their killer twisting their features.

"She loves killing killers," Rune said in apology as they walked past the two dying men.

Guards rushed to engage Sentara, some splitting off to strike at Mind and Rune. Those who chose Sentara thought her an easy target, but her blade whipped through tunic and armor, leaving dying bandits on the road.

One veered towards Rune, and she drew her sword, bright white flames blossoming on the steel. Rune flinched at the burst of magic, and argued with the Unnamed as to its purpose. The man stared at Rune before shifting direction towards Mind, who smoothly deflected his sword and dispatched the man. The men had once been soldiers, but a bandit's life had made them soft.

"You really think we'll find a secret room?" Rune asked.

Rune's hand snapped up as if controlled by another, and a giant fist of fire burst into view. It struck a guard in the face, knocking him sprawling, and then flicked him fifty feet into the estate wall. He groaned and slumped, while the enchanted limb backhanded a woman, launching her skyward. She screamed all the way to the wall, her legs

219

striking the top and flipping her end over end to land outside the grounds.

Rune winced. "Sorry!" she called.

"Enjoying your newfound magic?" Mind asked.

She allowed a small smile. "She is fun to have as a friend."

They reached the main doors of the home, where a dozen bandit guards had congregated, pointing spears and swords out the opening. Some held servants by the throat, putting the screaming women between themselves and the attackers. Mind heard the fear of the guards in their thoughts, who believed Mind and his companions were Griffin soldiers, come to seek justice for their crimes.

Sentara darted to them and leapt into a soaring flip over the extended weapons. One man's jaw dropped open when the ancient woman flew over his head and landed at his back. He spun, swinging his sword at Sentara.

"What kind of woman are you?" he demanded.

"The dangerous kind," Sentara said, and slashed once.

The entrance hall dissolved into chaos, and Mind strode into the conflict, his sword swinging at bandits. One held a trembling servant between them. Mind felt the woman's fear and her desire to fight. He reached down and picked up a sword.

"You come at me and I'll gut her like a fish," the man growled.

Mind darted in, driving the sword through the man's arm, plunging the weapon into the wall. The man bellowed in pain, releasing the woman, who spun and yanked the knife from the man's belt, plunging it into his heart. She stared at the dying bandit, her chest heaving, her face set in a grim line.

"Get the other servants out," Mind said.

"Are you with Griffin?" the woman asked.

"No," he said. "But by nightfall this home will burn to the ground. I suggest you all be gone." He paused, and then added, "And take whatever you want from the house, as a final payment."

She stared at him, and then inclined her head. Mind returned to the entrance hall and followed the trail of wounded and dead. Some had made the mistake of trying to strike at Rune's back, but the wall itself had reached out, wrapping around them and crushing them in its splintery embrace.

"You think the secret room lies below?" Sentara called back, casually dispatching a huge mountain of a man with a maul as a weapon. The man stared in shock at the woman that had dealt the lethal blow.

"Has to be," Mind said.

As the giant slumped, Lord Dallin appeared in a doorway. His eyes were wide with shock and anger, and he yanked the longsword from his side. He pointed it at Rune, who stood nearest to him, and released a strangled bellow.

"I will not permit you—"

His sword betrayed him, the metal bending and stabbing him in the chest. He cried out and stumbled back, shocked and bloodied. The sword continued to attack him, and he raised his arm in a vain attempt to fend off the rabid blade. Golden weapons leapt down from the walls, diving and striking his back, his legs, his shoulders. Screaming, he sought refuge under the table, but Sentara leapt to the surface of the table and drove her sword through the wood, into the wounded man.

"Shall we explore?" she asked, pulling her sword free.

"Rune?" Mind asked. "Why don't you make sure the rest of the servants get out."

"With pleasure."

The girl lowered her hand and the blades clattered to the ground. Then she turned and strode from the room. Mind turned to Sentara, who hopped down from the table and wiped her sword on Lord Dallin's pants.

"Let's find ourselves a secret room," she said.

He nodded, wondering why part of him remained reluctant. Recalling the interior layout of the estate from the minds of the bandits, he exited and turned to the stairs leading down. If Serak had a secret room, he would find it, and use whatever he found against the Father of Guardians.

Chapter 32: Serak's Heart

Mind and Sentara left the main floor behind and entered the first basement of the house. Mostly filled with crates and barrels of goods for winter, it also contained a pair of training chambers. Crossing the first training room, Mind grasped a shield on the wall and rotated it, turning a lever that opened a hidden door behind, a secret he'd learned from the minds of the bandits.

The stairs beyond the secret door turned inward, leading to the second basement. Wide and open, the lower chamber lacked interior supports, providing an unbroken view of the treasure. Chests were stacked next to crates of furs, overflowing with coin. Enchanted weapons hung on racks, bags of jewels idly piled at their base, gilded chalices from the tables of kings tossed on top. A trove of ill-gotten goods from decades of robbery.

Sentara whistled. "Horndall is quite the saver."

"Indeed," Mind said.

"What are we looking for?" Sentara asked.

"A buried secret," Mind said. "Lord Dallin built the secret entrance to this room, but a few of the older men remembered this basement as a musty series of rooms filled with old furniture and rusted weapons. Serak has shown a deeply rooted instinct for keeping secrets, even more than Elenyr. I wager there is a secret chamber that connects to this level."

They set to searching, and Mind followed the right wall. He shoved chests of coin away, spilling gold onto the floor. Jewels glittered in the dim light. He examined the wall, every indentation, every bracket for light orbs, even the cracks in the foundation. A blast came from above, causing both to look up at the ceiling.

"Rune is still adapting to the transition," Sentara said. "But she would do better with some training."

"I'm sure the Hauntress would offer," Mind said, sidestepping the thinly veiled request.

Sentara's lips thinned. "Not going to happen," she said flatly.

Mind shrugged. "She's the best for the task, and you know it."

"The Unnamed has nearly an oracle's power," Sentara said, "but lacks the control. She is still highly impulsive."

"So is the fragment of Light," Mind murmured.

He'd noticed a pattern on the floor. He bent and shifted a pile of furs, revealing a faint indentation carved into the stone. He followed it, mentally shoving other objects aside, using his magic to knock chests and bags away.

"What is it?" Sentara asked.

He continued to follow the curved line to its end, where it doubled back and curved in another direction. Other lines intersected, and Sentara joined his effort, lifting and moving the contents of the room to reveal more lines. There were frequent breaks in the carving, and Mind had to search to find more. By the time they were finished, the grooves covered the whole of the floor.

"It's just a bunch of lines," Sentara said.

They'd retreated to the stairs to survey the room. Mind frowned as he examined the strange grooves. They seemed random, just curves and points, swirls and arcs. They could have been just a decoration carved into the floor, but Mind sensed a pattern.

He looked at it from every corner of the room, careful to not spill more coins on the sections they'd revealed. The more he looked, the more he was certain it was a pattern, but for what? Then Mind spotted a section of the carving, a slightly curving line merging with an arc. He knelt and touched it, a slight smile on his face. Rune's footsteps echoed on the stairs as he picked his way to the center of the room.

"You know what it is," Sentara said.

"She said you found it," Rune said. "What did you find . . ." Her eyes widened at the sea of wealth.

Mind stood at the center of the floor and reached out with his magic, grasping the gravity at his feet. Every section of the stone floor, cunningly built into seemingly random decorative grooves, began to shift . . .

Sentara jumped out of the way as the floor moved beneath her feet, gliding and shifting in a grinding of stone on stone. There were no gears. There was no need for gears, because the creator had possessed powerful earth magic, and the floor was meant to be turned with the same. But stone was beholden to gravity, and so the floor rotated.

The lines came together, the gold and jewels sliding about as the lines merged, rotating to complete a single image, a large concave triangle. A circle appeared on the inside of the triangle, the border of which connected with the triangle.

"It's the symbol of magic," Rune breathed. "The three points of mastery with the circle of magic at the center—she says the mastery is the hard part."

The symbol came together, and light glowed across the completed symbol, brightening the room, the magic shifting to the walls. Seams formed in the stone, and the walls turned into panels, which rotated in place, briefly revealing a second wall, the true outer wall of the basement, just a foot behind the false wall. The sections of wall pushed the wealth about, sliding chests and bags away as they turned like doors. Decorations and diagrams appeared from the other side, the records built of lightcast sheets, crafted to endure the weathering of time. The basement didn't lead *to* the secret chamber. It *was* the secret chamber.

The walls finished locking into place and Sentara released a bark of laughter. "Say what you will about Serak, but he certainly has a clever mind."

"What is all this?" Rune asked, pointing to diagrams and notes inscribed on the lightcast sheets.

Mind advanced to the nearest diagram, which contained information about the Krey Empire, a list of its worlds. The list was disturbingly long, and question marks indicated that it was not complete.

The diagram adjacent included an image of Guildmaster Elsin, the writing beneath describing her as Serak's beloved, the one who had

225

rescued him from the Empire. At least that explained why he'd loved the woman.

The lightcast sheets hung like curtains, each a part of the written archive detailing Serak's first years on Lumineia. This place had been his home, his refuge, his place of learning about Lumineia, and his place of teaching Elsin about the Krey Empire.

"Serak lived here before he became the Father of Guardians," Sentara called. "He writes of the wonders of magic, of his excitement at the possibilities."

"Elsin saved him from the Empire?" Rune's voice was uncertain, as if she didn't understand the words.

Mind answered over his shoulder. "It's why he loved her, why he volunteered to become the first guardian."

"He must have come back after he became a guardian and created the locking mechanism," Sentara said. "He didn't have stone magic until then."

Mind made his way from sheet to lightcast sheet, delving into the history of Serak. It was evident from the openness to the language that Serak never thought the room would be found. He spoke honestly of his worries, of his desires to protect Lumineia. He'd seen the Empire, knew its threat, and didn't understand why Elsin wanted to keep such knowledge a secret.

"It would have caused chaos," Mind murmured to himself. "The people were just not ready—still aren't ready for such a truth."

Mind read the next sheet, which detailed the beginnings of Serak's thoughts regarding the Dark Gate. He hadn't learned about it here, he'd learned about it as an Empire slave. Serak had considered using the Dark Gate then, even spoken of it to Elsin, but she'd wanted to rely on magic first. She'd had faith in her Verinai to conquer the nations, but Elenyr had proved the greater, and Elsin had died in the conflict.

As Mind worked his way around the room, the text gained a more hopeful air, and spoke less of his theory regarding opening the Gate. The tone of the journal shifted to his desires regarding the guardian charm, and he'd hoped to become an eternal warrior in the cause of freedom.

226

If I die, I die for my beloved. If I live, I will become as powerful as she, capable of standing with her against any threat, even the very Krey Empire.

"You should see this one," Rune called.

Mind stepped away from his examination and picked his way through the scattered wealth to reach Rune. The young woman stood before a panel obviously made after Serak had become a guardian, after Elsin was dead.

The Fragments of Draeken are even more powerful than I, Serak wrote. *They can do what I failed to do.*

"What did he fail to do?" Sentara asked.

Mind stepped to the preceding panel, a scowl on his features. "He tried to open the Dark Gate. He thought he could control the army, but failed." He bent to read the last line. "Looks like he managed to shut the Gate before the entity on the opposite side destroyed us all."

"And he thinks you can do what he couldn't?" Sentara asked.

Mind nodded. He noticed a scribble at the base, a notation about an outcast member of the Krey Empire. He'd learned her name before coming to Lumineia, or at least the woman's persona. She carried a lethal reputation, too dangerous for even the Eternals to invite into their ranks. The line through the name indicated Serak had decided against seeking her help. He gave the reason why he'd chosen to avoid her.

They call her Bonebreaker for good reason. She may be a foe of the Empire, but even for my plans, she is too dangerous.

Mind turned and gazed about the room, at the glimpse into Serak's past. The man who had become a guardian did indeed fight to protect Lumineia, but he did so by killing its people, by kidnapping and enslaving whole tribes of innocents.

Mind didn't like comparing himself to Elsin, but he agreed with the Verinai Guildmaster. He too believed the people of Lumineia capable of defending themselves. But was he a fool to believe that? Especially considering what he'd learned about Serak? The man had come from the Empire, been a slave to one of its houses, suffered abuses and ordeals Mind could not imagine.

But he'd unwittingly transferred those same abuses to the people of Lumineia. Every act done to him, he'd done to others. Some of the panels spoke of his life before Elsin. They didn't explicitly say he'd come from outside Lumineia. Apparently he'd thought that too dangerous a truth to leave in written form, but to Mind they were clear. Serak saw Lumineia as a morsel of meat before a ravenous Empire. Mind agreed with fighting the Empire, but he would do it on his terms.

The tension in his chest stirred, and he realized Draeken did not agree. Draeken liked the prospect of Serak's plan, craved the power being offered. Mind jerked his head but the tension remained, so he swept a hand to the chamber.

"We have what we need."

"What?" Rune asked, bewildered.

"Elsin is the key," Mind said with a nod. "And she will be his undoing."

Chapter 33: Lost

From her vantage point on the city battlements, Elenyr surveyed the growing camps outside of Terros. She sat on the top of a turret roof, leaning against one of the flag posts. The sun was setting, the icy wind blowing across the city, carrying the scents of sweat, smoke, and roast meat.

The gathered army camps stretched across the farmers' fields, with soldiers from many kingdoms, all gathered to face the threat of Serak. She felt a measure of pride at the sense of unity, the emotion mingling with her worry for Light and Shadow.

Below the tower, Fire and Water were speaking to a group of human soldiers from Erathan, quietly gathering information on their king. Elenyr still thought he was an imposter, but they lacked proof. She'd tried to talk to King Justin, but this time the man had refused her counsel. At least he'd lifted the bounty on her head.

Jeric had departed, saying he might be able to use krey technology to locate Light and Shadow, but he would not be back for a few days. In the interval, Fire and Water sought the information on King Numen, while secretly rooting out halls of the Order in Terros. The Order had been destroyed in the south, but a few halls remained in Griffin.

They'd hit two Order halls in the last week, decimating a tavern and a large home on the northern side of the city. Both had belonged to the Order of the Ancients, and the papers they'd found there pointed to another tavern, this time on the western side of the city, on the waterfront.

Water looked up and caught Elenyr's eye, and she dropped through the walls of the tower to reach the earth. Stepping out of the thick barrier, she turned corporeal and strode to join the two fragments, who separated from the soldiers. Lachonus joined them.

"What have you learned?" she asked.

"King Numen does not visit his soldiers," Lachonus said. "He gives orders entirely by messenger."

"Strange," Elenyr said. "But not entirely uncommon. Does he visit any known Order halls?"

"No," Water said. "Horn tracked him when he left the castle, but he didn't do anything suspicious."

Fire sniffed in irritation. "Why don't we just attack and force him to reveal himself?"

"A plan I can get behind," Lachonus said.

"No," she replied. "We need to watch and wait."

Horn appeared between the rows of tents and joined them, the tension in his expression showing he'd learned something new. He motioned them out of earshot of the soldiers and they drifted deeper into the shadow cast by the city wall.

"Numen traveled outside of the city today," he said.

"Where did he go?" Elenyr asked.

"South," he replied, "to a village a few hours ride from Terros. Sea Haven."

"I've been there," Fire said. "It's large, and mostly used by fishermen and trappers. Why would Numen go there?"

"Another hall belonging to the Order of Ancients?" Lachonus asked.

"Perhaps," Horn said.

"Only one way to find out."

"Should we collect Rynda?"

Water shook his head. "She was summoned to a war council at the fortress."

"I bet she hated being summoned," Fire said with a grin.

"We should see what Numen was doing there," Water said.

Elenyr hesitated, not liking the prospect of leaving Terros. Mind had said they should stay put, but she'd grown tired of waiting. They'd been in Terros doing nothing, and this looked like their best opportunity to investigate the imposter.

"Let's go," she said.

The group procured horses and departed the camps, working their way south. The village was not far, and they arrived a few hours after dark. Layered in snow, the village resembled any other sleepy coastal village. Ships bobbed on the sea, the nets gathered for the night. Even in winter, the fishermen cast their nets, a bitterly cold occupation, even if it was profitable.

Haphazard and scattered, the village boasted a motley collection of cabins surrounding the inn and blacksmith shop, both situated on opposite sides of the only street. The inn was larger than normal, with three levels, the bottom of which was used as a store and tavern.

"Owned by the Order?" Lachonus asked, his tone uncertain.

"I don't think so," Horn said. "The other halls we've attacked had a military air. This looks like any normal village."

"Then why would Numen come here?" Elenyr asked.

Horn shrugged. "He came and spent an hour at the tavern before departing."

"Did he speak to anyone?" Lachonus asked.

"I don't know," Horn replied.

Water shook his head in confusion. "Then what drew him here—"

The rumbling roar echoed in the distance, the sound tinged with menace. Those in the village straightened, a woman in the street freezing in shock. Elenyr blinked in surprise and turned to Water, both speaking at the same time.

"Dragon?"

The beast burst into view and soared above the village, the great wings visible in the silvery light of the moon. Those in the street scrambled to get inside, a woman dropping her sack of food, a man tripping on a step in his haste.

"Just passing?" Lachonus asked.

"We're not that lucky," Water said.

231

"There were rumors in Terros of a dragon sighting outside of Herosian," Horn said. "At a farm. Word is the dragon kidnapped a man before the place was burned to the ground—"

Elenyr frowned, wondering why that would be significant. A farm outside of Herosian. Could that be near her own farm? The one where Mind had left Gendor? The blood drained from her features as she thought of the four reported generals Serak desired, one of which was an assassin.

"How close to Herosian?" Elenyr demanded.

Confused by the sudden heat in her voice, Horn shook his head. "I'm not sure. Why?"

"You think the dragon took Gendor?" Water asked.

"The assassin," Elenyr growled. "Serak must have taken him."

"You think Serak is here?" Lachonus asked. He had his sword in hand as he eyed the sky.

"I certainly hope so," Fire said.

"We should spread out," Horn said. "Circle the village and send a signal if you see anything."

It was a sound strategy, but set Elenyr on edge. Something about Numen's visit to the town seemed out of place, but she couldn't explain her reasoning. She agreed to the plan and departed from the others, speeding through the trees to the west, before cutting back to reach the southern edge of the settlement.

She ascended out of a large boulder and stood atop, scanning the dark forest for any hint of Serak, or the dragon. The dragon rumbled again, and she spotted frightened faces in the windows of the village.

The wings appeared again, and the dragon abruptly dropped into view, sweeping above the homes and structures before rising again into the night sky. Flames kindled in its maw, and Elenyr began to fear it would attack the village.

Even as she tried to understand, she fought the anger. She should have seen the signs, should have realized Gendor would play a role in Serak's plans. Instead she'd ignored past foes, leaving them to be taken by their greatest adversary.

Shouts came from the buildings, with villagers arguing about whether they should abandon the village or stay. One family opted for the former, and bolted out of their door, racing into the trees. Another did the same, the father and mother carrying their two small children into the dark forest. The blacksmith appeared in his door and hissed for his family, and just as the woman appeared, the dragon returned.

It landed on the roof of the inn, wood crunching under its large claws. The red dragon slid down the roof but caught the pitch at the top, its claw digging deep. It reared back and released a thundering roar that sent the blacksmith scurrying back inside. A plume of fire burst from the dragon's maw, illuminating the village in garish red light. Then it dropped into the street, landing atop a horse that was tied to a railing.

He caught the animal in his jaws and ripped it apart, devouring the meat. Elenyr drifted forward, unable to sit idle while the dragon attacked the village. But where was Serak? Was this just an isolated attack? A coincidence?

The dragon rumbled its hunger and turned towards a nearby home. Screams came from within, and Elenyr burst from the trees. Ethereal, she charged the village, closing the gap in a rush. She passed through a house and caught a glimpse of a woman huddling in the corner with her daughter. Both screamed at Elenyr's passage, her cloaked figure appearing through one wall and disappearing through the opposite. She spotted a barrel in the street and leapt to it, using it to jump to a roof. Someone called her name but she was closing on the dragon, which had begun to claw at the roof, ripping a hole as it sought to reach those trapped inside.

"The Hauntress!" the innkeeper bellowed in fear.

The dragon turned and spotted her, and she cursed the man's cowardice. The dragon rounded on her and opened its jaws, the fire bursting through her ethereal frame. She passed right through the creature's jaws and darted to the side, where she turned to flesh and slashed at the dragon's throat.

Her blade cut a shallow line into the dragon's scales. The dragon turned on her and snapped its jaws, but she'd dropped through the roof into the interior. The man bellowed as she appeared and brandished an old sword.

"Get out the back," she barked. "I'll draw him away."

Without waiting for a response, she leaped through the door and raced into the street. The dragon spotted her and dropped from the roof, charging in pursuit, it's claws ripping the street as it opened its jaws again. She turned ethereal but did not deviate in her course. She spotted Horn atop a nearby roof, a crossbow in hand as he aimed at the dragon. Lachonus stood on the opposite side, an elven long bow drawn to his ear, the arrow glowing faintly.

They had positioned themselves ahead of her, and she raced towards the ambush. The dragon roared at her back—and abruptly launched itself into the sky. It's great wings brushing the inn, sending wooden shingles raining down into the street. It flapped for height and banked over the trees, disappearing from sight.

Confused, Elenyr came to a halt, wondering why the beast had fled. Lachonus and Horn dropped from the roofs and approached, bearing matching expressions of confusion. Horn pointed to the trees.

"What just happened?"

"Why did it flee?" Lachonus said. "Dragons are notorious for fighting to the death, only fleeing when they've been grievously injured."

"I don't know," Elenyr said, a touch of foreboding in her gut.

The dragon had hardly attacked the village before departing. Perhaps a younger beast would have behaved in such a manner, but the dragon had been large enough to be a real threat. Why did it leave unless . . .

"Where's Water?" she asked, spinning about. "And Fire?"

The street was empty, the villagers still too afraid to enter. Seized with fear, Elenyr raced down the alley and ascended the slope to where Water and been. She dove into the dark forest, searching for one of the fragments.

She searched in trees and behind boulders, racing about with increasing fear. Where were the fragments? They would not simply depart, not without leaving a message, an entity to inform her of where they went. But there was nothing.

"Tracks here!" Horn called.

Elenyr turned midstride and bolted to Horn, arriving just as Lachonus did. Horn was on one knee, examining the boot prints. He shifted and followed them, working his way to a vantage point next to a tree, where the tracks came to an abrupt end. Moisture in the soil indicated it had been Water.

"Water watched the dragon from here." Horn shrugged helplessly. "The tracks just end. Can he fly?"

Elenyr shook her head, dread seeping into her soul. First Light and Shadow, and now Fire and Water? She had no evidence aside from the cryptic words of the Order members in the attack of Rynda's camp, but she felt it in her bones. The fragments had been taken by Serak, and the dragon strike had just been a feint to draw them out. Mind was right, and she should never have left Terros.

"They're gone," Elenyr said. "Serak has taken them."

"The dragon," Horn said, rising to his feet. "The attack was a ruse."

"If that's true, how do we find them?" Lachonus asked.

"I'll find them," she said.

She turned and leapt into the trees, ignoring the shouts of her companions. In ethereal form she sped through trees and stones, racing back to Terros. Her sons had been taken, and she would not stop until she'd forced the words from a member of the Order. Her features set in a grim line, she accelerated, driving herself forward, fear rising in her chest.

Chapter 34: Homeland

After the conflict with Serak, Tardoq and his two companions retreated into the forest before the kings' soldiers could arrive. Word of a dragon sighting spread like wildfire, the people panicking at the mere mention of an attack. The trio went north, and despite her and Rake's injuries, Senia kept them moving until they reached the edge of Blue Lake. They camped on the edge of a shallow ravine, where a river had cut through the stone.

"You really should see a healer," Rake said, checking the bandages on Senia's wounds.

"You and me both," she said. "But time is short, and a healer would recognize me."

Tardoq stood at the edge of the ravine, watching the sun set on Blue Lake, marveling at the serenity to what he would have called a slave world. He'd spoken of unharvested worlds as filthy bogs. How little he'd known.

"Why do the people fear dragons so much?" Tardoq asked.

"They are unaware of the treaty between the oracles and dragon kind." Senia winced as Rake tightened the bandage. "Dragons rarely come to our lands, and those that do have been cast out by dragon kind. They are exiled, angry, and hungry. They come to kill."

"Dragons are native to Lumineia," Tardoq said. "Did you know that?"

"What do you mean?" Rake finished the bandage and stepped to the small fire.

"Humans, dwarves, elves, gnomes, and all the other races were not born on Lumineia," Senia said, wincing as she examined her wounds. "We were brought by Ero and Skorn. Dragons and reavers were already here."

Rake's features were forlorn. "The more time I spend with you, the more I miss my ignorance."

"You have but scratched the surface," Tardoq said.

Tardoq claimed a seat by the fire and examined the chunk of meat cooking over the coals. They hadn't killed it, rather it had come from the stock of a farmer they'd passed, one Senia had helped several years ago. When they'd made camp, Senia had laid a bed of coals and used magic to shape a trio of rods, on which she placed the thin strips of meat. She'd added a touch of seasoning, and the meat smelled better than any food Tardoq had had in the diamond halls of the emperor.

"That should be done," Senia said, pointing to the meat.

Tardoq picked it up right off the hot metal, his thick flesh keeping him from being burned. He ate a bite, pleased by the crusted exterior and the pink interior. He nodded his approval and settled back against a tree, wondering when his life had taken such a strange turn. He sat for a meal with a modified human that could see the future, and a human that could change his very flesh to become a mighty beast. He began to laugh, causing Senia to raise an eyebrow.

"What amuses you?"

"This." He swept his hand at the fire. "When I stepped through the Gate to Lumineia, I would never have imagined I'd end up here."

"Do you regret the choices?"

Tardoq shrugged. "I doubt I would have done any different. Wylyn chose her fate, as did her son. I fought for them because that's what I'd been raised to believe, that we were superior to you. Yet in all my years fighting for the krey, I never felt more at home than I do at this fire."

"Now we're home to you?" Senia had a small smile on her face.

"I meant the steak," Tardoq said.

Senia laughed, and Rake grinned. Extricating another steak from the fire, Rake handed it to Senia and then gathered his own meal. Then he claimed a seat on a fallen log. As he cut a piece for himself, Rake's expression turned serious.

"What now? Serak has one of his four generals, and his plan appears to be working."

"His goal remains the fragments of Draeken," Tardoq said.

"They will fight that fate," Senia said, steam rising from her dinner, wreathing her face and giving her an otherworldly look. "If they succeed, our efforts will not be needed. But if they fail, our actions will be all that stops the impending destruction."

"Then what's our next step?" Rake asked. "Another general?"

"Bartoth," Tardoq said. "The rock trolls hold him prisoner. If we hasten, we can get there before Serak does."

"And then what?" Rake asked. "Serak knows we're coming now."

"True." Senia's features were knit in thought. "But I suspect our presence will slow his plans. He cannot risk failure, and he is one that plans ahead."

"Then we go north," Tardoq said. "A ship?"

I could fly us.

"Isray?" Senia asked at the mental words. "Are you certain?"

Rake grimaced. "He says we can."

"You expect me to ride on your back?" Tardoq asked.

"Only out of necessity," Rake said. "We'd get there much faster, and it seems that is our goal."

"You have our gratitude," Senia said.

Tardoq wasn't fooled. The woman had known all along that Rake would offer. He wondered how much she really did see, and if the glimpses provided hope, or madness. He finished the meal and then stood.

"I'll take watch."

He stepped into the trees and walked a short distance. Finding a spot behind a boulder, he settled in to watch the dark trees. His enhanced hearing helped him listen to his companions despite the distance, and he smiled to himself, guessing that the Demoness had

238

been right. Rake was falling in love with the oracle. Tardoq idly wondered if she returned the affection.

The night grew still, the forest steeped in dim light from the partial moon. Animals flitted about, keeping their distance from him. He did not move, but he listened to the surroundings, prepared to attack or defend. After the battle with Serak at Gendor's farmhouse, he'd thought the Father of Guardians might retaliate, but not this night.

Tardoq stayed in place throughout the night. He could go days without sleeping, but rarely had to test that limit traveling with humans. Rising with the sun, he returned to the camp to find Senia and Rake already packing their gear.

Tardoq began to feel apprehensive about the plan to ride a small white dragon across the sea. His weight alone would be too much for even the sturdiest of steeds. Rake turned into his dragon form, his body swelling, muscles rippling beneath the white skin, wings sprouting from his back. Beautiful and captivating, the transformation reminded Tardoq of all the Empire could not do. They had limited control over changing physical form, and very expensive amulets had the power and ability to alter the body of one into another. But to turn into a dragon? Even the krey could not perform such feats.

The dragon dropped onto its forearms, lowering its body to the ground. It was smaller than the red it had fought, but the back was as tall as Tardoq, the wings wide and powerful. Senia climbed onto Isray's back without hesitation, and then the beast's head swiveled to Tardoq.

You're not as heavy as you look, outlander.

The voice was not Rake's. Deeper and more resonant, the voice was that of the dragon, an entirely separate consciousness merged with the mind of the human. Tardoq reluctantly placed his foot onto the beast's forearm, using it to swing his leg over the dragon's neck behind the oracle. The dragon spread its wings, and then dropped over the cliff.

Tardoq tightened his grip on the bony ridges extending from the dragon's back. The spark of fear came suddenly and brought a laugh to his lips. Then the dragon banked out of the dive and curved over the water, his powerful hind legs brushing the surface. The beast emitted a mental chuckle before flapping hard for altitude.

"I should not have doubted you," Tardoq said ruefully.

Never doubt a dragon, Isray replied.

Tardoq did not feel fear at heights, but riding the back of a dragon into the clouds left him apprehensive. He kept tight rein on the emotion, unwilling to let his companions notice. He found his own pride amusing. He was actually concerned about the opinion of people he'd once called slave. Now he would call them friend.

The realization that he'd fully joined himself with the people of Lumineia was disconcerting. Thousands of years of training and tradition, undone by six months on Lumineia. He would have thought they were manipulating him, but he'd been trained to resist such interrogation. No, they were being sincere, and that was what left Tardoq so shaken.

The anger was sudden and cold. He viewed the last few months in their entirety, and realized just how far he'd fallen. He was a Bloodwall, and he'd resorted to begging foes for aid, even helping them on their own menial tasks. What did he care of the threats on Lumineia? He was sworn to protect the Empire, and should be eliminating all of them, including the Eternals. Then he could seize a Gate home and return with an armada to watch Lumineia burn.

That is what he *should* do.

He sighed and the anger melted away. It would never happen. The prospect of fighting Senia, of killing Rynda, proved more abhorrent than facing the breadth of the Empire. At some point since Wylyn had been killed, he'd crossed a line. He'd switched sides, and even if he could, he wouldn't go back. Astride a dragon flying over a bright blue sea, he realized he'd abandoned the Empire.

He pondered the ramifications of the choice as they flew north. They soared above the sea, and stopped to rest at the islands of Azure, landing at night to avoid being spotted by the island race. Then they departed the next day, attempting to avoid a storm.

He'd flown above storms before, but in the confines of a ship, the black clouds seemed distant. Astride a white dragon, he felt the thunder in his bones, and saw the storm's might beneath his feet.

Three days after departing Talinor, they reached the northern deserts known as the Fractured Plains. From the sky, the thousands of cracks, canyons, and gulleys made the landscape look like a great hammer had struck the earth, shattering the smooth stone of the great plateau. In the distance a great tower of rock rose into the sky, and Isray banked towards the natural citadel.

"That's Astaroth," Senia said over her shoulder. "The largest rock troll clan lives inside, and it's Queen Rynda's home."

"How will they react to a dragon approaching?" Tardoq asked.

Not well, Isray said.

"We should land and walk from here." Tardoq said.

"Not enough time," Senia said, her voice suddenly tense. "It looks like Serak got here first."

Tardoq squinted, his enhanced vision allowing him to see the citadel, and the smoke curling up from the summit. Black and thick, it stained the white clouds, too much to come from a fire. They were under attack.

"We're too late," Senia said.

Tardoq shook his head. "That smoke is recent." He smiled in anticipation. "We're right on time."

Chapter 35: The Fallen King

The white dragon folded his wings and they dropped from the sky. Tardoq gripped the bony ridge, sweeping the citadel with a searching look. As he would have expected from the rock trolls, the tower of stone boasted formidable fortifications, even though some were unfinished.

Balconies lined the exterior, many under construction. The summit was in the process of being hollowed out, providing natural walls against attack. The quarried stone had been placed around a courtyard at the foot of the fortress.

Smoke belched from one of the doorways in the top, and rock trolls sought to extinguish the flames. Several spotted the white dragon and rushed to arms. Isray released a rumbled warning as Senia raised her voice. Tardoq winced when her voice came out as a roar.

"I am the oracle of Lumineia. We have come on Queen Rynda's request."

That's a lie, Isray said.

"We're just trying to land without getting killed," Tardoq said.

The rock trolls hesitated, obviously still suspicious. Their array of weapons was impressive, and Tardoq eyed the large axes, hammers, swords, and mauls, each crafted by their wielder. That and the wealth of tattoos marking their kills showed the identity of individual trolls. Many had picked up enormous crossbows and laid them on the partially completed battlements, the barbed bolts aimed at the white dragon.

"They don't know they're under attack," Tardoq realized.

"What do you mean?" Senia asked as Isray landed on the rim, his claws grasping the rock.

Tardoq didn't answer. He pulled his hammer from his back and dropped from the dragon's back, landing on a section of scaffolding.

The wood crunched under his feet and several of the trolls turned their weapons on him.

"What *are* you?" one asked.

It was the best question. He was only slightly larger than a rock troll, but his armored body and horns set him apart. They wanted to know if he was a threat, and the soldiers arrayed against him made it clear they weren't taking any chances.

"Quiet, Kentor," another said.

Kentor grinned. "I just want to know how to grow bone armor like that."

"You don't," Tardoq retorted.

The young troll did not appear disappointed, his smile remaining on his features. He had a number of tattoos, but his eyes held an innocence the others lacked. He'd seen war, that much was obvious by the kills marking his chest, but it had not yet darkened his soul.

"Who are you?" the officer demanded of Tardoq.

"Where's Bartoth?" Tardoq asked.

"You don't ask the questions," he snapped, twirling his black axe.

"He already did," Kentor pointed out, to which the officer groaned.

"Kentor, do you need to be punished again?"

Senia dropped to Tardoq's side and the officer blinked in surprise. "Oracle Senia? What are you doing here?"

"Warshard Toril," Senia said. "We don't have much time. Where's Bartoth?"

"In his cell at the base of the tower," Toril said. "Why?"

"Because that fire is a distraction," Tardoq said. "And I'm guessing you pulled most of your forces to extinguish it."

Toril's eyes narrowed. "The fire was caused by an ember from a fire. Nothing more."

"I expected more from Rynda's people," Tardoq sneered.

Weapons were pointed their way and Senia placed a comforting hand on Tardoq's arm before stepping between him and Toril. The dragon released a rumble and the crossbows rose toward the beast.

"You must take us to Bartoth," Senia said. "If we are wrong, then it was just a fire. If we are right, someone has come to free him."

Toril's eyes flicked between Tardoq and the dragon, before settling on the oracle. He was obviously trying to decide whether to believe them, but ultimately caution won out, and he gave a motion to his forces. The gathered rock trolls reluctantly lowered their weapons.

"I will take you to him," Toril said. "But your mount stays outside."

I'm not a—

Senia cut Isray off with a warning look. "As you will." She then added mentally. *You're no use to us inside, and we may need you outside if that red dragon returns. Stay alert.*

Tardoq heard the unspoken exchange and agreed with a curt nod. The dragon dipped his head and folded his wings on his back. Tardoq fell into step beside Senia, noting the quartet of rock trolls taking the position at his back. All boasted countless tattoos, their scars revealing their legacy of combat. Kentor claimed the fourth position, flashing Tardoq a grin. In the lead, Toril guided them into the interior of the citadel.

Much of the fortress was under construction, the echo of hammers clanging in the background. The recent growth was obviously necessary due to the large population. Tardoq spotted young rock trolls training in the hallway while dwarves labored to carve out a new training chamber. All stopped to watch Tardoq pass, their eyes going wide at the armored dakorian.

Tardoq carried his hammer in his hand, preparing himself for a second fight with Serak. The man was devious and powerful, and Tardoq reviewed everything he'd learned about his chosen foe, every tactic, every technique.

"Bartoth is in chains?" Senia asked.

"Gnome made," Toril said. "They keep him from using his magic."

Body magic. Tardoq had met Bartoth a few times before the troll had been defeated by the fragments. His magic allowed him to manipulate any aspect of his physical form, and he'd used strength, seeking to intimidate Tardoq. The effort had been futile, and Tardoq had shown his superiority. The encounter had proven Bartoth's brutal and ambitious nature. He was one to be despised, yet not dismissed.

"Has he tried to escape?" Senia asked.

"Twice," Toril replied. "But he underestimates his own people."

"What is Rynda's plan for him?"

"She means to execute him in front of the clan," Toril said.

The hatred in his voice was not for Rynda, but for Bartoth, who Tardoq knew had once been their king. A grunt of agreement came from behind Tardoq, suggesting the feeling was common among the clan.

The winding corridors descended past personal quarters, meal halls, and training halls. The citadel was more like a giant barracks than a city, with the shape focused on war rather than community. Tardoq did not see any taverns or merchants, suggesting supplies were provided to rock troll people by the military, which dominated their social order.

The parallels to dakorian society were impossible to ignore, right down to rank of the soldiers. Whelp children, naifblade youths, and warsworn adults. Dakorians might have different names and ages, but the social structure was the same. It made Tardoq question their origin. He'd thought rock trolls had been adapted from the race of man like the rest of the races. Could it be possible they had once been dakorians themselves?

Tardoq shoved the enticing but distracting questions aside. If Serak were present at the citadel, the impending conflict would be deadly. He needed to stay focused. He tapped his hammer on the wall, brightening the runes on the weapon.

"Nice hammer." Kentor sidled up to walk next to Tardoq. "What magic?"

"You'll see soon enough."

"I hope so."

Tardoq glanced to the troll, and again noted his youth. He nevertheless had as many kills as his companions, yet fewer scars. Kentor was a warrior with a large sword, an elegant weapon with a strange glimmer to the metal.

"Name?" Kentor asked.

"Tardoq," he replied.

"What are we facing?"

"If I'm right?" Tardoq pointed to the troll's cheek. "A kill for your face."

One of the other trolls grinned at that. Tattoos for the face were reserved for the most formidable kills, a hero, king, or dragon. But the youth frowned at the revelation, for it revealed the truth. The threat they faced would be deadly in turn. Good kid.

Tardoq thought of his youngest brother, Weldenton, whom he'd called Welt. Despite the large age gap, Tardoq had harbored a soft spot for the youth, even training him in his spare time. Gifted with any weapon, Tardoq had imagined him becoming a Bloodwall like himself, the two fighting side by side for ages. Welt had become a Bloodwall, but shortly afterward had disappeared, a fate when a Bloodwall was killed and the house did not want to show weakness.

"Have you any talent with that?" Tardoq asked, pointing to the hilt of Kentor's sword.

"Decent," he replied modestly, but the snort of irritation from another troll indicated the truth. Kentor was better, and the others were annoyed by his skill, a familiar sentiment that Tardoq had also experienced.

They passed a collection of forges, where young and old trolls labored over the flames, their hammers ringing on steel. Senia glanced back, a look of warning that Tardoq understood. Serak was here.

They descended further, into the depths of the fortress. Then they turned down a corridor which led to a large steel door. The mechanism of gears and bars was dwarven made, and would have required an

246

army to breach. But it lay open, and the two guards were on the ground.

Toril leapt to their bodies. "Dead," he hissed. "Tensin, summon reinforcements."

"That's what Tardoq is for," Senia said, stepping past him.

Toril rose and barred the way. "I can't let you go in there."

"Do you really want to stop me?"

Senia's voice was quiet, yet carried a seething threat. Toril glanced to Tardoq, who subtly shifted his feet, ready to spin and strike at the three trolls behind him. Kentor bore a wide smile, his arms folded like he couldn't wait to witness the attempt. Tardoq had faced Rynda, and if her people were anything like her, they would be well trained. Fortunately Toril scowled and inclined his head.

"I'm First Warshard," he said. "I go first."

Senia gestured in invitation and Toril drew his weapon. Striding to the cracked strongdoor, he eased through the gap, and Senia was quick to follow. Tardoq was forced to open the door wider, and he winced when it squeaked. The other three trolls followed him inside.

The prison chamber was larger than he had expected, and obviously a natural cavern. The cave lacked much of the floor, the darkness of the abyss surrounding a raised platform. A cold breeze emanated from the depths. Rather than an ornate cell, the rock trolls had opted for simplicity. A giant chain, each link as thick as Tardoq's neck, bound Bartoth to the platform. With the chasm on three sides, the only point of entrance was the front, where two more dead rock trolls lay. But Bartoth was not alone, and Serak turned at their entrance.

"Oracle," Serak said evenly. "You're gaining a habit of disrupting my plans."

"My pleasure," Senia said.

She drew a dagger from her side, and ignited white flames across the steel. Tardoq let his hammer head fall to the stone, the impact filling the last of the runes on the weapon, and sending a chilling ring through the chamber. Serak scowled, a hint of displeasure.

247

"You were a fool to join them," Serak said.

"I didn't have much choice," Tardoq said. Senia glanced his way and raised an eyebrow, at which he rolled his eyes. "Plus I like them better."

Senia smiled.

"Submit and we will not kill you," Toril said to Serak.

Bartoth was on his feet, the giant chain clinking against the band around his neck. "You don't even know what you face," he mocked.

"I have no intention of fighting you," Serak said to Senia.

"What?" Bartoth rounded on Serak. "What do you expect me to do?"

Serak smiled at the bound rock troll. "I expect you to destroy them."

Bartoth rattled the chain, his voice darkening. "How am I supposed to do that?"

Serak reached out, and the ground rose up at his sides. Tardoq expected a weapon and was not disappointed. A giant sword was lifted into view, and a matching war helm. The black helm seemed to absorb the light.

"That looks exciting," Kentor said.

"Kentor," Toril groaned.

Senia began to advance and Tardoq joined her, the group crossing the smooth stone leading to the raised prisoner platform. Serak seemed unperturbed, and pointed to the enormous sword and helm.

"The helmet and sword of a giant." Serak reached out and touched the metal, which glittered with power, as if it wanted to be worn. "The elves should have destroyed such powerful relics, but instead they were sold and eventually placed in Mistkeep, where they were foolishly put on display. Now they belong to my future general, the mightiest of my horsemen."

"That's not my soulblade," Bartoth growled, retreating a step from the offering.

"Your soul doesn't belong to you anymore," Serak said.

248

"Serak," Senia said, advancing towards him. "You don't understand what you're unleashing."

"Yes." Serak held her gaze. "I do."

"Serak," Senia called. "Trust me. You seek a fate you will never obtain, and before this is over, you will be the one bound in shackles."

The timbre to the oracle's voice sent a shudder throughout the cavern, and even Tardoq raised an eyebrow. The words were spoken by one in authority, who'd seen the future. It was not a guess. It was a prophecy.

Serak glared at her, a flicker of doubt appearing in his eyes. Then he jerked his head. "An oracle's words," he sneered. "So full of lies."

With that he clenched a fist, and the stone holding the helmet turned into hands that lifted the helm up and placed it on Bartoth's head. The rock troll reached up and sought to dislodge the helmet but it refused to budge. Then he released an unholy scream, the sound reverberating in the confines of the cavern. His body began to glow, and he screamed again, falling to his knees.

Tardoq lunged forward, sprinting past the shocked Toril and ascending the slope onto the pedestal. So quick was his charge that none managed to follow. Tardoq closed the gap and swung his hammer with all his might, intending to end Bartoth before Serak's plan could take shape. His hammer swung for Bartoth's head, the blow backed by all his tremendous strength. Bartoth raised his arm.

And caught the weapon in his bare hand.

Chapter 36: Warmind

Bartoth held the head of the hammer, his bones unbroken. Bartoth's chest heaved from exertion, his body swelling in size. He stood, his body rising, his flesh darkening to a dull grey. He towered over Tardoq, a full head higher. His tunic had torn from the growth, leaving only the pants, which had stretched to the breaking point.

Tardoq wrenched his hammer free and swung again. Bartoth reached for the dark sword. Tardoq whirled and leapt, using the rotation to enhance the speed of his hammer, which came down on Bartoth's arm. But the rock troll moved with shocking speed, withdrawing his hand before the impact. He reached out and struck Tardoq in the chest, knocking him backwards. Tardoq recovered and rolled to his feet, raising his hammer to face the still bound Bartoth.

"What have you done to me?" Bartoth's voice was one of horror.

"The helmet has unlocked every facet of your body magic," Serak said, his eyes on Tardoq. "Every charm, every augmentation effect, all are now active. You are stronger and faster than anyone on Lumineia—including a Bloodwall."

"Doesn't mean he has my mind," Tardoq snarled.

He leveled his hammer and released a full blast of the embedded magic. Bartoth snatched the wide sword and raised it, deflecting the blast into the ceiling. Stone exploded and crumbled into the abyss.

"I have my own training," Bartoth said, excitement coloring his voice.

"Kill him," Toril barked. "Before he escapes the chain."

The Warshard and his three trolls charged Bartoth. Chained and against four of the mightiest soldiers on Lumineia, Bartoth stood his ground, the black greatsword spinning right and left, parrying and striking.

By the time Tardoq reached the conflict, two were dead, both bodies tumbling into the abyss, their broken weapons disappearing into the darkness. Only Toril and Kentor remained, both fighting for their lives.

Tardoq entered the fray, reaching his hammer out to deflect a blow meant to take Kentor's throat. The impact still knocked Kentor to his back, his head striking the ground. Senia took his place, her form tiny in the midst of the towering combatants.

She evaded Bartoth's blows, the black greatsword passing above her head, and then missing her stomach by inches. She closed the gap and sliced across Bartoth's leg, cutting deep. Bartoth snarled and swung his sword, but Senia leapt and jumped off Tardoq's hammer, flipping over and slicing Bartoth across the arm. More blood spilled down his body, and Bartoth glanced at Serak, who watched the battle from the back of the outcropping.

"If you cannot survive against them, you aren't good enough for me," Serak said evenly.

The lull in the conflict allowed Tardoq to hear the sprinting of many feet, of hundreds of rock trolls charging down the tower. Tardoq wiped blood from his cheek, where Bartoth's blade had nicked him across the jawline.

"I can stop you," he said.

"Maybe," Bartoth acknowledged. "But not without your hammer."

Bartoth darted at Toril, striking him in the face with his free hand. Then he lunged at Tardoq, his large blade whistling as it came down. At the last instant the sword shifted its path, and came for Senia. She cried out and leapt backward, but the hurtling sword would cleave her from head to foot. Tardoq recognized Bartoth's ploy. His hammer, up and horizontal, could be tilted to accept the blow, but it would not be at the right angle to prevent damage to his hammer.

He could save Senia's life.

At the cost of his weapon.

He tilted his hammer, catching the sword between the hammer head and the shaft. The sword cut deep, severing the hammerhead

251

from the shaft, releasing all the contained power in a single, powerful blast.

Tardoq stumbled backward with his broken hammer. Senia went flying sideways. Bartoth's greatsword sliced across her scalp, drawing blood but not a lethal blow. She landed hard, and Tardoq stepped between them. Alone and weaponless, he stood against a foe with strength and speed greater than his own.

Bartoth turned and swung his sword, unleashing a single, massive blow that severed the chain. Coiling the chain around his arm, he began to advance, a chuckle of anticipation coming from beneath the helmet.

Tardoq darted in, evading the flashing sword and catching the chain. With a twist and a savage yank, he knocked Bartoth onto the floor of the cavern. Then he leaned out and opened his hands in Kentor's direction. The youth had recovered but wisely feigned weakness until Tardoq noticed his half-open eyes.

"Need a blade?" Kentor asked with a smile, and tossed his soulblade to Tardoq.

Tardoq caught the hilt of the sword and twisted it in his grip, plunging it through Bartoth and into the stone. He bellowed in pain and Tardoq yanked the weapon free, intent on finishing his foe.

The stone rose up beneath him, flinging him backwards. He rolled and came to his feet. Kentor joined him on his right, Senia on his left. Serak stepped to the writhing Bartoth and shook his head in disgust. As the stone settled around them he pointed to Senia.

"Next time, I'll make sure he has armor to match the helm. Then he'll be unstoppable."

"Not against me," Tardoq spat.

Serak regarded him with thinly veiled hatred. "Perhaps you're right."

Serak gathered his hand and the ground rose up, shaping into a scorpion's tail, and pointing at Tardoq's chest. Tardoq twisted, attempting to evade the incoming strike, but the tail snapped forward.

Tardoq knew it was coming, saw the tail aimed for his heart, gauged its speed, and knew it was too late. He'd faced death thousands of times and thought he was prepared, but not at the hands of Serak. He growled his anger and braced for the lethal blow.

Kentor stepped in front of Tardoq, the stone shard piercing his chest, shoving them both backward. Tardoq caught a glimpse of Serak and Bartoth stepping off the outcropping and disappearing into the abyss. Then the stone tail came to a stop, pinning him against the side of the cavern.

Senia darted to the tail and swung her dagger, shattering the stone. Tardoq groaned as he fell to his knees, and Kentor dropped at his feet. Clenching his hand against the wound, Tardoq rolled the young troll onto his back.

"Why would you do that?" he demanded of the troll.

Kentor coughed, blood on his lips and face. "A troll is taught to recognize a captain. It was my honor to die for you . . ."

He smiled and then relaxed in death. Tardoq stared at the boy's body, shocked by what he'd done. The boy had saved Tardoq's life, at the cost of his own. Why? They should have been enemies, and under other circumstances, Tardoq would have killed him without a thought. Now? Anger pooled in his belly at the killing.

Tardoq rose to his feet and pursued Serak, intent on tearing him apart with his own hands. He stumbled, but refused to go down. Blood spilled down his chest but he kept moving, ignoring the hands attempting to hold his arm.

"Serak!" he bellowed. "Get back here and fight!"

He reached the end of the outcropping and fell to his knees. He fought to ignore the pain by clenching a hand to the wound, but the ache continued to mount. He began to feel dizzy as he roared into the abyss.

"I'll kill your pets and rip your bones from your flesh!"

"Tardoq!"

The voice was like thunder at his side, and he turned to find Senia yanking on his arm. He tried to pull free but she grimly held her grip.

He wanted to shout at her but the dizziness continued to buzz in his ears.

"What!" he snapped.

"You're losing too much blood!" She sought to reach his wound. "It's going to kill you!"

Her logic warred with his desire to follow Serak. But instinct confirmed her words, and he looked down at the gaping hole through his body. Even his advanced healing would not stop his death, and he fell backward, grimacing in pain.

"I'll kill him for this," he hissed.

"I know," she said, and fought to staunch the bleeding with her own clothing. "Get a healer!" she cried to the rock trolls bursting into the room.

Tardoq growled at his helplessness, at the cold seeping into his body. He reached up and gripped her tunic, pulling the oracle down into his face. Her eyes were bright blue and tight with fear. She was frightened *for* him.

"Keep me from dying and I will stop him."

"I'm not a good healer."

"Then burn it with fire!" he roared.

She bellowed for a healer and then shook her head, her features writ with worry. Then she gathered fire into her hand and raised it above his wound.

"Are you certain you want to do this?" she asked.

"Are you even asking?" he snapped.

She put her burning hand onto his wound and he arched his back, sucking in a breath as his flesh seared together, closing the wound. The pain was worse than the wound, like a hot coal that fell into his soul.

"Tardoq," Senia said. "Thank you for saving my life."

"You owe me a hammer," he said.

She laughed, the sound tinged with relief as a rock troll woman knelt at Tardoq's side. A soothing sensation came from the wound, the relief of pain robbing him of his reason to stay awake. He growled and fought the desire to sleep, but even his mighty strength was not endless, and darkness claimed him, his last thought of Kentor and Serak.

The foe he'd chosen.

Chapter 37: The Alliance Council

Mind stood on the hill overlooking the ashes of Lord Dallin's estate. It had been several days since they'd discovered Serak's secrets and set the structure on fire. Mind remained on the hilltop, watching the wind pick up the ashes.

"Are you just going to watch it burn?" Sentara asked, clearly annoyed.

"Yes," he replied.

"Don't you have a foe to fight?" Rune asked.

"Eventually."

Sentara and Rune departed shortly after, and he acknowledged them long enough to express his gratitude for leading him to the estate. He would not have found it on his own. Clearly confused by his silence, Rune cast him a final look before she and Sentara left.

Alone, Mind leaned against a tree, considering all he'd learned in the last few weeks. He guessed that Serak had his brothers by now, but he was not inclined to hasten. Serak had planned for ages for this confrontation, and if Mind wanted to be victorious, he needed to be cautious.

Serak wanted Mind to come to him. He'd even given him a destination, albeit one he had to search for. Blackwell Keep. He'd looked for the name in Serak's secret room, but there had been no mention. He must have discovered the citadel after he'd used the secret room.

Serak expected Mind to go to the King's Library. From there he would discover the location of the fortress, and then arrive alone. By now, Serak expected him to be suspicious of Elenyr. If he did go to the library, Serak would know he was coming. But Mind would be noticed in the King's Library, and even if he erased memories, someone would notify the king that he'd been searching archives. His allies—and especially Elenyr—might even figure out what he was searching for, and worry that he'd turned to Serak.

Mind frowned as he realized that was probably Serak's intent, to show Elenyr that Mind was no longer her son. As much as Mind wanted to find Blackwell Keep, he wasn't willing to do that to Elenyr. Mind needed an alternative source of information, one that would appear to follow Serak *and* be perceived as an attack against him. Fortunately, he knew just the person. His plan set, Mind turned away from the empty hilltop and took his journey west.

A month remained of winter, the snows deep across the ground. Mind used his magic to lighten his own body. He couldn't fly without the other fragments, but he could be light enough that he could walk across the snow. At the nearest inn, he rented a steed and accelerated.

It took him several days to reach Terros. As he approached the city, thousands of soldiers from across Lumineia patrolled the roads. Mind slipped through their ranks to reach the city, and the host of armies that had gathered in various camps.

Elves from Orláknia, rock trolls from the northern deserts, dwarves from the Tyndrik mountains. They gathered with orcs and goblins, humans from all three kingdoms, and even a handful of giants had joined the assembled races. It was the greatest assembly of races in the history of Lumineia, but Mind couldn't shake the feeling that it was all part of Serak's plan.

He worked his way past the elven camp, picking details of Elenyr, Fire, and Water from the soldiers. Water and Fire were both missing, as Mind had expected. What came as a surprise was the news that the Hauntress had disappeared as well.

Serak could have taken Elenyr with the other fragments, but Mind suspected that if he could, he would have killed her. Mind guessed Elenyr had departed on her own volition, probably searching for the fragments. He frowned, and on impulse shifted direction.

He reached the rock troll camp as the sun dipped low on the horizon. Unlike those in the other camps, the rock trolls had felled trees and lifted boulders, building a fort. They had come as allies, but they were not taking chances. Children from the city hovered outside, whispering and hoping to catch a glimpse of the mighty warriors.

Mind tied his mount to a tree and strode to the entrance to the fort. He wished he could pick their minds for the truth, but rock trolls were trained for all types of combat, physical and mental.

"Is Queen Rynda present?" he asked.

"She's at the war council," one said, jerking his chin towards the castle in the distance.

Mind returned to his steed and guided his horse into Outer Terros. Dozens of towers dotted the farmland, where much of the forces from Erathan and Talinor now resided. Teeming with cavalry and infantry huddled around fires, the farms resembled an army camp rather than the tranquil outskirts of a city.

Mind passed through the guard stations with ease, manipulating the minds of the common guards to reach the city, which proved to be overcrowded. Soldiers not on duty wandered through the streets, searching for ale and amusements. Women flirted with the soldiers, and children marveled at those from foreign lands. Urchins sought to pickpocket the foreigners.

Mind threaded his way through the crowd and turned north, to the castle. The empty minds of the guards were easy to alter, and soon he strode through the castle's main gates. A servant led him to the top floor of the structure, to the council chamber.

The council chamber sat atop the fortress, adjacent to the king's office. Mind had been there before as an ally to King Justin, but could not approach as the fragment of Mind. The bounty against the fragments and Elenyr had been lifted, but they were still not welcome, especially in the king's castle.

The guards flanking the council doors scowled when he approached, and he dipped into their thoughts, manipulating their perspective before they recognized him. They blinked in confusion, and then straightened at his new appearance. Mind assumed the haughty demeanor of Lord Eron while projecting the man's face into their thoughts.

"My Lord Eron," the guard said, bowing to Mind. "We were not expecting you."

"I arrived early," he replied. "I must speak to the king."

"He is in council with the other monarchs," the other guard said. "You should return another time."

"Open the doors," Mind ordered. "The king will wish to hear what I have to say, unless you wish to tell his son why his father perished at an assassination attempt."

They exchanged a look, and then one of the guards bowed. "Of course."

The two men caught the handle and swung it open, allowing Mind to enter the council chamber. Mind dropped his magic as he entered. His appearance ended the conversation at the council, and brought the three human kings to their feet.

"You!" King Numen spat.

Mind swept the room with his gaze. King Justin, as the resident monarch, sat at the head of the table. King Porlin flanked him on his right, while the one with King Numen's face sat on his left. Lining the table, Queen Alosia of the elves and King Dothlore of the dwarves claimed the right seats. Queen Erisay sat in the seat furthest from Justin, the dark elf regarding Mind with a curious expression. Adjacent to her, Queen Rynda stood at the foot of the table, and she nodded in approval at Mind's entrance.

"It's good of you to come," she said. "Perhaps you can talk sense into such stupid men."

King Justin stabbed a finger at Mind. "I should summon the guards and have you in shackles, fragment."

"For protecting your people?" he retorted.

"For trying to kill me," Numen snarled. "King Justin, I demand you have this man imprisoned."

"I won't be long," Mind said, advancing around the table.

His casual approach caused King Porlin to stumble back, and brought the other monarchs to their feet. But Mind only had eyes for the one on King Justin's left. The imposter that looked like King Numen.

"King Numen," he said evenly.

259

"The fragment of Mind," he snapped. "You are interrupting a council of kings. Guards!"

"I'm not here for games," Mind said, ignoring the soldiers swinging the door open. "I wish to know the location of a hidden fortress, one called Blackwell Keep."

A flicker of recognition passed across his eyes but he shrugged, feigning confusion. "A question better put to historians."

"I'm betting you know the answer," Mind said. He reached the end of the table and Numen palmed the hilt of his weapon.

"Mind," Justin said, motioning to the guards. "You should not have come. The guards will detain you until I can determine your fate."

"Good luck with that," Rynda snorted in scorn, causing Justin to scowl.

"You are angry with me," Mind said, cocking his head to the side. "Why?"

"Because you ally yourself with the Hauntress," Justin said. "She who nearly killed King Numen on the grounds of this very castle. You have meddled in the affairs of my kingdom for ages, and that meddling is at an end."

Mind burst into a mocking laugh, the sound bringing the approaching guards to a halt. Elenyr had been right, and the imposter was using King Justin, had already warped his mind. The touch of purple in his eyes revealed the subtle tinge of magic.

"To be honest," Mind said. "I care nothing for your complaints, except for one. You impugn on the honor of one who has more integrity than your entire royal family."

"She tried to kill *me*," King Numen shouted, gripping the hilt of his sword.

"Draw your weapon and I draw mine," Rynda said.

"You would side with *them?*" Numen demanded.

"I would think that would be obvious," Rynda replied.

Erisay stood and joined her. "If we're choosing sides, I prefer yours. Do you mind?"

"Not at all," Rynda said with a smile.

Dothlore grinned and rose to stand with them. "Every alliance needs a good dwarf."

Porlin looked between his two human king allies and the others at the foot of the table. "I'm not sure what is happening here," he said evenly. "I thought we were discussing how to attack Xshaltheria."

"You have someone that can answer that," Mind said, and pointed to Numen.

"Me?" he scoffed. "I'm the reigning monarch of Erathan. The only thing I know about Xshaltheria is that we were held prisoner there."

"That's not entirely accurate," Mind said.

The room went quiet, and King Justin jerked his head, as if he were trying to discard a confusing thought. But the magic warping his thoughts remained rooted. Mind could simply rip it out, of course, but that risked impairing the king, permanently. Mind needed him to start believing his words first.

"What are you talking about?" Porlin asked.

"It's happened," Numen snarled. "We all know he's just a piece of a single soul. He's gone mad. He could even be working for Serak, for all we know." He barked an order, summoning his own guards. Soldiers entered the room, but Rynda drew her sword and pointed it at them. She didn't need to speak for them to stop in the door. They looked between her massive blade and King Numen.

"I must admit it's a bit complicated," Mind said. "We all thought the real King Numen a captive, when in fact, he was an assassin by the name of Carn, who served Serak."

"Are you going to listen to this absurd tale?" Numen demanded. "He's a guardian, and we all know the tales of how they went mad. This man isn't even a—"

His voice cut off. He continued to move his mouth, but all sound had been extinguished. Mind recognized the use of a muffling charm, probably by someone in the room. Perhaps a guard had sound magic?

"So you're saying this man is an imposter?" King Porlin asked as Numen fought to speak.

"Of course," Mind said. "And the Hauntress warned King Justin of this fact. Didn't she?"

He faced Justin, who blinked in confusion and stumbled backward, reaching for his head. He mumbled a few words, but the doubt Mind had inserted had done its job. Mind stepped to the king and placed a hand on his shoulder, as if to determine his wellness. Instead he used the contact to reach into his thoughts.

The spell altering his thoughts was flawless but easy for Mind to discern. He found the threads of purple magic in his mind and removed them. When Mind stepped back, King Justin straightened, and then his eyes settled on Numen. He yanked the sword from the scabbard on his hip.

"*You*," he snarled. "She was right. You are an imposter."

King Numen glared at the group, all of which were now arrayed around him. He retreated towards his guards, but Rynda stepped between them, and the confused soldiers backed to the entrance. Facing a hostile room, Numen growled his anger.

"You weren't supposed to be here," he said to Mind. "You were supposed to be following the clues to your brothers."

"Who are you?" Mind asked.

The man looked to those in the room. He had several monarchs and a dozen soldiers arrayed against him, and even if he could convince the Erathan guards to join him, he wasn't making it out. He shrugged, and pulled the amulet from his neck. The illusion about his features faded, revealing a dark haired man with small, beady eyes. Mind had never met him, but several in the room knew his name, and Rynda's laughter was pure delight.

Zenif, first servant to Serak himself.

Chapter 38: The Imposter

"Zenif?" several voices chorused, and the kings were suddenly more hostile.

"Zenif," Rynda said, twirling her sword. "I've dreamed of removing your heart. You have my gratitude for making that easy . . ."

"You *dare* to come into my castle?" Justin demanded. "I will have you hanged for what you did."

Mind picked up the history from those in the room, their anger baring their thoughts as if they were shouting. Zenif was Serak's first lieutenant, a mind mage with a talent for sleeping charms. He'd been instrumental in the capture of all the monarchs, even subduing Queen Rynda.

"Where is the real King Numen?" Dothlore asked.

"Dead," Zenif said. "And the fragment speaks the truth. He served Serak for decades."

Justin swore under his breath. "I thought he was a friend."

"He was," Zenif said. "He just believed in a different cause."

"What do we do with him?" Erisay asked, her voice uncharacteristically harsh.

"I see no reason to delay the execution," Rynda said.

"We should learn why he was here in the first place," Justin said.

Zenif swept a hand to the gathered kings. "Isn't it obvious? I was tasked with ensuring you all gathered for war."

"Serak *wanted* us to come?" Dothlore asked. "Why?"

"You'll find out soon enough," Zenif said. "And since I doubt that you'll disband for any reason, my work is complete. I'll see you on the battlefield."

"You think we'll let you escape?" Justin growled.

He smiled in a way that inspired a sense of foreboding. "Who said anything about permission?"

Zenif drew his sword and plunged it into the floor. Imbued with lightning, the weapon's power exploded outward, bolts of lightning striking the table, walls, and windows. Guards and monarchs dove for cover. Rynda raised her sword in front of her, the wide blade deflecting one bolt, another grazing her leg. Heedless of the lightning, she charged Zenif.

Zenif leapt backward, alighting on a cabinet of fine ales. Rynda's sword came down on him but he stepped to the side, the weapon crashing through the cabinet, shattering bottles and sending ale across the floor. Zenif stabbed a finger towards the rock troll and she stumbled, reaching to her head, the sleeping charm striking heavy.

"Not this time," Mind said.

He reached out and caught the sleeping charm. It was powerful, but no match for him. He clenched a fist and the magic disintegrated into sparks. Zenif scowled and retreated again, leaping Justin's swinging sword and landing at the door leading to Justin's office. He reached for the handle, but a dagger of pure orange light thudded into the wood.

"I wouldn't," Erisay said.

She stood with her dark eyes hard, another orange dagger in her hand. A sound mage? Mind had not known, or even suspected. He raised an eyebrow to the woman as the other kings expressed their shock.

"Wait," Zenif said, raising a hand to placate those in the room. "There is more I can tell you."

"You have nothing left," Mind said.

He smiled. "I have one more card to play, or did you think I'd infiltrate your war council alone?"

Mind frowned and turned to the room. The guards were just guards, their minds open, worried about the rising tension. That left just the kings. Was it possible that another king was a traitor?

"He lies," Rynda spat. "He's just a desperate man about to die."

The kings approached, as did the guards, driving Zenif to the wall. He retreated, but his expression remained unconcerned. He locked eyes with Mind, a slight smile on his features. Mind again searched the room with his magic. The blades came closer to Zenif.

"Don't worry," he said. "Serak has made his intentions clear for all of you. We won't kill you."

"Is he alone?" Justin asked Mind.

Just as Mind turned, Rynda's blade smashed Mind in the face, the flat blade landing heavy and knocking him to the floor. His vision swam, and he instinctively recognized that Rynda had not been the one wielding the weapon. Whoever had landed the blow had used metal magic.

Shouts rang out in the room as weapons betrayed their masters, the blades turning and sweeping, attacking neighbors and allies. One guard fought his own spear as the spear of his companions plunged into his leg. Others fell onto their backs, fighting to keep their swords from piercing their own hearts. Other swords swung wildly, clashing into light orbs, plunging the room into flickering light.

"Metal mage," Rynda growled. Grasping her sword with both hands, she lunged at the wall, driving the blade deep into the stone. It trembled as if it wanted to move but could not break free. Rynda turned on the nearby guards. She caught one sword and hurled it through a window, the force of her throw sending it spinning into the snowy gardens. She reached to the nearest chair and picked it up. Using the chair like a club, she waded into the fray, knocking weapons flying. With her dagger made of pure sound magic, Erisay deflected swords and spears, her gaze fixed on Zenif, who stood at the door to Justin's office.

Mind shook his head to clear it, and scanned the room. The magic could have come from Zenif, but his smug smile and his previous comment suggested it came from someone else. Someone in the room. The guards were all struggling to hold their weapons, and most of the monarchs were similarly occupied. In the gloom, one man stood out.

King Porlin.

The king stood at the center of the fray, his hands outstretched, his face a mask of determination. Mind had known him to be a timid and nervous man, a far cry from the rigid discipline being displayed.

Rynda too, noticed Porlin, and her eyes narrowed. Instead of going for a weapon, she reached for the large council table. Catching the edge, she heaved it off the floor and hurled it at Porlin. He saw it too late and flinched. Mind recognized his opportunity and reached up, shifting the table in mid-flight so it came down at an angle, obscuring him, Porlin, and Zenif from view.

Mind caught Porlin's wrist and shoved him to the door of the king's private office. Kicking it open, he pushed them through and then slammed the door behind himself. The table had struck Porlin a glancing blow and his head was bleeding, but he glared at Mind with suspicious eyes.

"Why did you save me?"

"Answers later," Mind warned.

He jumped to one of the windows and smashed it with the hilt of his sword. Then he jumped onto the angled roof, sliding to the roof of the guest quarters. Zenif and King Porlin exchanged a look and then leapt after. As the trio sprinted across the castle roof, the table was yanked away from the door and Rynda charged into the empty office. Shouts rang out, and King Justin bellowed an order for the guards to pursue the fleeing pair. Glancing backward, Mind fell back and motioned the others ahead. Both remained suspicious but did as requested.

Mind brandished his sword and sprinted after, making it seem like he was giving chase as Rynda appeared in the window behind. Mind smiled as her voice called to the others, informing them that Mind was in pursuit.

"What is your intent?" Zenif cast over his shoulder, too quiet for Rynda to hear.

"I told you," Mind replied. "Answers later. Now get moving before we're caught."

Mind cast a look back and spotted Rynda sliding down the roof, her metal hand ripping into roof tiles. She hit the flat roof and accelerated into a run, quickly gaining ground. Mind scowled. If she caught up, his plan would be for naught.

"Through the window," he hissed, pointing to the window leading to the top guest chambers. "Into the closet."

Porlin scowled, an expression uncharacteristic on the man. "You can't expect us to—"

"Do it if you wish to escape."

Porlin looked to Zenif, who nodded, and the pair crashed through a window into one of the guest chambers. They leapt to the closet as Mind pointed to the door. It swung open and crashed against the wall. Diving inside the closet, Mind shut the door moments before Queen Rynda leapt through the window. She raced to the open hallway door and disappeared into the corridor, her heavy footfalls fading.

"She's going to realize she lost us," Zenif growled in the dark closet. "Then she's going to come back."

Mind pushed through the heavy coats provided to the noble guests. At the back of the closet, he fumbled for the hidden latch, causing the rear of the closet to swing open. He stepped inside and reached up to the light orb bracketed above the hidden stairwell. The others followed and he shut the hidden door, a whisper of a gear sealing the opening.

"Five generations ago a prince installed this passageway so he could privately visit his frequent trysts. Few knew of the passageway then, and none know of it now."

"Good," Porlin said. He pulled a dagger from a sheath at his belt and placed it on Mind's throat, driving him back against the wall. "Then no one can hear you die."

"He's the fragment of Mind," Zenif said, his voice warning. "He is not to be harmed."

"He came here," Porlin hissed. "He should be traveling to Blackwell Keep but he came here and exposed you, forcing me to reveal myself. He's chosen his side."

"I needed them to believe I was still their ally," Mind said. "And I didn't know about you."

It was true. Mind hadn't known of Porlin, and considered the revelation a fortunate discovery, under the circumstances. Porlin looked on him with suspicion, while Zenif remained uncertain. Mind frowned.

"I just saved you, didn't I? If I wanted you dead, I could have let Rynda crush you with a table."

"Why did you come?" Zenif asked.

"Isn't it obvious?" Mind asked. "I want to know the location of Blackwell Keep."

"Serak told you where to find the answer," Porlin said.

"Of course he did," Mind snapped. "But that was not all he told me. He said it was imperative that Draeken remain in the good graces of the kings."

The lie was a gamble. Serak could have told Zenif and King Porlin everything he'd shared with Mind, but Serak had shown himself to be secretive, and Mind doubted he would ever share more than what was necessary. King Porlin reluctantly lowered the dagger.

"Blackwell Keep was once part of the same collection of cities as Xshaltheria," Zenif said. "It lies west and north of the volcano forge."

"I've traveled the region," Mind said. "Never seen an old fortress."

"That's because it lies beneath," King Porlin said.

"Then that is where I make my destination," Mind said.

"You should hurry," Zenif said. "He's expecting you."

"One question before I go," Mind said. "What happened to the real King Porlin?"

"What makes you think I'm not him?" Porlin asked, a smirk appearing on his face.

"The Porlin family has no history of magic," he said. "Yet you displayed the magic of metal, shadow, and mind. Who are you?"

Zenif and Porlin exchanged a look, and Zenif inclined his head. Mind expected Porlin to bear a matching amulet, removing the persona to reveal his identity. Instead Porlin straightened and pointed to Zenif.

268

"You know the father," he said. "Now you know the son."

"Zoric," Zenif added.

Mind regarded them with a strange look, noting the clothing on Porlin, subtly enhancing his shape, making him appear overweight. His features were also altered, a touch of coloring here, a hint of darkening beneath the eyes.

"And King Porlin?" he asked. "Is he still alive?"

Zoric smiled. "The previous king of Talinor never had a son, and I took his place. Porlin didn't die. He never existed in the first place."

Chapter 39: Blackwell Keep

Mind allowed Zenif and Zoric to depart unharmed. He would have preferred to give them to Rynda, but doing so could tip his hand. If Serak thought he'd made his choice to remain loyal to Elenyr, he could strike at the other fragments.

They departed through the secret tunnel and Mind returned to the castle, joining the search for the escaping imposters. Once they were gone, he took his leave. Slipping away, he retreated through the city and found his way to his horse. Just as he mounted, Rynda stepped out of the trees.

"Fragment," she said.

Her sword was in her hand, low and ready. Mind glanced to the blade, annoyed he hadn't evaded the rock troll queen. Rynda's mind was shut to him, but he should have been able notice her anyway. Perhaps he was more distracted than he thought.

"Rynda," he said, coiling the reins through his hand in case he had to run. "Is there something you need?"

She snorted. "The only reason you have your head is my respect for the Hauntress. Why'd you help them escape?"

Of course she'd figured it out. He sighed. "Serak has taken my brothers, and wants me to come to him. He thinks I will switch sides."

"Will you?"

Mind held her gaze. "I'm not betraying my family."

The odd tension spiked, and he realized Draeken did not agree with his choice to remain loyal to Elenyr. But Draeken was not in control. Not now. Mind may be a piece of a soul, but he was still the master of his own fate.

Rynda held his gaze and then sheathed her sword. "What do you need?"

"Just like that?"

She grinned. "I don't like being excluded from a fight."

Her offer was unexpected, but not unwelcome. He considered refusing her offered aid. But Serak expected him to come alone. Wanted him to come alone. And that provided an opportunity. He smiled, and then suggested a plan. When he finished Rynda smiled in turn.

"I'll be there."

Mind inclined his head in gratitude, and then turned his horse onto the road. Heading east, he followed the trail out of the assembled camps and into the open. The road grew quieter the further he traveled from Terros, until only the wind rustled empty branches.

A recent snowfall had deepened the carpet of white, and his horse picked its way over the frozen ground. Mind settled into his saddle, pondering what lay ahead. He felt a note of finality in approaching Serak. Had he considered every choice? Every option?

Draeken was also eager for the impending confrontation. His emotions were visible in a sudden surge of eagerness, a touch of apprehension, a flicker of worry. Mind could not feel more of Draeken's thoughts, not without another fragment, but he could feel portions of his thoughts. Draeken wanted to speak to Serak and feared what Mind intended.

Mind disliked being at odds with Draeken. It felt wrong, but the recent conflict had divided the fragments as no conflict had before. Water was falling in love with Lira, Fire had fallen for Soreena, and Light had begun to control himself. Even Shadow had changed, and learned how to make a friend.

Mind had also changed, if he was honest. He'd seriously considered betraying Elenyr and joining Serak, an option he never would have considered before. He'd even let Rynda help, and he would be the first to acknowledge how he did not like working with others.

He could have traced the changes to Serak, but they went deeper. In the last few decades the fragments of Draeken had acted with more maturity, more reasoning. Serak would have undoubtedly noticed the

271

growth, and perhaps that was the reason for his timing in summoning Wylyn and initiating this war.

Mind threaded his way north and east, passing through villages steeped in snow. Despite the recent snowfall, the air had just started to warm, a hint of the coming spring. Those in the village halls looked forward to the spring melt, the trappers and merchants eager to ply their trades. Mothers called their children in for dinner, the tiny offspring cold from playing in the piles of snow.

Mind passed through the villages, watching the people go about their lives, struck by the sense of permanency. The race of man had a short life span, especially compared to the fragments, yet they lived every day expecting the following day to come. They didn't know Serak loomed over them, or that they lived under a constant chance of krey invasion. He'd always looked down on them for their ignorance, but this time he felt a touch of envy for their happiness.

Departing the eastern villages and cities, he made his way north, into the foothills. From there he located one of the ancient dwarven mines. He and Fire had hunted a rabid reaver at one time, and the beast had taken refuge in the mines. The underground workings connected to all the other mines, a labyrinthine network of underground tunnels, mine shafts, and natural caves.

Mind entered the mine shaft and activated a light orb, which he tossed above his head, using his magic to place it in a hover. Then he descended into the dark and musty depths. For anyone else the network of tunnels would have left them trapped forever, but Mind sent his magic outward, sensing the ripples of gravity, feeling their hold on the rocks and stones, their passage through the empty caverns. Hundreds of feet in all directions, his magesight allowed him to feel all the tunnels, allowing him to bypass dead ends and cave-ins.

The markings on aged mining equipment revealed the network of settlements to be dwarven, and the tracks were easy enough to discern. Like all dwarven mines, these connected to a central fortress, the location to which all ores and metals were sent. Once he'd figured out the right direction, it was easy to solve the labyrinth, and he followed the correct tunnels to the citadel at its heart.

The air was warm, and occasionally musty when he passed areas where water had found its way inside. The tunnels were mostly natural, the miners following the existing caves and crevasses.

Streams gurgled through the empty mines, the iron long since depleted. More than likely the ore had been used to create the fortress of Xshaltheria, the metal forged into the giant chains that held the citadel inside the volcano's mouth.

Structures and fortifications were visible, the metal rusted, the stone doors open. Barracks and forges were layered in decay, as were long stretches of emptiness. As Mind approached Blackwell Keep, he slowed, listening and watching for golems. He had no desire to repeat what had happened in Beldik.

Two days after entering the caves, Mind approached a vast cavern. He had yet to encounter another living soul, or even a golem, but he slowed and came to a halt. From the opening recessed in the cavern wall, Mind surveyed the fortress.

The cavern was enormous, easily a mile across. The chamber lacked a floor, just a great well of darkness plunging into the earth. At the center of the abyss, a fortress sat on a column of stone. Arched bridges connected the fortress to the outer wall of the cavern, the spans seeming precarious and thin against the backdrop of darkness.

The fortress boasted a quartet of turrets, each situated at one of the four corners of the keep. A wide courtyard surrounded the fortress, with walls segmenting the space. An outer wall ringed the column of stone, the barrier just feet from the plunging abyss.

Golems stood on every battlement, in the courtyard, and on the roof. All carried weapons. All ready to fight. These weren't like the worker golems at Beldik. This was an army. Mind surveyed their positions, watched them patrol the battlements. He then watched the windows, noting when light spilled from within, and when they went dark. Hours turned into days, and Mind frequently retreated to seek other vantage points. From various openings and corridors, he watched and waited, preparing himself for a final confrontation with the Father of Guardians.

Chapter 40: Elenyr

"Speak," Elenyr snarled.

She stood in what remained of an Order of Ancients hall in Terros. Men and women groaned on the floor, the survivors laying beside the dead. All had fallen to Elenyr, and she stood in front of the captain, a woman named Lilac, a pretty name for a pretty woman, a noble, if her clothing and demeanor were any indication.

"I don't know what you seek," she said, quivering in fear.

Elenyr put her sword on the woman's throat. She'd been trained for combat, but her sword was also on the floor of the small tavern, her brief attempt to stop Elenyr resulting in a slash across her shoulder.

"Give me a destination," Elenyr said. "Or you'll find out why they call me the Hauntress."

The woman turned white and pressed herself into the wall, her memory pendant bouncing on her throat. Elenyr knew better than to rip it from her neck. Mind had said doing so would erase her memories. But the presence of the pendent indicated she was a senior acolyte.

Elenyr leaned in, pressing the tip of her sword on the woman's throat, drawing a bead of blood. "Serak has four of my sons." Her words were so dark the nearby survivors sought to crawl away. "The fifth is on his way to Serak's lair. Do you know what a mother will do for her children? Do you know what I will do to you?"

The woman swallowed. "Blackwell Keep."

"Where?" Elenyr barked.

"I don't know—I swear!" She trembled so much Elenyr's sword cut her anew. "No one knows the location, not even Zenif."

"How can I find it?" she demanded.

"We were told to avoid the King's Library," she cried out. "Serak said the fragment of Mind would need it. I wager he was supposed to go there to find the location of the fortress."

Elenyr whirled and darted from the space, the woman so frozen in fear she did not move until Elenyr passed through the wall. Then she sank to her knees, tears flowing freely as she cursed.

Elenyr rushed through the trees of Terros, her passage sparking fear in soldiers and commoners. She didn't care, her only thought on reaching the library and searching the archives for the location of the hidden fortress.

She passed through the outer wall to enter the King's Library. It had not operated since the Order had attacked her and the fragments, but many of the archive chambers were still intact. She scanned them for number eighteen, the map room, and charged upward, through the stone to reach the chamber. Inside, she touched a light orb and threw herself into the books.

The minutes ticked away, and she tossed books aside, diving deeper and deeper. The pile of books grew, the papers flattened, the spines open. She'd always been tidy, but she took no thought for the books. Each useless book increased her tension to the boiling point.

Serak had her sons, and Mind was on his way to Blackwell Keep. She was going to be too late, and her sons would become Draeken, forever a tyrant. She'd failed, and her sons would die.

Elenyr stood and threw the latest book against the wall, anger overpowering restraint. Her chest heaving, she glared at the bookshelves, cursing them for their useless maps. She clenched and unclenched her hands, the sensation of helplessness gripping her spine.

Was it Xshaltheria? No. She knew in her gut it would not be the location she sought. From what the monarchs had said, there was no place for caging four powerful fragments. That suggested it was somewhere else, somewhere Serak had prepared for the final confrontation. So far, Elenyr's effort had been futile, and her sons were in the hands of her foe.

"Where are you?" she growled at the stack of books.

They were scattered, the books haphazard and strewn across the table and chairs. The room was one of those to survive the battle when Wylyn had attacked the library, and she was destroying it anew. Abruptly weary, Elenyr sank onto a seat, where she stared into the fire. How had Serak defeated her? At every turn, he seemed to know what they would do, where they would go, even who would be their ally. She'd never felt so helpless.

She reached up and grasped the crystal hanging around her neck, her record of the fragments. It contained her memories of her sons, how they'd saved each other, how they'd fought together, and laughed together. It meant everything to her, and Serak was about to take that away. A knock came at the door, and when she did not respond, it swung open, revealing Jeric.

"How did you find me?" she asked, her voice wooden, unfeeling. She'd lost Fire, and now she was going to lose them all.

"Hundreds saw your mad dash from the tavern in Blue District to the library," he said. "You weren't exactly subtle." He entered the room but stopped on the threshold.

"We're too late," Elenyr whispered, the words like gravel across her teeth. "Serak is going to win."

"Don't lose hope," Jeric said. "Mind disappeared only yesterday."

"You heard what happened," Elenyr said. "He came and left."

"He chased Serak's spies out of the fortress," Jeric said.

"He went *with* them," she said. "There's no way he would have chased them and *not* caught them."

Jeric didn't reply. They both knew it was true. King Porlin might be a traitor, and Zenif had proven his ability, but even together they could not stop the fragment of Mind. The plausible answer was that Mind had gone with them.

To join Serak.

She spotted a broken book and sighed. Dropping to her knees, she began collecting the papers, stacking them into a neat pile. She wondered what Serak would do to the library when he invaded with the army from the Dark Gate. Would he burn it to the ground?

"Is there anything Ero can do?" she asked.

"I tried," he replied, his voice pained. "The Eternals are scattered across the Empire. Nothing I possess will help us find Serak quickly."

"I cannot let him have my sons," she said, rising and putting the book on the table. "I *will not* let him have my sons."

"You raised them to choose," Jeric said softly. "You cannot rescind what you have taught."

She clenched her hand into a fist and struck a table, cracking it down the middle. He was right, but the truth hurt more than Carn's lightning. She would never have guessed the fragments would be manipulated in such a way. Would she have to fight them? She shuddered at the prospect.

"What I wouldn't give for a shot at Serak," she said.

"I might be able to arrange that."

Both turned to find Queen Rynda in the doorway. "Queen Rynda," Elenyr sighed. "We are in no mood for amusement."

"I don't jest," she said. "I came to see if you'd like to join me for an assignment."

"What are you talking about?" Jeric asked.

She entered with a smile on her face, followed by a pair of followers. Lorica, guildmaster of the Assassins Guild, entered first. She nodded to Jeric as she stepped to the side, allowing space for Willow, her tattoos visible in the firelight.

"What is this?" Elenyr asked Rynda.

"Rynda caught me outside of Terros," Lorica said. "You should listen to what she has to say."

"I spoke with Mind before he left Terros," Rynda said. "I know where he's going."

"You know of Blackwell Keep?" Elenyr felt dizzy.

"Mind told me to gather these individuals," Rynda swept a hand to the group. "Sorry it took me a day."

"It is fortunate that Mind knew our location," Willow said.

"Not sure how he did," Lorica said, a touch of irritation in her tone. "But I cannot deny the opportunity. Rynda tells us the fragments are in trouble?"

Elenyr and Jeric exchanged a look, and Elenyr released a bark of relief. "You have no idea." Then she realized what such information implied. "So Mind didn't help Zenif and Porlin escape?"

"Oh he did," Rynda said. "But he had a reason. Serak thinks he's going to join his cause, and Mind wanted Zenif to tell him as much."

"Yet he told *you* where he was going?" Jeric sounded doubtful. "He's playing both sides. Could it be a trap?" Elenyr cast him a withering glare and he raised his hands in defense. "I apologize for my candor, but it's possible. Serak has done everything to manipulate the fragments. I'm not sure we can trust them."

"They are my sons," she snapped. "I will always trust them."

"As you should," Rynda replied with a firm nod. "I believe Mind remains our ally."

"Then how do we get there?" Elenyr asked.

The hope burst across her frame, her fingers trembling until she clenched them into fists. Mind was not lost, and if he had not turned to Serak's persuasions, then that meant he intended to fight, to defy Serak, to destroy him. She'd wanted a chance to fight and now it had come, a gift from her son, who'd chosen to extend an invitation. He was not lost. At least not yet.

"The fortress lies in the ancient dwarven mines northwest of Xshaltheria," Rynda said.

"That place is a labyrinth," Willow said.

"You've been there?" Lorica asked.

She swept her hand at the floor. "I've traveled far in the Deep, and the mines of which you speak are expansive, hundreds of miles of tunnels, empty mine shafts, and dead ends."

"We have a scout," Lorica said, motioning to Elenyr.

She smiled, the expression one of grim anticipation. "If Serak has built a fortress there, I will find it."

"Then what are we waiting for?" Willow asked, impatience in her voice. "It seems we are already a day behind Mind."

Worry fleetingly gripped Elenyr. Mind could have found her and spoken directly to her. Instead he'd spoken to Rynda, who'd gathered the others. Mind and Elenyr could have taken their journey together, yet he'd traveled ahead, alone. The only reason was because he wanted to speak to Serak, without the interference of anyone else. He was putting himself in the hands of the enemy, and if Serak was prepared for him . . .

"Gather your weapons," Elenyr said. "If we are careful, we can finally put an end to the Father of Guardians."

"It's about time," Rynda said.

Abandoning the books and the vain hope within, Elenyr joined Rynda at the head of the small group. A rock troll queen, inked warrior from the Deep, guildmaster of the assassin's guild, and Ero himself, head of the Eternals, all allied with her, the Hauntress. She felt a chill as they departed Terros and entered the frozen trees. They were either headed into victory, or Serak had planned the ultimate trap. She clenched her jaw against that fate. Serak would not be victorious this time.

Chapter 41: Wounded

Tardoq woke with a start, his first thought of pain. He pushed past it, listening to the sounds in the room, the scents, the heat of a single body. She was breathing slowly, not asleep, but close to it. The oracle. He couldn't tell how much time had passed, and the last thing he recalled was the conflict in the cell. And Kentor's death. He sat up, an involuntary groan escaping his lips.

Senia rose and came to his bed, placing a small hand on his shoulder. "You should lie still. The healer couldn't do much. She said your body was too different for her to know how to repair your wound."

"My wounds will heal on their own," he growled.

He looked down at the injury. The hole was still several fingers across. The bloody bandage managed to cover it, but Tardoq could feel where it had pierced all the way to his back, narrowly missing his heart. Kentor had saved his life.

"Are we still in Astaroth?" he asked.

She nodded. "It's been two days. I was worried."

"You're worried about me?" he scoffed. "An outlander?"

He finally noticed her expression, and saw the lines creasing her features. She hadn't slept much, and the fatigue was obvious. He guessed she had not left his side, a needless gesture, yet one for which he was grateful.

"I'll heal," he said.

She offered a faint smile and settled back into her chair. The room was sparse, just a pair of large beds, a chair, and a small table containing food. He reached for it, and relished the taste of cheese and bread.

"You could have gone without me," he said. "Undoubtedly Serak has already moved on to the remaining horsemen."

"I wasn't going to leave you," she replied. "Not after what you did for me."

He grimaced as he recalled his broken hammer. At the Empire he probably could have fixed it, or acquired a new one, but here, he lacked the materials or tools. For the first time since his youth, he would fight without his weapon.

"I liked that hammer," he sighed and leaned against the wall. "It saved my life more times than I could count."

"Yet you gave it up to save the life of a slave."

He shrugged. "It's possible I've grown fond of you."

She raised an eyebrow. "Only possible?"

He rolled his eyes. "You know what I mean."

She regarded him with a slight twist to her lips. She did know what he meant, that against all odds, against all factions or wars, they were friends. Tardoq might have attempted to explain it away because they were both alone in their own way. But that was not the sole reason. He liked her, and wasn't about to see her die. Even if it cost him his hammer.

"Could we replace your hammer?" she asked. "More than forty dakorians came through the Gate with you and Wylyn. Surely we can locate one of their weapons."

"We could," he said, "but they were inferior to mine. I doubt they could stand against Bartoth's sword."

He shrugged, and immediately regretted the motion. It pulled at his wound, clenching the tendons and torn sinews. Some of his organs had been lacerated, but he could feel them on the mend. He hated the itch coming from inside his ribs. It could never be scratched. The door swung open and Rake entered.

"You're alive," he said, catching sight of him.

"You thought I'd die?"

"You lost a lot of blood," Rake said.

Tardoq looked to Senia, who nodded in agreement. "It was *a lot*."

"I've survived worse," Tardoq said.

281

He had, but only a few times. Tardoq had once lost an entire limb. Even with only one hand he'd managed to kill the one that had taken his arm, and the four rebels with him. Regrowing a limb was worse than repairing organs. He still hated the itch though. He scratched his ribs above the bandage, as if that would help.

Rake sank into a seat on the second bed. "I'm glad you survived. After Senia described what happened, I'm starting to think we need you."

Tardoq grimaced as a tendon reconnected, gritting his teeth as it stretched taut against a bone. When it settled into place he sighed, and drank deeply of the mug from the table. Rock troll ale was not like those of the other races, and he appreciated its strength.

"What now?" he asked.

Rake and Senia exchanged a look, and then Senia pointed south. "Last night we received word from Rynda. The full rock troll army is departing in the morning."

"Joining the alliance at Terros?" Tardoq asked.

"Winter will be over soon," Senia said. "And the gathered races are ready to assault Xshaltheria."

They exchanged a worried look and Tardoq frowned.

"What aren't you telling me?" Tardoq asked.

"All five fragments of Draeken are missing," Senia said.

He scowled. Their time was short. He forced himself to his feet, and both of his companions rose to stop him. A glance kept them in place. He stumbled to the door, catching himself against the stone and cursing his weakness.

"Where do you think you're going?" Senia asked.

"I need a weapon," he said.

"And where do you think you'll get one?" Rake asked.

"The dwarves," Tardoq said, and shot them a look. "If you want me to fight Bartoth again, I'm going to need something stronger than my hammer."

"A weapon like that is going to take time," Senia said. "And we need to find the Hauntress."

"Too late for that," he said, working his way down the hall.

"If you start bleeding again," Rake warned, and then shuddered, "I'm not going to clean it up."

Tardoq spotted a balcony through a training room and passed through it. The two trolls training inside retreated at Tardoq's appearance. Both made to approach but Senia spoke to them and they departed. Tardoq stepped onto the balcony and looked to the night sky.

"You can't think to travel in your condition," Rake said.

Tardoq gripped the railing. "I told you. I'll heal."

"Tardoq."

Her voice brought him to a stop, and he released a long breath. "Please," he said. "I'm not letting Bartoth live after what he did to Kentor."

"He's killed thousands," she said softly. "Why did Kentor matter?"

He grimaced, both at the memory and at his muscles pulling at the wound. It had started to bleed again. He thought of Kentor stepping into the blow, giving his life, for him, a dakorian. The troll had died with a smile on his face.

"He was a fool," Tardoq growled. "He didn't owe me anything." Rake and Senia stood silent, and Tardoq struck the railing of the balcony. "He'd lived a score of years, and I've lived thousands. Why would he die for me? Why?"

He turned on Senia, who held his gaze. "Rock trolls are warriors from birth," she said softly. "He saw in you the same thing he is trained to recognize in his people, a leader of caliber."

"But I'm a dakorian!" he shouted. "I've sworn to kill him—and you. I should be slaughtering you just for existing, and summoning an armada to enslave you all."

"Would you do that?" Rake asked.

Tardoq growled and turned away, his anger bleeding away. He sighed and shook his head. "My oath is broken."

Senia came and stood beside him. "If you returned to the Empire, what would you do?"

"Do you know what happens to dakorians that disobey?" He jerked his head at the memories of the few he'd witnessed. "Their bones are removed, one by one, leaving them scarred and vulnerable. Then they are cast into the streets of rot-infested worlds, left to fend for themselves with a hefty bounty on their horns. Most don't survive the week."

"Have none of your kind stood against the Empire?"

"One managed to evade the punishment," he replied. "They call her the Bonebreaker, because she is known to shatter the bones of dakorians sent as assassins. She was once a Bloodwall to the Emperor himself, until she tried to kill him."

"Rake," she called. "Go and bring Ara."

"Why?" Rake seemed confused.

"She will know," Senia said.

"I'll see if I can find her." Rake turned and departed.

Senia placed a hand on Tardoq's arm, her tiny fingers on the bony ridge of his forearm. "It is not your armor that defines your strength, Tardoq, it is the strength of your conviction. Wars have been ended based on the strength of a single soul. You are a Bloodwall, but with Wylyn gone, you must decide what your blood will now protect."

"You?" he asked with a faint smile.

She chuckled and shook her head. "As much as I am enjoying a protector of such caliber, I think you would be selling yourself short."

"Then what?" he asked.

"You protected the head of a krey house," she said, her blue eyes piercing. "But you're capable of more."

"What are you suggesting?" he asked.

"That you become an Eternal."

284

He snorted in disbelief. "I've killed thousands of humans."

"So did Ero," Senia said. "And other Eternals. They each chose a different life."

"You don't understand," he said. "Even if I wanted to be an Eternal, they would never trust me."

"I think they will," Senia said. "If you show them how your heart has changed."

"How would I do that?" he asked. "I don't have a weapon."

"Will this help?"

She reached out of sight and produced a small object. She offered it to him and he accepted, confused by what she meant. It looked like a tiny wooden sword. Then he recognized the toy and his expression softened.

"Where did you find this?"

"It fell off your belt when we moved you."

He smiled and hefted the tiny weapon. "A human girl gave it to me in Talinor," he said, and briefly related the tale. "I don't know why I kept such a trinket."

"She saw you as a protector," Senia said. "And if a child can see what you are, I'm confident the fragments and the Hauntress can as well."

"You knew what happened?"

She shook her head. "I saw the toy and wondered why you had it."

"She was so small," he said. "But she did not fear me."

"She even gave you a weapon to fight with," Senia said.

"You expect me to fight with this?" he raised the tiny wooden sword and smiled faintly.

"I think you'll find it has more value than any blade." She grinned and pointed over his shoulder. "But perhaps there is a suitable replacement."

He rotated just as the door opened. Rake and an unfamiliar troll entered the room. Female, and obviously a soldier, the woman carried

285

a package wrapped in leather. She crossed the room and offered it to Tardoq.

"What's this?" he asked.

"A gift," Ara said.

He glanced to Senia and she nodded, so he reached out and accepted the offering. It was heavy, and obviously a weapon. With great care he unwrapped the leather bindings, revealing a black sheath and an enormous sword.

The hilt was wide and strong, built for two hands or one. The blade itself was elegant, with a core of dark metal, the outside lighter. The spine of the blade had ridges down its length, resembling the teeth of a saw, a weapon for slicing on one side, and shattering on the other. Tardoq had seen the weapon before, in the hands of Kentor.

"I cannot accept this," Tardoq protested.

"He would have wanted you to possess his sword," Ara said. "He forged it with his own hands, and it has few equals, even among our people. Steel core, mithral edge, and a special augmentation, allowing the user to adjust the weight, making it lighter or heavier."

Emotion clogged Tardoq's throat, and he grasped the hilt. Pulling it from its scabbard, he held it aloft, feeling the weight, the balance. He noticed the rune on the handle and pressed it with his thumb, the weapon growing heavy enough for him. Heavy enough to shatter stone. Or Bartoth's armor.

"I cannot express my gratitude," Tardoq said.

Ara inclined her head. "May his blade serve you well."

She turned and departed, leaving him to admire the new weapon. "Who was she?" he asked.

"Kentor's sister," Senia said.

"Yet she gave his blade to me?" he asked in surprise.

"Rock trolls believe a warrior possesses a spirit of combat," Senia said. "That such a spirit can be discerned by other warriors."

He gave the sword a final admiring look, and then gently slid it home. Joining the Eternals seemed absurd, and yet he could not dismiss the idea. But the decision could wait, for Bartoth and Serak remained alive.

"I assume you know where to go?" he asked.

"I do," Senia said with a faint smile. "And it's time to find out if Draeken has fallen to Serak."

"If he has?" Rake asked.

Senia's expression turned grim. "Then we must kill him."

Chapter 42: Draeken's Truth

Mind stepped into the light and approached the bridge to Blackwell Keep. The stone crossed the giant chasm, leading to the great pedestal holding the fortress. From his examination, Mind had discerned little of the ancient mining hub, and most of the aged walls had recently been replaced. Towers and fortifications, battlements and courtyards, all had been built deep in the earth, hidden from the eyes of man and elf. Serak's personal refuge. His home.

The air smelled faintly of sulfur, rising from the well of darkness. After watching for two days, Mind finally advanced across the bridge, his gaze fixed on the guards at the gates. When he crossed the midpoint, they came to an abrupt halt, the echo of their final footsteps reverberating throughout the massive cavern. As Mind closed the gap they parted, and the gates opened. Mind walked in their midst, eying the long weapons, hammers and swords, shields and mauls, many absorbing the light coming from the exterior light orbs of the fortress. Anti-magic weaponry. Serak was prepared for mages. He was prepared for the fragments of Draeken.

The doors to the great hall opened before him, and light came from within. He kept his gait even as he approached, and came to a halt on the threshold. Four figures were chained to the four corners of the room.

Fire was on his right, his head bowed, his eyes closed. Thick chains of anti-magic bound his wrists, while more chains of water magic connected to a band about his neck. He appeared unharmed.

On Mind's left, the fragment of Light was similarly shackled with anti-magic chains as well as crystalline chains made of glass, the material refracting the light fluttering off his body. He was also asleep.

At the other corners of the great hall, Shadow and Water were also bound, both in the same manner, both asleep. The chains were crafted for a single purpose, to contain the fragments. Devoid of pillars, decorations, or banners, the great hall lay empty except for the throne on the opposite end. Its occupant rose to his feet.

"Serak," Mind said evenly.

"The final fragment," Serak said with a smile. "Please come in."

Mind regarded Serak, struggling to contain the surge of anticipation. The Father of Guardians came to his feet and approached cautiously, coming to a halt at a distance. The two regarded each other.

"You did not go to the King's Library," he said.

"I preferred a more direct source of information," Mind said.

"Was it necessary to unmask my lieutenants?" Serak asked.

Mind swept a hand to the bound fragments. "Are these chains necessary?"

"My apologies," Serak said, his dark eyes filled with cautious optimism. "But you must understand. They lack your intelligence, and would not understand."

"That you want to protect Lumineia?" Mind asked. "By killing its people?"

Serak had obviously thought Mind would be more amenable, because his eyes narrowed. Mind's accusation set them both on edge, and the doors at the entrance gradually shut, the stone turning on a whisper of well-oiled hinges.

"I am not a cruel man," Serak said. "I didn't kill needlessly or seek wanton destruction. The lives I've taken have been necessary for the protection of the people."

"Tell me," Mind said. "What would Elsin think of the blood on your hands?"

His casual comment brought a frown from Serak. "Elsin was my beloved, but she did not understand."

"I think she did," Mind began to stroll around the room. "She had her own evils, but she believed magic was strong enough to stand against the Empire."

"You forget that I've seen the power of the krey," Serak said. "They could destroy our world without ever setting foot on its surface."

Serak was confused, his features closed. He'd thought Mind would arrive an ally. Instead Mind antagonized him, belittled him. For all Serak's planning, he had not prepared for this, and it left Mind in the position he desired.

"Elsin married another," Mind mused. "Isn't that right? A shadowmage, by all reports."

Serak's frown deepened into a scowl. "My cause has nothing to do with her."

"Did she love you at all?" Mind wondered aloud. "Or did she view you as merely a pawn for her ambitions?"

"She was my *beloved*."

The sudden heat to Serak's voice brought a smile to Mind's lips. "I think she grew to hate you," he pressed. "Hated what you became as a guardian, what you represented. You were just a source of information to her, a fount of knowledge regarding the Empire."

His boots clicked on the floor as he strolled around Serak. As Mind passed the fragments, he sent a thread of magic in their direction, using Serak's distraction to wake them up. His plan wouldn't work if he was alone.

"Do you know why she turned you into a guardian?" Mind asked. "Because you were expendable. Because if you died, she would just try with someone else."

"That's not true."

"Are you certain?" he asked. "You talked to her of the Dark Gate, tried to convince her that it could be opened. She refused, of course. She may have been cruel and ambitious, but she was no fool. Not like you, anyway."

"Elsin would have seen reason," Serak growled. "If the surviving oracle didn't kill her."

"She'd already turned away from you." Mind stabbed a finger west. "She'd already imprisoned you in the krey outpost, left you to die because she didn't think you were trustworthy. She feared what you'd become."

The stone floor began to tremble, and Serak clenched a fist. Mind pressed the advantage, waking Water as he drifted around Serak. Water's eyes snapped open, and Mind reached into his thoughts before Water spoke and gave away Mind's plan.

Eyes closed. Get ready to fight.

Water relaxed, feigning unconsciousness. Mind kept the pride from showing on his face. Serak had underestimated the fragments. Mind came to a stop in front of Fire, looking up at him with dispassionate eyes.

Fire, he mentally said. *Please don't burn anything.*

What happened? Fire groaned, his eyes twitching.

Serak wants Draeken. We're going to stop him.

"You thought you could get me to turn on my brothers?" Mind's voice was mocking as he walked towards Shadow. "That I would abandon my family for someone like you?"

"I thought you were intelligent," Serak sneered. "But perhaps I was mistaken."

"Elsin thought you a fool," Mind said, subtly waking Shadow. "And I must admit, I think the same. You planned for thousands of years, believing I would join you because your plan had merit. You are cunning, but still a fool."

A ghost of a smile appeared on Shadow's face but he otherwise remained still. Mind drifted around the room while Serak rotated to stay in focus. He'd probably guessed what Mind was doing, but his eyes were fixed on Mind, hatred pooling in his gaze.

"The Empire must be defeated."

"Perhaps I'm being harsh," Mind mused. "You did come from the Empire, so you probably know nothing of family, or what it means to be willing to die for them."

"Mind?" Light groaned. "My head hurts."

"I told you to be quiet," Mind said, smiling faintly.

Light grimaced. "Sorry."

"Light," Shadow chuckled. "You just had to speak, didn't you."

Fire smirked at the eagerness in his brother's voice and pulled at the chains. "Don't worry, Shadow. We'll all get the chance to kill Serak."

"Normally I'd advocate for justice," Water said. "But in this case, justice will probably mean death."

Mind came to a halt, again at the center of the room, and Serak glared at him. The floor trembled again, and again Serak clenched his hands into a fist. Mind had come and mocked Serak's plan, his intention, his intelligence, his beloved, and he struggled to keep his anger in check.

"You see, Serak, we may be fragments of a single soul, but we are also brothers. I wouldn't betray them for all the wealth of your Krey Empire."

"Then you'll see them die by the Empire," Serak hurled the words at him.

"You asked me to trust you," Mind said. "And I must admit I considered it. Your plan has merit, even if it's cruel and tyrannical. It *would* work. But I'm afraid I must decline. My brothers are my blood, and I'd rather die fighting the Empire with them, than be victorious with you."

Light giggled. "Look how angry Serak is."

"He should be," Shadow said. "We just turned him down."

"And now we're going to kill him," Fire said.

"Probably," Water said.

Serak continued to glare at Mind. Abruptly all the anger faded, his expression turning to cold hatred. The floor had settled, and Mind prepared himself for the fight. Serak swept a hand to the chained fragments, his eyes never leaving Mind.

"I'm afraid I must insist."

"That we become Draeken?" Mind scoffed. "We're not going to do that."

"It was a question before," Serak said. "But now it's an order."

Mind gathered his magic, eying Fire's chains. Break those, and Fire would free Water. Then they would go for Shadow and Light while Mind kept Serak occupied. He sent the plan to the others and they leaned against the chains, eager to join the conflict.

"War and Death," Serak said.

Mind frowned—and then retreated a step when a large figure stepped out from behind the throne. Easily twelve feet in height, he wore dark armor that covered every inch of his body. The helmet on his head exuded power, as did the enormous sword in his hand.

"Look out!" Water called.

Mind whirled to face the entrance. A second figure detached itself from the shadows behind the door. Cloaked and cowled, he carried a lethal scythe, the weapon pulsing with red veins of power. His hands were not flesh, but bone, and within the cowl, the red eyes were like burning coals.

"You should have killed Gendor," Serak said. "And Bartoth, for that matter. But your inability to do what is necessary is the very reason you are here. You call me a fool, yet bring me exactly what I desire."

Mind eyed the new combatants, picking the truth from their thoughts. Gendor fought the magic binding him to Serak's command, but the cloak he wore leashed his will. He resisted, but could not even speak, for Serak had willed him to silence. And Bartoth, all the might of body magic, every spell he possessed, all flowing through his blood, his muscles and sinews. He'd be stronger than a rock troll, as fast as a dragon, and backed by the cunning and devious mind of the former rock troll king.

"Two of my horsemen," Serak said as the pair flanked him. "After today, we will seek the final two, and then the Dark Gate will be opened."

"I'm not going to join you," Mind said.

"It's not *your* loyalty I seek," Serak snapped, his voice rising. "I never wanted the fragments. You are weak compared to the sheer might of Draeken."

He raised his hands and clapped them together. The floor raised up, closing about Mind's feet. The ceiling dropped down and grasped his hands, pulling him in four directions until his body could not stretch further.

"I'll rip you apart," Fire snarled, and the other fragments strained against the bindings.

Serak ignored them as War kicked the throne from its pedestal. He began to chuckle as he grabbed the pedestal hidden beneath, and pulled the secret lever. Five panels opened in the ceiling, and spikes of pure glass extended toward each of the fragments. The spikes of glass glowed to life. Light leaned away from the chains but his body began to shimmer, his magic flowing off his body.

"What is this?" Water demanded as he too began to glow, his magic glowing blue, the light swirling above and around him.

"You say you care about the other fragments?" Serak snarled. "Then this is your chance to save their lives."

Shadow cried out in pain, the shadows swirling about him like smoke and rising into the spike of glass, sinking into the shard. Fire snarled in pain as he fought against his bindings, the anti-magic glowing from heat, but not cracking. Mind grimaced as the spike above his head charged, the light brightening, and purple light flowed off his body.

"It's a version of a horrending dagger," Serak said. "Elsin built one to kill guardians that went mad, to rob them of their magic. It will siphon your magic away until there is nothing left."

"You track us for ages just to kill us?" Mind grimaced at the mounting pain.

"If I have to," Serak said. "The only choice you have is to become Draeken. Heal the shattered soul and destroy your bonds."

Serak reached out and the other four fragments slid toward the center of the chamber. Sections of floor and ceiling moved in tandem, the chains moving with them, all four fragments joining Mind at the center of the room. They were all straining against the bonds, all except Light, who whimpered in pain.

294

I'm sorry, Mind growled to his brothers, his anger overpowering his guilt. He'd thought to outthink Serak, but the Father of Guardians had prepared for him. Wanted him to become Draeken. Willing to kill them if they refused.

It's not your fault, Water said. *It's always been Serak.*

"Is he stupid?" Fire laughed at Serak through the pain. "None of us are going to join him."

"It's not up to you," Serak said, his eyes on Mind.

Mind reached out to Gendor. *I could have killed you at Mistkeep, and now you help him?*

I have no choice, he replied, and Mind felt the anger in his voice.

Light cried out and Shadow groaned. "We should become Draeken and rip his arms off."

"He *wants* us to become Draeken," Water hissed through clenched teeth.

"Why?" Fire spat at Serak. "He is not going to help him any more than we would."

"We don't have a choice," Shadow growled. "Unless you want to end up as ash on the floor."

The light in the glass spikes mounted, and all five of the fragments growled, their magics swirling upward. Weakness washed over Mind, like blood draining from an open wound. His magic flowed about him, a swirling of tremendous power, contained by his shackles and siphoned by the horrending spike.

"We aren't going to be your master," Mind growled, desperately searching for a way out.

"Your choice is not his."

"We *are* Draeken!" Mind shouted.

"No." Serak's eyes glowed in triumph. "This is the truth long kept, the secret Elenyr feared, the truth you never understood." He advanced until he stood just inches from Mind. "Mind, Fire, Water, Shadow, and Light, five fragments of a single shattered soul. But that is a lie, for there are not five fragments."

295

"What are you saying?" Mind demanded.

Serak's eyes bored into his. "There are six fragments, and Draeken is the fragment of Power."

Chapter 43: Draeken's Rising

Mind stared at Serak, stunned by his words, and suddenly everything locked into place. Draeken was a sixth fragment, but his was divided among the other five. He thought differently from Mind because he *was* different from Mind. He had his own thoughts, his own consciousness, and only became whole when they merged.

"Look at him finally understanding," Bartoth rumbled in amusement.

"You see," Serak said, "all that you have ever done, all the mighty deeds, the legendary feats, all was due to the fragment of Power that resides inside your flesh."

"You lie," Fire snapped.

"No," Mind jerked his head. "It's true."

He sensed it, the power roiling inside, for Draeken *wanted* to join Serak. He'd heard the call, listened to the invitations and reasons, and he agreed with the Father of Guardians. Mind realized the truth. If they merged this time, they would never part again, and Draeken would reign supreme, no longer fragmented, but whole, a mighty conqueror.

The pain mounted and he snarled at Serak. "I'm not going to do it."

"Then you will die."

"If we die, your plan will fail," he retorted.

"It would fail without you," Serak said. "Either you join, or I have nothing."

Mind heard the unwavering will in Serak's voice, saw it in his face. He would not stop the horrending, would not yield. He would continue until the fragments perished, or they joined as Draeken and broke their bonds.

Mind wanted to fight, yearned to defy Serak, but becoming Draeken would kill them all. It was a simple choice, death as a fragment, or life as Draeken. Perhaps in the future he would be able to separate from Draeken. Perhaps all the fragments could, and continue to fight. It was a small hope but the only hope.

His magic was being torn from his flesh and he cried out, but the real pain came from the shouts of his brothers. They were dying. He felt it in his bones. Heard it in their voices. Light was afraid. Water and Fire were angry. Shadow was laughing, because he was Shadow, but he too recognized their approaching end.

"Join as one," Serak urged. "Save them, and perhaps one day you can fight Draeken from within."

"Don't listen," Fire snarled.

"Would you rather die?" Mind shot back.

"I'd rather die defiant," Fire snapped.

"He's the fragment of anger," Serak leaned in, his voice persuasive. "But you are the fragment of intelligence. You can either lose forever, or preserve a chance to fight in the future. It is a simple choice."

"Mind," Water called, his voice turning weak. "Don't give him what he wants."

"It's our only way to fight Draeken," Mind snarled.

Mind reached for the others, and Serak's eyes widened in victory. All five fragments turned ethereal, their bodies flickering, their magics leaving the horrending spikes, turning towards Mind, beginning to merge.

He sensed Draeken's gathering strength, his consciousness gaining power as the other pieces joined. Draeken rushed to the foreground of Mind's thoughts, shoving Mind aside. Angry and despairing, Mind wanted to resist, but the sense of defeat would not be conquered. Even as he relinquished control to Draeken, he sought for another option.

Don't mourn your passing, Draeken spoke in his thoughts. *It was inevitable.*

Mind could feel the other fragments also resisting, their doubt slowing the merging. *You've never remained cohesive*, Mind retorted. *You won't last long.*

You've spent eons preparing to be me, Draeken said. *You cannot now undo what you have become.*

You cannot stop us, Fire said, his voice distant but approaching.

We will fight, Water said.

Can I be your nagging doubts and fears? Shadow asked. *I'd be good at that.*

When do we go home? Light asked. *I miss Willow.*

Draeken chuckled at his response. *You are the parts. I am the whole. You were never more than fragments. You will never be your own masters.*

Mind? Light asked, his voice growing weaker. *What is he saying? Am I going to see Willow again?*

Mind grimaced but Shadow answered first. *You'll see her soon*, Shadow lied, his voice uncharacteristically kind. *I promise.*

The other fragments began to dim, their magics flowing into Mind. His features began to change, a smile forming on his face, the smile of Draeken. Mind clenched his jaw, unwilling to relinquish control. Not yet.

Fire sent him a private thought. *We can't let Draeken do this.*

We either die or fight him from within, Mind responded.

I already died, Fire said. *I think I choose the fight.*

Water tried to keep his thoughts private, but his heart turned to Lira, his love tinged with regret. He'd never told her how much he felt for her, or his hopes to be an Eternal. Unwilling to let Draeken mock Water's fears, Mind caught the thoughts and swept them aside. It was a pointless effort. In a few moments Draeken would know everything, but at least Water would be spared Draeken's scorn.

Anger blossomed in Mind, sudden and wrenching. He'd failed. All his planning, all his effort to defy Serak's plan, it had been for naught, because the real foe was inside. How could he possibly defy Draeken? How could he conquer what lurked inside his own soul?

To his surprise, he'd seen the question before, in the thoughts of others. A farmer who lusted after the woman living down the street, a tavern owner who stole coin from travelers, a young woman who lacked the courage to stand up to her accusers, a king who betrayed his people for more power. They had endured the same doubt, and also feared what lurked within. They had feared succumbing to their ambitions, their greed, their addictions. Mind had always seen himself as different, but inside of him lurked the same craving for power.

The other fragments groaned, their magics merging together. Draeken sucked in his breath, his smile widening, the other fragments fading from sight. Mind sensed the coming end, felt the loss, the fear, the anger on behalf of his brothers, the guilt and doubt. He could not fight himself. It was the one foe he could not conquer . . .

"Mind!"

His eyes snapped open, and all eyes turned to the door, where a woman had leapt through. Blood stained her tunic and cheek, but the fierceness to her gaze pulled Mind from the brink. Elenyr had arrived. And she was furious.

"Kill her!" Serak barked.

Hope blossomed in the fragment of Mind as he met Elenyr's gaze. He expected her to lunge into the fight, but instead she reached to the pendant at her throat and ripped it from her neck. She raised it high and smashed it on the floor.

Chapter 44: Requiem

Elenyr led her companions west and north, chafing at every delay. She yearned to turn ethereal and cross the landscape at a sprint, speeding through trees and rocks, willing herself to her sons. But Rynda advised restraint.

"If he wanted you to join him, he would have invited you when he left," she said.

Elenyr hated her logic.

Despite Elenyr's impatience, the group traveled in haste. Rynda set the pace, a loping, powerful jog that devoured the miles. Lorica flew above the trees, her cloak turning into wings. As krey, Jeric's body already possessed enhanced faculties. Willow struggled to keep up, but she'd been training her whole life, and she managed to keep the blistering pace.

They reached the mountains and Elenyr dove into the earth. She'd visited the mines before and knew some of the entrances. Directing the others to one, she searched ahead, frequently returning to direct the path of the others.

Her chest continued to tighten the deeper into the earth they traveled, and she raced ahead and back, guiding the group. Then she spotted the first memory shard. Obviously left by Mind, the tiny spark of magic gave her a direction, and she knew she was close. She rushed back to the others, and guided them deep into the earth, to the giant cavern that held Blackwell Keep. They came to a halt on the threshold, and Lorica sucked in her breath.

"It's disturbing how much lies beneath the earth."

Willow offered a faint smile. "I find it disturbing what lies on the surface."

Her response made Lorica chuckle. Elenyr never took her eyes from the fortress, watching the golems arrayed on the battlements and in the courtyard. Then she spotted the light through a gap in the main entrance.

"They're here," she said.

Trembling with the desire to rush into the conflict, she stepped onto the road and crossed the bridge, the others at her back. All were silent, their blades and weapons out. Elenyr's gaze remained fixed on the doorway ahead. Just as they reached the outer gates, a shout of pain came from inside the fortress. She knew the voice, and lunged for the door.

Rynda grabbed her arm, bringing her to a halt. "We should strike together."

She turned ethereal and stepped out of reach. Then she raised her cowl, turning into the Hauntress. "My sons are dying. Don't tell me to wait."

Rynda hissed her name but she was already through the main doors. She dropped into the floor and charged towards the main keep, rising to the entrance doors. She reached a hand through the stone— and struck the barrier of energy. Moving at such speed, she was knocked backward, her vision flickering. She landed in the courtyard and skidded to a stop at the feet of a golem. Dazed, she groaned and crawled to her feet, but the golem dropped a sword at her eye.

She rolled, the blade grazing her cheek, drawing blood. She rose to her feet, driving her sword through the golem's body before twisting, cutting it in two. Another golem struck her side, and she growled in sudden rage. She attacked in a fury, obliterating the golems keeping her from the doors.

The front portcullis crashed inward and Rynda darted in, her greatsword sweeping through a pair of water golems in her way. Both lost their heads, the water splashing to the courtyard stones. She spotted Elenyr and scowled.

"He knew *you* would come," she said. "He didn't account for *us*."

Elenyr heard the wisdom in the troll's words. Serak knew to anticipate her, and had buried lightning charms throughout the stone walls of the fortress. She could not enter unless through an open door, just like anyone with flesh.

"We must get inside," she said, darting into the fray.

"Wait!" Jeric called, but she was already gone.

Lorica dropped from above. She folded her wings and landed in the midst of the golems on the balcony. They carried bows, which they fired at the sudden attackers. Lorica swept through them, her sword sending water tumbling to the floor of the courtyard.

Elenyr saw a gap and lunged for the gates, but a rumbling roar echoed, and she snapped to the side. Her eyes widened as she watched the hundreds of humanoid golems begin to merge, the water flowing together into powerful claws and great wings. A giant head took shape, the teeth hardening into rigid spikes.

"A *dragon* golem?" Lorica demanded. "What's with you people and your magics?"

The dragon leapt across the courtyard, its jaws reaching for Rynda. She rotated and slashed upward, her blade cutting deep into the dragon's throat. But the water sealed quickly, and a great claw swiped at the rock troll, knocking her through a stone wall. She disappeared in a cloud of dust, her sword tumbling from her hand.

Lorica flew onto the dragon's back, allowing her sword to carve a deep line through its flesh. The dragon roared and spun, slashing upward with a giant claw. Lorica folded her wings and dove, slicing across the dragon's hip on her way to the ground.

Rynda appeared covered in dust and picked up her sword. Spitting blood from her lip, she charged the dragon, and plunged her weapon through its wing, embedding her sword into the wall of the castle. Unfortunately that connected the dragon to the lightning embedded in the walls, causing the water to crackle with power.

"Did you have to make it stronger?" Willow called.

Willow had her crossbow in her hands. From behind a pillar she fired at the dragon, pummeling its face with dark bolts. Rynda cursed and ripped her sword free, releasing the dragon, but the damage had been done, and the dragon now had a body charged with magic.

"I didn't know it would do that," Rynda retorted.

"The lightning will fade," Jeric shouted as he carved his way to the dragon's hind legs. He slashed once and darted away. "Every injury will bleed the magic faster."

Elenyr ducked a wing and charged the main doors. She caught the handle and hissed in pain as lightning coursed through her arm. But she retained her grip and yanked, wrenching the door from its hinges. Both doors fell, tumbling into the courtyard, but a curtain of energy covered the opening.

Elenyr's eyes widened, fear stilling her heart. In the center of the cavern, the five fragments were bound together, each in enchanted shackles. Spikes of glass pointed down from the ceiling, siphoning their magics, the objects a disturbing match to a horrending dagger. At the center, Mind had his eyes clenched shut, his features gradually turning to Draeken. Serak stood in front of him, his features bright with excitement.

Elenyr saw her worst fears on full display. Serak had forced the fragments to combine, to become Draeken. He knew there were six fragments and had unified Draeken into a single purpose. To ally with Serak.

"Mind!" she shouted his name, but the crackling energy in the doorway kept her voice from behind heard.

"Lorica!" Rynda called. "Bring me the body of a golem!"

"On it."

Lorica turned away from the golems not part of the dragon and leaned down, catching a golem as she flew by. Lorica flew upward and tossed the body to Rynda, who caught the struggling water golem and charged the main doors of the keep.

"You might want to stand back," she called.

Elenyr ducked around the corner and Rynda tossed the golem into the open doorway. The golem hit the lightning, shattering into water and smoke, absorbing the sheet of lightning. Elenyr darted forward and dove through the hole, ignoring Jeric's shout of her name. It sealed behind her, leaving her trapped. Serak turned at her appearance, as did his two companions, a towering armored soldier, and a cloaked figure bearing a powerful scythe. But Elenyr only had eyes for the fragment of Mind.

"Mind!" she bellowed.

His eyes snapped open, and he looked to Elenyr with a desperate hope.

"Kill her!" Serak barked.

Bartoth and Gendor charged. Elenyr gripped her sword, but knew she would never reach her sons in time. One glance at the two horsemen revealed the power in their weapons. So she reached up and ripped the amulet from her neck. With all her might she flung the amulet to the floor.

It shattered, the crystal parting into a thousand shards, releasing the embedded magic. Images burst inside the room, filling every corner, the thousands of memories pouring forth in quick succession. Elenyr leapt back as the horsemen came for her, but the flood of images would not be stopped.

"Remember!" Elenyr shouted. "Remember what you are!"

Chapter 45: Conquerer

Mind flinched away from the surge of images, confused by Elenyr's choice. She should have fought her way to him and shattered the horrending spike. Why release memories? Then his eyes widened when he realized they were not memories of Elenyr.

They were memories of him.

He saw an afternoon from their first year, of Fire and Shadow arguing, of Light laughing, of Water admonishing them to obedience. The memory was tinged with affection, with even Shadow offering a smile.

He saw the day Water had been stabbed in the chest because he'd stepped in front of a spear meant for Mind's back. He'd bled all over Shadow, who'd complained that his favorite tunic was ruined.

Light, giggling as he fought beside Shadow.

Fire charging into a battle with Mind guarding his flank.

Mind, directing his brothers, protecting them, planning to keep them alive. So they could return home, together.

"Stop the memories!" Serak shouted.

"How do you expect me to do that?" Bartoth snarled, locked in mortal combat with Elenyr.

Mind didn't hear them. The flood of memories swirled around him, all from Elenyr's perspective, her vantage point providing a lens to watch the life of Draeken. His life with the fragments, fighting, building, of being a family.

" . . . I told you the bandit was dangerous," Mind said in one image.

"You didn't say they had an anti-magic ballista," Fire protested. "I didn't even know those existed . . ."

"They exist," Shadow offered helpfully.

Elenyr's laughter in the memory merged with another moment, of Water rebuilding an elven home, the walls having blown down in a storm. Shadow wielded a hammer nearby, and Mind stopped him before he drove a nail through Light's foot. Shadow's disappointment was palpable, until Light thought it gave him permission to do so, and jammed a nail into Mind's toe. He still had the scar.

Inside Mind's consciousness, Draeken railed against the images. He'd been present for all the memories, but he'd sulked in the background, divided, angry. He'd seen Elenyr as a captor, always keeping him apart. She'd known what he was. But she was right.

The malicious touch to Shadow's fragment, the fury in Light, Fire's pleasure in the punishment of others, even Mind's dark ambition, all had been Draeken. And Elenyr had spent entire lifetimes teaching them to control Draeken, to prevent his rise to strength.

"I am the fragment of Power!" Draeken bellowed, the words coming from all the fragment's lips. "I will not be defeated by . . ."

His words were lost in the next image, a memory of Mind consoling Fire on the death of a woman he'd cared for. Mind recalled the moment, felt the compassion touch his heart. In that moment Mind's worry for his brother had cooled. He'd thought he lacked the ability to feel such an emotion, but it was Draeken who didn't care about Fire. To Draeken, the fragments were merely vessels of his power, reservoirs of his being.

More and more, the images filled the room with light, the memories a sea of talking voices, of five fragments being brothers, forging unshakable bonds of family through thousands of years of battles and companionship. And throughout them all, Elenyr, always watching, always advising, always loving.

Mind looked up and met Elenyr's gaze. Alone, she battled the two horsemen. Unable to land a blow, she struggled to survive, the powerful weapons nicking her flesh, leaving her bloodied. Tears were in her eyes, tears for him and his brothers.

"Remember!" she shouted again, her desperate voice louder than Serak's shrieking orders.

Serak reached to the stone in the walls and sought to crush the memories, the walls folding and smashing together, but the memories could not be constrained. The light flowed onto the shifting walls, continuously revealing the fragments' legacy. A legacy of bonds greater than blood.

From within Mind, Draeken surged forward, attempting to seize control from Mind. Already partially merged, Draeken pulled on the threads of magic from the other fragments, pulling them into Mind.

Mind recoiled, and he was not alone. All five fragments fought, the memories galvanizing them to action. The flow of magics moved back and forth between Mind and the fragments, the light blinding and swirling about them, the sheer power slicing into the bonds that bound them.

Shackles broke away, unable to endure the shredding magic. One of the horrending spikes exploded, and then another. The remaining three detonated simultaneously, spilling glass shards on Serak's head.

"NO!" he roared.

Bound only by the inner struggle, the five fragments stood together, wrestling with Draeken, the fragment of Power. At the center, Mind sensed Draeken's fury, his drive for power, and recognized the precipice. Draeken would not be contained again, not inside the fragments. He would never stop subverting them, never stop pushing them to weakness, to fall to their darker desires.

Mind groaned at the choice. Keep Draeken inside—and watch him destroy the fragments—or merge and let Draeken stand alone. The fragments would be dead. But in that moment Mind saw a third option. Gathering all his magic, he reached for the portion of Draeken inside his body—and began to force him out.

Draeken clawed inside his skull, tearing and rending, and Mind fell to one knee, snarling at the effort. Draeken's power was considerable, but he was not stronger than Mind. He'd been taught by Elenyr how to conquer himself, to conquer Draeken.

"You cannot do this!" Draeken roared.

"Watch me," Mind said.

In his thoughts, he shoved Draeken to the edge of a cliff, where he clung to the precipice. Mind gathered his magic for a final push, collected all his magic into a giant fist, and smashed Draeken from his skull.

Green light burst from his body and poured into the center of the fragments, swirling and broken. But Mind's struggle was not his own. Linked as they were, he'd been pushing Draeken from all their thoughts, and green light poured from the other fragments, flowing into the center, where the stone began to melt. A face formed in the green light and screamed. Draeken's face. Draeken's fury.

"What have you done?" Serak demanded, his eyes wide in horror.

He tried to leap into the midst of the fragments but the whirlwind of power cut his flesh, drawing blood and forcing him back. He screamed his helplessness and prowled the exterior, the room forgotten, his entire plan pooling on the floor between the fragments. He lifted his arms and stone hands flowed out of the floor, each reaching for a fragment. Four of the stone hands were torn apart by the whirlwind, and only one made it through the cutting magic.

It grasped Water about the waist and yanked him out of the circle. He cried out as he was sent tumbling backward, bouncing off the floor and colliding with the wall. Serak leapt into the gap but it was too late.

The last of the green light fell to the floor and Mind sucked in a breath like his lungs had never been used. The link binding the fragments crumbled and the fragments stumbled backward. The green light at the center brightened to blinding, and then exploded, knocking everyone in the room from their feet. The ceiling shattered, stones falling on Serak. The floor crumbled, taking him and Shadow into the basement below. Shadow managed to catch the edge and Fire jumped, grasping his hand.

"What just happened?" Shadow exclaimed, shaking his head in confusion.

"I think Mind just killed Draeken."

Mind rose to his feet, feeling alive for the first time in his life. All the reserve, the doubt, the greed, had been stripped away like shackles had been removed, and he saw clearly. He took the room at a glance.

Rynda fought to pierce the lightning door and a fierce battle raged outside. Mind caught glimpses of Lorica, Willow, and Rynda, allies, loved ones, friends. Bartoth and Gendor were pulling themselves to their feet, both dazed by the falling ceiling. More importantly, Water was just feet from Bartoth's sword, and was the only one unconscious. Elenyr had been close to the blast and been thrown into a wall. Her eyes fluttered and she fought to pull herself out from under the debris, the charged stones preventing her from turning ethereal.

"Shadow," Mind said. "Get Water out. Fire, distract Gendor. Light, help Elenyr."

They obeyed the orders, leaping away as Mind raced to Bartoth. Under the fortress, the stones rumbled, and Serak bellowed his fury. Bartoth saw Mind coming and whirled, catching up his sword. Mind reached for his magic, enormously grateful to find it still present. It lacked the might it had when he held a piece of the fragment of power, but it was enough for Mind to enhance his jump and flip over Bartoth's flashing blade.

He landed near the door and cast over his shoulder. "You missed."

Bartoth snarled and spun, swinging his enormous sword with inhuman speed. Mind retreated, darting one way and then another. He had no weapon except speed, and he used it to avoid the empowered blade.

"You can't escape forever," Bartoth said.

"I don't intend to," Mind said.

His seemingly random and desperate attempts to evade brought him close to the sheet of lightning over the door. Bartoth bellowed his victory and lunged, driving his sword toward Mind's stomach. Mind sidestepped, and used a touch of gravity to nudge the blade to the side—into the lightning.

The empowered sword met the sheet of lightning, and both exploded. Bartoth was knocked onto his back. He tumbled across the floor and fell into the hole, a shout indicating he'd collided with Serak. The lightning shield had broken, and although the outer wall remained charged, the doorway stood open. Rynda entered and swept the room with a disappointed look.

"I missed it."

"There's plenty more to fight," Elenyr said, leaning heavily on Light, who carried her past the rock troll.

Shadow carried Water out, his body slung over his shoulder. Water had been torn away from the separation. Was his consciousness damaged? Was he dead? Mind's gut clenched in fear, but Shadow smirked.

"Just like Water to take a nap in the middle of a fight."

"Willow!" Light shouted. "Look who I found! Remember Gendor?"

He pointed to Gendor, who stood in the center of the space, his scythe at his side. As the others retreated, Mind joined Rynda, eyeing Serak's assassin. Rynda sniffed and pointed her blade to the man.

"Can I kill him?" she asked.

You should go, Gendor replied mentally, and Mind realized he still could not speak.

"We must go," Mind said. "Before Serak seeks revenge."

If I am ordered to kill you, I will have to obey, Gendor warned.

"Keep fighting him," Mind said to Gendor. "We'll be back."

Gendor inclined his head, and Mind retreated out the door. Casting the hole another reluctant look, Rynda followed. The entire castle trembled again, more violently than before, and the entire group sprinted past the broken dragon, its wounds caused by all the allies.

Mind raced for the bridge, crossing with the others. On all sides, the fragments and their allies bore smiles and laughter, with Light gushing words so fast only Willow seemed to understand him. Mind felt relief, unrestrained by Draeken's influence.

"We should kill Serak now," Rynda said, using her sword to point at the fortress. "We have them in our grasp."

"Serak just lost what he most desired," Elenyr said. "He's going to be furious. And he has two of his horsemen."

"We won't have a better opportunity," Rynda said.

"We are wounded and he still has an army," Mind said.

Rynda grunted in irritation, but the dragon golem released an enraged bellow and charged the bridge. The group retreated into the corridor, far enough that the dragon's maw could not reach. Shadow taunted the beast as they fled.

"What happened back there?" Jeric asked.

"I feel different," Fire said. "Happier."

For the first time in his existence, Mind felt complete. Without the piece of Draeken, without the link to the others, he'd been changed. Permanently. He was alone, yet surrounded by his family and friends, he did not stand alone. Then he sucked in his breath as he realized the source of the emotion.

He was no longer a fragment.

He was whole.

Chapter 46: Alliance

Mind stumbled into the snow and caught the trunk of a tree. The others exited the mine entrance, equally exhausted. Water groaned as he leaned against a boulder, and held the wound on his side.

The wind whistled through the trees, a touch of warmth in its passage. The snow had begun to melt, the trees dripping water from melting ice. The valley stretched out below them, the mountains rising in the east, hiding the fortress of Xshaltheria. Smoke curled up from chimneys in a sleepy village in the valley.

"Why do I feel so weak?" Light demanded, examining the blood on his arm with shocked eyes.

"The fragment of Power has been stripped from your flesh," Elenyr said.

Fire sparked flames up his hand. "My magic feels weaker."

"Draeken enhanced your magic," Elenyr said.

"What does that mean?" Shadow asked.

Elenyr grimaced. "You're no longer a guardian."

Mind could feel it in his bones, the weakness, the vulnerability. He'd felt it through the minds of others, but never in his own body. He raised a hand and found it to be trembling, and his stomach ached.

"I'm hungry," Light said, as if surprised.

"Your strength is no longer tied to your magic," Willow said, digging into her pack and offering Light a crust of bread. "I suspect you'll need to eat more than you did before."

"I feel so . . . tired," Shadow said, scowling. "I don't care for it."

"Fatigue is a state of being for the rest of us," Lorica said with a faint smile. "You get used to it."

"Any way to put us back together again?" Fire asked.

Mind shook his head. "It was either die and let Draeken take control, or rip him out of our bodies. We are not fragments anymore."

Water shook his head in confusion. "I don't feel the same weakness."

Mind recalled how Serak had tried to break the link, sending Water tumbling away from the circle. The piece of Draeken inside Water had not been removed, meaning his power remained. Fire grunted and stabbed a finger at Water.

"You still have Draeken inside you."

"Is that bad?" Water asked.

"No," Elenyr said. "You had the least of Draeken to start with."

Mind shivered, shocked to find the chill even colder than before. For the first time since the separation, he realized what he'd done. He'd removed what gave them strength against time, kept them alive through ages. Mind hadn't been victorious, he'd ensured their destruction.

"I'm sorry," Mind groaned and leaned against a tree. "I've doomed us all."

"No." Jeric removed a cloth from his pack and bandaged Light's arm. "You've given us the only chance we have."

"How can you say that?" Mind demanded. "We couldn't defeat Serak before—and now we have to do it without being guardians? I was a fool."

"Jeric is right," Elenyr said. "as long as Draeken was inside you, there was always the risk, the chance that the five of you would turn into him. If that happened, our fates would be sealed. What you did," she shook her head, her expression one of admiration and hope, "you ensured we would be able to fight our foes—with you at our side."

"But I'm so weak," Shadow protested.

"That feeling will pass," Elenyr said. "You won't return to your previous might, but you are still powerful—more so than a normal mage."

"We're no longer fragments," Mind said bitterly. "We're nothing."

314

"You are your own soul now," Elenyr said, sweeping the fragments with her gaze. "You can never be bonded again, never merged into Draeken. From this day forth, you will live your own life, free to choose your own destiny, your own battle to wage."

"I just killed us!" Mind shouted. "We're weaker than we've ever been, because of me!"

"I'm not that weak," Shadow protested.

Mind turned on him. "We all are. I didn't *save* us. I *destroyed* us!"

The anger coursed though him, bitter and rancid. He'd thought that pulling Draeken out of the fragments would stop Serak, but it had made them all mortal. They would heal slower, and suffer more damage. All could be killed, because Mind had made them vulnerable.

"Of all the foes we have fought," Elenyr said, "I thought you would have learned the greatest enemy is the one lurking within our own souls. We all possess a dark side, and you didn't just fight it, you *conquered* it."

Mind's anger could not withstand the hope and pride in Elenyr's face. She'd carried the secret of Draeken for thousands of years, fearing what they could become, and preparing them to be victorious. She'd even embedded memories that would remind the fragments of their true strength, not the bond of a shattered soul, but the bond of brotherhood.

"Serak was stronger than us *before* I removed the fragment of power," Mind said. "We cannot defeat him with magic."

"You defeated him by your intelligence," Elenyr said. "And we must do it again, one last time."

There was a shuffle in the snow, and all whirled to the trees, expecting to see a new threat. Mind drew his sword when a towering figure stepped into view, followed by an elf and a human. Rynda lowered her sword in surprise.

"Tardoq? What are you doing here?"

In answer he pointed to the elven woman. "I'm with the oracle."

"Senia?" Elenyr embraced the woman. "It is good to see you."

"You as well," Senia said, and swept the group with a look. "Is it done? Is Draeken separated?"

"You knew what would happen?" Jeric asked.

"I did not," she said, and her eyes settled on Mind. "The more likely future was Willow and Lorica standing in this clearing, the rest having perished when Draeken became whole. I hoped I would find myself proven wrong."

"Serak lives," Rynda said.

"Then it appears the final war has begun," Senia said.

"Who is that?" Shadow asked, pointing to the third man. "He looks squirrely."

The man snorted. "No more than you."

Lorica grinned and nudged Shadow. "I like him."

"You would," Shadow muttered.

"Do you have any food?" Light asked.

"Rake is a friend," Senia said, and tossed Light her pack. His eyes lit up when he opened it to find a stash of bread, meat, cheese, and even cake.

"I love the oracles," he crowed.

"Rake doesn't have a sword," Rynda said, pointing to the apparently weaponless man. "What is he supposed to do?"

"He can turn into a dragon," Tardoq said.

"Epic," Light breathed, pausing in shoving food into his mouth to stare at Rake.

"I assume you have a plan?" Elenyr asked Senia.

"I don't." Senia shook her head and turned to Mind. "But he does."

"Me?" he protested. "I'm the one that got us into this mess."

"Serak was always going to kill you," Senia said. "And if Draeken had become whole in Serak's castle, you would have never seen the light of day."

316

"Doesn't mean I have a plan," Mind said.

"Of course you do," Shadow scoffed. "You always have a plan."

Mind shrugged, but couldn't resist the small smile spreading on his face. With the addition of Tardoq, Senia, and Rake, there just might be a way to destroy Serak for good. But it was not a plan Ero would like.

"Jeric?" he asked.

"Yes?"

"I need you to send a message."

"To whom?" Jeric asked.

"Serak thinks he knows our allies," Mind said. "He believes he knows our strengths and weaknesses. But he looks only at who is here, not beyond."

"Who lies beyond?" Elenyr asked.

"The one the Krey Empire fears," he said. "I believe they call her the Bonebreaker."

Tardoq cursed, loud and abrupt. Jeric didn't take his eyes from Mind, his expression inscrutable. Mind did not retreat from his request. The Eternals were all occupied, Ero had made that clear, but that did not mean Lumineia did not have allies. After an interminable moment he inclined his head.

"She's more dangerous than you can imagine," he said.

"I certainly hope so," Mind said.

Tardoq stepped forward. "I'll be the messenger."

"You?" Jeric asked.

Tardoq inclined his head. "If you will allow it . . . I will protect Lumineia with my life."

"Us too."

Sentara and Rune appeared at Mind's side, bursting from nothingness. Rune stumbled to the ground but Sentara stood tall. She grinned at the swords pointed at her, unperturbed. Rune fell to her knees and vomited into the snow.

"I'm not dead yet, so that means I get to fight," Sentara said.

"Did she have to teleport us like that?" Rune asked, wiping her mouth. "We were standing right over there." She pointed to a nearby clump of trees.

"It appears we are gathered," Mind said with a firm nod. "And as Senia said, the final conflict is upon us."

"Can I say it?" Shadow asked.

Mind grinned and swept a hand to his brother. Shadow smirked, his voice turning determined. "Let's find some food."

"That's not what you were supposed to say," Fire protested.

Light laughed. "I think he's right."

Rubbing his forehead, Water groaned. "That's what you came up with?"

"Sorry," Shadow said. "I can do better." His expression turned serious. "Let the hunt for cheese begin . . ."

Light laughed, and several of the others cracked a smile. Mind chuckled as his brothers argued, and noticed Elenyr with a smile on her face, an expression of joy and hope. Mind realized in that moment that Serak could not win for a simple reason. He was alone. The fragments had family, and it wasn't magic or might that gave them power. It was the union of brotherhood, the bonds of the family Elenyr had built. As Mind watched the others join in the attempt to express their mission, Mind finally understood. Serak could manipulate, destroy, even kill, but they would stand defiant. Elenyr was right.

Serak didn't stand a chance.

Epilogue: The Fragment of Power

Serak stood in the courtyard, his baleful gaze fixed on the tunnel where the fragments had escaped. How had Mind found the strength? How had he cast Draeken from the fragments? The questions beat on the inside of his skull, his hands trembling in rage.

"They escaped," Bartoth said.

Gendor joined him, and even though Serak could not see his face, the man's smile was evident. Serak had given him specific orders, but he kept finding ways to insert his own will into that of the cloak. Serak resisted the urge to kill him.

"You let Elenyr enter," Serak ground the words out. "You let the fragments escape. You let them win."

He stabbed a finger at the destroyed doors of his great hall. The interior lay in ruins, piles of rubble from the collapsed ceiling, a great hole in the floor where Draeken had been expelled. All the destruction because of Elenyr and her fool companions.

Bartoth grunted in irritation. "Perhaps you are not as strong as you think."

Serak whirled and lifted a hand of stone, smashing the rock into Bartoth. He flew into the courtyard wall, the stone blasting outward. Bartoth managed to catch the edge before tumbling into the abyss, but Serak coiled a length of stone about his foot and raised him up.

"You think me *weak*?"

He bellowed the words as he smashed Bartoth into the courtyard.

"You think yourself *greater*?"

He raised a hammer from the earth and struck Bartoth in the helmet. The armored rock troll crashed through the wall of the fortress, blasting through furniture and glass before bursting out the opposite side. Serak caught him before he fell into the abyss, and brought the

319

hand crashing into the courtyard again, the brutal impact cracking stones.

"You want to prove yourself superior?" he shrieked.

Bartoth groaned where he lay, his mighty armor cracked, blood on the chest plate, his sword fallen nearby. Serak advanced upon his broken form, red obscuring his vision, a sword the size of a castle wall rising from the courtyard.

"I am the FATHER OF GUARDIANS!"

He raised the sword, the thundering in his veins compelling him to kill the troll. To kill someone—anyone. How had Mind done it! How had he found the strength! The failure could not be Serak's. It must come from his general, the warmind he'd thought impervious.

"I wasn't serious," Bartoth growled, his voice pained.

Serak raised the giant sword anyway, ready to extinguish the troll's life as the price of his failure. He dropped his arm, the sword coming for the rock troll, driving for his body—but a burst of light caused him to flinch.

The sword grazed the rock troll king and struck the stone, crumbling apart. Serak whirled, Bartoth's failure forgotten as he stared at the doors to the keep, at the light spilling forth from within. It was not white like light orbs, rather it was a different color.

Green.

He sprinted through the broken doors and rushed to the hole. Rising from the gaping opening, green light coalesced into shape, forming a torso, legs, arms, and head. The light swelled and brightened, sparking green lightning that arced into the walls.

"The Fragment of Power," he breathed.

The shimmering magic turned to flesh, the bright eyes darkening to a cold black. He floated forward in the air, whole and unshackled by the restraint of the fragments. Draeken's eyes settled on Serak, and Serak fell to his knees.

"Master," he whispered. "I thought you were dead."

Draeken floated forward and alighted at the edge of the hole. "Serak," he said. "You have done well."

320

Serak shivered at Draeken's voice. Such power! Never had he thought to see Draeken stand alone, to be separate from the fragments and the influence of Elenyr. Serak could see it in his eyes, the unbridled strength, the cold, calculating strength of will.

"Your throne awaits," Serak said.

"My reign will be endless," Draeken said. "But first the Dark Gate must be opened, and my former fragments must be conquered. The final conflict has begun . . ."

The Chronicles of Lumineia
By Ben Hale

—The Shattered Soul—
The Fragment of Water
The Fragment of Shadow
The Fragment of Light
The Fragment of Fire
The Fragment of Mind
The Fragment of Power

—The Master Thief—
Jack of Thieves
Thief in the Myst
The God Thief

—The Second Draeken War—
Elseerian
The Gathering
Seven Days
The List Unseen

—The Warsworn—
The Flesh of War
The Age of War
The Heart of War

—The Age of Oracles—
The Rogue Mage
The Lost Mage
The Battle Mage

—The White Mage Saga—

Assassin's Blade (Short story prequel)
The Last Oracle
The Sword of Elseerian
Descent Unto Dark
Impact of the Fallen
The Forge of Light

Author Bio

Originally from Utah, Ben has grown up with a passion for learning almost everything. Driven particularly to reading caused him to be caught reading by flashlight under the covers at an early age. While still young, he practiced various sports, became an Eagle Scout, and taught himself to play the piano. This thirst for knowledge gained him excellent grades and helped him graduate college with honors, as well as become fluent in three languages after doing volunteer work in Brazil. After school, he started and ran several successful businesses that gave him time to work on his numerous writing projects. His greatest support and inspiration comes from his wonderful wife and six beautiful children. Currently he resides in Missouri while working on his Masters in Professional Writing.

To contact the author, discover more about Lumineia, or find out about the upcoming sequels, check out his website at Lumineia.com. You can also follow the author on twitter @ BenHale8 or Facebook.

Made in the USA
Las Vegas, NV
05 February 2022

43216733R10194